THE PIONEERS —to them no world was too distant or dangerous to conquer if the payoff was big enough . . .

THE DIPLOMATS —they were masters at the art of turning enemies into friends by making them someone else's enemy . . .

THE OLYMPIANS—the symbol of Man's supremacy, they were sworn to beat any alien at any sport under any circumstances . . .

THE BIOCHEMISTS—their task was a simple one—to make Man into Superman . . .

THE CONSPIRATORS—their desire for power could topple Man's entire empire . . .

BIRTHRIGHT: THE BOOK OF MAN

BIRTHRIGHT:
The Book of Man

by

Mike Resnick

A SIGNET BOOK

NEW AMERICAN LIBRARY

TIMES MIRROR

PUBLISHER'S NOTE

This novel is a work of fiction. Names, characters, places, and incidents are either the product of the author's imagination or are used fictitiously, and any resemblance to actual persons, living or dead, events, or locales is entirely coincidental.

Copyright © 1982 by Mike Resnick

SIGNET TRADEMARK REG. U.S. PAT. OFF. AND FOREIGN COUNTRIES REGISTERED TRADEMARK—MARCA REGISTRADA HECHO EN CHICAGO, U.S.A.

SIGNET, SIGNET CLASSICS, MENTOR, PLUME, MERIDIAN AND NAL BOOKS *are published by The New American Library, Inc., 1633 Broadway, New York, New York 10019*

FIRST PRINTING, FEBRUARY, 1982

1 2 3 4 5 6 7 8 9

PRINTED IN THE UNITED STATES OF AMERICA

To Carol, as always,

And to my parents,
William and Gertrude Resnick

Contents

PROLOGUE: The Beginning

Eons passed, and Man slithered out of the slime, sprouted limbs, developed thumbs. He stood erect, saw the stars for the first time, and knew that they must someday be his.

Still more eons. Man grew taller, stronger, broader. He strode the face of his world, taking what he needed, spreading his seed across the length and breadth of it. He became clever, if not wise; strong, if not indomitable. Earth was his, remade in his own image, yet Man was not satisfied.

He reached the moon, and in short order had erected settlements on Mars and the inner planets. The asteroid belt came next, and by the dawn of the twenty-fifth century his ingenuity had allowed him to place metropolis after metropolis on the moons of the outer planets.

And there he came to a halt. A trip to the moon took a mere ten hours; even a journey to Pluto, while it required four years, was conceivable. Conceivable and possible, as three growing cities gave testimony.

But the stars were another problem altogether. The nearest was almost five light-years from Earth, an inconceivable distance even for this technically oriented century. Not only would the trip require half a dozen long-lived generations, but the ship would need an enormous amount of room for oxygen-giving plants, making the venture both financially and physically unfeasible.

1

So Man looked elsewhere for a solution. The concept of hyperspace was tackled by every scientific mind in the Solar System for more than a century; the sole conclusion, reached countless times in countless experiments, was that hyperspace was a myth.

And then, in the early years of the twenty-seventh century, a young Tritonian scientist devised a theory for an engine that would propel a ship at a faster-than-light speed. The scientific community scoffed at him, citing the long-standing theories that made a Tachyon Drive impossible; but the Solar Government, in overpopulated desperation, funded his project. Within two years the ship was complete. It was taken out into space some 75 million miles beyond Pluto and set into motion.

It disappeared immediately, and neither ship nor pilot were ever seen again. However, the total transmutation of mass into energy and subsequent explosion predicted by the men of science was also undetected, and more ships were built around the faster-than-light principle. As Aristotle's earth, air, fire, and water had kept Man from discovering the true nature of atoms and molecules for an extra thousand years, so had Einstein kept him from the stars for half a millennium.

But no longer!

There were immense problems at first. Forty-three ships disappeared from the sight and knowledge of Man forever before one returned; and the one that did come back plunged into the sun—and continued right on through it.

It was another century and a half before an acceptable braking system was developed, and sixty additional years before the ships could maneuver and change directions in terms of mileage rather than light-years.

But by the advent of the thirtieth century, Man was ready for his rendezvous with the stars.

Proxima Centauri was the first star he visited. It turned out to have no planets. Neither did Alpha Centauri, Polaris, or Arcturus.

Man discovered planetary bodies in the Barnard and Capella systems, but they were huge, cold, ancient worlds, totally devoid of life.

He made his first alien contact on the fifth planet of the Sirius system. The inhabitants were small, fuzzy little fluff-balls with no sensory organs whatsoever. Since the Sirians had neither eyes nor ears nor, apparently, brains, Man couldn't ask them for living space on the planet, so he simply took it. It was only after a small atomic war between two human cities a century later, which totally obliterated the Sirian population, that Man discovered the little creatures were empaths who had been killed by involuntarily sharing the agony of the war's victims. By that time it didn't matter, though; Man was the dominant life form on Sirius V, just as he was on a hundred other planets sprinkled across the galaxy. He trod with a cautious foot when necessary, a diplomatic foot when expedient, and an iron foot when possible.

After seven more centuries of exploration, colonization, and selective imperialism, Man had built himself an empire of truly galactic scope. He lived on only fourteen hundred planets, while two million worlds were inhabited by other life forms, but there was no doubt as to who was the master of the Galaxy. It was Man the Industrialist, Man the Activist, Man the Warrior, and more than one doubting world had been decimated to prove the point beyond question.

Man had been prepared for his conquest of the stars. He had the technology, the gumption, the will. The taking of the galaxy had been almost inevitable, completely inherent in his nature.

However, the administration of his newfound empire was another matter altogether. . . .

First Millennium:
REPUBLIC

1: The Pioneers

. . . As man began expanding throughout the galaxy, the most vital part of this undertaking was carried out by the Pioneer Corps. Beginning with a mere two hundred men, the Corps numbered well over fifty thousand men by the end of the Republic's first millennium, and their bravery, intelligence and adaptability form a chapter unmatched in the annals of human history . . .

> —From *Man: Twelve Millennia of Achievement*, by I. S. Berdan (published simultaneously on Earth and Deluros VIII in 13,-205 G.E.)

. . . If any single facet of Man could be said to present the first harbinger of what was to come, it was his creation of the Pioneer Corps. These technicians of expansion and destruction roamed the galaxy, assimilating what they could for the Republic, frequently destroying that which could not be annexed with ease. It was a bloody preface to Man's galactic history, and while one can objectively admire the intelligence which led to the annexation of many extremely inhospitable worlds, one cannot but wince at the end results. Perhaps no early triumph of the Pioneer Corps better illustrates this than the assimilation into the Republic of Zeta Cancri IV. . . .

—from *Origin and History of the Sentient Races*, Vol. 7, by Qil Nixogit (published on Eridani XVI in 19,300 G.E.)

It even *looked* hot.

It hung in space, a small, blood-red world, circling a binary at an aloof distance of a third of billion miles. Its face was pockmarked with craters and chasms, crisscrossed with hundreds of crevices. During what passed for winter, it could make lead boil in something less than three seconds. But winter had just ended, and wouldn't come again for thirty Earth years.

There were no clouds in the traditional sense, for water had never existed here. There were, however, huge masses of gas, layer upon layer of it in varying densities. Here and there one could see the surface, the ugly jagged edges, but for the most part there was just a billowing red screen.

The surface was as red as the gas, red and grizzled, like a man badly in need of a shave. There was no dirt, but the vast shadows managed somehow to make it look dirty. Dirty, and hot.

And, sometimes frequently, sometimes infrequently, there were the wildly flashing lights.

The planet, with its deep gouges and explosive brilliance, was as much an enigma as the ship orbiting it was a commonplace.

And common it was, with its Republic insignia, its oft-repaired hatches, and its two sloppily efficient tenants. It was no newcomer to space, this ship that had known a dozen owners and ten times that many worlds. If sound could travel through the vacuum, the ship would doubtless have sputtered as it glided around the tiny red world. For decades now, each takeoff had been a death-defying challenge, each landing a death-inviting proposition. The ship's exterior was covered with the grime and soot of more than one hundred worlds, which may well have been what held it together. It was prone to periods of deafening and body-wrenching vibrations, which

6

was one of the few ways its occupants knew it was still functioning.

They sat before a viewing screen, unkempt, unshaven, unshod—and unhappy. One was tall and gaunt, with hollow cheeks and deepset, brooding blue eyes; the other was of medium height, medium weight, and nondescript hair color, and was named Allan Nelson.

"Has the damned thing even got a name?" asked Milt Bowman disgustedly as he gazed at the screen.

"Not to my knowledge," grunted Nelson. "Just Zeta Cancri IV."

"We named the last one after you, so we'll christen this one Bowman 29," said Bowman, jotting it down on his star chart. "Or is it 30?"

Nelson checked his notebook. "Bowman 29," he said at last. He glanced at the screen and muttered, "Some world."

"Three billion worlds in the damned galaxy," said Bowman, "and they decide that they've got to have this one. Sometimes I wonder about those bastards. I really do."

"Sometimes they must wonder about us," said Nelson grimly. "I didn't see them beating off volunteers for Zeta Cancri IV."

"You mean Bowman 29."

"Well, whatever the name, there can't be more than a couple of hundred idiots around who'd open the damned place up."

He was wrong. There were only two: Bowman and Nelson. The Republic, vast as it was, couldn't spare anyone else, for Man had traveled too far too fast. In the beginning, when Sol's planets were first being explored, Man's footholds were mere scientific outposts. Later, as the planets were made habitable, the outposts became colonies. Even after the Tachyon Drive was developed, the handful of planets Man conquered were simple extensions of Earth.

But things soon got out of hand, for planets, with planetary civilizations, were a far cry from outposts and colonies. They were the permanent homes of entire populaces, with environments that had to be battled and tamed, urbanized and mechanized. And, before Man was quite ready for it, there were fourteen hundred such planets. It didn't sound like a lot, but precious few of them were even remotely similar to Earth, and Man needed all eleven billions of his population just to keep things running smoothly.

More than a third of the planets—those with alien life

7

forms—were under martial law; this required an unbelievably huge standing army. Another four hundred planets were used for scientific research and mining, which required twenty more agricultural worlds to supply them with food and water. Another three hundred and fifty were just being settled, and required massive efforts on the part of their populations to replace jungles, swamps, deserts, mountains, and oceans with human cities.

But fourteen hundred worlds represented only the most insignificant portion of the galaxy. Man hungered for more, and so he remained fruitful and multiplied. He sought out still more worlds, explored them, populated them, tamed them.

This was where the Pioneer Corps came in. Unlike the pioneers of old, the dispossessed and downtrodden who sought the freedom that new land would bring them, the Pioneer Corps was composed of experts in the field of terraforming—opening up planets and making them livable. Highly skilled and meticulously trained, the men and women of the Pioneers were civilian adjuncts of the Republic's Navy. Their relationship to the Republic was somewhat akin to government contractors, in that they were not officially under the direct command of the government, but were free agents whose membership in the Corps enabled them to receive lucrative contracts from the Republic.

Frequently their jobs consisted of nothing more than adapting alien dwellings to human needs. Sometimes they were required to kill off a hostile alien population, and occasionally they were forced to exterminate nonhostile populations as well. Among their ranks were engineers who, with the aid of the Republic's technology, could turn streams into rivers and lakes into oceans, who could thoroughly defoliate a planet twice the size of Jupiter, who could change the ecology of an arid world and turn it into a planetary oasis.

The Pioneer Corps numbered some 28,000 members, but the Republic, still suffering growing pains and testing its sleeping muscles, dreamed in terms not of hundreds but millions of worlds, and thus the Corps was spread very thin. And as the Republic's needs became more specialized, so did the tasks of the Pioneers.

One such need was for energy. All the worlds of the Republic had long since converted to total atomic technologies, and there could be no turning back. But the supplies of radium, plutonium, uranium, and their isotopes, even on newly discovered worlds, barely met their needs. Solar power conversion plants were erected by the tens of millions, but Man had not yet found an economical method of conserving sunpower. And, since almost half of the Republic's commerce depended on interstellar travel, new energy sources headed man's list of priorities.

Then Zeta Cancri IV was discovered. A tiny but massive world, its very high rotational speed combined with the exotic elemental makeup of its core to form enormous magnetic fields of fantastic energy. Ions injected into these fields were accelerated to speeds manyfold higher than those found in Man's most powerful cyclotrons. The interaction of the planet's electrical and magnetic fields, plus the formation of different ions from the vaporization of the surface elements, created almost ideal conditions for nuclear transformations.

In other words, random sections of Zeta Cancri IV's surface tended to go Bang with absolutely no warning.

The brilliant visual displays Bowman and Nelson saw from their ship were merely the end result of fission reactions on the planet's surface. The lower-atomic-number atoms were built up to higher nonstable molecules by these nuclear transformations—and then all hell broke loose. What were highly specialized laboratory conditions on Earth were simple natural phenomena on Zeta Cancri IV. A continuous series of atomic explosions rippled the surface, exposing even more virgin material to the electrical and magnetic forces. The explanation may have been simple, but the realities were awesome.

The Republic was inclined to waste men and money with passionate abandon, but it couldn't tolerate a waste of energy such as occurred daily on Zeta Cancri IV, so Bowman and Nelson had been contacted and offered the job of making the planet safe for a select group of 235 "miners," skilled scientists who would find some way to put all that wasted energy to better use. The men had made a bid, the Republic had not even bothered to haggle, and the job was contracted.

The explosions, as it turned out, weren't the only little detail the Republic had failed to mention. The gravity was nothing to write home about either. Only the most powerful of the Republic's mining ships would be able to land on the planet without being crushed to a plup . . . and that was in winter. In summer they would melt before they got within twenty miles of the planet's surface.

For along with the explosions and the gravity, the climate

9

was no bargain either. The planet moved in an elliptical orbit that took thirty-three years to complete. In winter it was a third of a billion miles from its huge binary parent, but by summertime it would be within 150 million miles. And at *that* distance, nothing the Republic had yet developed could withstand the heat. Thus, even if they were successful in opening the planet up, it could only be "mined" for a few years at a time, and would then have to be abandoned until it had again moved a sufficient distance from Zeta Cancri.

And, to top it off, the atmosphere was totally unbreathable.

"Except for these little difficulties," said Bowman, who had been cataloguing them aloud, "the job's a cakewalk."

"Yep." Nelson grinned. "Can't figure out why the government felt it had to force two million dollars on us. Almost like a paid vacation."

"Well," said Bowman, sipping a cup of coffee, "any ideas?"

"Most of them relate to the guys who sold us this bill of goods," said Nelson. He sighed. "At least it's only springtime. We've got a little time to mull the problem over."

"Think anything could be alive down there?" asked Bowman.

Nelson shook his head. "I doubt it like all hell. Still, there's no way to be sure without landing. In which case," he added, "there probably still won't be any life, including us."

"Very comforting," said Bowman. "I appreciate the Republic's confidence, but I'm beginning to wish that they had bestowed it elsewhere. We can't land on the damned planet, we can't find any friendly natives to do our work, and we can't chart those goddamn explosions."

"The explosions are the tricky part, all right," agreed Nelson. "If it weren't for them, we might actually get the job done."

"If it weren't for them, there wouldn't be any job," grunted Bowman. "I've had the computer working on them for the better part of three hours, and they're absolutely random. You could get two in the same spot an hour apart, or you might go half a century without one. And without being able to chart or predict them, there's no way we can get close enough to the surface to learn any more than we already know."

"I suppose we could just orbit the damned thing for a few weeks, and then return and tell them we couldn't hack it," said Nelson.

"And forfeit two million bucks?" demanded Bowman.

10

"I'd say the cards are stacked against us, Milt," said Nelson. "Item: The gravity is too heavy for us to land. Item: The air is both unbreathable and radioactive. Item: Even if a Pioneer-type ship could land, it would melt before we could take off again. Item: No permanent base could be set up, even if we solved all those problems, because the planet's temperature is going to double in another ten years. Item: If none of the preceding items were enough to dissuade us, we still don't know when an explosion will come along and blow us straight to hell and back. Item—"

"Well, they never said it was going to be easy," said Bowman with a smile.

Three days later the smile was long gone and forgotten. The ship's sensing devices had logged 129 more explosions, and the computer had verified that all were totally spontaneous and patternless.

"And if that isn't enough," said Bowman, checking the readout, "it looks as if the planet is getting smaller by the minute. Not enough so you'd notice it, but enough so it will finally blow itself to pieces in another four or five thousand years."

"Well, what next?" asked Nelson.

"I'm running out of ideas," said Bowman. "I was up all night with the computer. According to our mechanical comrade, all we have to do is get a superstrong mining ship and develop immunities to heat, radiation, and things that go bang in the night."

A week later things weren't appreciably better. The two Pioneers had shot a dozen probes into the planet; one had been demolished in an explosion within minutes, and the others were deactivated by heat and radiation shortly thereafter. They had sent a mechanical drone out to take a sample of the upper layer of the atmosphere, and the gravity had pulled it to the planet's surface, destroying it before it could feed its findings into the computer. They had tightened their orbit, and had barely escaped with their lives. They had shot two nuclear devices into the planet's stratosphere and exploded them, with no noticeable effect in either creating or alleviating the natural explosions. And they had played 3,407 hands of blackjack, also without producing any solution to their problem.

"You know," said Bowman, "a person could go absolutely nuts trying to crack this planet. How the hell do you take a world that's having nuclear fits and turn it into a nice place

11

to visit? Well, back to the drawing board," he finished, turning to the computer.

The drawing board was no help. There were simply no analagous situations stored within its memory banks.

"We could tie in with the Master Computer on Deluros VIII," suggested Nelson. "It might know something that our baby is overlooking."

"Sure," said Bowman sarcastically. "And pay out a million-dollar fee for the privilege. Hell, I'd sooner forfeit the contract. I hooked in once when I was a novice and spent my next five contracts paying it off."

"Then what do you suggest?"

"I don't know. We'll just keep trying. Sooner or later we've got to learn something about this goddamn planet."

Bowman was right. They *did* learn something, two days later. The Pioneers had sent off their last dozen probes with very little hope of any results, but one of them remained functional long enough to report the presence of life on or beneath the surface.

"That's crazy!" said Bowman. "What in hell could possibly be living down there?"

"We're not going to know until we can get our hands on some more probes," said Nelson.

"We've got to find some way to make contact with them," said Bowman. "They're the only way we're ever going to beat this dizzy world. You know all that bitching I did about the Master Computer a few days ago?"

Nelson nodded.

"Forget it," said Bowman. "This time I think we're going to need it."

Nelson offered no objection, and a few hours later their ship's computer was tied in. It fed the Master Computer every piece of data available about the planet and waited for the gigantic machine to hypothesize the makeup of the inhabitants. Its conclusion was less than comforting.

"According to the Big Brain," said Bowman, checking the readout, "the little bastards feed on energy. Which figures, I suppose; I don't know what the hell else they could feed on. But it also means that they're not going to bend over backwards to help us siphon it away from the planet." He paused. "As long as we're still tied in, and in hock for half the contract, we might as well see what it says about landing our miners on the surface."

12

It said *no* about as emphatically as a computer can say anything.

There was still time for one more question, so Bowman decided to see if the Master Computer could come up with any alternative to forfeiting the contract.

It could.

"Well, I'll be damned!" said Bowman as he looked at the readout.

"What does it say?" asked Nelson.

"It says, in effect, that since we can't bring Mohammed to the mountain, our alternative is to bring the mountain to Mohammed."

"Translated from the Biblical, what does that mean?"

"It means that instead of trying to land men on Bowman 29, we can funnel off the energy into a force field and send it across the galaxy."

"Do you know anything about force fields?" asked Nelson.

"No," said Bowman. "Do you?"

"Nope."

"I'll bet the Big Brain does, though," said Bowman disgustedly. "There goes our other million. There's more to this computer business than meets the eye."

"While you're at it," said Nelson, "you'd better ask it how to chart the field as it travels through space. We don't want any ships running into it, and we don't want it to collide with any stars or planets along the way. And you might also have the Big Brain figure out just how we're supposed to tap and utilize all this energy once it gets where it's going."

"Let the Republic pay for that last answer," said Bowman.

"Before you tie in again, Milt," said Nelson, "we've got a little ethical problem that we're going to have to solve first."

"You mean the energy-eaters?"

Nelson nodded. "They'll starve, you know."

"Not right away," said Bowman.

"I didn't know slow starvation was any better than fast starvation," said Nelson.

"It's not," said Bowman. "But there's the other side of the coin to consider."

"Our money?"

"That, too," agreed Bowman. "But I was thinking of the life expectancy of the race. After all, at the rate it's blowing itself up, the planet can't last another five thousand years before there's nothing left of it. And these creatures aren't ever going to migrate to anywhere else. Hell, there *is* nowhere else for a race that can live here."

"How about a star?"

"Not a chance. Any star the size of Zeta Cancri would sizzle them before they got close, and even if it didn't, it's still a totally different environment. Besides, they're never going to come upon space travel. The only fuel they've got is their food, and as long as they've got food, why leave?"

"Because you're not the only guy in the galaxy who knows the planet's dying."

"Maybe," said Bowman. "But we're presupposing that they're intelligent. I think it's far more likely that they're not."

"Why?"

"Because this is obviously a young planet. It's going to die in its adolescence, so to speak. That's barely enough time to develop life of any sort, let alone intelligent life. Besides, no creature could adapt so greatly that it can become an energy-eater if it was something else to begin with. And, assuming that these beings have always eaten energy, why should they have developed intelligence? There was no environmental need for it."

"Not so," said Nelson. "The probe said they're living underground. They may have had to develop intelligence to keep one step ahead of the explosions."

"The probe said they were on *or* under the surface. There's no reason to assume one rather than the other."

"The hell there isn't. You've seen the explosions, Milt. Nothing could survive those."

"If they've evolved anything," said Bowman, "it's probably an instinctive awareness of what areas to avoid at what times."

"Maybe," said Nelson. "But it sounds like so much rationalizing to me."

Bowman sighed. "You're probably right. Still, we've got a job to do. We've signed a contract, we're a million dollars in the hole already, and about to shell out another million. After expenses, we're not going to break even, but we'll come close. The alternative is to forfeit the contract and pay off the Master Computer from future jobs."

"I guess that's what it boils down to in the end," said Nelson.

"I guess so," agreed Bowman grimly. "We'd better reach a decision."

14

The silent, peaceful natives of Zeta Cancri IV were blissfully unaware of the discussion going on hundreds of miles above them. They went about their business, which was unintelligible to anyone but themselves, hopefully planning for the future, thankfully praising their God for this land of plenty He had provided for them.

Their decision made, the Pioneers tied in to the Master Computer once again; and, light-years distant, the Republic chalked up another world on Man's side of the ledger.

2: The Cartographers

. . . Unquestionably the greatest scientific achievement up to its time, and well beyond it, the Department of Cartography—and most especially the complex at Caliban—soon took on an importance undreamed of by the populace at large. For the first time since Man had reached for the stars, the military was totally subservient to a scientific arm of the Republic, and the expansionist movement took on a high degree of order and direction.

The various segments of the Cartographic Department first coalesced under the inspired leadership of Robert Tileson Landon, an almost unbelievably perceptive scholar who had been given total control of Cartography in 301 G.E., and proceeded to shape and mold the budding science into something far more vital than even Caliban's original planners could have anticipated. During the fifty-six years that Landon headed the Department, phenomenal gains were made in . . .

> —*Man: Twelve Millennia of Achievement*

. . . The Department of Cartography, established on Caliban in 197 G.E., was an almost perfect example of the transformation of a pure science into a vehicle for continued territorial aggrandizement. The chief motivational force behind this perversion was a Dr. Robert T. Landon. Spending as much time on his public image as on his appetite for Empire, Landon managed to die a beloved hero in the eyes of his people, which in no way alters the fact that he was responsible, directly or indirectly, for . . .

—*Origin and History of the Sentient Races*, Vol. 7.

Vast, thought Nelson, was an understatement.

Even before the ship entered the atmosphere, the building stood out. Though he had never been to Earth, he didn't see how it could possibly house any structure larger than the Big C. It stretched some sixty miles by forty miles, its solid shining steel reflecting the reddish-yellow rays of the sun, a silver iceberg with well over nine-tenths of its bulk beneath the ground, even though it rose some six thousand feet above the surface.

Yes, vast was an understatement, but then, the word hadn't yet been created that would do the Big C justice. The Big C wasn't its real name, of course; but somehow, the Department of Cartography just didn't conjure up enough grandeur, and so the Pioneers had come up with their own term for it.

Nelson had never seen the Big C before, though he had heard a great deal about it. Any structure that cost more than ten trillion dollars and housed half a million full-time staffers was bound to receive more than casual attention from the media. Parts of it were open to anyone with minimal security clearance, but not too many people bothered taking the tour. For one thing, the planet Caliban was well off the beaten track in a galaxy that was quite underpopulated in terms of humanity; for another, it would require a minimum of two days just to walk from one end of one level of the Big C to the other. As for learning exactly what went on there, it would take considerably more than a lifetime.

Not that each of the Big C's levels were open for walking all that easily. Nelson had complete clearance and was there by invitation from Landon himself, and it still took him the better part of three hours to be admitted to the Director's outer office, and another hour before Landon was able to greet him.

17

He'd never seen the Director in the flesh, but the man's visage was as familiar to the public as was the complex that he ran with an iron hand. Landon was middle-aged—Nelson guessed he was in his late forties—and had a somewhat unkempt curly brown beard. If the men of his family had ever possessed a humorous or kindly twinkle in their eye, it had been bred out of the line before Landon was born. Nor did Landon look haggard or worn, as one might expect of a man with his responsibilities. If there was one intangible quality about the man, the hard-set line of his jaw, the precise measured movement of his hands, it was total self-confidence.

"Nelson?" The Director extended his hand in greeting. "I'm Landon."

"Pleased to meet you, sir," said Nelson. "Shall I call you Doctor, or Mister, or . . . ?"

"Just Landon will do," said the Director. "Come on into my office and have a seat."

Nelson followed him into a room that was almost Spartan in its austerity. He hadn't known quite what to expect, but this certainly wasn't it: a plain wood desk, three chairs, two intercom devices, a small bookcase, a couple of rather common pastoral paintings which he suspected were prints, and a tray containing a pitcher of water and four glasses. The floor was badly scuffed, and made of a type of wood with which he was unfamiliar.

Landon pulled a sheaf of papers from one of his desk drawers and began thumbing through them, glancing at Nelson from time to time.

"Bartholomew Nelson," he said, half reading, half musing. "Seventeen years of service with the Pioneer Corps, degrees in geology, chemistry and sociology. Given twenty-four contracts, fulfilled sixteen, forfeited seven, one being processed in the courts." He looked up. "Not a bad record, given some of those planets. You any relation to the Nelson who helped open up Bowman 29?"

"He was my grandfather, sir," said Nelson.

"Good man. Never met him, but I've heard him spoken of very highly. Did a beautiful job on Delphini VII and VIII after Bowman died. However, I didn't bring you here to talk about your progenitors."

"I assumed as much, sir," said Nelson.

"Right," said Landon. "I've got a job for you, if you want it."

"Excuse me, sir," said Nelson, "but isn't it highly irregular

18

for the Director of Cartography to make assignments of this nature? I mean, I've always dealt with the Navy, or with some member of the Department of Geology."

"Absolutely right," agreed Landon. "It's highly irregular. Never been done before."

"Might I ask why the change?"

"You might indeed. Don't let the answer throw you."

"I won't."

"All right, as long as we're being frank: I have a job for you that the Navy knows nothing about, and would doubtless never approve if they did know."

"Doesn't that amount to treason, sir?" asked Nelson, more puzzled than shocked.

"Depends on your point of view," said Landon. "If it'll make you feel any more secure, you'll be working for the most powerful single organization in the galaxy."

"But you're just a bunch of mapmakers!" Nelson blurted out.

Landon stared at him coldly for a moment, then continued as if there had been no interruption. "And, in all modesty, you'll be working for the most powerful man in all of human history: me."

"I'm not sure I know quite what to say, sir," said Nelson. "I have a feeling that I'm being made the butt of some practical joke."

"Feel anything you like," said Landon. "However, if you complete the job to my specifications, I'm prepared to offer you half a billion dollars, or one hundred million credits, if you prefer this new-fangled currency." He dug into his desk again and withdrew a check. He slid it over to Nelson, who studied it and let out a low whistle. "Still think I'm joking?"

"Let's say my reservations are weakening," said Nelson. "There's nothing wrong with being a rich traitor; at least, not this rich a one."

"There's no treason involved," said Landon. "Once you've completed the job, you'll very likely be a bigger hero than me. It's just that things tend to get bogged down in red tape back on Earth, and it would take years to get this done through normal channels. If the damned fools would just listen to me, they'd move the whole government lock, stock, and barrel over to Deluros VIII: twenty times as big as Earth, same climate, and a hell of a lot closer to the center of things. It's inevitable, but they do love to drag their heels. Makes it damned hard for me to conquer their galaxy for them. I'll do it, of course, but they could make my job a lot easier."

Nelson blinked his eyes several times. This was obviously no dream, and the Director wasn't like any madman he had ever seen before, but everything he said was terribly out of focus. Mapmakers just didn't offer Pioneers half a billion dollars to commit treason, and then complain that the government was hindering their conquest of the stars.

"You look dubious," said Landon dryly.

"Stunned is more the word for it," said Nelson. "If what you say is true, it's a pretty big revelation. If not, then they've got a totally unbalanced egomaniac in charge of a pretty important governmental department. Either way, it's not something I was prepared for."

Landon laughed for the first time. "That's what I like about you Pioneers. Who else would tell the Director of Cartography that he's off his rocker? Tell you what. Why not come and take a little tour with me? It might help you make up your mind. And always remember: Mad or not, government checks don't bounce."

"That's what's kept me here so far," said Nelson frankly.

"Good for you. I don't trust a man who doesn't watch out for his own interests. Come along." With that, he rose and walked out the door into his outer office, followed by Nelson. As he left the larger enclosure, a quartet of security officers joined him. He walked over to a small battery-powered cart, motioned Nelson to sit beside him, waited for the officers to grab handholds, and began driving rapidly down a long corridor. Nelson tried to follow the various changes of direction Landon took, but soon became confused and settled back with a sigh. At no time did the cart move farther than fifty yards from one of the huge outside walls, and it seemed to Nelson that they were continuously ascending, although at a very slight angle.

At last the cart screeched to a halt, and Landon and Nelson got out. The security officers dismounted, but made no effort to follow them. The Director led the Pioneer to a small doorway.

"Not prone to vertigo, are you?" he asked.

"No, sir," said Nelson.

"Good. When we walk through this door we'll be on a balcony. It's quite long and of more than ample width, but every now and then somebody starts getting dizzy on me; sometimes it's vertigo, sometimes it's just the map."

Landon walked through the door, and Nelson fell into step behind him.

And stopped.

And stared.

And almost fell off the balcony.

Below him stretched the galaxy. Not a map, not a bunch of dots on a wall chart, but the *galaxy*.

As far as the eye could see and farther, as deep as the eye could see and deeper, it spread out before him in all its gargantuan vastness, all its delicate beauty. Millions upon millions of stars, worlds without end, natural and artificial satellites spinning crazily in their orbits, here an interstellar comet, there a meteor storm, way over there huge clouds of opaque gaseous matter.

"What do you think of it?" asked Landon with the air of a proud father.

"I never imagined . . ." muttered Nelson, unable to tear his eyes away. "I never guessed . . ."

Landon chuckled. "Quite a piece of work, isn't it? It's 57.8 miles long, 6.2 miles deep, 38.1 miles wide. It contains every star in the galaxy, bar none, as well as every other body we've charted. For example, there are well over two million asteroids between Sirius XI and XII, though we'd have to magnify the field to show even the bigger ones."

"It's awesome," said Nelson fervently.

"And accurate," said Landon. "It's moving far too slowly for you to perceive, but the entire galaxy is rotating at its natural speed. So are the planets, and all the other bodies. All solar storms, ionic and otherwise, are charted. We've even got a fix on every ship the Republic owns, plus a number of alien vessels as well."

Nelson only half-heard the Director. He was lost in the majesty and grandeur of the map . . . though *map* was such an inadequate word for it. As he looked more closely, he saw that the colors of the various stars had been maintained: There were red stars, yellow ones, white dwarfs, blue giants, binaries, trinaries, even long-dead black stars. Though he couldn't see any of them clearly, he'd have bet his last dollar that the topography of the myriads of planets was painstakingly accurate.

"This, of course, is just a beginning," Landon's voice came through to him. The Director pressed a small button on the railing of the balcony and spoke into a microphone.

"Control Booth, this is Landon here. Let's see Earth, and put it on high magnification."

Immediately a light flashed far out on one of the spiral arms of the simulated galaxy. It was a good five miles from where Nelson stood, but so bright that it immediately drew his attention.

"Earth," explained Landon. "And now, if you'll be so good as to look above you . . ."

Nelson's eyes followed Landon's extended finger. Somewhere above his head, though he couldn't say how close it really was, floated Earth, spinning serenely beneath its swirling cloud layers.

"Bad weather today," apologized Landon, "or you'd be able to see something more than Australia and Antarctica. I could have them remove the clouds, but I'm sure you know what the rest of it looks like. And here," he added, pulling a number of cards out of a slot next to the button he had previously pressed, "is a complete readout on Earth: land area, sea area, gravity, average temperature of all major land masses, dominant forms of life, population, political systems now in power, major religions, economy, military potential, stellar alliances, technology, languages, varieties of the major races, aquatic life, age of planet, life expectancy of planet, rare elements, atmospheric breakdown, and just about anything else you need to know."

"And you can do this with every planet in the galaxy?" asked Nelson.

"To greater or lesser extents, yes," said the Director. "It all depends on how much information we have about the stellar body in question. If cards aren't to your liking, you can get the information on tapes, microfilm or voiceprints."

"It's fantastic!" said Nelson.

"It has its uses," agreed Landon, placing the cards back into the same slot. "I'm about to show you its major purpose." He pressed the button once more. "Landon again," he announced. "Put the whole map on dim."

The galaxy dimmed until the nearer and larger stars were barely visible, and the planets and more distant stars were not to be seen at all. It looked, thought Nelson, like the death throes of the universe.

"Okay," said Landon. "Give me Earth again, on bright." Five miles away a tiny light flashed on, brighter than the brightest sun. "Fine. Now, starting with Sirius V, flash every planet we control, put them on bright yellow, and leave them on. Give me a rate of five a second."

Nelson watched for almost seven minutes as a cascade of brilliant yellow dots rippled forth from Earth to Deluros VIII, then spread radially throughout the core of the galaxy. And all had originated from Earth. A thrill of pride ran through him as he watched a two-millennium history of human endeavor take place before his eyes.

"Very good," said Landon. "Now pinpoint every Republic ship that bears arms, put them in green, and keep them flashing at half-second intervals."

Suddenly the pseudo-galaxy was alive with green. More than twenty million lights blinked on and off hypnotically, most of them within the periphery of yellow lights, but some—a million or so—well in advance of Man's frontiers.

"Fine," announced Landon. "Now, in blue, give me every planet capable of supporting human life, but not yet colonized by Man." He paused a second, then added: "Flash all those that are currently inhabited by intelligent alien races on a quarter-second blink."

In total silence, another forty thousand lights flashed on brightly, and now the hue of the galactic scheme took on a bluish tint. Nelson was overwhelmed by the scope of the blue worlds, and hazarded a guess that about a tenth of them were blinking on and off, while the rest remained constant.

"One last request," said Landon. "In very bright red, let me see every world possessed of sentient nonhumans that might have the potential to resist us militarily."

Another plethora of lights went on, well over three thousand of them, red and blinding.

Individually, except for the initial steps of Man's expansion into the galaxy, there was no pattern. But now, as Nelson stood back and let his eyes pour over the brilliant-hued panorama before him, he began to see channels of force and expansion, paths of greater and lesser resistance through which Man could thread his way.

"Do you begin to understand the significance of the Department of Cartography?" asked Landon.

"I think so," replied Nelson.

"We are, in a very real sense, the expansionist movement of the Republic. With our facilities here at Caliban, we and we alone are in possession of enough data to know which planets are of value, which are not, which may cause problems of an environmental or military nature, which aliens may behave in which ways. We carry the analysis of history one step further; we also see and study the ebb and flow of the future. We can, in much the same way I showed you our current position, literally fight wars on the map, safely predicting almost every logical outcome of every conceivable confrontation. We are not an arm of the Navy; the Navy is a physical extension of Cartography."

"If you can accurately predict every military outcome, why don't we embark on a full-scale war of conquest?" asked Nelson.

"A good question, which, alas, has two even better answers. The first is common knowledge: We estimate that well over ten thousand planets are inhabited by intelligent nonhuman species, which certainly puts the odds on their side. The second, however, poses far more of a problem: I did *not* say that we can *accurately* predict the outcome of every military action. I said we can *logically* predict it. There's a world of difference. Human logic is not entirely unique to Man, but it's not present in abundance throughout the galaxy. And it's damned hard to predict what a totally alien intelligence will do, or even what it's capable of. Don't forget: Of the thousand or so species we've already made physical contact with, we've been completely unable to communicate with ninety percent of them. They're *that* different. And since the big map was the product of human intelligence and endeavor, it projects outcomes based on strictly human logic and experience. We simply have no other type of philosophical system to program into it."

"I see," nodded Nelson. "For a while there, I was beginning to think the map had absolutely no limitations. It's still the most impressive piece of equipment I've ever seen or heard of . . . and I am now willing to admit that you probably aren't talking through your hat when you claim to be the most powerful man in history. I imagine no planet is explored or taken without your approval?"

"Right," said Landon.

"Very impressive," said Nelson. "I see where there have been half a dozen assassination attempts on the Secretary in the last year or two. Too bad they didn't know where the real power lay."

"Wouldn't do 'em any good," grunted Landon. "Most of our defenses aren't too obvious, but no place in the universe is better able to protect itself. Don't forget: No ship can get within a half a hundred light-years without our having it on

24

the map and knowing every single thing there is to know about it. I won't say we're impregnable, but no one is ever going to sneak in here and assassinate anyone."

"How *do* you get all your information?" asked Nelson.

"The map building itself is just a tiny part of the Cartographic complex," said Landon. "We employ more than four hundred thousand people whose sole duty is to collect and correlate information that pours in from all across the galaxy every day. Beneath the surface, we have a computer complex that positively dwarfs the map building. Someone once told me that there are more than eight hundred million miles of circuitry involved, though I don't know who'd bother to count it all. Results are the only things that matter, and we get them.

"The data is relayed to the map control room, also beneath the surface and adjacent to this building, which measures some two cubic miles. The information goes directly into the memory banks, and can be instantaneously translated into cartographic terms.

"When I spoke to the Control Booth a while back, the man at the other end merely punched some standard buttons that had been programmed into the Cartographic computer complex. What you saw seemed solid and three-dimensional, but was actually a hologram simulated by a few hundred thousand modified lasers. Anyway, the facets I showed you are static, or at least as static as the galaxy ever gets. Projecting our expansion takes a little more effort, and a hell of a lot of intuitive interpretation. As I said, you can't expect a five-hundred-year-old denizen of the Delphini system, a creature that is composed of silicon, breathes ammonia, excretes an oxygen compound, and has a metabolism that we can't even begin to analyze, to react to a situation quite the same way you or I would. And, that," the Director concluded, "is what makes it interesting."

"I could spend a lifetime here," said Nelson.

"The hell you could," said Landon. "I didn't bring you here to join my staff. You're here for an assignment, nothing more."

"Then why did you show me all this?" asked Nelson.

"So what I ask you to do won't seem quite so unpalatable to you," Landon replied. "At least you'll know that when Cartography makes an assignment, we've got a pretty damned good reason."

25

"Well, let's have it," said Nelson. "How many deities do I have to slaughter?"

Landon responded by pressing the button on the railing, picking up the microphone, and saying: "Landon here. Spin the whole damned thing around so the Gamma Leporis system is right in front of me."

The pseudo-galaxy tilted on its axis and began spinning so quickly that Nelson felt himself being drawn hypnotically into the vortex. Millions of stars swung by almost too fast for his eyes to follow them; and then, as suddenly as it began, the movement stopped.

"Very good," said Landon. "Now put its planets on flashing blue." A medium-sized binary just in front of the balcony was suddenly alight, surrounded by sixteen tiny flashing blue dots. "Fine," said Landon. "Let me have every aquatic world within ten parsecs, and also the home world of the Lemm." More tiny blue lights flashed on, blinking wildly, and Nelson saw a pattern developing. There was a ten-parsec line of worlds, a dozen in all—not counting the Gamma Leporis system—plus another that lay still five more parsecs distant. "Good," said Landon. "Now change the home world of the Lemm to green, and let me see every aquatic world they possess." The fartherest planet became a tiny dot of unbelievably bright green, and the other twelve worlds, plus three more worlds in the Gamma Leporis system, turned red. "One last thing," said Landon. "Show me the five closest worlds under our control." Five white lights flashed on, all of them more than a dozen parsecs distant.

"Well, Pioneer," said Landon. "That's our problem."

"*Your* problem," said Nelson. "It doesn't become mine until I know what you're talking about."

"It's very simple," said the Director. "The fourth, fifth, and sixth planets in the Gamma Leporis system are entirely aquatic. Which is to say that they consist of nothing but ocean. No continents, not even an island. Same with the other twelve worlds that are flashing red."

"So?"

"The ninth and tenth planets of Gamma Leporis are quite rich in numerous natural elements that the Republic needs: iron, lead, gold, even a little uranium."

"What has one got to do with the other?" asked Nelson.

"Not much, except for the Lemm," answered Landon. "We don't know much about them, except that they're quite similar to us in one respect at least."

26

"And what is that?"

"They seek after Empire," said Landon. "They've established bases, artificial islands, on the fifteen aquatic worlds in question."

"Why should that bother us, if we're after the material from the waterless worlds?"

"Good question," said the Director. "Let me put it this way: How would you feel about an alien power's establishing itself on Deluros V?"

"I wouldn't like it much," said Nelson.

"Why?"

"It's a big galaxy. Let them look elsewhere for what they want. The Deluros system belongs to us."

"They might be peaceful," said Landon.

"Then why are they expansionist?" said Nelson. "And why didn't they ask our permission?"

"Precisely," said Landon. "Well, it just so happens that *we* asked permission of the inhabitants of Gamma Leporis system."

"What does that have to do with the Lemm?"

"Lots," said Landon. "You see, the ichthyoid population of Gamma Leporis IV is an ancient race, some four billion years old. Their intellects have reached a point that Man can never aspire to, even in the distant future. But nature played a dirty trick on them: She made them totally aquatic. No race advances without technology, and ninety-nine percent of all technology is based on fire. Can't have fire on a water world."

"So the Lemm moved in and conquered them?" asked Nelson.

"Conquer isn't the word," said Landon. "The Lemm simply set up floating islands, dropped a few depth bombs that the ichthyoids couldn't cope with or respond to, and demanded that they begin mining their world and turning the various materials over to the Lemm."

"Sounds kind of like us," said Nelson, not without a touch of approval.

"To continue," said Landon. "It took us the better part of a year to communicate on even a basic level with the ichthyoids. They wanted nothing to do with us or the Lemm. The Lemm are a bit more technological; I imagine we could communicate with them in a matter of a couple of days."

"Why don't we?"

"No need to," said the Director. "We've got a pretty good

27

idea about their potentialities, their science, and their feeling toward outsiders."

"For instance?" asked Nelson.

"There are no domes on the water worlds. That implies the Lemm are carbon-based oxygen-breathers. Their science is obviously based on somewhat different principles than ours, or else they'd be more interested in Gamma Leporis IX and X, instead of water worlds. And we know they're an aggressive race that has nothing against an occasional conquest."

"Why not send the Navy against them?" asked Nelson.

"Two reasons. First, since their science is different from ours, we don't know what kind of fight they're capable of putting up. We're spread too thin throughout the galaxy to get involved in a major war just yet."

"And the other reason?"

"Simple. We're outnumbered a million to one in this galaxy. We'll win it, in time, every last piece of it. But if we make too loud a noise too early in our career, our opposition—both real and potential—may coalesce before we're ready for them. So the Navy says hands off."

"But you don't," said Nelson.

"Absolutely correct," said Landon. "We need those worlds." He picked up the microphone again. "Show all the worlds under current consideration in flashing white," he said, "and show me the fifty nearest human-controlled worlds as well." He waited a moment, then turned to Nelson. "You see?" he said. "It's a new line of expansion that would add another dozen systems to our collection, and put about three dozen more under our sphere of influence."

"And my job?" asked Nelson.

"Leave the Lemm home planet alone," said Landon, "but get the Lemm off the water worlds. Can you do it?"

"I suppose so," said Nelson, scratching his head. "If they're oxygen-breathers, it shouldn't be too hard to poison the air. A couple of really dirty bombs on each world . . ."

"No bombs," said Landon. "If I wanted a war, I'd send for the Navy."

"But they won't come," Nelson pointed out.

"Just the same, we don't want the Lemm figuring out what happened, or who is doing this."

"Okay," said Nelson. "Same principle: poisoning the air. It'll take a little more work, but it can be done."

"Secretly?"

Nelson nodded. "And I'll make it short-lived, something that will dissipate after a couple of years so we can move back in. Might as well put it on the solid worlds too," he added. "It might confuse them, and it'll stop them from retreating there. About how many Lemm will I be killing?"

"You don't want to know," said Landon.

"No, I suppose not," agreed Nelson.

"Any other questions?" asked the Director as he escorted Nelson back to his motorcart.

"Just one," said Nelson. "I'm doing this so we can move onto two worlds: Gamma Leporis IX and X. Yet your map projection showed seventeen new worlds."

"Eleven of those aquatic worlds are devoid of sentient life. And once the Lemm are driven off, I would imagine the ichthyoids would be happy to form an alliance with their saviors."

"And if they're not?"

"Well," said Landon with the trace of a grim smile about his lips, "if it comes down to cases, I would imagine Man can make a depth charge every bit as powerful as the Lemm's, wouldn't you?"

Nelson nodded vigorously.

3: The Miners

... It was during the period of 370–390 G.E., that the Federation of Miners made its first tentative steps toward a position of fiscal and political power, under the bold and visionary leadership of Jerim Coleman, a young legal student who took the cause of the miners as his own. Coleman, a deeply moral and religious man, was responsible for the heroic stands taken by the downtrodden miners of five major outworlds, including ...

> —*Man: Twelve Millennia of Achievement*

... Coleman, who reached the pinnacle of his power around the turn of the fifth century (G.E.), demonstrated all that was most distasteful in Man during the period of his greatest galactic expansion. Unyielding, uncompromising, he singlehandedly accounted for the deaths of more than five thousand members of his own species, as well as ...

> —*Origin and History of the Sentient Races*, Vol. 8

Coleman was met at the door by a Butterball.

This was not totally unexpected. He knew that the miners usually made alliances with the native life forms, occasionally because of mutual need, more often from sheer loneliness and boredom. And he also knew enough to remain where he was until one of the miners showed up. Any species that could call Gamma Leporis IX—with its bitter cold, raging winds, dust storms, and oppressive gravity—*home* had to be pretty tough customers if aroused.

The Butterball emitted an ear-piercing hoot, and a moment later one of the miners opened the door.

"What's up, Ferdinand?" asked the grizzled man. Then his eyes fell on Coleman. "You the man from the Federation?"

Coleman nodded.

"Well, come on in," said the miner. "Don't mind Ferdy here. He's pretty docile, all things considered."

Coleman followed the man into the large auditorium. Most of the seats were filled. He estimated the crowd at 350, which was not a bad turnout, given a world population of 422. He walked immediately to the dais, laid his briefcase out on the podium, withdrew a sheaf of papers, and gratefully noted a cup of hot coffee on the shelf directly beneath the slanted board that was meant to hold his papers, but would doubtless end up supporting his elbows instead. He considered taking his coat off, but decided to wait until he felt just a bit warmer.

He took a sip of the coffee, checked the microphone, and faced his audience.

"Gentlemen," he said, and waited for the various conversations to subside. "I'm pleased to see such a good turnout. I'm glad you felt this meeting was important enough to leave your videos." He had hoped for a chuckle with that, and was gratified to note one spreading through the assemblage. Gamma Leporis IX was more than a light-year from the nearest sending station. "Tell me," he said, blowing into his hands and rubbing them together, "when does summer come around here?"

"You're *in* summer!" shouted someone. "You ought to come by someday when it's nippy out!"

That brought the laughter he had been waiting for. If there had been any hostility, at least it would be suspended for a little while.

"Well, gentlemen," he said, "I'll get right down to business. My name is Jerim Coleman, and I represent the newly formed Federation of Miners. At present, the Republic has

31

843 mining worlds, and our Federation has been accepted on well over half of them—and there are a lot we haven't made presentations to yet. I've asked to speak to you this evening because I'd like to tell you a little bit about ourselves, and try to offer you some concrete reasons why joining the Federation will prove to be in your best interests."

He looked across the audience. So far, so good. Now for the silken hand disguised in a gauntlet of tempered steel.

"I know a number of stories have reached you concerning what membership in our organization entails, so I won't mince words. If you join, every one of you will be required to turn half his salary over to us for a period of five Earth years, and each of you will have to sign a contract guaranteeing that you will remain in the mining profession for a period of no less than fifteen years. You will also have to undergo extensive psychological conditioning."

He waited for the reaction that he had seen so many times in so many similar meeting places. First silence, then a whispered muttering which quickly turned into a series of outraged curses, cries, and questions. He waited a full four minutes for the noise level to subside before continuing.

"Gentlemen," he said at last, "please give me your attention for a little while longer. I know most of the objections that you want to raise, and will try my best to answer them right now. After I'm through, I'll be open to questions from the floor. All I ask is that you hear me out. Besides," he added, "if I get your blood boiling, it'll make the walk home a little easier."

There were a few grins at that, and one huge guffaw from somewhere to his left.

"Your major objection is probably that no organization can possibly do enough for you to merit half your income. After all, no single vocational group is paid as well as you. Not that you don't deserve it: You're not pick-wielders, but highly trained specialists, responsible for survey work, controlling robotic miners, and refining the ores that you come up with, which makes you well-nigh irreplaceable. Your second objection concerns the fifteen-year contract. You are highly paid because, due to environmental conditions, your work is extremely hazardous, and therefore each of you—or most of you, anyway—hopes to make a killing and get back to civilization to spend some of those hard-earned credits. Am I correct in my assumptions?"

There was a general nodding of heads.

"Good. Now, before I answer those and other objections, I'd like to spend a few minutes filling you in on the background of the Federation so that you may better realize exactly what it is that we have to offer. After all, we couldn't present such extreme conditions for membership unless we felt we could give you value received for time and money spent. And try to keep in the back of your minds the fact that eighty-three percent of the mining worlds that have been offered membership have accepted.

"Now, with that in mind, let's take a brief look at the mining industry as it now exists. The Republic controls almost thirty-five hundred worlds; almost a quarter of them are devoted exclusively to mining. The Republic boasts some thirty-seven billion citizens; less than two million are miners. So what we basically have here is a situation in which less than one ten-thousandth of one percent of the Republic's population is controlling well over twenty percent of its territory.

"And economically, the disparity is even greater. The Republic is powered almost exclusively by atomics; all but a fraction of their fissionable material comes from three hundred and seven mining worlds, of which Gamma Leporis IX is one. The Republic still backs its money with gold and silver; every last bit of it comes from one hundred and two mining worlds, including Gamma Leporis IX. The Republic needs metals for its ships and armaments; all of it, without exception, comes from the mining worlds, including Gamma Leporis IX."

"So they need us," broke in a bored voice from directly in front of him. "That's why they pay us so well."

"Ah, but do they?" said Coleman. "You, sir, since you seem willing to speak up: Would you consent to tell me how much your yearly salary is?"

"Why not?" said the man belligerently. "Seventy-five thousand credits."

"And your job?"

"I mine gold and silver."

"How much?" asked Coleman.

"Lots."

"More than a ton a year?"

"A ton a week'd be more like it," said the miner with a touch of pride.

"Do you know the going price on gold these days?" continued Coleman.

"Can't say that I do. Lots, I suppose."

"You suppose right, friend," said Coleman. "Fifty-three credits an ounce. The Republic pays your salary with what you mine in a day, and has money left over.

"And that's not the only way they're taking advantage of you," Coleman continued, speaking once more to the entire audience. "I learned in my briefing that there were originally a thousand miners on this world when operations began ten years ago. What happened to the other five hundred and seventy-eight?"

"The nelsons got 'em," said the man who had spoken before.

"And what, pray, are the nelsons?" asked Coleman.

"If you ever see one, you'll know what they are!" said the man devoutly, amid much laughter. "They were discovered about forty years ago by a guy named Nelson, the Pioneer who opened up this system. Big, fur-bearing creatures. They can't be carnivores, since there aren't any game animals on this world. I'd guess they ingest minerals, except that I don't know how that would produce fur. Anyway, whatever they are, they don't like people poking around in their supper troughs."

"In other words, they killed more than five hundred miners?" asked Coleman.

"Tore 'em to ribbons," said the man. "They'd probably have butchered the rest of us, too, if we hadn't run across the Butterballs."

"Butterballs?" asked Coleman, who knew perfectly well what they were.

"Big round yellow things with chubby little legs. You passed one when you came in. Tame as all get-out, but they're poison to the nelsons. I don't know exactly how it works, but they seem to emit some kind of radiation or electrical charge that just knocks nelsons for a loop. We found out that they love magnesium, so we give them all that we mine and they stick around and keep the nelsons from decimating us. Works out pretty well all the way around, except for the nelsons."

"So along with all the other hazards you have to contend with," pointed out Coleman, "you also have to fight off a belligerent alien population. And, in addition, and for no extra consideration, you have also made the Butterballs into a loyal ally of the Republic. Am I correct?"

There was a general agreement.

"Then I submit that the miners are the Republic's most ex-

34

ploited minority. Whatever they're paying you, it isn't enough. Whatever political and economic power you wield, it is minuscule compared to what you deserve. And *that*, gentlemen, is the reason for the Federation."

"We're all for getting a better deal," said a man in the back of the audience, "but you still haven't said how you intend to help us, or why you need so much of our money."

"I'm just getting to that point," said Coleman. "To begin with, the Federation cannot begin to function until at least eighty percent of the mining worlds are members; otherwise, we simply haven't the power. For this reason, we need time: time to build a powerful lobby on Earth and on Deluros VIII, time to get public backing for our demands, time for the government to realize they've no choice but to deal with us. We estimate a minimum of twelve years; therefore, we must demand that you remain on for fifteen years. Once we start the ball rolling, the only thing that could stop us would be defections among our ranks."

"Why the money?" asked another miner.

"For the same reasons: lobby, organization, and propaganda. And if you're to stay on this world for fifteen more years, you wouldn't have a chance to spend it anyway."

"What are you going to offer us in exchange for all this?" asked the same man, still dubious.

"Offer is the wrong word," said Coleman calmly. "We are going to demand a piece of the action. Every miner will get one three-hundredth of what he produces. No salary, no matter how astronomical, can possibly match that. We will also insist on political representation; the details of this haven't been worked out yet. Representation based on our population is wholly unacceptable to us; basing it on our economic power is too much to expect at this time. But we shall and will work out an equitable arrangement."

"And when the Republic says no?" asked a man.

"They won't say no," said Coleman.

"But if they do?"

"Then every mining world in the Republic will go on strike. For the next decade and more, you will be carefully and thoroughly conditioned to do whatever is required of you. And how long do you think the Republic could stand a galaxy-wide strike? A day? A week? Surely not a year. Think about it, gentlemen. Cartography may be the great force behind our expansion, but you, and you alone, are the major power insofar as utilizing what we already possess. You've been a sleeping giant up until now, but the time has come to arise and flex those long-dormant muscles."

There was a low buzzing in the room.

"Gentlemen, it is not my intention to rush you," said Coleman, "but I must ask for a vote tonight. Tomorrow morning I'm taking off to visit your less fortunate companions of Gamma Leporis X, and—"

"What do you mean, less fortunate?" demanded a miner.

"Your air may be cold," said Coleman, smiling, "but at least it's breathable. As I was saying, I'll be very happy to answer any questions at this point; but I must have your decision one way or the other, by sunrise."

To nobody's great surprise, least of all Coleman's, Gamma Leporis IX voted overwhelmingly to join the Federation of Miners.

It didn't take twelve years. Things had gone even faster than Coleman had expected, and now, seven years after his visit to the Gamma Leporis system, he stood before the Secretary of the Republic as that graying politician bounced from one tirade to the next, barely pausing for breath.

"Just what the hell are you trying to pull, Coleman?" he demanded for the dozenth time. "This is blackmail, plain and simple! The Republic will not be railroaded into any action by a bunch of miltant malcontents."

"I beg to differ, sir," said Coleman. "Respectfully, of course. But if the Republic wasn't scared out of its wits, I think our problem would have been handled at a lower level."

"Your only problem is your so-called Federation!" snapped the Secretary. "And I'm not going to *handle* it; I'm going to grind it into the dirt!"

"I think not," said Coleman. "May I sit down while we discuss it?"

"No!" bellowed the Secretary. "You may not sit down, and we will not discuss it! Had you come in here like a reasonable man, I'd have been happy to talk with you. But no, you toss a list of ultimatums on my desk and demand that the Republic knuckle under to a bunch of hooligans."

"Had I acted like a reasonable man," said Coleman, "and had I not come prepared with a list of demands which are absolutely nonnegotiable, I wouldn't be here. I'd be cooling my heels in office after office while everyone in the government hoped the problem would go away. My very presence here attests to the efficacy of our methods."

"Who the hell are you, anyway?" demanded the Secretary. "You're no miner. How did you come to be part of this organization? And where is the Federation's headquarters? Who are its officers?"

"I don't believe that I'm going to tell you," said Coleman calmly. "None of that information could possibly help our cause, and I can certainly conceive of numerous ways by which releasing any further facts about ourselves could only work to our detriment."

"In what way?"

"It is not inconceivable that knowledge of our headquarters would precipitate an immediate attack on them," said Coleman. "We have absolutely no intention of using force, but we do intend to protect our existence. Our power is economic and moral, not military."

"You're about to learn just how unmilitary your power is," said the Secretary. "When is this galaxy-wide strike supposed to take place?"

"At midnight, Earth time."

The Secretary pressed one button from among the multitude on his intercom set. "I want the 27th Fleet sent to Spica II immediately. At precisely midnight, Earth time, they will demand that the miners turn over fifty tons of iron. Should the miners refuse to do so, they are to take whatever action is deemed expedient to secure the iron. Is that understood?" He flicked off the switch without waiting for a reply. "All right, Mr. Coleman. Now let's see just how much gumption your Federation has."

Coleman pulled a small, transistorized communicative device out of his pocket and activated it. "This is Coleman." He waited until his voiceprint had been cleared. "It's Spica II, tonight. Get a camera there on the double." He replaced the communicator in his pocket and looked up at the Secretary with what he hoped was a confident smile. "It's your move now, sir."

"You talk about this as if it were a chess game, instead of a crime of treason against the Republic," said the Secretary. "But since you've made the ground rules, I hope you'll be willing to play by them." He flicked on the intercom again. "Intercept and detain all ships traveling within one parsec of the Spica system for the next five days." He looked steadily at Coleman. "Still think you have a chance?"

37

"Tell me when you're ready to agree publicly to our demands," said Coleman. He turned and left the office.

At exactly midnight, the Federation of Miners went on strike.

At eleven minutes after midnight, the flagship of the 27th Fleet demanded that the miners of Spica II relinquish their daily quota of iron.

At twelve minutes after midnight, the miners refused.

At fourteen minutes after midnight, the 27th Fleet gave the miners a ten-minute ultimatum, after which they stated that they would take the iron by force and arrest the miners.

At twenty-two minutes after midnight, the seventy-two miners who formed the total population of Spica II gathered by the largest single refinery on the planet and set off a series of three nuclear bombs.

And at three minutes after one in the morning, Coleman was ushered into the Secretary's office under armed guard.

"Just what the hell are you trying to prove?" demanded the Secretary, who had obviously just been aroused from a sound sleep.

"We're not trying to prove anything," said Coleman. "We're trying to win something: our rights. These miners have undergone three hours of intense hypnotic conditioning every day for more than a decade, and are fully prepared to die for their rights if need be. In fact, they are so completely conditioned that they have no choice in the matter; any opposition by the Republic will trigger this reaction. I assure you that there can and will be no weakening of our resolve."

"Dammit, you're the best-paid men in the Republic!"

"Not in relation to the service we render to the Republic," said Coleman. "Are you ready to agree to our demands yet?"

"You can blow every last mining world to hell before we'll submit to this kind of coercion!" snapped the Secretary.

"I doubt that, sir," said Coleman. "Once the Republic discovers how deeply these miners believe in their cause . . ."

"The public won't find out a damned thing," said the Secretary. "We stopped your ship, and we'll stop every other ship that attempts to approach a mining world."

"Then ultimately your own conscience will force you to yield to us," said Coleman with more confidence than he felt.

"Get him out of here," said the Secretary disgustedly.

"Is he under arrest?" asked one of the military aids.

"Hell, yes! Charge him with treason and lock him up!"

Coleman was escorted to an electrified cell. He was well fed, and was treated with the utmost cordiality. Each morning he was allowed to view the newstapes. He could find nothing about the results of the strike, nor even any acknowledgment of its existence, but he knew it would be continuing. The Republic could get along without the mining worlds for a week or two, possibly three. But then all interstellar traffic would come grinding to a halt. Before long the hospitals would be screaming for supplies. They'd be the first to feel the pinch, and for that he was sorry; but they'd be followed in short order by the huge spacecraft cartels, and they'd scream good and loud. Even the Secretary couldn't keep the lid on this for too much longer.

He spent exactly nineteen days, six hours, and twenty-four minutes in prison. Then he was once again ushered into the Secretary's presence.

The Secretary seemed to have aged perceptibly since the last time he had seen him. There were deep heavy lines around his eyes, and his pendulous jowls seemed to sag even more.

"If you ever had any friends on Praesepe II and VI, Alphard XVII, or Altair V, you'll never see them again. I hope that makes you happy."

"It makes me very sad," said Coleman sincerely. "And I know their deaths must weigh heavily on the conscience of the Republic."

"How about *your* conscience?" said the Secretary. "Doesn't the fact that well over four thousand patients have died because your strike has prevented our hospitals from getting vital materials bother you at all?"

"I deeply regret their deaths," said Coleman carefully. "But our stand has been taken. We are totally committed to our cause, and too many of us have died to back down now. If the Republic cares for either the rights of its miners or the lives of its patients, it has the wherewithal to end the strike this very minute."

"I told you before: We will not yield to threats."

"We can wait," said Coleman. "Time is on our side. Not even you, with all the resources of the Republic behind you, can keep this quiet for much longer. If you'd made it public to begin with, you might have been able to stir up sentiment for your side. But now the miners of five worlds are dead, and not a single member of the military has been harmed. Where do you think the public's sentiment will rest?"

"What's to stop us from surrounding every remaining mining world and moving in after every last miner blows himself to bits?"

"We're using exceptionally dirty bombs," said Coleman calmly. "It would be years before most of the worlds could be opened for mining, or before the mined material could be safely used. Do you think the Republic's economy can stand that?"

The Secretary closed his eyes and lowered his head in thought for a full minute. Then he looked up at his aides. "Will you leave Mr. Coleman and me alone for a few moments, please?"

When the room emptied out, he gestured for Coleman to sit down opposite him.

"If we agree to your financial terms, will you relinquish your request for greater political representation?"

Coleman shook his head. "You're going to sign it anyway, so why should we yield? Too many of us have died to start striking bargains now."

"What do *you* get out of this?" asked the Secretary.

"Justice."

"I mean, personally."

"I get a salary of a quarter million credits a year," said Coleman. "And I donate ninety percent of it to our medical program."

"I never could stand dealing with a thoroughly righteous man," sighed the Secretary. He pulled the miners' demands out of the drawer, picked up the seal of his office, stamped the papers, and signed his name.

Victory celebrations were in progress on almost a thousand scattered worlds, not the least of which was Gamma Leporis IX. Intoxicants flowed and happiness reigned supreme on this final night of idleness.

"Hey!" cried somebody. "Let's let Ferdy in and give him a drink! He's got as much right inside here as anybody."

Indeed he did, agreed Ferdinand silently. He had no auditory orifices with which to hear, but he had means of understanding what was said, and he'd been listening intently all evening.

He didn't especially like being inside the auditorium. It was warm and uncomfortable, the higher oxygen content of the air made his eyes smart, and his metabolism couldn't cope with the whiskey they were feeding him. But Men were a pretty pleasant species, and he was very happy to kill nelsons in exchange for magnesium.

Tomorrow morning, he decided, would be soon enough to present them with the Butterballs' list of demands.

4: The Psychologists

... Probably no field of study was more instantly expanded than that of psychology, for where Man originally had only himself as a subject, he now had literally thousands of races, many with such foreign values that simply separating sentient from non-sentient life forms became a titanic task. For half a millennium Man was able to communicate with less than five percent of the other races of the galaxy; as his new psychological skills improved, he was ultimately able to understand and exchange ideas with almost half of them ...

—*Man: Twelve Millennia of Achievement*

... Conceived as a pure science, Man's mastery of psychology soon became simply another tool to be used in his expansionist endeavors, often pointing out the weaknesses in an enemy's mental defenses. Nonetheless, in its formative years—100 to 600 G.E. —the purpose of alien psychology was still rather pure and idealistic. Some fascinating problems arose and were ultimately solved, and many of Man's methods have since been adopted by ...

—*Origin and History of the Sentient Races*, Vol. 7

Consuela Orta walked into the room and smiled politely at the Madcap. The Madcap immediately began eating its tail.

"Good morning," she said.

The Madcap growled hideously at her, then started battering its head against the padded wall.

"Would you like some water?" asked Consuela, placing a dish on the floor.

The Madcap giggled hysterically, took another bite of its tail, and lay on its back, its feet held rigidly in the air.

Consuela remained where she was for five minutes. Then, with a sigh, she opened the door to leave.

"Good morning," said the Madcap.

"Good morning," repeated Consuela.

The Madcap raced twice around the room, turned over its water bowl, and began licking the liquid up from the floor. Consuela closed the door behind her and stepped out into the hallway to join the man who had been observing her through a one-way mirror.

"That one's crazier than most of them, isn't he?" asked the man.

"It's well-named," agreed Consuela, walking toward the commissary.

"It's a fascinating creature!" said the man enthusiastically. "Just fascinating! Sometimes I think I went into the wrong field."

"And just what *is* your field, Mr. Tanayoka?" asked Consuela. "I was told to show you our facilities and extend every conceivable courtesy to you, but no one has yet told me why."

"I'll come to that in just a moment, Ms. Orta," said the small, black-haired man.

"*Mrs.* Orta," she corrected him.

"My mistake. Now, about the Madcap: Is it intelligent?"

"That is a very chancy question." Consuela smiled. "I have known many humans that I didn't think were intelligent. If you mean, is it sentient, I suspect that it probably is. No non-sentient life form could possibly come up with so many different aberrant reactions to the same stimuli. A life form incapable of all creative thought would fall into a set pattern, whereas yesterday, for example, the Madcap drank the water immediately, gravely shook hands with me, and then tried to stand on the ceiling."

"Maybe it wasn't thirsty today," suggested Tanayoka.

"Given its history of behavior, I'd suggest that it's just as likely that it wasn't thirsty yesterday and was dying of thirst today. No, the more I think about it, the more convinced I am that it's probably sentient. Unbalanced, perhaps, but sentient. Now all I have to do is make some degree of sense out of what it does." She uttered a grim laugh.

"If anyone can do it, I'm told you're the one," said Tanayoka. "You've succeeded in almost thirty-five percent of your cases; that's more than twice the norm."

"That's me: surrogate mother to the galaxy." Consuela paused, then turned to Tanayoka. "How did you know that?"

"I told your superiors that I needed their best alien psychologist. And with these credentials"—he flashed a plastic card before Consuela's eyes—"I usually get what I want."

"And you want me."

"So I'm told," agreed Tanayoka cheerfully.

"Well, what rare beastie am I to make sense out of for your department?" asked Consuela.

"Have you ever heard of the planet Beelzebub?"

"Sounds like something right out of *Paradise Lost*," commented Consuela.

"I very much doubt that it was ever a candidate for Paradise," said Tanayoka. "It's about forty-five light-years from here. I won't go into all its physical features, but it's pretty valuable. The place is simply lousy with gold, platinum, silver, and even uranium."

"I don't see the problem," said Consuela.

"The problem is that there happens to be a resident alien population on Beelzebub. We've been mining there for about eight months. They never tried to contact us or communicate with us, but they didn't hide their presence from us either. At any rate, we had no problems for thirty weeks. Then, eighteen days ago, when we began to load the processed ores onto our ship prior to moving to another area, they began ripping our miners to shreds. The Federation of Miners has gone on strike, and they won't go back to Beelzebub until the Republic can guarantee their safety."

"It's a big galaxy," said Consuela. "Why not do your mining on some other planet?"

"It's not generally known," said Tanayoka, "but the Republic is having more than a little difficulty backing its currency these days. We still use rare metals, you know, and though the days of gold-backed currency are definitely numbered, they're not over yet. We need what Beelzebub has to offer, Mrs. Orta, and we need it badly."

"Badly enough to exterminate an entire native population if it should turn out that they aren't sentient?" asked Consuela, a gleam of understanding coming to her eyes.

Tanayoka nodded. "Your primary job is to determine whether or not they're intelligent. We don't want another Doradus IV."

Consuela nodded. Ever since Doradus IV, when the Navy had destroyed an entire sentient population while defoliating the world prior to mining it—from the air Doradusians bore a striking resemblance to cabbages—a number of alien worlds had closed their doors to the Republic's commerce. The government had suddenly grown very sensitive about its public image, not without cause, and needed no new disasters.

"You mentioned my primary job as if there is a secondary one as well," said Consuela. "Is there?"

"Absolutely," said Tanayoka. "If they *are* sentient, we want you to try to convince them to let us perform our mining operations in peace."

"And if I can't?"

"Why consider unattractive alternatives?" said Tanayoka. "You're the best in your field. Let's just assume that you're going to get the job done."

Consuela suddenly remembered why she had devoted her life to dealing with nonhuman beings possessed of nonhuman motivations.

"I'll meet you at the spaceport this evening," said Tanayoka. "And Mrs. Orta, there is one other consideration."

"Oh?" asked Consuela, her eyebrows rising.

"My department is being pressured to come up with a solution, so I'm afraid I'm going to have to pass some of that pressure down the line to you."

"How much time do I have?"

"Twenty days."

"Twenty days!" she exploded. "Do you realize how long it takes to learn an alien tongue, or to discover what motivates an alien mind, or—"

"They originally gave me ten days," said Tanayoka apologetically. "This is the best I can do."

"Well, you can tell your department that I think it stinks!"

"I do have the authority to make you come," said Tanayoka softly.

"Oh, I'll come, all right. There's not much I can do in

45

twenty days, but these poor creatures deserve *some* consideration before you exterminate them!"

She was still fuming when she boarded Tanayoka's ship, and she hadn't calmed down appreciably by the time they landed on Beelzebub. Tanayoka escorted her to an armored groundcar and took her to the mining sight. Seven small mountains had been strip-mined. The miners had carefully restored the landscape before moving on, and had broken down their ore refinery, which had been at the base of the largest mountain.

"Where was their ship, and at what point were they attacked?" asked Consuela after she had given the area a cursory inspection.

"The ship was about two miles south of us," replied Tanayoka, "and the miners were attacked just about where you and I are standing."

"I assume they fought back?" she said dryly.

"Their contract gives them the right to defend themselves," said Tanayoka, "although it specifically prohibits offensive or aggressive actions."

"I don't suppose anyone thought to save an alien corpse?"

"I'm afraid our weapons fried them to a crisp," admitted Tanayoka. "However, I do have some photographs of the aliens taken by Elaine Bowman, the Pioneer who opened the planet up."

"Why didn't you show them to me during our flight?" asked Consuela.

"You never asked," said Tanayoka.

"May I see them now?"

He withdrew a pair of transparent cubes from his pocket. Inside each was a hologram of an inhabitant of the planet. They stood erect, though she couldn't begin to guess how tall or short they might be, since there was no point of reference. Their heads possessed rather large eyes, ample mouths, and barely discernible auditory orifices. She couldn't make out any nostrils, but assumed they must have been narrow slits, so tiny that they didn't show up on the holograms. The creatures possessed thin, leathery skin of reddish hue.

"Well, what do you make of them?" asked Tanayoka when she had finished studying them.

"So soon?" she said with a smile.

"I thought perhaps they might give you an inkling as to whether or not these creatures are intelligent."

"They tell me a lot more about the planet than the aliens,"

said Consuela. "Gravity about the same as Earth and Deluros VIII, or else they wouldn't be both erect and slender. Mean temperature between twenty-five and forty-eight degrees Centigrade; any less and they'd need hair or feathers or some other body covering for warmth, any greater and they'd probably be nocturnal, which these beasties definitely are not. Also, they don't come from a very mountainous section of Beelzebub, or their motor muscles would be much better developed."

"I know all about the planet," Tanayoka pointed out. "After all, we're standing on it. What I want to know is, are they intelligent? And, equally important, why did they decide to make war on our miners?"

"And you want me to tell you all that, based on beings and a culture I've never seen?" said Consuela. "I appreciate the Republic's confidence in my ability, but it's absolutely out of the question." She paused for a moment. "For what it's worth, the most important single fact now at our disposal is that they waited more than half a year to attack us, and that they did so only after we began making off with the ore."

"Does that imply intelligence?"

"Perhaps. Or it could just be territoriality. Many unintelligent creatures will protect what they consider to be their property. A dog and his bone, for example."

"How about the fact that they have neither clothing nor any other decoration?" asked Tanayoka.

"It's a warm planet," said Consuela. "And not all sentient beings feel the need to wear tokens and trinkets. No, I'm afraid I can't even begin to reach a decision until I've had the chance to observe one of them at close range."

"They've shown no desire to hide from us," said Tanayoka. "I can have one captured and brought to you in a matter of hours."

"Unharmed," said Consuela.

"Of course. My dear Mrs. Orta, what kind of monsters do you take us for?"

"If you'll be polite enough to take me back to the ship to await the alien, I'll be polite enough not to answer your question."

Tanayoka sighed, returned Consuela to her quarters aboard the spacecraft, and issued orders to capture one of the aliens. Two hours later he knocked on her door and informed her that her subject was in the brig, awaiting her pleasure.

When she arrived, she found an inhabitant of Beelzebub

47

pacing back and forth like a caged animal, which it indeed resembled. She pulled up a chair and sat down to observe it.

The alien uttered a loud hooting sound, glared at her for a moment, and then resumed its pacing.

"The jaw's built all wrong," said Consuela. "It must ingest by suction. It couldn't possibly have any teeth."

"Are you a physiologist as well as a psychologist?" asked Tanayoka.

"A little of both. Our field has come a long way since it was concerned with why husbands strayed from the fold."

"Touché!" said the little man. "I notice that it has well-articulated thumbs on its hands. Wouldn't that imply some intelligence? I mean, you need thumbs to build machines, and so on."

"There are still some apes and monkeys in captivity on Earth," said Consuela. "They have thumbs, but they've reached an evolutionary dead end, and hence haven't developed the power of abstract thought."

"What kind of dead end?"

"They're herbivores," explained Consuela. "Thus they have no need to do anything with their hands except peel bananas. There is no environmental need for them to think."

"Surely you're not suggesting that only carnivores can develop intelligence!" said Tanayoka. "What about the Butterballs of Gamma Leporis IX, or the—"

"You misunderstand me," said Consuela. "Being carnivorous has nothing to do with developing intelligence. In point of fact, only a very small percentage of sentient races spring from carnivores. Most meat-eaters evolve *physical* means of catching and killing their prey. What I said was that environmental need creates intelligence. Man developed it because he weighed about a hundred pounds and was trying to kill half-ton herbivores for dinner. No amount of physical equipment could have helped him. Other races develop intelligence for other reasons of need. However, many of them—most, in fact—get sidetracked somewhere along the way. Like the monkeys, for example."

"Then how can you tell if our alien here is intelligent?"

"I intend to ask it," said Consuela.

"How? You don't know anything about its language."

"It's quite possible that we have a language in common. May I have the loan of some paper and a pen?"

Tanayoka sent for them, and a moment later she was carefully drawing a right triangle and writing Pythagoras's theorem beneath it.

"What makes you think it has the slightest acquaintance with the square of the hypotenuse and its relatives?" asked Tanayoka.

"It's a pretty universal theorem," said Consuela. "I expect it is just as true on Beelzebub as on Earth."

She passed the paper through the bars to the alien. It looked at the figures, contorted its mouth into a snarl, and ripped the paper to shreds. Three more attempts brought forth the same results.

"Obviously it's not geometrically inclined," said Consuela. "I'm going to try some simple binary equations next, but technology is usually the forerunner to a knowledge of the binary system, and there's been no evidence of any technology on this world, so I rather expect our friend here to give this the same treatment."

The creature ripped up five sheets of paper before Consuela put her pen and paper aside with a sigh.

"Nonmathematical," she said. "Or noncooperative. Probably the latter."

"Unintelligent?" asked Tanayoka tentatively.

"Not necessarily. I have a son who could never make change, and now he's a newsman of some renown. His math is still absolutely abominable, but I hardly consider him unintelligent."

"I'm beginning to get an appreciation of the problems involved in your line of work," said Tanayoka with a grim smile. "It has also occurred to me that it may know perfectly well what you're doing, but feels obligated to offer you nothing but its name, rank, and serial number."

"That's quite possible," she agreed, without ever taking her eyes off the alien.

"And as a whole, psychology is coming up with about sixteen percent successes," said Tanayoka. "I'm amazed that you come up with even one percent!"

"Well, you can do a lot with percentages," said Consuela. "Usually the Republic considers us successful if we discover their weaknesses. Understanding them takes a little more work." She paused, looking at the alien for a long minute. "Has it had any water since it was captured?"

"Not to my knowledge," said Tanayoka.

"Good," said Consuela. "Let's see if we can't set up a little reward situation."

49

With the aid of some of the crew members she set up two transparent boxes, each containing a jiggerful of water. One box had an untreated red top, the other a blue top that emitted a mild electrical charge when touched. Then she heated up the room and raised the humidity until everyone in it, human and alien alike, was feeling uncomfortable.

The alien was then presented with the two boxes. It immediately opened the one with the blue top.

"Some of us just aren't born lucky," said Consuela, as the alien drank the half-ounce of water within the box. The boxes were removed, the missing water replaced, and they were offered to the alien again. This time it chose the red box.

It chose the blue and the red in order the next two times, and Consuela turned to Tanayoka.

"By now it should know which one is loaded," she said. "Let's start switching them around."

After thirty tries, the alien had chosen the blue box twenty-seven times.

"Some of us were just born dumb," commented Tanayoka.

"Not so," said Consuela. "An unthinking animal would get the right box fifty percent of the time, probably even more. Take my word for it, our friend knows the difference."

"Then why did it purposely shock itself almost every time?"

"Maybe it feels good. This isn't a human physiology we're dealing with."

"So is it intelligent?"

"More than a laboratory mouse," said Consuela. "That's all I can tell you today. Let's cool the room off and give it something to eat."

They left the brig area, and Consuela asked to be taken to the mining site once again.

"I'm having a little difficulty understanding why the aliens took no action against the miners the whole time they were extracting and refining the minerals," she said, her eyes scanning the landscape. "It would seem more sensible for them to attack the moment the miners began stripping the mountains."

"Maybe they wanted to make sure the ore was being removed before they committed themselves," suggested Tanayoka.

She shook her head. "There's no sign of any technology on

this planet. They couldn't know what a refining operation was for, so why did they wait?"

"Does it make that much of a difference?" asked Tanayoka.

"Certainly. If I can come up with a reason as to why they didn't mind raw materials being taken but objected to refined ore, that would prove they were intelligent."

"In what way?"

"Because, having no experience with refined ore, they would have had to extrapolate, by abstract thought, the uses to which it might be put."

"But why would they disapprove?"

"It doesn't matter. The mere fact that they could form a chain of reasoning that would lead to disapproval would be sufficient to prove they were sentient. Don't ask me to psychoanalyze their racial consciousness in twenty days. If I can show you they're intelligent, that ought to be enough to keep the Republic from annihilating them."

She walked from the refining site to the foot of the nearest mountain, then back again.

Then she shrugged, shook her head, and asked to be returned to the ship. She didn't visit the alien again that day, but spent her remaining waking hours poring over Pioneer Bowman's report on the planet.

It didn't tell her much. The alien civilization was totally nomadic—but so were many sentient races. They had a rigid tribal structure—but so did ants and baboons. Pioneer Bowman could discern no intelligible language—but Pioneers had no training in alien linguistics. True, they had no sign of any technology—but Man himself had existed without technology for well over a million years. In short, there was simply not enough information to form a decision one way or the other, which stood to reason: the aliens constituted only a miniscule section of the report, the bulk of which concerned the minerals to be found on the planet and the conditions under which the miners would have to work.

The next morning was spent drawing simple pictures and even simpler mathematical formulae for the alien, with absolutely no success. Then Consuela requested that some samples of raw and processed minerals be brought to her.

She showed and then offered each in turn to the alien, but elicited no response. Borrowing a laser hand weapon, she destroyed both samples. The alien ignored her. She offered it a piece of gold jewelry; it placed it to its lips, grimaced, and flung it back at her.

She spent the next two days alternately trying to communicate with the alien and to get it to demonstrate that it could differentiate between raw and refined minerals. If the alien understood or cared, it kept it a secret.

On her fifth day on Beelzebub, Consuela had two crew members construct a miniaturized spaceship and tiny human figurines. She placed them on a board in front of the alien, put tiny pieces of refined material in their hands, and slowly moved them across the board into the ship. The alien looked bored.

"Have you any inkling as to whether they are intelligent?" asked Tanayoka at dinner that night.

"None whatsoever," replied Consuela. "Nor do I have an answer to the more important problem of why they attacked the miners when they did."

"More important?" asked Tanayoka.

"Certainly. Even if they are not sentient, I don't wish to see them destroyed. If I can find out what precipitated their attack, perhaps we can avoid provoking them again."

On the sixth day, she had the crew members jerryrig a small smelting plant outside the ship. The alien was taken there, under heavy guard, and allowed to observe. It showed no interest at all.

On the seventh day, the alien was escorted to a nearby mountain, one which had not been mined. Consuela, again borrowing a laser weapon, carved a hole three feet above the ground level, exposed some precious minerals in their raw form, and accompanied by the alien and its guards, took the minerals from the site to the ship. There she smelted them as the alien watched, and waited for a reaction. There was none.

After another day of trying to communicate with the alien, Consuela approached Tanayoka.

"It's highly unlikely," she said, "but there is always the possibility, however slight, that you've captured their equivalent of the town idiot. Let's turn it loose and get another one."

Tanayoka gave the appropriate orders, and three hours later Consuela was attempting to make some sense out of a new subject. By the dawn of her sixteenth day on Beelzebub, she had released the second alien as well.

"We can bring you a third one if you think it will do any good," Tanayoka said gently.

She shook her head. "If I've done nothing else, I think I've proved that no one is going to communicate with these fellows in the time remaining to me."

"Then you're giving up?"

"Not at all. I'm just going to have to attack the problem from a different angle. Either our two subjects were going out of their way to be uncooperative, or else they don't give a damn about what we do to their mineral wealth. Since the Republic finds the former conclusion untenable, I'm going to have to assume the latter."

"I'm not quite sure if I follow you, Mrs. Orta," said Tanayoka.

"Since you're not going to stop mining anyway, and since the aliens don't seem to care about mining, I'll have to proceed as if something else precipitated their attack. Now, I'm not as versed in the physical sciences as I should be, but could any of our equipment have emitted a sound, possibly beyond our ability to hear, that could have driven them wild with pain or fury?"

"No," said Tanayoka. "We considered all possible physical causes before we contacted you. There were pungent odors, of course, but they had existed for weeks. There wasn't enough in the way of harmful radiation to have killed an insect. None of the miners went hunting aliens or anything else for sport or meat. We never used a megaphone or microphone in case the volume might startle them. We landed the ship in a totally deserted and desolate area to make sure we didn't damage any life forms."

"The men visited the ship during the first thirty weeks?" asked Consuela.

"Yes."

"Then what," she said, more to herself than to him, "could they possibly have done differently?"

"I wish I knew," said Tanayoka.

"Let me take another look at the site," said Consuela. They took the groundcar and arrived a few minutes later. She walked around, certain that the answer was staring her in the face if only she could rid herself of her preconceptions long enough to see it.

"You seem distressed," said Tanayoka gently after some time had elapsed.

"I'm just trying to clear my mind," she said. "You see, there is an enormous tendency on the part of alien psychologists to anthropomorphize, to give human traits and values to

53

aliens who simply don't possess them. I've got to force myself to stop wondering what would make *me* want to attack the miners, and start attacking the problem of why an alien would do so."

"I see," said Tanayoka.

"It could be something so odd or so tiny that a human would completely overlook it," she continued. "For example, did the miners build latrines or outhouses, or anything else that might be considered a desecration of alien ground?"

"Quite possibly they did," said Tanayoka. "But I couldn't begin to tell you where. We put everything back in order before we left. We even spent an extra day restoring the mountains."

"Is there anything else they could have done on the final day that they hadn't done before—hold a party, send a radio message to Deluros or Earth, anything?"

"Nothing comes to mind," said Tanayoka.

"Then why were they attacked?" she said, more irritated at herself than her companion. "The aliens watched them mine the mountains for half a year. What did they do differently?"

"I wish I could help you, Mrs. Orta."

"So do I," said Consuela.

She sighed, walked to the groundcar, took one last look at the terrain before returning to the ship—

—And then it hit her.

"Curious," she said.

"What is?"

She shook her head in wonderment. "Of course!"

"You know, don't you?" said Tanayoka excitedly. "What was it we did?"

"You know, too," said Consuela. "It's that damned tendency to anthropomorphize again. I should have figured it out two weeks ago."

"I haven't figured it out yet," said Tanayoka. "Won't you please tell me what you've found?"

"Just use a simple process of elimination," said Consuela. "What did our miners do when they were ready to move on to the next site? Well, they tried to load the ore onto the ship, but we are forced by necessity to assume that didn't trigger the aliens off."

"Why forced by necessity?"

"Because you and I both know that if that's the reason, it's too damned bad for the aliens, because the Republic is going to keep on extracting what they need from Beelzebub.

54

Besides, our two sample aliens showed no interest whatever in refined ores. And we know it wasn't the knowledge that the ship would soon be taking off, because they could have had no such knowledge. And we know the miners didn't create any disturbance in their exuberance at completing the first phase of their jobs."

"But there *is* nothing else!" said Tanayoka.

"Yes there is," said Consuela. "Look around you, Mr. Tanayoka, and tell me what you see."

"The mountains."

"And what did the miners do to the mountains when they were through mining?"

"Nothing," said Tanayoka.

"You still don't see it, do you?" said Consuela with a smile. *"They restored them."*

"Of course they did," said Tanayoka. "Surely you're not implying that . . ."

"Indeed I am," said Consuela. "It's the only other thing they did that they had not been doing for the thirty weeks that the aliens left them alone."

"But why should putting the land back the way we found it drive them into a frenzy? It doesn't make any sense."

"Not to you and me," said Consuela. "But it must make a lot of sense to an inhabitant of Beelzebub."

"It's the stupidest thing I ever heard of!" said Tanayoka, throwing up his hands in frustration.

"No, but it's probably the most alien thing you've ever heard of," said Consuela. "You must remember not to think of aliens as good or bad, smart or stupid. The only word that properly defines them is *different*."

"But why would they object to our restoring the mountains?" persisted Tanayoka.

"I have absolutely no idea," said Consuela.

"Can any race that reacts like that possibly be sentient?"

"I don't know," replied Consuela. "And to be perfectly frank about it, at this moment I couldn't possibly care less."

"But——"

"Please let me continue, Mr. Tanayoka. You brought me here to solve your problem. While there is always the possibility of error, I believe that I have solved it. But you must understand that the members of my profession are neither magicians nor omnipotent. It may take years or decades or even centuries to understand why they don't mind having their land ripped to shreds but are enraged at its restoration, and it may take even longer to determine whether they are truly sentient beings. Psychology is hardly an exact science. But I think I have discovered how to guarantee your miners' safety, and I trust I have bought the aliens enough time for future psychologists to answer all your questions about them. And now," she concluded, "if you no longer have need of my services, I'd like to return home."

Four months later Tanayoka paid her a visit.

"You were right," he said admiringly. "I don't think the miners or I really believed it, but it worked. When they finished strip-mining the next three mountains they left them just as they were, and there were no incidents at all."

"I'm gratified to know that everything worked out," said Consuela.

"I think you'll be further gratified to know that a team of three psychologists has been dispatched to Beelzebub to study the native population more thoroughly."

"Indeed I am," said Consuela.

"While I'm here, may I take you to lunch, Mrs. Orta?" asked Tanayoka.

"I'd love to, but I'm afraid I'm a bit late making my rounds today."

Consuela shook his hand, walked down the corridor, stopped at a faucet to fill a small pan with water, then sighed and opened a door.

Inside, the Madcap was happily munching on its tail.

5: The Merchants

. . . As these worlds were assimilated into the budding financial empire of the Republic, it became the duty of the merchants, and more specifically the Department of Commerce and Trade, to bring monied economies into being on these planets. Perhaps the most important single person in the galaxy during this period was Kipchoge Ngana, whose complicity in the death of the Republic has been debated for millenia . . .

—*Man: Twelve Millennia of Achievement*

. . . Foremost of these was Kipchoge Ngana (884–971 G.E.), a ruthless financial and organizational genius who studiously avoided all publicity. It was he who fought tooth and nail against granting the most basic rights to non-human races, and who probably kept the stagnant and decrepit Republic alive and running long past its life expectancy . . .

—*Origin and History of the Sentient Races*, Vol. 8

Kipchoge Ngana leaned his chair back on two legs, put his feet on his desk, and sighed. Things had been going well, both for his department and the Republic. The Gross Galactic Product had doubled for the sixth decade in a row, the brief trade war with Darion III was over, and Man had never had it so good.

It was a strange feeling. He should have been smug and complacent, but instead he felt like a man waiting for the other shoe to drop and not having the slightest idea where it would be dropping from.

He glanced at his appointment calender: two visits from minor officials in Cartography, a luncheon with a merchants' organization from the newly settled Denebian colonies, and a planning conference within his own Department of Commerce and Trade. It was the last that was his specialty, and he was utterly convinced that no single facet of the Republic was quite so important.

Certainly they needed the Cartographers to decide upon the patterns of expansion, and the Pioneer Corps and Navy to open the planets up, and of course Psychology had become the darling of the popularizers of science. But all those came before the fact; each science and parascience had a definite job to do, and once their function was fulfilled, they moved on to the next world. After that, after the planet was made habitable, after the alien contacts had been made, after the Republic had made a commitment to the new world, it was up to the merchants, under the expert guidance of the Department of Commerce and Trade, to move in, to graft the world onto the sprawling economic structure of the galaxy, and to bring it firmly within the Republic's sphere of financial influence.

The Republic had long since learned that military force was a last resort, to be used only in the most insoluble of situations. The trick—and this was Ngana's specialty—was to introduce monied economies to the various worlds until they were so dependent upon continued commerce with the Republic that revolt and isolationism became the most repugnant and unfeasible of concepts.

On about a third of the sentient worlds, the problems had been slight, for economic structures already existed. It was the remaining worlds that wound up as Ngana's pet projects. And he was very good at his work.

There was, for example, Balok VII, a small world possessed of a totally self-reliant society relatively low on the evolutionary scale, but sentient nonetheless. The natives, vaguely humanoid in type, were completely herbivorous, and the continual search for the vast quantities of food they needed to sustain themselves prevented them from developing many other skills. There was some attempt at farming, but the climate was too uncertain for crops to be depended upon, and the economy never developed beyond a one-for-one trading stage.

Ngana had looked the world over, ordered in some twenty thousand "agrarian assistants," and quintupled the amount of available food in three years' time, never once extracting any payment or promise of payment from the natives, and never once allowing them to discover the methods the Republic used to multiply the food supply. At the end of three years a noticeable increase in the population took place, and the agricultural equipment was then sold or leased to private interests within the Republic. It functioned for five more years, and then, at a word from Ngana, all "assistance" came to a halt. Amid hoarse outcries of misery, disease raised its ugly head, and the Republic sent in free medical supplies. After six months, the flow of supplies stopped.

The supplies were then sold to the Republic's merchants, who rented out the agricultural machinery to the natives in exchange for harvests of certain crops, and after the first payments were made on the machinery, the medical supplies were sold on credit against future crops.

Within five more years the natives of Balok VII had need of neither equipment nor medicine, being quite capable of manufacturing their own, but by that time they had a growing agricultural economy, and the first paper Republic credits had already been introduced into the society, with which they purchased newer and better farming machines. And, of course, the continuous introduction of more advanced equipment ensured the production of more and more crops, with the Republic as the only interested speculator.

That had been easy. Korus XVI was a little more difficult. It held a race of silicon-based life forms that inhaled ammonia, excreted a carbon compound, and had a very viable economy that was based predominantly on rare metals. The inhabitants were very happy to be isolated from the mainstream of the Republic's commerce and evinced no desire to trade with any race other than their own.

Ngana authorized fifty merchants to artificially reproduce the rarest of the rare metals that formed the staple of Korus

XVI's financial structure and to flood the planet with them, trading them to private individuals for elements that were of equivalent value to Man. Fifty percent of the merchants' profits went back into continuous market flooding, until the various coins of the Korusian realm became all but worthless. The remaining fifty percent of the profits were applied to "saving" the Korusian economy by putting it into synchronization with that of the Republic, for which the merchants were granted fifty years of exclusive trading rights to the planet. Within a decade, Korus XVI had been added to the list of the Republic's economic satellites.

Now and again a planet would attempt to withdraw from economic association with the Republic; rarely was it successful. Total trade embargo was the first means of reprisal. If this proved unsatisfactory, any medium of financial exchange used by the planet could be duplicated in huge quantities by the merchants in charge of commerce in that particular system. Except for fissionable materials, which were in ever-increasing demand across the galaxy, there was nothing so rare that Man couldn't spare a planetload of it to push an unruly economic entity back into line: diamonds, rare earths, drugs, water, chlorine, whatever an independent-minded planet held near and dear, would immediately be made worthless.

Most economies, whether natural or imposed by the Republic, dealt in essentially artificial mediums of exchange, made valuable only by the populace's confidence in them. There were a few worlds, however, where this did not hold true. If, for example, World X prized apples above all else, and apples were the prime medium of exchange, to be eaten when accumulated, introducing more apples into the society wasn't about to turn it into an economic entity that the Republic could influence and deal with. But finding something that destroyed apple crops, and then reintroducing them through the Republic's merchants, usually did the trick.

Yes, Ngana knew his job, and knew it well. More than four thousand sentient races had been discovered, and well over fifteen hundred of them were already integral cogs in the Republic's vast economic machinery. By the time he retired, Ngana expected to see that figure more than double.

But in the meantime, he was uneasy, and he couldn't quite put his finger on the reason for it. He'd been feeling apprehensive for more than a year now, filled with vague doubts about the wisdom of assimilating so many races so quickly. He did not fear any strivings for economic independence;

60

such problems could and would be dealt with quickly and efficiently. It was something else, something he sensed was more far-reaching, but it was like a glimmer of light he could see only out of the corner of his eye; when he turned full face to it, it was gone.

A buzzer sounded on his desk, and he pressed a button that activated the inter-office communicator. It was Renyan, the Secretary of Commerce and Trade, his immediate superior. The gray-haired visage on the small screen looked troubled.

"Kip," said Renyan, "cancel everything you have on for today and get over to my office right away."

"Something serious?" asked Ngana.

"Very."

"On my way," said Ngana, flicking off the intercom. He debated taking a note pad, but decided that the meeting would probably be on record if he needed to go over anything later. Five minutes found him seated at a large oval table with Renyan and an elderly woman he didn't recognize.

"Kip," said Renyan, "I'd like you to meet Miss Agatha Moore, a member of our trade commission to Lodin XI. Miss Moore, it seems, is the bearer of rather grim tidings."

"Well, what can we do for you, Miss Moore?" asked Ngana.

"Not a thing," said Agatha Moore. "But it's just possible that I can do something for you. Or, at least, prepare you for something that's going to be done to you."

Ngana shot a quick look at Renyan, who just raised his eyebrows and shrugged.

"Are you speaking of me personally?" asked Ngana.

"I'm afraid not," said Miss Moore. "I refer to you only insofar as you are a member of the Republic. And," she added thoughtfully, "because your consummate skill at your job has created the problem."

"I'm afraid I don't follow you at all, Miss Moore," said Ngana, running his fingers through his wiry black hair.

"If you were aware of what I was going to say, I wouldn't be here speaking to you," said Agatha Moore rather primly.

"I apologize," said Ngana. "Please continue."

"Mr. Ngana, I am no psychologist, and I don't imagine you are either. However, it shouldn't take a master of that field to realize what's going on."

Ngana looked at Renyan again, convinced that this was about to become some kind of elaborate joke.

61

"To continue," said Miss Moore, "let me ask you exactly what your specialty is, Mr. Ngana."

"My job is to create favorable economic conditions among alien civilizations and to open their planets up for trade with the Republic's merchants."

"In other words, you develop undeveloped planets and give them all the economic benefits that accrue to the Republic's member worlds."

"That is essentially correct," said Ngana.

"Are you aware of the GGP for the past twelve months?"

"160.4 trillion credits, or thereabouts," said Ngana.

"160.369 to be precise," said Miss Moore. "And are you aware of what portion of that product is due directly to the output of nonhuman worlds and populations?"

"No, I am not."

"88.321 trillion credits," said Miss Moore. "Does that imply something to you?"

"Only that we've done a hell of a good job incorporating them into the economy," said Ngana.

"That's your side of the coin," said Miss Moore. "They, on the other hand, seem to feel that they're economic slaves."

"Meaning?"

"Meaning they feel that if they're to supply such a large proportion of the Republic's capital, they want a share of the profits. Or, to be more precise, they want immediate enfranchisement."

"The other shoe," said Ngana glumly.

"What?" asked Renyan.

"Nothing," he replied. "How do you know this is so?"

"In your work, you deal with figures," said Miss Moore. "In mine, I deal with people, human and nonhuman alike. At a convention on Lodin XI, this was the prime topic of discussion among the alien members present, nor did they seem intent on hiding their feelings or their purposes. They want value received for their economic contributions to the Republic."

"So they want a piece of the action, do they?" asked Ngana. "How well organized are they?"

"Very," said Miss Moore. "As I said, Mr. Ngana, you've done your job too well. They now possess an economic club—a club *you* gave them—to threaten us with."

"Have we any corroborative reports?" Ngana asked Renyan.

"I've had feelers out all day," said Renyan, "and while the movement seems to be in its infancy, it definitely exists."

"Have you contacted Psychology yet?"

"No, Kip," said Renyan. "I thought we'd better discuss all our options first."

"I'll begin by assuming that the Republic isn't crazy about the notion of giving four hundred billion aliens the vote," said Ngana wryly. "Which means whatever action we decide upon must be aimed at preventing this movement from coming to fruition, correct?"

"May I remind you that it was only twenty-six hundred years ago that your own race was held in a slavery more severe than the economic bonds you now shackle these worlds with?" said Miss Moore.

"Your point is noted," said Ngana, "although my own ancestors never left the African continent until long after the American Civil War. And, to be honest with you, Miss Moore, if I were an inhabitant of the Denebian colonies, or Lodin XI, or any other recently assimilated world, I'd be very much in favor of complete and immediate enfranchisement, just as I would have been were I an American slave centuries ago. But I am neither. I am a ranking member of the Republic, charged with perpetuating the interests of my employer. Or to be blunt, I'm one of the Haves. The Have-nots' arguments appeal to me emotionally, but I run my job with my intellect, not with my heart. And if Man is to fulfill whatever destiny he has in the galaxy and claim whatever birthright is his, he'll reach his goal a lot sooner if he does not allow all of his achievements to become subservient to some alien's notion of fair play and morality, or even his own such notion."

"How noble!" said Miss Moore sarcastically.

"Nobility is a drag on the market. I'm paid for solving problems, not for moralizing them away. I'm sorry that you don't admire my ethics; but, on the other hand, I don't think too much of your pragmatism."

"Kip," broke in Renyan hastily, "wait in the anteroom for me, and check out the ramifications of the problem with Psychology. I'll be with you shortly."

Ngana took his leave, walked to the plush anteroom, and sat down. Renyan walked out a few minutes later, looking somewhat flustered.

"You know, Kip," he began, "when I called you in we had only one crisis on our hands. Now we have two."

"Oh?"

"She wants our jobs."

"Both of them?"

"Yours, for saying what you did; and mine, for not firing you on the spot."

"She's just a trivial old lady," said Ngana.

"A rich, politically potent, trivial old lady," corrected Renyan.

"How serious is the problem?"

"It depends who she knows. She could—"

"I don't mean the irritant," said Ngana bluntly. "I mean the problem. How serious are the outworlds about enfranchisement?"

"As I told you, I just learned of it a few hours ago, but there does seem to be considerable open sentiment for it, as far as we can tell."

"And the Republic is against it, of course?"

"Of course."

"How close is the association among the worlds? Can they act as a unified body?"

"Not yet," said Renyan. "But give them twenty years or so and there'll be no doubt of it. We have no trading, immigration, or traveling restrictions. If they want to get together, they'll have ample opportunity to do so."

"All right," said Ngana. "I imagine we ought to begin by having Psychology eliminate all those worlds that won't have the gumption or the temperament to stand up to us. That should knock about half of them out. As for the others, we'll start squeezing them so hard they can't quit."

"You're looking at it all wrong," said Renyan. "They don't want to quit. They want more power *within* the Republic, not total independence from it."

"I know," said Ngana. "But first we have to weaken their bargaining position."

"And we have to do it without cutting the Republic's financial throat," pointed out Renyan.

"I don't know how to put this diplomatically," began Ngana, "but . . ."

"But what?" asked Renyan.

"But you've got a remarkable facility for pointing out the obvious. I don't mean to hurt your pride. You were chosen for your post because you're a fantastic administrator. But solving this problem is simply beyond your realm of experience. May I respectfully suggest that you leave it to your Brain Trust?"

"Meaning you?"

"Meaning me, and my staff. You can modify our solution to suit the political and diplomatic and administrative necessities of the moment, but I'll get a lot more accomplished by returning to my own office than by jawboning here with you."

"You know what I hate about you, Kip?" said Renyan.

"What?"

"You can be the politest sonofabitch in the world when you're trying to prove a point to me, but when we both know you're right you can become one of the most distasteful individuals I've ever met."

Ngana flashed him a smile and returned to his office. He assembled four senior members of his extensive staff, explained the problem to them, and set them to work coordinating various details of the plan he had devised. That done, he had Psychology give him a thumbnail sketch on the characteristics of each race he would be dealing with. Some were loyal to Man, some were unable to summon the emotional independence to offer the Republic an ultimatum, and some simply didn't care. What remained were 845 worlds that could and would do all within their power to gain enfranchisement.

Enfranchisement, of course, was merely a word, a harbinger of things to come. But its meaning was absolutely clear: the ultimate passing of political power from Man to non-Man.

It was a knotty problem, and full of political obstacles. The Republic had no desire to keep the alien worlds in line through overt military force. After all, there were well over a billion suns in the galaxy; almost half of them possessed planets; and an average of one out of every twenty planets held life forms that were either sentient or someday would be. That was a lot of life forms to have massed against you.

Also, there were the 2,500 sentient races that had not yet accepted commerce with the Republic; throttling their brother creatures in too obvious a manner wouldn't exactly entice them into joining the Republic's economic fraternity.

And, finally, there were the potential Fifth Columnists, the humans who felt that the alien worlds had every legal and moral right to enfranchisement and a say in the political future of the galaxy. They would be the most bothersome obstacle, for Man needed to keep his exclusive little fraternity tightly knit at this point in his history; there were just too many outside interests picking away at him to allow internal strife to weaken his infant primacy in the galaxy. Yes, the solution must definitely handle the sympathetic humans with tender kid gloves. The brass knuckles, he decided, would remain hidden for the time being.

Reports began coming back to him. Gamma Leporis IV couldn't make any trouble; they were still entirely aquatic and could be cut off from all communication with the rest of the races. The Denebian Colonies were a trouble spot; it was suspected that they had nuclear weapons, and the capacity to deliver them. Binder VI's economy depended on atomics, but they possessed no native fissionable material; an embargo would probably bring them into line. Canphor VI and VII could withstand an embargo for more than a decade; they had a viable political system, and the last two governors had run on a platform of enfranchisement. And so it went, planet after planet, race after race, economy after economy.

By the end of the week the truth began to manifest itself to Ngana: There was indeed no way to keep the 845 worlds, and very likely all of them, from their share of the spoils. It was possible on a short-term basis, to be sure; but other than total assimilation, the only answer was total political and economic disenfranchisement.

"And that," concluded Ngana to his subordinates, "is the proverbial Pandora's Box. Ultimately half the worlds would revert to economic and possibly social barbarism. But the other half would eventually unite as a competitive entity. The competition would be economic in the beginning, but would sooner or later spread over into political and military competition as well. And Man simply cannot buck those odds at this point in history. I think we're better off to make the best accommodation we can, and make the transition slow enough and difficult enough so that Man can gather his forces and energies for another try at primacy sometime in the future. Any comments?"

"I'd hate to be around after the next election!" said one man fervently.

"We'll carry the next election, and the next twenty after it," said Ngana. "There's going to be a change in the power structure of the galaxy, a huge and vital change, though, let's hope, a temporary one; but none of us will be alive to see it. Surely you don't think we're going to turn the reins of government over to them without putting up a little resistance, do you? No, gentlemen, we are not. Our recommendations will be as follows:

"First, that the sectors of representation be redivided in the most favorable way. The ancient word for it was gerrymandering. This, plus a few rule changes in electoral procedures, will secure political power for us indefinitely even if all the nonhumans in the galaxy are given the vote tomorrow.

"Second, that no assimilated world will be enfranchised without paying a modest fee. The figure I propose is thirty-three percent of its Gross Planetary Product for a period of twenty years.

"Third, that representation be based on a planetary ratio, rather than a racial ratio. Thus, Man would be represented by almost ten thousand planets and colonies; no other race would have more than two dozen."

"They'll scream bloody murder on that one," said one of the subordinates.

"Let 'em. It'll take them fifty years to knock it down; that's fifty more years we've bought for Man.

"Fourth, that all military forces be placed under the rule of Man."

"They'll knock that one down, too," said the subordinate.

"Legally, yes," said Ngana. "But what human commander is going to turn his fleet over to an alien simply because an alien-dominated government tells him to?

"Fifth, and last, that a census be taken prior to enfranchisement. That'll buy us another twenty years or so."

The proposals were written up and submitted to Renyan, who, with the aid of his legal staff, worded them subtly, diplomatically, and legally. They were then sent to the Secretary of the Republic, who eventually gave them his stamp of approval and had them made into law.

The aliens weren't happy about it, but it was better than nothing, and one by one, world by world, they agreed to the terms. Which, decided Ngana, made a considerable amount of sense; not being enfranchised, they hardly had the power to object.

Weeks later he was summoned to Renyan's office, where once again he met Agatha Moore, now in charge of the newly formed Commission of Alien Rights. A brief discussion of minor problems followed, after which Renyan broke open a bottle of his finest liqueur, and passed glasses around.

"To Man," he said, raising his glass, "who may not have

come out of all this smelling like a rose, but who came out on top all the same."

"Do you really think so, Mr. Renyan?" asked Agatha Moore.

"Absolutely," said Renyan expansively. "In one fell swoop we've added twenty percent to the Republic's annual income, nipped what amounted to an insurrection in the bud, satisfied if not delighted our fellow races, and secured Man's political power for the forseeable future."

"And what do you think, Mr. Ngana?" she asked.

"I think Man has had it," he replied bluntly.

"*What?*" demanded Renyan.

"Oh, not tomorrow, or even a century from now. I bought us quite a bit of time," said Ngana. "But the handwriting is on the wall. We expanded too far too fast, tried to do too much too soon. In a matter of four or five hundred more years we'll have run out of stepping blocks to throw at the other races, and we'll be out in the cold. I've secured us enough military might so that we'll survive. In fact, we'll do more than survive; we'll thrive and prosper. What we will *not* do is rule the galaxy with an iron hand. Not yet, anyway. The first chapter in Man's galactic history is coming to an end. The best we can do is consolidate what we've got and try to hang onto it for a few millennia; then we'll be ready to move forward again."

"You sound as if we're about to enter a galactic Dark Age," scoffed Renyan.

"No," said Ngana. "But our first Golden Age is going to get rather tarnished in the years ahead. Am I correct, Miss Moore?"

"Absolutely," said Agatha Moore.

"Well, I'll be damned!" snapped Renyan. "You make it sound as if you sold us out!"

"Not at all," said Ngana. "I simply postponed the inevitable for as long as I could, and got us the best bargain I could manage. The problem—I won't call it a fault—was inherent in our basic dream of Empire . . . and make no mistake about it: Empire is what we were dreaming of. To control a world, you must control its economy, but for a world to have an economy it must be enlightened enough to ultimately desire fair payment for its labors. They happened to pick this point in history to extract that payment.

"If it will make you feel any better, Man will continue to be the most potent and powerful single race in the galaxy.

But a millennium or so from now, he will stand alone and apart from a galaxy that will be more or less united against him, or at least a galaxy with goals considerably different from his. Then Man will begin the second stage of his destiny. The first was to overcome the obstacles of Nature, and he succeeded with consummate ease. The next step will be to overcome the intelligent races of the galaxy, some of them a by-product of Nature, some bastard stepchildren of an illegitimate union between Man and Nature, for many of them would not have had their annoying drives and ambitions without our guidance and example. I'll be surprised if Man accomplishes that step as easily as he took the first one, but if he's to be the true master of the galaxy he'll have to do it sooner or later."

"Probably later," said Agatha Moore.

"Don't count us out too soon," said Ngana. "And now, if you will excuse me, I'm afraid I must return from the remote future to the problems of the here and now. The natives of Pinot VIII don't seem to give too much of a damn for the value of a credit these days, and since I'm still on salary, I imagine I'll have to look into the matter."

And, so saying, the man who had extended the life of the Republic while simultaneously signing its death warrant scurried back to his office, thoroughly enmeshed in his newest problem. The future would have to take care of itself; as for the present, he had work to do.

Third Millennium:
DEMOCRACY

6: The Diplomats

. . . It soon became apparent that the Democracy had taken on the proportions of a Frankenstein monster unleashed by Man upon himself. Almost every galactic office of influence was held by non-human races, and Man found himself dealing from a position of weakness heretofore unknown to him. To retain what political and economic power still remained, the diplomats took on new powers and functions, becoming not merely ambassadors but actual policy makers, as in the case of . . .

—*Man: Twelve Millennia of Achievement*

. . . Never one to take setbacks lightly, even those that occurred as a result of a galaxy-wide enfranchisement and the subsequent democratic restructuring, Man soon developed his Diplomatic Corps. Ostensibly they were ambassadors of goodwill whose sole purpose was to make new allies and iron out misunderstandings with old ones, but in actuality . . .

—*Origin and History of the Sentient Races,* Vol. 8

Eleven hundred years, reflected Hermione Chatham-Smythe, was a long time to be without glory.

She looked at one of the viewing screens as her ship sped through space, and a thousand million stars blurred into one huge sparkling curtain. Some of those stars Man had lost, others he still held. But he hungered for all of them, hungered so greatly that he could almost taste them.

The empty, gnawing lust was not new. Man had felt it before, had probably been born with it. And like a strong young giant, he had stalked across the galaxy, grasping at all within his reach. But in his youthful eagerness, he had grabbed more than his hand could hold, and bit by bit it began slipping away. Where once he had held twelve thousand worlds in his hand and reached for more, now he possessed a mere nine hundred, and had been seeking, for fifty generations, only to regain what had formerly been his.

The worlds were valuable in and of themselves, but were even more valuable as a symbol, a testament to Man's primacy.

And Man would get them back. Even now, with his back to the wall, he dreamed not of survival, but of laying claim once again to his galactic birthright. Success wouldn't come as easily as it had in the heyday of the Republic, but it would be built more carefully this time, more solidly; it would be built to last as long as Man himself.

And Man planned to last a long, long time.

The first steps were simple: Man consolidated what holdings remained to him. Bit by bit he began expanding again, but never did he move on to a new world or system until the last one was made secure. And always in Man's mind was the knowledge that pitted against him was an entire galaxy, a galaxy he had helped to unite in opposition to his claim upon it. It was a galaxy that, in whole or in part, still needed his trade, his science, his drive. But it was also a galaxy that was no longer playing by Man's ground rules.

Which, sighed Hermione, was where *she* came in.

She flicked an intercom device beside her and spoke into it. "Much longer?"

"About two more hours," replied the pilot. "Are there any final orders concerning our approach?"

"Not if our information was correct. As soon as we're close enough to see or sense what's going on, come to a dead stop."

She turned back to the viewing screen. Somewhere up

ahead was her destination, the site of a very minor little war between two very minor little races. And the powers-that-be on Deluros VIII (Earth had not been abandoned, but the bureaucracy had long since outgrown it) had decided that one or both races needed a friend. At least one thing Kipchoge Ngana had predicted two millennia ago had come to pass: Although Man's military and economic power was minimal compared to that portion of the galactic races that were arrayed against him, he was still the single most powerful race around. Which meant, of course, that as long as his relations with other races were on a one-to-one basis, he was usually able to call the shots.

Just under two hours later the pilot informed her that they were entering the system that housed the Ramorians' home planet. Hermione sent for Commodore Lucius Barnes, her young, super-efficient military adviser. "Does our basic information check out?" she asked when he arrived.

"Pretty much so," replied Barnes. "Ramor is not too different from Earth: about ten percent smaller, slightly higher oxygen content, rotates on its axis once every nineteen hours, solar year seems to be about 322 days or thereabouts. Theoretically, at least, they speak Galactic-O."

That last was a relief. No single language could be accommodated by all the varied races of the galaxy, but great strides had been made in the field of communications, foremost of which were the development of Galactic O,C,M,G, and N, the letters standing for Oxygen, Chlorine, Methane, Guttural, and Nonclassifiable. Almost eighty-five percent of the sentient races breathed either oxygen, chlorine, or methane, and one couldn't expect a crystalline methane-breather to be able to produce the same explosive sounds as a carbon-based oxygen-breather, and so on. So five forms of Galactic had been developed, and most of the races were capable of speaking in at least one of the variations. There never had been, and probably never would be, a translating mechanism that would instantaneously, or even slowly, translate the sense of every native language; but every galactic traveler possessed an incredibly miniaturized T-pack which could give immediate translations of Galactic. No more than one race in five even knew of the existence of the Galactic languages, but even that percentage made the traveler's work much easier.

"Can we assess the situation yet?" asked Hermione.

"Yes, ma'am," responded Barnes. "There are six planets in

the system. Ramor itself has two moons, and the fifth planet, a giant, has eleven. Most of them are colonized, and our spectroscopic analysis indicates that all of them could be mined for iron and some of the rarer metals, which is probably the purpose of the colonies. At this moment, the third and seventh moons of the fifth planet are under attack by what seems to be a rather small expeditionary force."

"That would be the Teroni," interposed Hermione.

"What have we got on Teron, ma'am?"

"Chlorine-breathers. Teron is in the nearest star system, some two parsecs away. We once controlled the fourth planet from their sun, but never had any interest in Teron, which is the ninth planet. From what we've been able to determine, Teron and Ramor had an agreement that allowed Ramor to mine the second planet in Teron's system, while the Teroni were given mining rights to the moons of Ramor's fifth planet. We don't know exactly what happened next, but six years ago all mining forces were withdrawn, all embassies closed, and all diplomatic relations broken off. Since that time there have been a number of minor skirmishes between the two races, but no all-out war as yet."

"Why not?"

"The Teroni would ultimately win, but not without first absorbing some devastating losses."

"Then why are we in Ramor's system rather than Teron's?" asked Barnes.

"Because," said Hermione, "it would appear that Ramor is in greater need of a big brother with muscle. Neither system has been willing to trade with Man for centuries, and both have some agricultural goods and rare earths that we need. My orders, which are delightfully vague, are simply to open up a line of trade with one or both of them. How I do so is my own business."

"And have you any ideas based on what we know?"

"Indeed I do," said Hermione. "In your considered opinion, how do their military ships stack up to this one?"

"No contest," came the quick reply. "According to our readout, it would take about twenty of them just to put a dent in us."

"And you consider there to be little or no difference between the Ramorian ships and those of the Teroni?"

"In structure, they're totally different," said Barnes. "In capabilities, they're two sides of the same coin."

"Now, as I understand it," said Hermione, "the Teroni

73

have a fleet of some fifty-five military ships, while the Ramorians have thirty-two."

"In that case," said Barnes, "neither has enough to adequately defend its own system against an all-out attack by the other. Sooner or later, one of the ships would have to get through."

"I agree," said Hermione. "Which is why they've limited their skirmishes to the mining colonies. It seems to be an unspoken rule of the game that massive attacks and massive retaliations are to be avoided at all costs. Tell me: How many Teroni ships are in the area of the Ramorian moons right now?"

"Sixteen that we've been able to spot; possibly one or two more."

"That ought to be enough," mused Hermione. Then: "Would you please open up a line of communication with Ramor for me?"

A few moments later she was conversing with a man who, if not the head of the Ramorian planetary government, was at least authorized to speak for that personage.

"The ship *Haiti*, out of Deluros VIII, race of Man, bids you welcome," said Hermione.

"We bid the *Haiti* welcome," came the reply, "and respectfully request its purpose."

"Too long have our races lived in mutual isolation," said Hermione, being very careful that she allowed for no misinterpretation of her Galactic-O. "We humbly suggest that the time has come for our races to renew our brotherhood and open our space routes to free trade once again. As a gesture of our goodwill, we bear a cargo consisting of machines that will synthesize artificial fabrics, which we know that your miners will value highly. We ask nothing in return except the right of free trade with you."

"I am afraid that is out of the question," replied the Ramorian. "Centuries ago our people had a taste of what free trade with Man means, and the memory of it still stings bitterly. You will not be molested, but you are forbidden to land on any world in our system. We appreciate your gesture of friendship, but we cannot and will not accept this or any other inducement to reopen any form of commerce with Deluros VIII or any other planet housing the race of Man."

Hermione cut the communication off, then turned to Barnes.

"Ma'am?"

"I think the time has come for a more forceful gesture," she said. "You say there are sixteen Teroni ships attacking the moons of the fifth planet. Can we destroy about a dozen of them without any great risk to ourselves?"

"Absolutely."

"Then have the crew do so, and chase the Teroni survivors out of this system in the general direction of their home planet."

The *Haiti* reached the beleaguered moons in a matter of minutes. With no warning whatsoever it blasted five Teroni ships out of existence before they even knew it was among them.

With the *Haiti*'s speed, maneuvering power, and defenses, the remainder of the job was just a mop-up action. Its armaments—the end product of an arms race that had existed since the first caveman discovered the first femur bone—were devastating, and a few moments' time saw it chasing the four surviving ships back toward Teron.

"Is there any way we can fake a disabling hit to the *Haiti*?" asked Hermione.

"Right now?" asked Barnes.

"Well, before the Teroni are beyond sight and sensor range. Then have the ship limp back to Ramor just fast enough so that they can't overhaul it."

The pilot did as Barnes instructed, and the Teroni returned to their home planet with the false knowledge that the *Haiti* wouldn't be able to do too much damage until repairs were made.

Before long, Hermione was once again in communication with the Ramorian spokesman.

"The ship *Haiti*, out of Deluros VIII, race of Man, sends you greetings and felicitations."

"Our position remains unchanged," was the terse reply.

"We do not doubt your sincerity," said Hermione. "But to prove our own goodwill toward all the people of Ramor, we have recently engaged a number of Teroni ships in the vicinity of the moons of your fifth planet."

"And?" The radio didn't record it, but Hermione had a strong suspicion that there was a long gulp in there somewhere.

"And we achieved a stunning triumph for the people of Ramor. We flew no colors, so the glory of victory will be credited solely to your planetary government. We trust you will accept this as a further proof of our friendship, and will—"

"Did you destroy them all?" came the imperative question.

"Let me consult my figures," said Hermione, smiling as she allowed the Ramorian spokesman to sweat for an extra minute. "No," she said at last. "But twelve Teroni ships were totally demolished with absolutely no Ramorian casualties. Four ships did indeed escape, but we have doubtless secured your mining colonies for the foreseeable future."

"You're sure four of them escaped?"

"Yes," said Hermione calmly. "We could have hunted them down, but how else would the tyrants of Teron know that they may no longer harass our Ramorian friends with impunity?"

Something resembling a groan came across the radio.

"And now, to further show our goodwill, the *Haiti* will return to Deluros VIII, and will never again trespass into Ramorian space until such time as you, our brethren, actively pursue a trading treaty. We bid you farewell, and earnestly wish that your Deity may smile upon you."

She cut communications, and was not surprised to note an immediate attempt to reopen them.

"Wait!" came the Ramorian's frantic supplication. "You can't leave our system now!"

"Why not?" asked Hermione innocently. "We realize that it will doubtless take you time to consider all the implications of our act of brotherhood. We are prepared to wait until you come to us freely and openly. It is not Man's way to apply force of any type."

"But what if the Teroni return? They still outnumber us!"

"Why would they return?" asked Hermione sweetly. "Not only did we teach them new respect for the forces of Ramor, but they have never previously launched an all-out attack on you."

"They were never so blatantly provoked before," said the Ramorian bitterly.

"I feel," said Hermione, "that your worries are needless. After all, I am certain that the four Teroni survivors were too far away to tell that our ship was severely crippled."

"Please explain yourself!" came the desperate demand.

"As we were pursuing the survivors, a chance shell exploded against our hull, crippling us. But I'm sure the Teroni could not have seen it happen. After all, they were some ten million miles away when it occurred."

"Their sensing devices have a range of twice that distance!" said the Ramorian. "Now they'll know that it is safe to retaliate against us! They can be here in less than two days!"

"I'm so sorry!" exclaimed Hermione. "The repairs required to make our ship totally efficient again would take less than half a day, but I fear the journey to Deluros VIII, in our present condition, will consume almost a year. If only there were some other place where we might make repairs . . ."

"Please stand by," said the Ramorian. The radio went dead for a few minutes, then came on again. "I have been instructed to inform you that you will be permitted to make your repairs on Ramor, or in orbit about us if that is more convenient to you."

"How charitable of you," said Hermione. "However, I realize that we have blundered and caused you considerable mental and emotional distress by our meddling. Therefore, I feel it would be unfair to impose on you any further. No, we will follow our original plan and return to Deluros VIII, to repair the ship and await your decision about the reopening of trade."

"But the Teroni will destroy us!"

"Surely you overestimate them," said Hermione. "However, if you were to consider an immediate trading treaty, we would, as a further gesture of brotherhood, remain in your star system until such time as the Teroni are convinced that Ramor is virtually invincible."

Hermione leaned back, shut her eyes, and smiled. It was too bad, she decided, that neither the Ramorians nor Galactic-O had an analog word for "blackmail."

Within two hours, Hermione Chatham-Smythe, ambassador-at-large, and the premier of Ramor's planetary government had affixed their signatures to a treaty that once again allowed Man to deal commercially with the inhabitants of the Ramorian system.

After sending the news on to Deluros VIII, Hermione invited the pilot and Commodore Barnes up to her suite for a brandy.

"Where to next, ma'am?" asked the pilot.

"It's been quite a long time since we've established a reciprocal trade agreement with any chlorine-breathers in this sector. I'm sure that, given time, we can convince our Teroni brethren of our friendship and good intentions. Don't you agree?"

She smiled sweetly and took a sip from her delicate long-stemmed glass.

7: The Olympians

... Like the Pony Express, which earned a place in human history far surpassing the importance of its accomplishments in its eleven-month lifetime, so did the cult of the Olympians receive an amount of publicity totally out of proportion to its achievements during its brief, twenty-two month existence. This in no way is meant to denigrate those romantic idols of the early Democracy, for at that time Man needed all the heroes he could get, and certainly no group ever filled that need with the zest and flourish of the Olympians ...

—*Man: Twelve Millennia of Achievement*

... Perhaps worthy of a passing mention are the Olympians, for it is doubtful that any other segment of humanity so accurately mirrored Man's incredible ego, his delight in humiliating other races, and ...

Origin and History of the Sentient Races, Vol. 8

There were fifty thousand beings in the stadium, and countless billions more watching via video. And every last one of them shared the same goal: to watch him go crashing down to defeat.

"Big moment's coming up!" said Hailey, who slapped life into his legs as he lay, face down, on the rubbing table. "Today's the day we'll show 'em, big fella."

He stared dead ahead, unmoving. "You hope," he said.

"I know," said Hailey. "You're a Man, kid, and Men don't lose. Ready to meet the press yet?"

He nodded.

The door was unlatched, and a flood of reporters, human and nonhuman, pressed about him.

"Still think you're going to take him, Big John?"

He nodded. Olympians were known for their reticence. They had managers to answer questions.

"It's one hundred and thirty degrees out there," said another. "Not much oxygen, either."

He simply stared at the reporter. No question had been asked, so he offered no answer.

"Boys," said Hailey, stepping in front of him, "you know Big John's got to get emotionally up for this, so shoot your questions at me. I'll be happy to answer any of them." He flashed a confident grin at one of the video cameras.

"I didn't know Olympians had any emotions," said a Lodin XI reporter sarcastically.

"Sure they do, sure they do," jabbered Hailey. "They're just too professional to show 'em, that's all."

"Mr. Hailey," said a space-suited chlorine-breather, using his T-pack, "just exactly what does Mr. Tinsmith hope to prove by all this?"

"I'm glad you asked that question, sir," said Hailey. "Very glad indeed. It's something I'm sure a lot of your viewers have wondered about. Well, let me put the answer this way: Big John Tinsmith is an Olympian, with all that that implies. He took his vows four years ago, swore an oath of total abstinence from sexual congress, alcoholic stimulants, detrimental narcotics, and tobacco. As a member of the cult of the Olympians, his job is identical to that of his brethren: to travel the length and breadth of the galaxy as an ambassador of Man's goodwill and sportsmanship, challenging native races to those physical contests in which they specialize."

"Then why haven't any Olympians challenged a Torqual to a wrestling match?" came a question.

"As I was saying," continued Hailey, "the natives of Emra

IV pride themselves on their fleetness of foot. Foot racing is their highest form of physical sport, and so—"

"It wouldn't have to do with the face that the Torquals go twelve hundred pounds of solid muscle, would it?" persisted the questioner.

"Well, we hadn't wanted to make it public, but Sherif Ibn ben Iskad has challenged Torqual to put up its champion for a match next month."

"Sherif Iskad!" whooped a human reporter. "Now, that *is* news! Iskad's never lost, has he?"

"No Olympian has," said Hailey. "And now that that's settled, I'll get back to the subject. Big John Tinsmith will be running against the very finest that Emra IV has to offer, and I guarantee you're going to see . . ."

On and on Hailey droned, answering those questions that appealed to him, adroitly ducking those he didn't care for. Finally, fifteen minutes before post time, he cleared the room again and turned to Tinsmith.

"How do you feel, kid?"

"Fine," said Tinsmith, who hadn't moved a muscle.

"Herb!" snapped Hailey. "Lock and bolt the door. No one comes in for ten minutes."

The trainer's assistant secured the door, and Hailey pulled out a small leather bag from beneath the rubbing table. He opened it, pulled out a number of syringes, and began going over the labels on a score or more of small bottles.

"Adrenalin," he announced, shooting a massive dose into Tinsmith's arm. "Terrain looked a little rough, too. Better have a little phenylbutazone." One dose was inserted into each calf. "Something to make you breathe the air a little easier . . . here, this'll ease the heat a bit . . . yep, that's about it. Getting sharp?"

Tinsmith moved for the first time, sitting up on the edge of the table, his long, lean legs dangling a few inches above the polished floor. He took two deep breaths, exhaled them slowly, and nodded.

"Good," said Hailey. "Personally, I was against this race. I think it's a little soon for you yet. But Olympians can't say no, so we stalled as long as we could and then agreed to it." Tinsmith lowered himself to the floor, knelt down, and began tightening his shoes. "Now, this guy's fast, make no bones about it," said Hailey. "Damned fast. He'll knock off the first mile in under three minutes, which means you'll be so far back you probably won't be able to see him. But the Emrans

81

are short on staying power. Figure he'll get the second mile in three and a half, the third in three and three-quarters. Save your kick until then. It's four miles and eighty yards. If you run like you trained, you ought to pull even with him a good quarter mile from the finish." Hailey chuckled. "Won't that be something, though! Have that bastard pull out by hundreds of yards and then nip him at the wire just when every goddam alien from here to the Rim thinks an Olympian has finally gone and got himself beat. Sheer beauty, I call it!"

"Ready," said Tinsmith, turning to the door.

"Just remember, kid," said Hailey. "No Olympian has ever lost. You represent the race of Man. All of its prestige rides on your shoulders. The first time one of you gets beat, that's the day the Olympians disband."

"I know," said Tinsmith tonelessly.

Hailey opened the door. "Want me to go with you? Give you a little company till you reach the track?"

"Olympians walk alone," said Tinsmith, and went out the door.

He strode through a long, narrow, winding passageway, and a few minutes later reached the floor of the massive stadium. The air was hot, oppressive. He took a deep breath, decided that the shot was working, and walked out to where the throng in the stands could see him.

They jeered.

Showing and feeling no emotion, looking neither right nor left, he walked to where his opponent was awaiting him. The Emran was humanoid in type. He stood about five feet tall, and had huge, powerful legs. The thighs, especially, were knotted with muscle, and the feet, though splayed, looked extremely efficient. His skin was red-bronze, and both body and head were totally without hair. Tinsmith glanced at the Emran's chest: It seemed to have no greater lung capacity than his own. Next his gaze went to the Emran's nose and mouth. The former was large, the latter small, with a prominent chin. That meant there'd be no gasping for air through his mouth during the final mile; if he got tired, he'd stay that way. Satisfied, and without a look at any other part of the Emran nor any gesture of greeting, he stood at the starting line, arms folded, eyes straight ahead.

One of the officials walked over and offered him a modified T-pack, for it was well known that Olympians spoke no language not native to their home worlds. He shook his head, and the official shrugged and walked away.

Another Emran began speaking through a microphone, and the loudspeaker system produced a series of tinny echoes from all across the stadium. There were rabid cheers, and Tinsmith knew they had announced the name of the home-world champion. A moment later came the jeers, as he heard his own name hideously mispronounced. Then the course of the race was mapped—thrice around the massive stadium on a rocky track—and finally the ground rules were read.

A coin was flipped for the inside position. Tinsmith disdained to call it, but the Emran did, and lost. Tinsmith walked over to his place on the starting line.

As he stood there, crouching, awaiting the start of the race, he glanced over at the Emran and studied him briefly. He was human enough so that Tinsmith could see the awful tension and concentration painted vividly on his already-sweating face. And why not? He was carrying a pretty big load on his shoulders, too. He was the fleetest speedster of a race of speedsters. The Emran, aware of Tinsmith's gaze, looked at him and worked his mouth into what passed for a smile. Tinsmith stared coldly back at him, expressionless.

He had nothing against this being, nor any of his past opponents; just as Iskad had nothing against all the beings he had destroyed with his muscle, just as the brilliant Kobernykov had nothing against the thousands of beings he had defeated at the gamesboards. He didn't want to cause this opponent the shame of defeat before this vast audience of his peers.

But Olympians had no choice but to win. If any Olympian, anywhere, lost, the mythos they were building about Man's invincibility would be shattered, and they would be just one more race of talented competitors on the gamefields of the galaxy. And *that*, he knew, was unacceptable. More than that, it was unthinkable.

It was not for the adulation of Man that the Olympians competed. That was a side benefit, and an occasionally bothersome one. They lived only to hear the jeers of the other races when they stepped onto the field, a little less vocal at each successive event, and to hear them diminish throughout a contest until there was a respectful silence, perhaps mixed with awe, at the conclusion. The awe was not for the individual Olympian, but the race he represented, which was as it should be.

There was no time for further reflection, for the race began and the Emran sprinted out to a quick lead. Tinsmith

83

tried briefly to keep up with him, then fell into stride, his long, lean legs eating up the ground with an effortless pace. For the first quarter mile he breathed through his nostrils, testing the efficacy of the stimulants; then, satisfied, he resumed his normal method of breathing, one gulp of air to every three strides.

Far ahead of him the Emran was increasing his lead, pulling out by first two hundred, then three hundred yards. The Olympian paid no attention to him. Hailey had told him what the Emran could and couldn't do, and he knew his own capabilities. If Hailey's information was right, he'd be pulling up to the Emran in about eleven minutes. And if Hailey was wrong . . .

He shook his head. Hailey was never wrong.

The crowd was cheering, screaming the name of its champion, and across the galaxy 500 billion viewers watched as the Olympian fell so far behind that the video picture couldn't accommodate both runners. And every single one of them, Tinsmith knew, human and nonhuman alike, was asking himself the same question: Could this be the day? Could this be the day that an Olympian would finally lose?

Everyone but Hailey, who sat quietly in his box, stopwatch in hand, nodding his head. The kid was going well, was obeying orders to a T. The first half in 1:49, the mile in 3:40. He picked up his binoculars, saw that his charge was showing no signs of strain or fatigue, and leaned back, content.

At the end of the second mile the Emran's lead had not diminished, and even the handful of humans in the stadium sensed an impending upset. But then, slowly, inexorably, Tinsmith began closing the gap. After three miles, he was once again only two hundred yards behind, and as they turned up the backstretch for the final time, he had narrowed the Emran's advantage to one hundred and fifty yards.

And there the margin stayed, as first the Emran and then, more than twenty seconds later, Tinsmith hit the far turn. The Olympian peered ahead through the dust after the flying bronzed figure ahead of him.

Something was wrong! The Emran should be coming back to him by now, should be feeling the strain of that torrid early pace on those heavy, burly legs, should be shorter of stride and breath. But he wasn't. His legs were still eating up the ground, still keeping that margin between them.

Tinsmith knew then that he couldn't wait any longer, that the homestretch was too late, that his body, already beginning to feel the strain, would have to respond right now. There would be no breather for him, no tired opponent to pass at his leisure, if he was to attain the anonymity of victory, the knowledge that he was just another addition to an immense list of triumphs, rather than the last Olympian.

He spurted forward, spurred on more by fear than desire. His legs ached, the soles of his feet burned, his breath came in short, painful gasps.

Into the homestretch he raced, his body screaming for relief, his mind trying to blot out the agony. Now he was within seventy yards of the Emran, now fifty. The Emran heard the yells of the crowd, knew the Olympian was making a run at him, and forced his own tortured legs to maintain the pace.

On and on the two raced, each carrying a world on his shoulders. Tinsmith was still eating into the Emran's margin, but he was running out of racetrack. He looked up, his vision blurred, and willing the spots away from his eyes he focused on the finish wire. It hung across the track, a mere two hundred yards distant. He was thirty yards farther from it than the Emran.

He was going to lose. He knew it, felt in in every throbbing muscle, every bone-shattering stride. When they spoke of the Olympians in future years, on worlds not yet discovered, *he* would be the one they'd name. The one who lost.

"No!" he screamed. "*No! Not me!*"

His pace increased. He was not running after the Emran any longer, he was running from every human, living or yet to be born, in the galaxy.

"*NO!*"

He was still screaming when he crossed the finish line five yards ahead of his opponent.

He wanted to collapse, to let his abused body melt and become one with the dirt and the stone on the floor of the stadium. But he couldn't. Not yet, not until he was back in the dressing room.

He was vaguely aware of one of Hailey's assistants breaking through the cordon of police and officials, racing up to support him, but he brushed him away with a sweep of his long, sweat-soaked arm. Someone else came up with a jug of water. Later he'd take it, later he'd pour quarts and gallons into his dry, rasping throat. But not now. Not in front of *them.*

The fire in his lungs was beginning to diminish, to be replaced by a dull, throbbing ache. Suddenly he remembered the cameras. He swallowed once, then drew himself up to his full height. He glanced calmly, disdainfully, at the throng of reporters, then turned and began the slow, painful trek to the dressing room.

Hailey moved as if to accompany him, then stopped. Another of Hailey's aides began to walk after him, but the trainer grabbed his arm and held him back. Hailey understood.

Olympians walked alone.

8: The Barristers

. . . As the Olympians fought for Man on the fields of honor, so, in a far more meaningful way, did the barristers fight for Man in the courts of law. The problems were both new and immense, for a million alien worlds with a corresponding set of mores, laws, and statutes were the battlefields, and as often as not the lawbreakers had not the slightest notion that they were violating planetary ordinances. In many cases the laws were simply incomprehensible, totally meaningless to someone raised in a human culture; but even then, Man looked after his own, and, however hopeless the case, one or more barristers were sent in to defend their errant brother. Perhaps no other barrister during the period of the Democracy achieved quite the measure of fame that Ivor Khalinov did. Born at the huge complex on Caliban, he grew to maturity on that incredible world prior to . . .

> —*Man: Twelve Millennia of Achievement*

Khalinov (2399–2484 G.E.) came to prominence as a result of a number of admittedly brilliant cases in the courts of Lodin XI, Binder VI, and Canphor VII, worlds where no Man had ever won a decision before. Unquestionably possessed of one of the greatest legal minds of his era, Khalinov's courtroom and pretrial tactics were nonetheless . . .

—*Origin and History of the Sentient Races*, Vol. 8

"Son," said Khalinov, peering out from beneath his gray, bushy eyebrows, "I'm going to be perfectly honest with you: I'd much rather be prosecuting this case than defending it."

"Thanks a lot," said the blond youth glumly.

"Oh, I didn't say I wouldn't take the case," said Khalinov. "Your parents are paying me far more than you're worth. More than anyone's worth, really. I just remarked that I don't think the odds are in our favor."

"You've bucked the odds before," said the youth, almost pleadingly. "That closing argument of yours in the blasphemy case on Lodin XI is still required reading in every school in the Deluros system."

"Well, not quite *every* school." Khalinov smiled. "But be that as it may, your case is a little different from blasphemy through ignorance of local custom. You are charged with killing fifty-seven sentient entities on the planet Atria XVI. Admittedly it was an involuntary action, compounded by carelessness, and it could not possibly be construed as malicious. But the fact remains that you did indeed cause their deaths."

"But . . ."

"Furthermore, Atria XVI has no plea-bargaining. Manslaughter, murder three, involuntary homicide—none of these terms exist in Atrian law. You either killed them or you didn't, regardless of circumstances. And son, you killed them."

"Then why defend me at all?"

"Aside from the money, you mean?" asked Khalinov. "I guess it's because I still believe that every man has the right to a defense—and on Atria XVI, you need a good defense about as much as any man I ever knew. You know, the simple act of resisting arrest and returning here to Deluros VIII merits the equivalent of a life sentence. You knew we'd extradite you, didn't you?"

"I wasn't thinking," said the youth. "I just couldn't believe what was happening. What's the penalty if I'm convicted, Mr. Khalinov?"

"There's only one penalty for murder in the Atrian system," said Khalinov. "Death by heat."

The youth's body seemed to shrink into itself. "I kind of guessed that."

"Don't give up the ship just yet, son," said Khalinov. "All the odds mean is that we'll have to fight a little harder." He pressed a button on his desk, and four armed guards came in. He nodded to them, then turned back to the boy. "They'll be taking you to Komornos, a moon of Atria V, to await trial. I've got your preliminary hearing and bill of indictment here, along with transcripts of our interviews, so unless something comes up, I won't be seeing you until the trial."

As the youth was led out, Khalinov pressed two more buttons to summon his junior partners, Kominsky and Braque. Neither of them ever saw the inside of a courtroom if it was possible to avoid it, for neither had anything approximating Khalinov's eloquence, but that didn't mean they were drawing their salaries for nothing. Kominsky, an Orthodox Jew in an age when almost every other religion had atrophied from lack of interest, knew more about nonhuman criminal law than Khalinov could ever hope to learn, while Braque, a former governor of Praesepe III, was the man who handled the miles upon miles of red tape that magically appeared every time a human stood trial on an alien world. There were other partners and assistants as well, twenty-seven of them to be exact, but most were concerned with corporate law and interstellar commerce, vital fields but totally devoid of the type of publicity that surrounded Khalinov's more famous cases.

"I hear we've got a real stinker this time," said Braque, pulling out a long yellow legal pad. (Some customs never changed.)

"If I were a betting man," said Khalinov, "and were feeling extremely conservative, I'd offer five million to one that our boy is tried, convicted, sentenced, and executed inside of three hours."

"What did he do?" asked Kominsky.

"He sneezed."

"Then what?" asked Braque.

"Then he resisted arrest and fled to Deluros VIII."

"That's all?"

"Yep."

"You're pulling my leg," said Braque.

"Am I?"

"Not necessarily," said Kominsky, his eyes alight with interest. "Where did this happen?"

"Atria XVI."

"A methane world?"

Khalinov nodded. "The damned fool had his T-pack off."

Kominsky nodded grimly, but Braque just looked puzzled. "I don't see the problem," he said.

"The problem," said Khalinov, "is simply this: The Atrians are a crystalline race, methane-breathers living at an awfully cold temperature. Young Heinrich Krantz—yes, the Commander's son—was there as a military aide on a trading mission. I don't know if he was drunk or sober, but, for whatever reason, he voluntarily or involuntarily—he swears it was the latter—turned off his T-pack while walking down a major Atrian thoroughfare. And then, with nothing to blot out or muffle the sound, he sneezed."

"So?" asked Braque.

"So fifty-seven Atrians shattered like so much fine crystal," said Khalinov. "Then, when confronted with the civilian police, he panicked and decided to come back here."

"How did he get away?" asked Braque.

"He threatened to remove one of his protective gloves. The heat of his body would have killed every Atrian within two hundred feet of him. He'd have died too, of course, but that doesn't help his case any. So they let him go, radioed ahead, and we took him into custody the second he landed. I've spent the better part of two weeks cajoling and threatening Henderson over at Extradition, but it's no go: we can't keep him. Seems we're cultivating the Atrians' friendship, so he's got to stand trial."

"Won't you look cute, though," said Kominsky, "standing there in fifty pounds of protective covering and having all those delightful histrionics come out so soft and tinkling through your T-pack."

"Don't remind me," said Khalinov, wincing. "Anyway, the trial is set for three weeks from now."

"The Atrians don't waste any time, do they?" said Braque.

"They seem to like their justice swift and sure," said Kominsky with a grimace.

"Indeed they do," agreed Khalinov. "Which means that we've got a lot of work to do and not much time to do it in." He turned to Braque. "I want you to arrange accommodations for the three of us, half a dozen reporters—not all friendly—and at least two cameramen. If they need any equipment to muffle the heat and noise of their cameras, or even the scratching of their pens, see that it's supplied. Also, if I need any special outfit to enable me to stalk around the courtroom or stamp a foot or anything like that, get me two sets of it. Then find out the political situation there and if we can offer a couple of gifts to the lord high mufti without offending anyone else. Figure out what an animated chandelier would like and get something appropriate. If possible, have us stay on Komornos; it'll probably be more comfortable for us, and we won't have to worry about accidentally shattering any more Atrians. Finally, find out what form their visual media take and hunt me up a couple of experts in it."

He dismissed Braque with a wave of his hand, then turned his attention to Kominsky.

"Okay," he said. "Fill me in."

"It may come as a shock to you, Ivor," said Kominsky, "but even *I* don't have fingertip data on every race in the galaxy."

"Then tell me what you can about methane-breathers in general before you run off to the library, or wherever it is you run off to when you're trying to convince me you're a genius."

"In general," began Kominsky, "about ninety percent of all methane-breathing races are crystalline. They're extremely sensitive to sound and heat, but beyond those two forces they're just about unkillable. If you could hit the average methane-breather with the force of a small grenade but without the accompanying heat, he probably wouldn't even feel it. Another interesting point is that since they are virtually indestructible, most methane beings are extremely long-lived, usually surviving thousands of years. This tends to make them pretty placid and contemplative, which is one of the reasons they haven't accomplished a hell of a lot—in human terms, anyway. Also, due to their physiology and the mental attitude that accompanies an eons-long life span, very few methane races are at all advanced technologically. There's never been much research done on their ESPer qualities, but I'd assume they're a little higher than average in telepathy, and almost at the bottom of the scale in all other such talents.

"Being basically static in their social outlook and mobility, I imagine that their penal codes would be both simple and very stark. They'd have little experience with lawbreakers, almost no misdemeanors, and would rid their society of felons swiftly and efficiently.

"Of course," he concluded with a smile, "none of the above may apply to this particular race of methane-breathers."

"Thanks," grunted Khalinov. "Anything else you can think of off the top of your massive head?"

"It's my brain that's massive," corrected Kominsky. "My head simply houses it. As for any further information, I can only add that since they could never have been carnivora, they probably aren't going to view even an accidental murder in the most rational or lenient of lights. Murder's an ugly thing even to a race that once depended on killing for its survival; I would think that it's incomprehensible to a methane-breather, especially since most of them are sexless and therefore can't even have had any experience with crimes of passion."

"Okay," said Khalinov. "I'd sure hate to hear you expound on a subject you know something about." He stood up. "Find out everything you can about the Atrians, check into any court cases they may have won or lost on *other* planets, and get back to me in a couple of days."

While his staff went about their duties, Khalinov went down to the library stacks in the building's basement and began finding out what he could about Atrian law.

It wasn't very encouraging.

Five non-Atrians, none of them Men, had been tried for murder during the twelve centuries that Atria XVI had been a member of the galactic community. All had been found guilty, and all had been summarily executed.

Atrian criminal law was a composite of childishly simple codes and shockingly severe penalties. Most of the crimes were meaningless to Khalinov; they evidently could be committed only by one Atrian against the person or property of another. But for those crimes that could be committed by non-Atrians, they were meaningful in the extreme.

Anyone who knowingly or unknowingly caused the death of an Atrian, for any reason whatsoever, including self-defense, was guilty of murder. The penalty: death.

Anyone who entered an Atrian domicile without written permission was guilty of the Atrian equivalent of breaking and entering. The penalty: death.

Anyone who took possession of any Atrian property or artifact without first proffering a fair and agreed-upon payment was guilty of robbery and/or burglary. The penalty: death.

And *that*, in toto, was their penal code for alien races.

It told Khalinov almost as much about the race by its omissions as by what it said. For one thing, it was obvious that Kominsky was right about their near-indestructibility, for there was no mention of assault or battery. He was probably also correct about their being a race of philosophical bent, since, unlike most of the races of the galaxy, there was no mention of blasphemy or of giving lip service to local religious mores. Probably the surest bet of all was that they were indeed long-lived, for nowhere was there any sentence other than death; and it stood to reason that prison sentences would be meaningless to a race that was virtually immortal.

The transcripts of the five non-Atrian murder trials were almost identical. In every case the argument was made that the act had been accidental. In only one case did the court disagree, but it seemed to make no difference. If a non-Atrian caused an Atrian death, his own life was forfeit. Period.

He read more. The defendant did not have to be present; if he was, he could not confront his accusers unless they agreed. Trial was by a randomly selected jury of five, but the jury could be waived by the defense. And, finally, there was only one court on Atria, because of the relative absence of crime. As a result, its verdict was final; there was absolutely no procedure by which a decision could be appealed.

Krantz had been given a preliminary hearing on Deluros VIII, at which time he was indicted of the lesser crime of resisting arrest and making an illegal claim of sanctuary. They decided, further, that he qualified for extradition. As yet, his case hadn't been heard on Atria XVI, for on that unthinkably frigid world there were no bills of indictment, no pretrial hearings, nothing but a simple verdict of innocent or guilty.

After two more hours of poring over what little was written concerning Atrian law, it began to look more and more as if this wasn't going to go down in history as one of Ivor Khalinov's more brilliant cases.

He started up from his book, suddenly aware of another presence in the room. It was Kominsky, back from wherever he went to do his research, and looking as grim as Khalinov.

"Well?" demanded the barrister.

"To draw a rather poor parallel," said Kominsky, "if your

93

boy Krantz were a horse, we could save a lot of time and money by shooting him right now."

"It looks that bad?"

"It sure doesn't look good," said Kominsky. "I'll give it to you point by point. First, the only Atrian who won a court case on any other world was executed upon returning to Atria XVI, because they thought the judgment had been too lenient. Second, they're more fragile than most methane-breathers; there can't be any doubt that a good loud sneeze, amplified by passing through an unfiltered and unmuffled T-pack on Krantz's oxygen helmet, would shatter every Atrian in his vicinity. Third, they subscribe to the laws of the Galactic Commerce Commission insofar as their interplanetary and interstellar trade is concerned, but they seem to do it as a necessary and irritating inconvenience; none of the more sophisticated codes, such as mercy, applies in planetary matters. Fourth, they have no religion, and even if they did, I very much doubt that their god would be the forgiving type. Fifth, they are definitely asexual, and reproduce by a form of budding, unbelievable as that sounds. Sixth, the average life span is upward of three thousand years. Seventh, there's never been a trial that lasted more than two hours. And eighth, I could use a drink."

"I'll agree with your last point," said Khalinov, pulling out a hip flask.

"How about the first seven?"

"Oh, I agree with them, too. That's why I'm drinking with you." He uttered a long "Ahhh," wiped his mouth off, and passed the flask to Kominsky. "I want you to hunt up Braque as soon as you can. Assuming he hasn't been sleeping all afternoon, he should have figured out what form of communication passes for video on Atria XVI. Have him line up a couple of guys who can use the medium, and have them make a five-minute recording."

"Of what?"

"Of an Atrian whose protective glove accidentally comes off while visiting Deluros VIII, thereby freezing fifty-seven Men to death."

"Okay," said Kominsky dubiously. "But . . ."

"But what?"

"But I think the Atrian judge may sentence the actor to death for even pretending to take someone else's life."

Khalinov just glared at him.

The courtroom was filled by the press, Krantz's parents and their influential friends, Khalinov's staff and assistants, and a handful of beautiful, blue-white, glasslike creatures. Khalinov himself, terribly uncomfortable in his modified heat-and-oxygen suit, sat at a table some twenty feet from a large crystalline figure, who was either standing, sitting, squatting, kneeling, or lying down, Khalinov couldn't decide which.

"Has the defense anything to say before sentence is passed?" said the Atrian. The words were like delicate chimes, but they came out in flat, unaccented Galactic-O through Khalinov's T-pack.

The lawyer rose to his feet.

"Your honor," he said, "I have not even heard the charges against my client."

"Were you not sent a copy of our penal code, along with a report of Man Krantz's actions?"

"Yes, but it is customary for the prosecuting attorney to state his case prior to the opening statement of the defense."

"Whose custom are you referring to, Man Khalinov?" asked the judge. "Yours or ours?"

"My apologies, your honor," said Khalinov, bowing deeply. "That being the case, I would like to enter a plea of innocent to the charge of premeditated murder."

"I do not recall that the word 'premeditated' was included in the charges," said the judge.

"But it must have been implied, your honor," said Khalinov, "or else some crime other than murder has been committed."

"That is for me to decide," said the Atrian. "You have waived trial by jury, for reasons best known to yourself. Therefore, you have placed all responsibility for all decisions and interpretations solely upon me. My interpretation is that under Atrian law, murder need not be premeditated, but is defined simply and explicitly as the taking of one or more Atrian lives, by any means whatsoever, with or without motive or preknowledge. Therefore, your claim is disallowed, on the grounds that the charge is not premeditated murder."

"If my client pleads guilty, the trial will end immediately, will it not?" asked Khalinov.

"Yes."

"Then Heinrich Krantz pleads not guilty to the charge of murder."

95

"Even though you yourself know that he did in fact commit the crime?" asked the Atrian.

"Even so," agreed Khalinov, studying the Atrian's face for an expression of some kind, but finding none. "Later we may change the plea, but how else can I argue my client's case? After all, I am only obeying the rules of the court."

"Using them to serve your own purposes," corrected the judge.

"Agreed," said Khalinov. "Is it not my job to protect my client's interests in any way I can? We are ready for the prosecution to present its evidence now."

"I am also the prosecution," said the judge. "I know as absolute fact that Man Krantz caused the death of fifty-seven Atrians in the following manner . . ." The T-pack droned on and on with an explicit recounting of the crime.

When the Atrian had finished, Khalinov arose again. "Your honor," he said, "with the court's permission I should like to present a visual display." He nodded toward two assistants, and they approached, bearing the Atrian equivalent of a tridimensional video receiver.

"Does this exhibit bear directly upon your case?" asked the judge. "Or, more precisely, will it in any way prove that my information is faulty and that your client is innocent of the crime of murder?"

"Not directly," admitted Khalinov, "but it does have some relevance to the subject of murder on the planet Atria XVI, and as such—"

"The exhibit is disallowed," interrupted the judge.

"But your honor!"

"Man Khalinov," said the judge, "the rulings of this court are not subject to debate or question. Your exhibit will not be permitted. If you cannot prove, absolutely and beyond question, that Man Krantz did not cause the deaths of fifty-seven Atrians, then you are wasting the court's time."

"I gather you've got plenty to waste!" snapped Khalinov. "A man's life is at stake here. I intend to see to it that he gets the best and most comprehensive defense of which I am capable."

"Well spoken," said the Atrian, "but irrelevant."

"No more irrelevant than the lives of fifty-seven Atrians," said Khalinov. "My client is a sentient being, just as the deceased Atrians were. What is more relevant than his defense?"

The judge remained silent for a long moment, then spoke. "Continue."

"Thank you, your honor. With the court's permission, I should like to call as a witness Professor Nigel Patrick, of the University of—"

"One moment," said the judge. "Was Man Patrick on Atria XVI at the time of the crime's commission?"

"I object, your honor," said Khalinov. "No crime has yet been proven."

"Your objection is overruled. In point of fact, the crime has not yet been *dis*proven."

"Then in answer to your question, no, Professor Patrick was not on Atria XVI at any time during his life prior to yesterday."

"Then how," asked the Atrian, "can Man Patrick possibly testify in support of your client?"

"Professor Patrick holds a doctorate in Criminology and another in Ethics," said Khalinov. "The defense shall attempt to show that on many similar worlds—"

"Disallowed," said the judge.

"Dammit, your honor!" bellowed Khalinov, though only soft tinkling chimes came through the T-pack. "How can I present a defense when you disallow all my exhibits and all my expert testimony?"

"They are not germane to the case at hand," said the Atrian. "If your exhibits and your witnesses cannot disprove the truth of the charges, then they are irrelevant."

"They are not irrelevant! It is your law that is irrelevant!"

"Man Khalinov," said the Atrian calmly, "our law is not on trial. Your client is. Please continue."

Khalinov lowered his head in thought, painfully aware of the fact that the newsmen and cameras were catching every instant of this fiasco. He was also aware that he had to keep talking, for the moment he stopped he'd be conceding defeat.

"Your honor," he said, "you made a remark about your law not being put on trial. Has any law of yours ever stood trial?"

"No."

"Why not?" asked Khalinov.

"Because laws are neither guilty nor innocent, and therefore cannot be tried."

"But laws can be good or evil," persisted Khalinov. "What would you do if you discovered that a law was evil?"

"Laws in themselves cannot be good or evil," said the Atrian. "Therefore, your question is irrelevant."

"But laws *can* be practical or impractical, can they not?" said Khalinov. "For example, a law that required me to argue before you without a T-pack would be impractical, wouldn't it? Or a law demanding that I not wear an outfit incorporating life-support systems?"

"Agreed," said the Atrian. "But we have no such laws."

"Please allow me to continue, since you've disallowed every other line of defense," said Khalinov.

"You may continue," said the judge.

"Thank you. May I ask you for a legal opinion, your honor?"

"Yes."

"*Why* would a law requiring that I appear here without life-support systems be impractical?"

"Because you would die, obviously," was the answer.

"Would a native of Atria XVI die were he to appear before you without life-support systems?"

"Of course not," said the judge.

"Would a law requiring a native of Atria XVI to wear my particular life-support system be impractical?"

"Naturally. The Atrian would die."

"Would you then admit, your honor, that there are at least some instances where a law cannot be applied practically to both Atrian and non-Atrian alike?"

"I so admit," said the judge, "and I can appreciate your line of reasoning. However, this was merely a hypothetical case. In the case of Man Krantz, he destroyed fifty-seven sentient beings."

"I'm coming to that," said Khalinov. "Let me hypothesize further. If, in the next instant, my life-support system should fail, due to a malfunction that is clearly the fault of the manufacturer, a tremendous amount of heat would shortly escape my protective suit, enough heat to destroy every Atrian in the room. Who would be responsible for this: myself, the manufacturer of the suit, the salesman I purchased it from, the quality-control expert who didn't catch the flaw, or perhaps the company that manufactures the machines upon which such suits are constructed?"

"I cannot answer that without further data," said the Atrian.

"I agree," said Khalinov. "Would you go so far as to say,

however, that I was not guilty of the deaths that would occur?"

"Tentatively, I would agree that you were not guilty," said the judge slowly. "However, may I caution you once again that this is merely a hypothesis? Man Krantz's T-pack was examined and found to be in perfect working order."

"All right," said Khalinov, stalking back and forth before the judge, his hands clasped behind his back. "Let's get on to the case of Heinrich Krantz. And let us also keep in mind that you have found—hypothetically, to be sure—that a law can be impractical, and that the death of an Atrian is not necessarily the responsibility of the destroying agent.

"Now, then, let us examine exactly what happened. Heinrich Krantz, a man with no prior criminal record, found himself on a crowded Atrian thoroughfare. For whatever reason, his T-pack was turned off—and let me remind the court that the reason for this hasn't yet been determined. It may well have been through an act of carelessness on Krantz's part; but, on the other hand, it may just as easily have been jostled into that position by the pressing crowd of Atrians.

"At any rate, the T-pack was off. Now, on oxygen worlds, the T-pack is a hand-carried portable instrument. But on worlds where atmospheric conditions are such that we must wear protective covering and life-support systems at all times, the T-pack is built into the transparent facial mask. The reason is obvious: We are frequently so encumbered by our outfits that this is far more convenient than having to hold the T-pack in our hands. There is one other fact concerning this structure: Since Men rarely travel alone on such worlds, when the T-pack is turned off, it is still possible for them to communicate with each other. The T-pack, when working, muffles our voices and transmutes them into more pleasing, more coherent, and, in your case, less lethal sounds; but when it is off, the sounds are not muffled at all. For this, you may blame the manufacturer or the designer, if you wish, but you certainly cannot blame my client.

"So we have Heinrich Krantz walking down your thoroughfare with, for a reason as yet undetermined, his T-pack off. And what did he do?

"I don't know if there is an analog word, even in Galactic-M, but he sneezed. This is an involuntary action due, one might say, to a biological deficiency in our race. Had someone pointed a deadly weapon at Heinrich Krantz and told him that it would be fired if he made a sound, no matter

99

how great his fear and his desire to live, he could nonetheless not have kept from sneezing at that instant in time. It was an action which was not unique to my client, but one which has been bred into him for untold thousands of generations. I have with me scientific testimony to the effect that sneezing is common not only to Man, but to more than eighty percent of all oxygen-breathing races." He walked to his table, withdrew a file of papers from a folder, and placed them before the judge.

"Your honor," he concluded, "I will now restate my client's plea. According to Atrian law he must plead guilty, for he was indeed the agent whereby fifty-seven of your citizens died. However, based on the arguments I have offered, and the hypotheses you yourself have agreed to, I strongly request—no, I *demand*—that due consideration be made of the circumstances surrounding the act in question. No race that has a life span as long as yours can be totally devoid of mercy and compassion. If you cannot find my client innocent, then surely you can agree that he should not be made to pay so high a penalty for an involuntary action that he was and still is physically incapable of avoiding.

"On Deluros VIII, as on most of the worlds in the galaxy peopled by Man and non-Man alike, our penal codes allow for degrees of leniency based on degrees of guilt. If your honor could bring himself to delay passing sentence until such time as you can look through our codes—and I will be happy to supply numerous experts, at my own expense, to discuss them with you—I feel that both my client and the cause of Atrian justice will be better served.

"I thank you for your patience and tolerance, and hope that in your wisdom you can come to a decision that will be fair both to my client and to the memory of those deceased Atrians, who, though victimized, were no more innocent than was Heinrich Krantz."

Khalinov sat down, sweating profusely. He wished he could see an expression on the Atrian's face, wished he could get an inkling of what the delicate, blue-white, crystalline being was thinking, but there was no way to tell. He'd just have to sit and wait.

The Atrian judge remained motionless and silent for the better part of an hour. Then, at last, he looked up, and a hush fell over the court as both human and nonhuman waited to hear his verdict.

"Man Khalinov," said the Atrian, "you have caused me to

think deeply and seriously over all you have said. It is my regretful conclusion that Man Krantz must be found guilty. He is hereby sentenced to die by heat tomorrow."

"But your honor!" cried Khalinov, leaping to his feet again.

"Allow me to continue," said the judge. "The court appreciates your arguments, and will go so far as to admit to their validity in certain cases, including the case of Man Krantz."

"Then why not give him a lesser sentence?"

"Man Krantz's life span is, in your terms, between ninety and one hundred and ten. Is that not correct?"

"Yes."

"The expected life span of an Atrian is approximately thirty-four hundred years. While I will admit that a sentence of perhaps fifty years, or possibly even less, would be appropriate from the point of view of the defendant, you must consider that this would be a worse insult to the families of the deceased and the general populace of Atria XVI, than would be a verdict of innocent. You are fond of hypotheses, so allow me to pose one of my own: What would your reaction be if an entity convicted of slaying fifty-seven Men on the planet Deluros VIII were to be given a prison sentence of two months?"

Khalinov closed his eyes. There was no argument to be made. "Thank you, your honor," he said, and turned to leave.

"Man Khalinov," said the judge. The barrister stopped. "This does not mean that your logic and efforts have been for naught. If you have time prior to your return flight to Deluros VIII, please accept my invitation to join me in my chambers, and bring along some of your legal books. I would very much like to exchange ideas with you."

"I'd consider it a rare privilege, your honor," said Khalinov, wondering if he had won or lost. "Is there any particular subject you'd like to cover?"

"I think we shall begin," said the Atrian, "with involuntary manslaughter."

And then he knew: Krantz had lost.

But Man, just possibly, had won.

9: The Medics

... So while it took Man countless eons to develop his medical science to the point where almost all human diseases could be diagnosed and treated with some degree of certainty that a cure would be effected, he was forced to cover the same ground a thousand times over in an infinitesimal portion of the time when contact with other races was made. And, as if this weren't enough of a problem for those medics who boldly strode toward these new and incredibly varied horizons, there was always in the background Man's precarious position in the political schemata of the galaxy ...

—*Man: Twelve Millennia of Achievement*

(No mention of the Medics can be found in *Origin and History of the Sentient Races.*)

"What's *wrong* with it?" snapped a haggard Darlinski. "Hell, I don't even know what keeps the damned thing alive!"

"I'm not paying you enough for you to turn prima donna on me," said Hammett harshly. "Keep making tests until you find out what's affecting him."

"First," said Darlinski, "you've got to prove to me that it's a him. Second, you're not paying me enough to do very damned much of anything. And third—"

"Cure him and you've got a raise," said Hammett quckly, with more than a touch of irritation.

"I don't want a goddamn bloody raise!" yelled Darlinski. "I want a healthy specimen of whatever this is so I can see what the hell the difference is!"

"He's all we've got."

"Didn't it have any friends or subordinates?" demanded Darlinski.

"For the twelfth time, no," said Hammett.

"Then, for the thirteenth time, what in blue blazes is a planetary ambassador doing without even a single subordinate around?"

"I keep telling you, I don't know. All I know is he screamed once, collapsed, and couldn't be immediately revived, so they brought him here."

"Of course they couldn't revive it. Hell, if they slapped its face they might have broken every bone in what seems to pass for its head. And for all I know, it'd melt if anyone threw cold water on it."

A light on an intercom unit flashed, and Darlinski pressed a button.

"Pathology here, boss," said a laconic voice. "Got anything for us to work on yet?"

Darlinski uttered a few choice but unprintable words into the speaker.

"Don't get sore, boss. All you got to do is figure out what makes it tick."

"I know," snarled Darlinski. "The fat bastard that runs this shop just promised me a raise if I get it right."

"Boy, am I impressed," said the voice. "The fat bastard who runs the planet just promised us a war if you get it wrong. Have fun."

"What are you talking about?" demanded Hammett, walking over to the intercom.

"Haven't you seen a newstape?" said the voice from Pathology. "Hell, you've had the damned thing up there for six hours."

"Just tell me what's going on," said Hammett.

"Seems this joker's buddies back on Pnath are claiming we've either kidnapped or killed it. I gather it was here on a peace-making mission—a very private little war the powers-

103

that-be didn't see fit to tell us about—and evidently they think we're doing them dirt. According to the media, a tiny skirmish is about to become a full-fledged war unless we can convince the Pnathians, or Pnaths, or whatever they call themselves, that we're acting in good faith."

"Have any of those geniuses down at Central thought to ask for a Pnathian medic?" asked Darlinski.

"Yep. But the Pnathians think we've killed or brainwashed this one and they won't send any others until it's returned whole and healthy."

"Beautiful," said Darlinski. "What if the damned thing dies on me?"

"Well," chuckled the pathologist, "I guess the Navy can always use another bedpan scrubber. Ta-ta."

The intercom switched off.

Hammett waited until Darlinski's stream of curses had left him momentarily breathless, then walked over to the Pnathian ambassador.

"I didn't realize it was going to turn into this kind of incident," he said. "Let's get back to work."

"What do you mean, 'Let's?'" snapped Darlinski. "You wouldn't know a tumor from a wart. Go on back to your goddamn office and worry about how to pay for next week's heating bill."

He turned back to the patient, and Hammett, shrugging, left and closed the door very carefully behind him.

Darlinski took a deep breath, sighed, and looked at the notes he had scribbled down during the past few hours. They weren't much. The Pnathian breathed an oxygen-nitrogen compound, but there was no way of telling whether a dose of forty percent oxygen would revive it or kill it; ditto for a ninety percent nitrogen dose. Its skin was extremely fine-textured, but he didn't dare take a sample, or even a scraping; for all he knew, the Pnathians, or at least this particular one, were chronic hemophiliacs. And for that reason he couldn't take a sample of the being's blood, either.

Nor could he even make a guess about the gravity of the Pnathian's home world. It had three legs, allowing it a tripodal stance, which implied a heavier gravity; but the structure seemed much more fragile than a heavier gravity would allow. And, of course, he didn't dare X-ray it for fear of a fatal, or at least terribly adverse, reaction.

There were no hands or arms as such, but instead a trio of tubular appendages, all extremely flexible, not quite tentacles

104

but far from hands. He tried to figure out what function they served, but couldn't. Obviously, the race was intelligent, and had developed the machinery of space travel and war, but when he tried to imagine the control panel of one of their ships, his mind came up blank.

As for the head, it extended on a long thin stalk of a neck and contained not one but four orifices that might or might not have been mouths. They were arranged perpendicular to the ground, and the third orifice was the only one that fogged the crystal of his watch. However, he had never come across any being that required four mouths, nor did it seem likely that the remaining orifices could all be breathing apparatus, unless the being had the equivalent of three stuffed noses. They *could* be ears, but it seemed unlikely; in every species he had ever examined, human and nonhuman, sapient and nonsapient, the ears were set much farther apart for greater efficiency. Urethra and anus? Possibly; but, if so, which was which, and how could he differentiate them from the mouth? He grinned at the thought of some alien physician pouring the equivalent of hot chicken broth into his rectum, then frowned as he realized that it would only be funny *after* he cured the patient.

Or, he admitted honestly to himself, *if* he cured it.

The Pnathian had two eyes. The lids were over them, but he had lifted them and seen that they were quite dull, with the pupils reacting only very slightly to light stimuli. Just above the eyes was the cranium, an oblong structure stuck atop the rest of the face at a 45-degree angle, almost like a baby whose head was terribly misshapen due to a difficult birth.

Its pulse was almost twice that of his own, but that could simply be because of the gravitational difference. Or it could be a sign of impending death. Or . . .

Darlinski cursed once again, stepped back, and stared at the Pnathian. He felt terribly oppressed. Hell, oxygen-breathers weren't even his specialty. But Jacobson was on vacation somewhere on Deluros VIII, so they'd pulled the boy genius out of the chlorine ward, pointed him in the direction of the Pnathian, patted him on the head, and said Go.

The question, of course, was: Go where?

Hammett broke his concentration, such as it was, by calling on the intercom.

"Any ideas yet?"

"All of 'em pertain to what I'm going to do to you once I get this patient out of my hair," said Darlinski disgustedly.

"I hope we're both still here long enough for you to have a chance," said Hammett. "I've been checking up on the story, and it's true. The government's bought us a little more time, but if we haven't got our ambassador on its feet and ready to exonerate us in a few days, that's it."

"I don't suppose anyone has yet thought to get me any useful information from a Pnathian medic?" said Darlinski.

"Yes and no," said Hammett.

"And just what in blazes is that supposed to mean?"

"Yes, they thought to ask, and no, nobody got you anything. You don't understand the political situation. I can hardly believe it myself. I don't know if this race is composed of nothing but paranoids or what, but they won't send anyone here or even feed us any information about their physiology until they know their ambassador is all right."

"Thereby making sure that it's never going to be all right," said Darlinski grimly.

"I did learn that it's a female, and her name is . . . well, it's not really pronounceable, but the closest human analog is Leonora. And no, she's not pregnant."

"They told you that?"

"Not in so many words, but I gather that she's only recently reached childbearing age."

"Then why in the name of pluperfect hell is she their sole ambassador to a race they're at war with?" demanded Darlinski.

"How should I know?" said Hammett. "We've got Psychology working on it, but they've got even less to go on than you do."

"I hope you don't expect me to feel sorry for Psychology."

"Nope. Muff this one and you can spend the rest of your life feeling sorry for you and me."

"Very funny," growled Darlinski.

"No," corrected Hammett. "Very serious. I'd rather have you kill her by accident than have her just lie there and die for lack of treatment. I don't care if you begin by ripping her heart out with your bare hands, but you've got to do something. Is there anybody I can send to assist you?"

Darlinski roared a negative and cut the intercom off. Then he walked back to the Pnathian and examined her again, armed with the knowledge that she was a female. This implied some bodily cavity that would be absent in a male, but

106

as he went over her, inch by inch, he concluded that the only orifices on her entire body were the four pseudo-mouths on her head. One was obviously for breathing, which meant that of the remaining trio, one was for ingestion, one for sexual congress, and one was of undertermined properties. And, for the life of him, he still couldn't figure out which was which.

He glanced at a clock, and realized that he'd been on his feet for more than twenty hours and would shortly be in a state of near-collapse. That meant he had to get something down to Pathology that they could analyze while he slept. He ordered a pair of nurses into the room and prepared to take small skin scrapings from each of the patient's tentacular appendages, another scraping from the trunk of the body, and smears from each of the three nonbreathing orifices.

Careful as he was, he noticed that on the last scraping, a small amount of pinkish fluid began oozing out. It had to be blood, and he immediately placed it on a slide and sat back to see whether or not the bleeding would stop by itself. It did, almost immediately, and he instructed one of the nurses to take everything down to the Path lab.

"Get me a report within six hours, hunt me up a room, see that it has a hot shower, and have someone bring me some breakfast and a stimulant in five hours."

So stating, he waited until he'd been assigned some nearby sleeping quarters, and, with a sigh, put them to good if brief use.

He awoke feeling no better rested, and within a matter of minutes was standing next to Jennings of Pathology as they took turns viewing slides in the latter's lab.

"Not that having very few red corpuscles proves a damned thing," Jennings was saying. "It could, of course, indicate a serious blood deficiency. On the other hand, maybe the damned beast doesn't *need* red corpuscles. I think, though, that we'd better go under the assumption that this blood count is pretty near normal."

"Any reason why?" asked Darlinski.

"The best." Jennings grinned. "If it's not normal, we're out of luck. I've broken down the blood structure, and there's no way we could synthesize red corpuscles of a type this thing wouldn't reject before it died for lack of them. So, pragmatism being what it is, we'll pretend that whatever else is wrong, the blood count's normal."

Darlinski nodded his head and grunted his assent. "How about the tissues?"

"You mean the scrapings?" asked Jennings. "Well, we might be running into a little more luck there . . . or worse luck, depending on your point of view."

"Suppose you tell me what my point of view is," said Darlinski warily.

"If your point of view is that of a doctor looking for something to cure, we might have something for you. Here, take a look."

Darlinski bent low over the powerful microscope and peered through it. A tiny skin sampling was on the slide, and even without resorting to the highest magnification Darlinski was aware of an enormous amount of cellular activity.

"What's happening?" he asked.

"Can't say for sure," said Jennings. "But by all rights, that ought to be a very dead piece of skin, and it just as obviously is not. For the life of me I can't figure out what's feeding it or supplying it with whatever it needs in the way of blood and oxygen."

"Speaking of oxygen," said Darlinski, "what kind of dose can I give her?"

"Based on the blood structure, I'd say she's living in her equivalent of an oxygen tent right now. I wouldn't want to be the guy responsible for giving her a higher dose. It just might burn her lungs out."

"How about the smears?"

"Now, that's something really interesting," said Jennings.

"You found something?"

"Nope. I found absolutely nothing."

"You're an easy guy to interest," said Darlinski.

"Hold on a second, boss," said Jennings. "Let me ask you a question first: Who the hell told you that this was a female?"

"Hammett."

"And who told him?"

"The Pnathians."

"Yeah? Well, you can't prove it by me."

"What did the smears show?" asked Darlinski, scratching his head.

"Nothing. Or, rather, nothing even remotely sexual. I've labeled the three smears One through Three. Now, Smear One, taken from the bottommost orifice, showed traces of water, a couple of enzymes, and the residue of two or three other organic liquids. From this, and the fact that they're not broken down, we've got to figure that its sole purpose is the ingestion of liquid nourishment. Smear Two has numerous traces of solids, plus a few decay germs and something which seems to act as a mild preliminary stomach acid. Ergo, that's where the solid nourishment goes. Smear Three is a problem, but I'd be willing to wager that its function is strictly vocal."

"But, damnit, one of those orifices has to be the equivalent of a vagina!" snapped Darlinski. "They're the only orifices on the whole goddamed body, and the subject is definitely a female."

"Maybe so, but she doesn't kiss and copulate in the same general area," said Jennings. "There is absolutely no trace of any sexual hormone, lubricant, or other secretion known to science, and since she's a warm-blooded oxygen-breather, I have to think that her sexual hormones wouldn't be that hard to spot."

"Could the orifice be used for excretion?" asked Darlinski.

"Highly doubtful," said Jennings. "No, I'll make it stronger. Definitely not. I would certainly have found something to indicate it if that were the case. Sorry to give you a problem, boss, but that's the way I read it."

"*A* problem? Hell, you've given me a pair of them."

"Yeah?"

"First, I've got a female patient with no discernable sex organs. And second, I've got an eater with no discernable means of excreting waste products."

"Maybe that's what's wrong." Jennings grinned. "Maybe she ate too much and is due to explode."

"Thanks a lot," said Darlinski. "Well, I'd better get back down there and see if I can figure out what to do next."

When he arrived a few minutes later he found the Pnathian gasping weakly for air. Its face, and hence its breathing orifice, was covered with a foul-smelling substance which seemed to be coming from its food-ingesting orifice. Quickly summoning an intern to help him, Darlinski managed to turn the Pnathian on its side and, taking an antiseptic wipe, began cleaning its head off. In a few moments the breathing became normal again, and, instructing the intern to keep a watchful eye on the patient, he took a sample of the substance up to Pathology.

"Well," said Jennings after some thirty minutes of testing, "we've solved one of your problems. It seems that the same mouth, or orifice, does double duty: it both ingests the food and excretes it. Very inefficient. In fact, uncommonly so."

109

"You're sure it's not vomit?" asked Darlinski.

"Absolutely," said Jennings. "Vomit would still have some partially undigested food left. This stuff is all broken down. The body's taken most of what it needed, and this is what's left."

"We're learning things all the time," said Darlinski. "I bet if they left the damned thing here for another year or so, I might even figure out what's killing it."

"According to the newstapes," said Jennings, "you've got considerably less than a year."

"Don't remind me. What are the chances of it dying if I take some X-rays and fluoroscope it?"

"I don't think the X-rays will do any harm. Under normal circumstances I'd say that fluoroscoping was out of the question until we knew more about it, but these are hardly normal circumstances, so you might as well go ahead."

Two hours later Darlinski was looking at a number of X-rays that were laid out before him and cursing furiously.

"Well, boss?" asked Jennings on the intercom.

"It can't have any broken bones," said Darlinski. "The damned old girl doesn't have a bone in her entire body!"

"Learn anything from the fluoroscope?"

"Not a thing. I've seen insects with more complicated digestive systems. The food goes in, is carried to just about every cell in the body, and what remains will be coming out again in a day or so. All that's left is brain damage, and how the hell do I know whether it exists or not until I've seen a working model of an undamaged brain?" He loosed another stream of curses. "This stupid creature just doesn't make any sense!"

"Agreed," said Jennings. "You know those scrapings?"

"What about them?"

"They're growing. Another week and they'll cover the whole damned slide."

"Could it be a form of cancer?" asked Darlinski.

"No way," came the reply. "No cancer I know of ever acted like this. These scrapings haven't been cultured; by rights, they should be dead and decaying."

"Besides, if there was some kind of skin cancer, I'd have spotted it before now," agreed Darlinski. He stood up. "This is crazy! The respiratory system is working, the digestive system is working, the circulatory system is working. What the hell can be wrong with it?"

"A stroke?" suggested Jennings.

110

"I doubt it. If there were a blood clot in the brain, something else ought to be hampered too. I figure we can rule out a heart attack, too; we haven't made the slightest attempt at treatment and yet the condition, whatever it might be in regard to the norm, is completely stable. It seems to me that if anything sudden hit her, she'd either degenerate or start improving. But she doesn't do either."

"If you're looking for some paradoxes," added Jennings, "you might figure out why everyone keeps calling it a female."

"I've got enough paradoxes of my own to work on," said Darlinski. "I don't need any of yours."

"Just trying to be helpful, boss. See you later."

Darlinski went back to the patient, muttering obscenities to himself. It just didn't add up; even a virus, left unattended, would either have killed her or been partially fought off by antibodies by now. Perhaps the weirdest part of the whole insane situation was the fact that the ambassador simply refused to change, either for better or for worse.

Okay, he decided, let's look at it logically. If the Pnathian's condition remained unchanged, it must be because something in her internal or external environment was also unchanged. Since he had established, insofar as was possible, that her internal systems were all functioning normally, and since Jennings had as yet been unable to detect any microbes, bacteria, or viruses that might be harmful, he would operate on the hypothesis that the cause was either a blood clot or tumor in her brain, which he couldn't possibly cure or even find, or else that the problem lay in the external environment.

And, if the external environment was the cause of her problems, the most likely place to begin changing that environment was with the atmosphere and the gravitation.

He began by changing the pressure within the room to zero gravity, with no visible effect. Then, gradually, he increased it to three gravities. The breathing became slightly more labored, but there was no other reaction, and on a boneless being he didn't feel he could increase the pressure any further.

He then placed a respirator over the Pnathian's breathing orifice and lowered the oxygen content to fifteen percent, then twelve percent. When he got it down to eight percent he thought the patient would surely begin to choke, but instead, he detected a noticible twitching of one eyelid.

111

Encouraged, he dropped it down to a four percent oxygen compound—and all hell broke loose!

The Pnathian ambassador began whispering incoherently, and her tentacular appendages started thrashing wildly. Darlinski easily avoided them, strapped the trunk of her body to the table, and settled back to observe her. Her eyes were open, but seemed unable to focus, and her motions, even after ten minutes, were so disjointed as to convince him she would never in a dozen lifetimes learn how to bring food to her mouth, let alone pilot a spaceship.

An idea began dawning somewhere in the back of his mind, but first he had to check out a few facts. His first act was to call Jennings.

"Tell me," he asked the pathologist, "exactly what would happen to a human, used to breathing a nineteen percent oxygen compound, if you doubled the oxygen content on him?"

"He'd probably laugh his fool head off," said Jennings promptly.

"I know," said Darlinski. "But is there any possibility that he might pass out instead?"

"I doubt it. Why?"

"What if you quadrupled it—got it up to seventy-six percent, or even a little bit higher?"

"It's been done many times in emergency cases."

"Does it ever knock them out?"

"Once in a while. Rarely, though. What are you getting at?"

"One final question and I'll tell you."

"Ask away," said Jennings.

"What if you stuck a man into a ninety percent oxygen atmosphere—"

"No problem," came the quick reply.

"You didn't let me finish," said Darlinski. "What if you put him there and left him there for a week?"

"It's never been done to my knowledge. It'd probably burn out the brain and the lungs, in that order. . . . Wait a minute! Are you trying to tell me that . . ."

". . . That our ambassador breathes a four percent oxygen compound, or less, and that she's been living in our equivalent of a ninety percent oxygen tent since she arrived. At first it was probably invigorating, perhaps even intoxicating. But ultimately it hit her, hard, and she's been in a state of collapse ever since."

112

"Then you've solved it!" exclaimed Jennings. "Pretty simple at that, wasn't it?"

"I haven't solved it at all," said Darlinski. "I'd wager that she hasn't got enough brainpower left to rattle around in a thimble. Totally uncoordinated, eyes can't focus, unaware of surroundings, drooling slightly out of her two ingestion orifices. It's my opinion that right now she ranks considerably lower than a Mongoloid idiot on whatever scale they use to measure intelligence. She may be cured, but she's as nonfunctional as a rock."

"If it'll make you feel any better, she was probably like that within an hour of her collapse," said Jennings.

"Makes me feel great," said Darlinski, cutting the communication.

The idea was rounding out, but he still had to check with Hammett. He explained the entire situation to him, then waited while Hammett checked with the government.

"Nice job," said Hammett an hour later, "but the Pnathians aren't buying. First, they think we're lying to them, and second, they think that if we're telling the truth we're responsible for what happened to her. So we came close, but no cigar. The truce ends in two days' time, so if you can't come up with a way to cure a mental vegetable by then . . ." His voice trailed off.

"Let me ask you one question," said Darlinski.

"Shoot."

"How do you know that the ambassador is a woman?"

"The Pnathians—or, to be more accurate, the Pnathian spokesman—told us so."

"Told you it was a female?"

"Yes."

"What were the exact words?"

"I'm not quite sure. A general expression of regret that Leonora had just recently reached that point of physical maturity where she could have offspring."

"Is that an exact, word-for-word translation?"

"Not quite. But it's as close as our translators could come with a race that doesn't speak Galactic."

"Our heterosexual male and female translators," said Darlinski.

"What are you getting at?" asked Hammett.

"Don't ask," said Darlinski. "Now, let me get one fact straight in my mind: Whether the ambassador lives as a vege-

113

table or dies tomorrow makes no difference in the Pnathians' stated plans, correct?"

"Correct."

"All right. I've got a favor to ask of you."

"I'll do what I can," said Hammett.

"I want you to cordon off Surgery Room 607 and the adjacent recovery room. Then I want you to set up the capabilities for an atmosphere of three and a half percent oxygen, ninety-five percent nitrogen, and one and a half percent inert elements in both rooms. Standard pressure. And finally, post a guard and see that no one except Jennings is allowed in without my express permission."

"Give me two hours and it'll be done," said Hammett. "But—"

"No questions. Oh yes, I'll want one other thing, too. Give me a vat, one cubic yard, of the most highly concentrated nitric acid we have, and place some opaque covering over it."

"Acid?"

"Right. And don't forget the covering. I'll be down in surgery in two hours."

True to his word, Hammett had the rooms in order when Darlinski and a nurse wheeled the Pnathian in at the appointed hour. Jennings was waiting for them, a curious expression on his face.

"You know," he said, "I've been wracking my mind trying to figure out what kind of operation you plan to perform. I keep coming up with the same crazy answer."

"Far from being a crazy answer," said Darlinski, "I've got a sneaky suspicion it's the only sane one. You can act as my anesthetist."

"Will you need one?"

"Shortly. Nurse: you, Jennings and I will now don our oxygen masks." This done, he ordered the atmosphere lowered to three and a half percent oxygen. "Okay, Jennings, set the respirator up to thirty-five percent and knock her out."

Jennings placed the nozzle over the Pnathian's breathing orifice, and the ambassador lost consciousness almost immediately.

"Is the acid vat here?" asked Darlinski. He looked around until he found it. "All right, nurse. We will now prepare for amputation."

"What are you amputating, sir?" asked the nurse.

"The head," said Darlinski.

114

"I knew it!" said Jennings. "You've got to be out of your mind!"

"What've we got to lose?" asked Darlinski, unmindful of the nurse's horrified reaction. "Mindless or dead, the war starts; this is the only way to stop it."

And, so saying, he made an incision midway on the long stalk that passed for a Pnathian neck. His hands moved quickly, expertly, until the neck was all but severed.

"Nurse," he said, looking up for an instant, "it will doubtless bother you no end, but I don't want this sutured or closed in any way. We will apply a tourniquet for about ninety seconds if you wish, but it must then be removed."

The nurse, pale and horrified, nodded weakly.

"Jennings, you know what to do with the head?"

"The vat?"

Darlinski nodded. "If I'm right, it's going to be screaming bloody murder anyway, so we'll destroy it as quickly as possible."

"Wouldn't the incinerator have been more humane?"

"Doubtless. However, I don't relish taking a babbling, decapitated head down five levels and through crowded corridors to the incinerator. Do you?"

"I see your point." Jennings grinned. He grunted as the head rolled off the Pnathian's body, and, averting his eyes as best he could, he quickly took it to the opaque vat and placed it inside. When he got back to the table he found Darlinski removing the tourniquet. No blood poured forth.

"It probably doesn't need it, despite the absence of its mouth, but let's open up the neck a bit and insert a breathing tube. Then you'd better run up to Pathology and figure out what kind of solution we can give it intravenously until it can eat for itself, though with all that subcutaneous fat I doubt that it'll be necessary." Jennings left, and Darlinski turned to the nurse. "Until I know the outcome of all this, I'm afraid you're going to be confined to quarters. You are not to discuss this with anyone except Mr. Hammett, Dr. Jennings, or myself. Is that clear?"

The nurse nodded.

"Fine. Stick around a bit longer, until we can hunt up a replacement. And call Hammett and tell him to get his tail down here on the double."

It took Hammett exactly four minutes to arrive, at which time Darlinski explained the operation to him.

"You see," he began, "the whole problem was that the ambassador is very definitely *not* a female. That threw me for a while, but I couldn't give it my full attention until I figured out what had caused its problem in the first place. But there were so many hints I should have seen it even sooner: the fact that its tissue kept growing, even when it wasn't cultured; the fact that we couldn't find any sexual apparatus; the fact that there were no outlets for spores. So of course, what could it be but an entity that is capable of reproduction by fission, and hence of regeneration? I should have guessed something like that the first day, when only one of my scrapings drew any blood at all, and that coagulated in just two or three seconds."

"But can it grow a head?" asked Hammett. "After all, you've removed its brain and all its orifices. Even a starfish has to have part of the core remaining to regenerate."

"I think it will. If not, the body and head would probably have died immediately. Neither did, which is why I destroyed the head: I didn't want that mindless pseudo-cranium growing another body. Also, if I can coin a word, we occasionally tend to Earthomorphize, to give certain Earthly qualities to all forms of non-Earthly life. It seems unlikely to me that any creature could survive with its head severed, but the fact remains that it is indeed surviving. However, the really major problem still remains."

"And what is that?" asked Hammett.

"The new brain won't know that it's an ambassador, or that we saved its life—so I think we'd better prepare for a little war."

10: The Politicians

. . . Thus it was that, toward the end of the Democracy's first millennium, a wave of sentiment swept across the human worlds and colonies of the galaxy. Long had they waited for Man to reestablish what they considered to be his rightful position of primacy among the sentient races, and the prevailing mood was almost akin to that ancient credo of "manifest destiny." And, indeed, it was fast becoming manifest that Man had served his galactic apprenticeship and would no longer be content to play a secondary role in the scheme of things.

It was at the height of this crisis of conflicting philosophies and overviews that Joshua Bellows (2943–3009 G.E.) began his meteoric rise to power. Immensely popular with the masses, he was originally opposed and later lauded by certain elements within his own party. For if it is true that great events summon forth great leaders, then . . .

> —Man: Twelve Millennia of
> Achievement

. . . That Bellows had considerable charm and charisma as a politician cannot be denied. However, those writings and tapes of his that still exist would

117

seem to imply that he had neither the capacity nor,
originally, the motivation to have accomplished what
he did without some powerful behind-the-throne
assistance . . .
    . . . Although the Democracy survived him by
more than twelve centuries, there can be no doubt
that Bellows was responsible for . . .

*—Origin and History of the Sen-
tient Races,* Vol. 8

Josh Bellows sat behind a huge desk, its shining surface
dotted here and there with papers and documents, a score of
intercom buttons by his right arm. Immaculately tailored and
groomed, he presented the ultimate picture of dignity, with
his heavy shock of gray-black hair, the firm, hard line of his
jaw, and the tiny smile wrinkles at the corners of his clear
blue eyes. He looked every inch a leader of men, which was in
fact what he was.

"So how's it going?" he asked.

The figure approaching his desk was almost his antithesis
in every respect. Clad in wrinkled, crumpled clothes, squint-
ing through lenses so thick that one couldn't see his eyes behind them, what hair he still possessed in total disarray, he
seemed as out of place in these majestic surroundings as anyone could be.

"The natives are getting restless," said Melvyn Hill, pulling
up a beautifully carved chair of Doradusian wood and un-
ceremoniously putting his feet on the desk.

"The natives always look restless when you're staring down
at them from the top," commented Bellows. "When I was one
of them I was restless too. That's how I got here."

"That was a little different, Josh. You were restless for
power. They're restless for you to exercise that power."

"I know." Bellows frowned. "But what the hell do they expect me to do? Declare war?"

"No," said Hill. "Although," he added thoughtfully, "not
one out of five would be adverse to it."

"I won the Governorship of Deluros VIII with sixty-four
percent of the vote," said Bellows. "I think that shows a mandate of some sort for my judgment."

"I'll agree with the first half of it, Josh," said Hill. "It
shows a mandate of some sort."

"You know," said Bellows, grinning, "you are the one

member of my staff who continually makes me wonder about the wisdom of not surrounding myself with yes-men and sycophants."

"You're paying me too much to simper and suck my thumb and tell you that everything you do is right," said Hill, swinging his feet back to the floor with a grunt. "Someone in this damned Administration ought to tell you the truth."

"Which is?"

"Which is that you are in considerably more danger of impeachment than you realize."

Bellows just stared at him for a minute, his face expressionless. "Nonsense," he said at last.

Hill got to his feet. "Let me know if and when you want the rest of my report." He turned to leave.

"Hold on a minute!" snapped Bellows. "Get back in your chair and let's have this out."

Hill returned and took his seat again. "Shall I begin?" he asked.

Bellows nodded.

"All right, then. You ran for the Governor's chair based on a campaign of human primacy. So did your opponent, but it was you who began proclaiming that it was manifest destiny that Man once again rule the galaxy."

"Just politics," said Bellows.

"No, sir, it wasn't just politics. Just politics would have been promising to exterminate the Lemm, or some other race who's been a thorn in our sides. A quick little battle like the one we fought a couple of centuries ago against Pnath; it had no business taking place, but we won pretty easily and everyone felt pretty cocky about it. *That's* politics. You've done something more. You've given them a dream, a promise that our race will return to its former position of supremacy. You hammered away at it for almost a year. Now, I'll admit that you were forced into it or else you'd never have won, but your constituency put you here, and they're getting a little restless waiting for you to lead them to the promised land. You've been in office almost three years now; that's sixty percent of your term, and you haven't produced yet.

"So," he continued, "they're taking matters into their own hands. There have been pogroms on a number of worlds which we cohabit with other races, there have been some minor skirmishes in space between ships from our outworlds and those of various aliens, and your legislature has been dragging its feet on every recommendation you've sent them.

The human race has a standing battle force of some sixty million ships and ten billion men throughout the galaxy, and they're getting restless.

"As for your impeachment, the media is just now starting to talk about it, but I've done a head count, and they're only about a dozen votes short."

"Twenty-eight votes," said Bellows.

"That was *last* month," persisted Hill. "Josh, you just can't sit on your hands. You've got to *do* something."

"Like what?" said Bellows softly. "What the hell do they want me to do—launch a sneak attack on Lodin XI and the Canphor Twins? Am I supposed to kill off every alien in the galaxy just to make them happy? I'm not the President of the human race, you know. I'm just the Governor of one world."

"Deluros VIII is more than one world, and we both know it," said Hill. "Since we moved our bureaucracy here from Earth, we've been the social, political, and moral headquarters of the race of Man. For centuries the Governor of Deluros VIII has been the most powerful human in the galaxy; for all practical purposes, the job is identical to being President of the human race. If you give an order, every military unit from here to the Rim will obey it without question; if our economy goes up or down, every other human world follows suit in a year or so. We set the fashion, physically and philosophically, for every human everywhere. So don't hand me any of that crap about being the leader of one small, insignificant little world."

"All I ever promised was to give Man back his dignity," said Bellows. "I said it was our manifest destiny to rise to the top of the heap, and it is—but not by pulling the other fellows off. We'll do it by working harder, producing more, being smarter—"

"Bunk! You couldn't deliver on that promise if your term of office was ten thousand years and you lived to the last day of it. Look," said Hill, clasping and unclasping his hands. "You were born handsome, articulate, and likable. I mean it. I've always liked you, and I like you even now, when you're throwing both our careers down the drain. You come on like a forceful but benevolent father that everyone automatically trusts. Just give the mess to Josh; he'll take care of it. The problem is that you've never had to use that thing you call a brain a day of your life. Everything comes easy to Godlike father images, and when you needed some dirty work done,

120

someone like me has always been around to do it. Not that we've minded. But now you're Governor of Deluros VIII, and there's no higher office a human can aspire to the way the Democracy's set up. Now you've finally got to deliver instead of going after the job of the guy who's next in line above you. And if you can't make the decision and take the kind of action that's required, then let me or someone else do it in your name, or that handsome, noble face and lordly demeanor are going to get expurgated from the history books faster than you can imagine."

"Well, I'm sure as hell not going to go down in history as the man who started the first galactic-scale war!" said Bellows. "I don't plan to be remembered as the greatest genocidal maniac of all time."

"It's not a matter of genocide," said Hill. "It's simply a matter of testing the opposition, pushing and probing until you find a weak spot, then plugging the gap and looking for more. No one's advocating cutting off our noses to spite our faces; we need the other races as much as we ever did, perhaps more. But we need them on our terms, not theirs."

"We've been through all this before," said Bellows, glancing down at his appointments calendar.

"Evidently it hasn't done much good up to now," said Hill. "Dammit, Josh, I know that you've got reservations about it, but the Governorship is no place for vacillation. Sooner or later it's got to come, and it might as well be sooner."

"If it could be bloodless, I'd have no hesitation," said Bellows. "But these are sentient beings, Mel, not so many pieces on a gameboard."

"Begging your pardon, but we are *all* just pieces on a gameboard. A politician is successful or unsuccessful by virtue of how well or poorly he manipulates the pieces."

"Mel, if Man is to rule the galaxy—and I'm convinced he is—he's got to do so by exhibiting leadership in those areas that truly show his worth: industry, dignity, intellect. No simple show of force will make us fit to rule; if anything, it goes to prove the point that we're not yet capable of doing so."

"That's beautiful rhetoric, Josh, and I hope you put it in your memoirs," said Hill, "but it's a bunch of ivory-tower gobbledegook. Religion, morality, and Joshua Bellows to the contrary, Man is neither good nor bad, pure nor impure. He is simply Man, and his destiny, if he has one, is to make the most of all of his gifts, without attempting to place values

121

upon them. If he has a notion to grasp at the stars, then it's his duty to do so in the best and most efficient way he can; and if he fails, well, at least he did his damnedest. But Man can't just spout pretty platitudes while there's anything in his universe lacking accomplishment. I've heard it said that Man is a social animal. Some deeper thinkers have concluded that he's a political animal. I've known women who swore he was a sexual animal. None of them are totally wrong, but they haven't quite got around to the truth of it. Man is a *competitive* animal. Philosophers dream of utopias in which every need is cared for, and there is an inordinate amount of time for contemplation. Utopia, hell—that's madness! Man's living in utopia right now, a time filled with as many challenges as he can handle. But he can't start meeting those challenges until you give the word."

"And you say they're preparing to throw me out of office if I don't give it."

"They don't want to do that, Josh," said Hill. "With the magnetism you've got, they'd back any action you took. The legislature would be much happier with you than without you, but you've got to play ball with them."

"I'm still as popular as ever in the polls," said Bellows. "What if I force them into a showdown, make them put up or shut up?"

"You'd lose," said Hill promptly. "Your popularity is due, in large part, to stories I've leaked to the media about how our forces are massing and how we're ready to begin reasserting ourselves. The day they find out that those are phony, you won't have to wait for the legislature; the voters'll throw you out on your ear."

Bellows excused Hill for an hour while he attended another meeting, then summoned the gnarly adviser back to his office.

"Where would you begin?" asked the Governor bluntly.

"Ah," said Hill, smiling. "Someone else told you the same thing."

"What they told me is my business," said Bellows. "Your business is to make suggestions."

Hill chuckled. "They must really have spelled it out for you, huh? Okay, Josh, how's this for a bloodless starter: Convert every T-pack so that it'll just translate Terran, rather than Galactic-O."

"You're crazy!" exploded Bellows. "Do you know what that would do to our commerce and trade, to say nothing of our Diplomatic Corps? No one would be able to understand a word we said!"

"They'd learn," said Hill softly. "Or better still, get rid of T-packs altogether, and make it illegal for any Man to speak Galactic. Force the other races to start playing in our ball park. We're still the most potent single military and economic entity in the galaxy; sooner or later it'll become essential to their self-interest to give in."

"But in the intervening time we speak to nobody except Men, is that it?" said Bellows.

"How much time do you think will elapse?" countered Hill. "More than two thousand worlds depend on us for medical supplies, and almost ten thousand more require produce from our agricultural planets. Now, maybe some of the others will drag their feet, but that's a hard twelve thousand worlds that will learn Terran within a month. And don't forget, this is just symbolic, simply a means of asserting our identity."

"Consider it vetoed," said Bellows. "It would cause too much confusion, kill half the methane-breathers we tried to communicate with, and I'll be damned if I'm going to cut off vital medical supplies to millions of beings just for the sake of making a gesture."

Hill took a deep breath. "All right, then. Instead of taking them all on at once, take on the biggest."

"Meaning?"

"Canphor VI and VII."

"Are you seriously suggesting that I start a war with the Canphor Twins?" demanded Bellows. "That we blow them all to hell just to get the legislature off my back?"

"I am," said Hill. "But with reservations."

"That's a comfort. I didn't know you had reservations about anything."

"Where it concerns physical or political survival, I'm the most reserved person you know," said Hill. "I do not suggest that we launch an attack on the Canphor Twins or any other worlds. We have our image to consider."

"Then what are you talking about?"

"I suggest that we repel an attack by the Canphor worlds on Deluros VIII," said Hill. "You would have no objection to fighting them under those conditions, would you?"

"None at all," said Bellows. "However, I don't think they're any likelier to attack than we are."

"It's a pity that I wasn't born with your looks and that

123

deep, thoughtful, resonant voice of yours, Josh," said Hill with a little smile. "I could have achieved godhood within my own lifetime."

"I assume you're telling me how stupid I am," said Bellows dryly.

"Correct," said Hill. "Not that I hold it against you. That's what you've got *me* for."

"I'm not exactly sure *what* you're here for, but it's not to start wars for me," said Bellows with finality. "Consider the subject closed until such time as I personally reopen it."

Hill left the Governor's office and returned to his own, where two of his aides were waiting for him.

"Any luck?" asked one.

Hill shook his head. "He just doesn't realize how much trouble he's in, and he's basically too humane to do anything to alleviate the situation." He closed his eyes. "God save us from decent and moral leaders!" he added fervently.

"What's next?" asked the other.

"I'm not sure," said Hill, scratching what little remained of his once-bushy head of hair. "For Man's sake and for his, we ought to do something. The problem is that he can countermand anything I do."

"If he does, they'll kick him out and make you Governor," said the first aide. "What's so wrong with that?"

"You're going to find this hard to believe," said Hill, staring at him, "but I'm not totally unidealistic myself. I know what Man has to do, and a lot of it isn't going to be very pretty. We need a Governor like Josh Bellows, one who can convince us that everything we're trying to accomplish, and the means we're using, is not only acceptable but basically moral. If Josh told us to wipe out twenty sentient races tomorrow, we'd be absolutely sure it was the proper thing to do; if *I* ordered it, everybody would think I was a power-mad dictator with delusions of grandeur. The people need a leader they can love, respect and damned near worship. Josh fills the bill, so we've got to see to it that he's the one who actually gets the ball rolling."

"Did it ever occur to you," asked one of the aides, "that the reason Josh commands so much respect is that most of what has to be done is unthinkable to him?"

"The thought has crossed my mind on occasion." Hill grinned. "You know, it's low-down bastards like me who change history; but it's people like Josh who get the public to like it."

124

"I repeat: What's next?" said the second aide.

"Well," said Hill, "there's not a hell of a lot of sense trying to get Josh to knowingly take an *active* role in all this. He may have some pretty outmoded scruples, but he's not dumb, and he won't willingly let himself be pushed into anything. We'll simply have to work around him at first."

"How?"

"I am not totally without power in this Administration," Hill said softly. "Who's in command of our fleet in the Canphor system?"

"Greeley."

"Fine." He walked over to a recording device, picked up the microphone, and sat down.

"To Admiral Greeley, 11th Fleet," he began. "For your ears only." He waited the customary five seconds it would take for Greeley's thumbprint to unlock the protective clacking and scrambling mechanisms. "Greetings, Admiral. This is Melvyn Hill, Communications Code . . ." He paused, turning to his code book. "Code 47A3T98S. In view of what I'm about to say, I'd like you to check my code and voiceprint against your computer banks so there will be no doubt in your mind as to my identity." He waited long enough for such a check to have been run, then continued. "It has come to our attention, Admiral, that a number of pirate vessels which have been harassing our trade routes may well be doing so under the unwitting protection of Canphor VI. As a result, we have made a secret agreement with the government of Canphor VI to the effect that all nonmilitary vessels flying that world's colors will also have a special insignia prominently displayed on their starboard sides, the form of which is"—he looked down at some of his scribblings on a scratch pad and randomly chose a design—"an octagon within a circle. Any nonmilitary ship not carrying such an emblem is likely to be a pirate vessel. Your duty will be to demolish the first three such ships you encounter, then report directly to me. Under no circumstance is this to be discussed over subspace radio waves of any length, as we fear some of our communications may be monitored. Also, no more than three vessels are to be destroyed, as this preliminary act is merely to show any and all concerned parties that our vessels are no longer to be considered fair game. An all-out campaign will be mapped later. Good luck." He turned off the device and tossed the recording to one of his aides.

"Take this to Greeley personally," he said. "Don't leave

125

until he's got it in his hands." He turned to his remaining aide. "From this point forward, all alien correspondence to leave this office will be in Terran. That includes oral tapes as well as written documents."

"What if the boss says no?"

"He's got a pretty big planet to run," said Hill. "I don't think he'll bother reading anything that comes out of here. If he does, just play dumb and refer him to me."

This done, Hill settled down, went about his business, and waited for a report from Canphor VI. In less than a week it came in:

Mission accomplished. Any further instructions?
Greeley

And, moments later, he was once again in the Governor's sumptuous office.

"Suppose you tell me just what the hell is going on?" demanded Bellows.

"Sir?"

"Don't 'sir' me, Mel! The Canphor VI government is screaming bloody murder that we've shot down three of their cargo ships, and I can't get a straight answer out of Greeley. He keeps telling me to ask *you* about it."

"All I told Greeley was to keep his eyes peeled for pirate vessels," said Hill.

"There hasn't been a pirate ship within fifty parsecs of the Canphor system in a century, and you know it!" snapped Bellows. "I want an explanation and I want it quick!"

"I have none to make until I look into the matter," said Hill. "For the present, I'd suggest that we write a profusely apologetic note to Canphor VI immediately. I'll do it if you like, and send you a draft for your personal approval."

Bellows stared across the huge desk at his adviser. "I don't know what you're up to, Mel, but you're on very shaky ground at this moment. Past friendship aside, I won't hesitate to dump you if I find it necessary—and I'll find it necessary if there's one more incident like this."

Hill returned to his office, dictated the note of apology, and sent it to Bellows. It came back with the Governor's approval.

"Okay," he said to his secretary. "Send it off."

"In Galactic, sir?" she asked.

"In Terran," said Hill calmly.

126

Within hours the government of Canphor VI sent back a message that the apology was unacceptable.

"What will the Governor say to that one?" said one of Hill's aides, looking at the transcribed reply.

"I haven't the slightest idea," said Hill. "However, I don't think he'll say too much."

"Oh? Why?"

"Because I've released copies of our apology and Canphor VI's answer to the media." The intercom lit up, and Hill pressed a button. "Hill here."

"Mel, this is Josh. I don't know why Canphor VI turned your note down, but I've got a pretty good suspicion. Did you send it in Galactic?"

"I can't recall," said Hill.

"That's it!" bellowed the Governor. "You've got two days to put your affairs in order and clear out. You're fired!"

"I wouldn't release that to the press for a few hours yet, Josh," said Hill.

"And why not?"

"It won't make the headlines until they're through running the story about Canphor VI turning down our apology."

The intercom flicked off without another comment from Bellows.

"We haven't got much time," said Hill to his aides. "Three hours from now every human in the Deluros system will be screaming for war, and by tomorrow morning the rest of the human worlds will be out for blood too. If Josh wants to keep his political scalp, he'll have to attack—and if I know Josh, he'll procrastinate until it's too late."

"I don't see that you can do anything about it," volunteered one of the aides.

"That's why I'm your boss instead of the other way around," said Hill. "Send the following message to Greeley, unscrambled." He paused, trying to get the words straight in his mind, and then began dictating.

Admiral:
The content of this message is of such import that we've no time for code. The planned attack on the Canphor system will take place in five days' time. The delay is regrettable, but the bulk of our fleet is engaged in maneuvers on the Rim. Do not—repeat, do not—move in until that time, as you can expect no assistance from Deluros

127

VIII prior to the return of the fleet. Should there
be any doubt whatsoever concerning your orders,
return immediately to base at Deluros V.

Melvyn Hill,
Assistant to the Governor

Hill looked up. "What's the latest frequency that Canphor
VI has cracked?"

"H57, about a week ago."

"Good. Send it on H57, but in Terran. We don't want to
make it look too easy for them."

"What if Greeley attacks?" asked an aide.

"He won't," said Hill. "He doesn't know what the hell I'm
talking about, so he'll come racing back to base, just in time
to help fend off the Canphor fleet."

Hill walked out his door and strolled casually over to Bellows's office. He smoked a cigar, checked his watch, decided
that the message would have been sent and intercepted by
now, and walked in. The security agents had already been instructed that he was no longer a member of the staff, and
they barred his way. After sending through his formal request
to see the Governor, he was kept cooling his heels in the
outer office for another hour before he was finally ushered in.

"I don't know why I'm wasting time like this," began Bellows. "I've got nothing to say to you."

"But I've got a lot to say to you, Josh," said Hill. "Especially since this is probably the last time we'll ever speak
together. May I sit down?"

Bellows stared hard at him, then nodded. "Why did you do
it, Mel?"

"I suppose I should say I did it for you," said Hill, "and in
a way I did. But mostly, I did it for Man." He paused. "Josh,
I don't want to startle you, but you're going to have a war on
your hands in less than a day, and there's no way in hell you
can get out of it, so you'd better make up your mind to win
it."

"What are you talking about?" demanded Bellows.

"Canphor VI," said Hill. "And possibly Canphor VII too.
They'll be attacking Deluros VIII very shortly. It'll take very
little effort to beat them back, and not much more to defeat
them. They're operating on the assumption that we're unpro-
tected." Bellows reached for his intercom panel, but Hill laid
a hand on his arm. "No hurry, Josh. Greeley will be back
ahead of them, and has probably got everybody in an uproar

128

already. Let's talk for a few minutes first; then you can do anything you want to me."

Bellows sat back in his chair, glaring.

"Josh, I'm not going to tell you how this came about. It's so simple you wouldn't believe me anyhow, and besides, you'll be able to speak with a little more forcefulness and moral outrage on the video if you don't know. But the thing is, it's started. Man's about to make his first move back up the ladder, and you're going to go down in history as the guy that did it. It won't be completed in your term, or your lifetime, or even in a millennium, but it's started now and nothing's going to stop it.

"You've got the people behind you," Hill continued, "plus the unswerving loyalty of the military. This battle won't amount to anything more than a minor skirmish, and knowing you, I'm sure you'll offer very generous terms to Canphor when it's over. But the very least the legislature will demand is that the Canphor system become a human protectorate. They'll want more than that, but I imagine you'll get them to compromise there. Whatever the result, the Canphor worlds will contribute their taxes to Deluros VIII, and our tariffs will reflect their change in status.

"And once you find out just how easy this is, it'll occur again and again in some form or another. You're going to be riding a tidal wave of sentiment, and you're either going to steer it where it wants to go or get thrown out of the saddle within a month. You'll be very careful and meticulous, and you'll always pay lip service to the Democracy. Perhaps it will even remain as a figurehead of galactic power, but the handwriting will be on the wall. Man's going to wind up calling the shots again.

"I don't know what you think you've done," said Bellows, "but whatever it is, it can be undone. If there really is an alien attack force on the way from Canphor, I'll see to it that it's called back."

"Uh-uh, Josh," said Hill. "They've heard what they've been expecting to hear, and they're not going to believe anything you tell them."

"They'll believe me when I tell them we're standing ready to repulse any attack."

"I'm afraid not," said Hill. "There's no way you can turn it off, Josh. You'd better start thinking about how you're going to tell the people that you're the leader they've always wanted you to be."

129

Hill stood up and slowly walked out of the office.

Bellows spent the next two hours confirming the truth of what he'd been told, and two more hours after that frantically but fruitlessly trying to avert the coming conflict.

As night fell, the Governor of Deluros VIII sat alone in his semi-darkened office, his hands clasped in front of him, staring intently at his fingers. He considered resigning, but realized that it wouldn't have any effect on the tide of events. He even considered having Hill make a full public confession, but knew even as the thought crossed his mind that the populace would approve of Hill's actions.

Bellows was an essentially decent man. He didn't want to destroy anyone. At heart he believed that Man would emerge triumphant in the galactic scheme of things by virtue of his own endeavors. Furthermore, Man was still immensely outnumbered by the other races. The course Hill had charted would be so perilous, so fraught with danger at any misstep . . . Man would have to divide and conquer on a scale never before imagined. He'd have to be quiet about it, too; would have to accomplish most of his plan before the galaxy awoke to what was happening, or everything would come down on his head, hard.

And yet, if Man was capable of pulling it off, didn't he deserve to? After all, this wasn't exactly survival of the fittest so much as ascendancy of the fittest. The races of the galaxy would continue to function, and under Man's leadership they would very likely function all the more efficiently.

Or was he just rationalizing? Man was capable of such splendid achievements, such generosity to other races, why did he have to have this aggressive, darker side of his nature? Or was it a dark side at all? Was Man, as Hill had said, merely making the most of every single one of his attributes, including this one?

Bellows reached for the intercom button that would summon the press. As they filed into his office, he made his decision—or rather, he thought with a bemused detachment, he acknowledged the decision that had long since been made for him. For while he had many other qualities—goodness, judgment, integrity—all had failed him in this crisis, and he was left with the foremost quality that any politician possessed: survival.

"Gentlemen," he began, staring unblinking at them from out of his clear blue eyes, "it has come to my attention that a fleet of military ships has just left Canphor VI for the purpose of perpetrating a heinous sneak attack on Deluros VIII. Neither we nor any other world housing members of the race of Man will tolerate or yield to such an unprovoked action. Therefore, I have instructed the 7th, 9th, 11th, and 18th fleets to take the following steps . . ."

Sixth Millennium: OLIGARCHY

11: The Administrators

(No mention of the Administrators, as such, can be found in *Man: Twelve Millennia of Achievement* or in *Origin and History of the Sentient Races*.)

The Democracy did not die rapidly, nor did Man particularly want it to. From the instant that the fabled Joshua Bellows had repulsed an abortive attack on Deluros VIII by the Canphor Twins and followed up by winning a quick series of battles and putting the entire Canphor system under martial law, the handwriting had been on the wall. For the second time in galactic history, the Cartography complex at distant Caliban had become the most important single factor in Man's expansion, but this time it was a more mature Man, a Man who knew the bitter aftertaste of expanding too rapidly, who began gathering his empire about him.

This was no hit-or-miss proposition, this expansion. There was no settling or winning of strategic systems and then moving parsecs away to new challenges. Man was more thorough this time, more methodical, more grimly efficient. Radiating out in all directions simultaneously from Deluros VIII, Earth, and Sirius V, Man took each world as it came. When a major military power stood in his way, such as Lodin XI, he leveled it; but by and large, he still preferred the more permanent and more devastating method of economic warfare to bring rebellious worlds into line.

As the fourth millennium of Man's galactic influence drew to a close, he controlled almost half the sentient worlds in the galaxy, though the Democracy still stood. Another ten centuries saw him in possession, either militarily or economically, of some eighty percent of the populated planets, and the Democracy died without a whimper.

In its place there appeared the seven-seat Oligarchy. Ostensibly there were no restrictions on any of the seats, but all were held by Men, and had been thus held since their creation. Nor did the alien races suffer overmuch from this change, for Man was still a doer, a builder, a force for movement, and he took care of his possessions more meticulously than the alien-dominated Democracy had ever done.

The administration of the Oligarchic empire was by no means an easy task. In point of fact, it redirected and sapped Man's energies for more than two centuries, as well it should have in view of the vastness of the undertaking.

There were, at the dawn of the Oligarchic era, some 1,-400,000 inhabited planets in the galaxy; 1,150,000 were eagerly, or willingly, or tacitly, or resentfully, within the political and economic domain of the Oligarchy.

The problems posed by such an empire were immense. For example, all member worlds paid taxes. Although the planetary governments were responsible for raising the revenues, they did so under the supervision of the Oligarchy, which supplied an average of twenty men to each nonhuman planet, and fifty to each planet populated primarily by Man. Thus, the Taxation Bureau employed more than twenty-five million field representatives, and another six million office workers. And like all the other agencies, it was woefully undermanned.

The military bureaucracy quickly expanded to unmanageable proportions. The Oligarchy had inherited a standing task force of some twenty-five billion men. To have deactivated even half of them once the Democracy had breathed its last would have destroyed the economies of literally hundreds of thousands of worlds, and so they remained in the various branches of a service which numbered far more officers in peacetime than it ever had during its days of battle.

Agriculture posed a special problem. There would never be a crop failure, not with more than fifty thousand agricultural worlds. But the creation of equitable tariffs and the channeling of certain goods to certain worlds were unbelievably complex. A side product was the reintroduction of widespread narcotics addiction, complicated by the fact that there was simply no way to outlaw the growth of harmful plants. For example, the natives of Altair III found that wheat was a powerful stimulant and hallucinogen to their systems, while opium was the staple diet of the inhabitants of Aldebaran XIII.

Before two decades had passed the bureaucracy had outgrown the confines of Deluros VIII, despite its 28,000-mile diameter. Cartography confirmed that while there were a handful of larger planets hospitable to human life, none were of sufficient size to warrant abandoning Deluros VIII.

Ultimately a satisfactory solution was reached, and implementation began shortly thereafter. Deluros VI, another large world, though not quite so large as the Oligarchic headquarters, was ripped apart by a number of carefully placed and extremely powerful explosive charges. The smaller fragments, as well as the larger irregular ones, were then totally obliterated. The remaining forty-eight planetoids, each approximating the size of Earth's moon, were turned over to the largest departments of the Oligarchy. Domes were erected on each of the planetoids, construction of worldwide complexes was begun, and life-support systems were implemented. Within half a century almost the entire administrative bureaucracy had moved from Deluros VIII to one or another of the Deluros VI planetoids. The orbits had been adjusted, the planetoids circled huge Deluros millions of miles from each other, and tens of thousands of ships sped daily between the ruling world of the Oligarchy and its forty-eight extensions. Here floated Commerce, a massive red-brown rock reflecting the sunlight blindingly from its billions of steel-and-plastic offices; there raced the smallest of the planetoids, Education and Welfare, spinning on its axis every sixteen hours; on the far side of the sun was the massive Military complex, taking up four entire planetoids, and already choking for lack of room.

And halfway between daytime and evening was the Investigations planetoid. With some 80 million bureaucratic appointments per year, plus the huge narcotics trade and the various alien acts of rebellion, it could hardly be said that the department lacked for work.

None of the planetoids found their work easy. The Bureau of Communication was involved with implementing the first ruling passed by the first members of the Oligarchy: that Terran was to become the official language. The Treasury planet-

134

oid was continually balancing tendencies toward inflation and depression, and was not abetted by the fact that with such a multiplicity of worlds in the Oligarchic empire, there was simply no single substance rare enough to back the currency with. Four-fifths of the Labor Department was devoted to keeping the miners happy without yielding too much power to them. No one knew exactly what occurred on the Science planetoid, but there were 122 vast buildings, each hundreds of miles long, devoted to the 122 major sciences, and no one seemed to be suffering from boredom.

But as she looked out her window at the twinkling, shining mini-worlds, Ulice Ston knew that the Department of Alien Affairs was currently sitting on the biggest problem of all; and that she, as Director, was sitting on the Department of Alien Affairs.

The bulk of her business concerned the legal wording, ratification recommendations, and enforcement of some half million treaties per year. All wars not involving humans were also in her domain. So were all complaints of mistreatment of aliens.

And so, she sighed, was Bareimus.

The Bareimus situation was, simply stated, a stinker. By rights it should have gone to Science, or perhaps some sector of the Military, but since it concerned aliens, the problem was all hers. And a hell of a problem it was.

Bareimus was a star about eight parsecs from the Binder system. It had seven planets circling it at distances of from 34 to 280 million miles. Two of the planets were inhabited; five were totally devoid of life. The Astronomy Department had decided, by means she could barely begin to understand, that Bareimus was going to go nova, or possibly supernova, within two years.

Her job was to evacuate the indigenous populations of Bareimus III and V before the cataclysm took place. The natives of Bareimus V, a docile, philosophically-oriented race of chlorine-breathers, were more than happy to relocate around a stable sun, and the problem there was merely one of logistics. Though "merely," she reflected, was hardly an adequate adverb to describe the task of moving some two billion beings and their possessions halfway across the galaxy in a year's time.

Her troubles—and her incipient ulcer—were being caused by Bareimus III. There was nobody in the department, indeed in the whole Oligarchy, lacking an opinion on the matter.

With one notable exception: Psychology couldn't make up its collective mind, and that was the root of the problem.

The whole thing had begun some five years earlier, when a botanical survey ship made a landing in a clearing near one of the more densely forested regions of Bareimus III. They had thought they were setting down amid some lush green vegetation, but when the crew left the ship they discovered that the tail-first landing had placed them down on a small, barren patch of dirt.

Nobody had thought too much about it until the time came to collect samples to bring back to their lab—and some of the small green plants they were approaching began running away. They finally caught a couple by hurling a large net at them, and discovered, when they tried to take the plants back with them, that they were once again rooted.

They dug up both the plants and the surrounding dirt, took them back to the ship, and determined that they were semi-carnivorous. They didn't *have* to eat insects and rodents, but they were equipped to do so, and indeed seemed to thrive better with occasional additions of small living things to their menu. They seemed healthier and more vibrant after such meals, and their color turned brighter, leading one of the crew to dub them Greenies, a name that stuck.

The next unusual occurrence came later on that same survey trip, when a botanist casually threw a still-lit cigar onto the turf—or onto what had been a Greenie-filled turf an instant earlier. As he released the cigar, the little plants scurried away, giving it a wide berth.

Curious, the botanist returned to the ship, lit a cigar, and held it near one of the Greenies. There was no reaction. Then he dropped it on the plant. Despite the fact that the base of its stem was badly burned, it made no attempt to uproot itself and move away. Further experimentation proved that the Greenie samples in the ship showed none of the self-preservational instinct they had manifested in their natural habitat, nor did a reward-oriented experiment using small animals cause them to act in any manner other than that of exotic cousins to Venus Flytraps.

The observations and experiments were written up, logged, and forgotten. Then, some two years later, another ship landed in the Bareimus system. During their stay among the chlorine-breathers of Bareimus V they discovered a malfunction of their life-support systems, and since the planet-bound population could afford them no help, they sent a message back to the nearest world where they could reasonably expect repairs to be made, and decided to await the arrival of the rescue ship on Bareimus III, where they wouldn't be forced to use any more of their limited supply of oxygen. Their observations of the Greenies were identical to the earlier reports, although they attempted no experiments. However, upon returning to the Deluros system, they presented their information to the Biology planetoid, and eventually someone who was interested enough to read it gathered all the reports together, and still another expedition was sent to Bareimus III, but this time with the express purpose of learning what made the Greenies tick.

The ship landed, and the scientific crew noted all the usual traits of Greenie behavior. Five of the plants were "captured" and taken back to the ship's greenhouse, where they failed to respond to any stimuli. Then they were marked, and placed back where they were found, amid thousands of other Greenies. And now, back among their fellows, they once again responded to heat and other threats.

The experiment was repeated numerous times with different Greenies, and always the results were identical. Under laboratory conditions, they acted like any other plant; but placed in their natural environment, they protected themselves at all costs.

Next, a number of Greenies were moved not to the ship's greenhouse, but to a patch of ground a few miles from the other Greenies. They still responded, but slowly, as if they were befuddled. Their confusion increased proportionally with the distance between them and their home colony, until, at exactly 5.127 kilometers, they once again became inert.

The next step was to move larger and larger quantities of Greenies 6 kilometers away from the home colony. When some 2,000 were assembled, from a colony of 11,500, they began to react, but again, very slowly and in much obvious confusion. As their number increased, so did their efficiency, until, with 4,367 Greenies present, they functioned as well as they had in the original colony. And, conversely, as the original colony was depleted to where only about 1,500 remained, all reaction to stimuli stopped.

The implications were staggering. Here, undoubtedly, was a group mind at work. Each plant acted as a single cell of that mind. With only 1,500 cells, the mind was mere potential; at 2,000 cells, it was kinetic but unbalanced; and at 4,-367 or more cells, it functioned at peak efficiency. The

137

Greenies' mass mind represented a phenomenon heretofore unknown in the galaxy, even among those few races possessed of telepathy.

The next problem facing the scientists was of equal or even greater import. Granting that the Greenies, as a group, had a mind, was it an intelligent one? Simply having a functioning brain was no proof of sentience; for every intelligent life form that Man had found, there were thousands that lacked the power of abstract thought.

The task was an intricate and complex one, for no vegetation had yet been discovered that even hinted at having the Greenies' capacity for intelligent action. And no one quite knew how to test a plant for intelligence.

Scores of reward situations were devised, usually with rodents native to Bareimus III. In every case, the Greenies devised ways to catch them. But did that make them intelligent, or merely coldly efficient hunters with thousands of outlets for their senses? No one knew.

An entire Greenie colony was transported back to the Biology Department and studied. Thousands of botanists and psychologists created literally millions of tests. Most were discarded out of hand; those that were administered could not produce definite results. The Greenies could crack almost every maze or hunting situation devised, but they showed no interest in anything else. They solved feeding problems that would have stumped even Man, but, once fed, they became mentally inert. Nor could any divisiveness be imposed; feeding one half of the colony while starving the other half did not produce a small-scale vegetable war. And, the scientists concluded, how could it? If half a brain lacks blood or oxygen, it doesn't take up arms against the other half.

Still, no one was totally convinced that the Greenies were intelligent. It was simply a case of nobody being able to guess what kind of thoughts were entertained by a Greenie's mind. Some telepaths from the distant world of Domar were called in; they all agreed that there was some sort of mentality there, but it was so alien that none of them could either make contact with it or begin to figure out how it functioned.

That was where matters stood when it was discovered that Bareimus was about to go nova.

And since no one knew what the Greenies were or were not, they had thankfully given the problem to Ulice Ston, who had never even seen a Greenie, and knew next to nothing about botany and alien psychology.

138

Her first step had been to ascertain the cost and the logistics of evacuating the Greenies from Bareimus III. This required an initial expenditure in excess of two billion credits simply to locate and chart the Greenie colonies. Then Cartography was asked to find a world approximating the atmospheric and gravitational conditions of Bareimus III. Some 3,096 worlds filled the bill, but only four of them had the requisite insect and rodent population. Evacuation usually posed no ecological problems on a race's new world, but, as in all other things, the Greenies were an exception: They would ingest nothing but live food, and there was no way that 45 billion transplanted Greenies would fail to make a dent in any planet's ecological balance. That knocked out two of the four worlds, and the other two seemed to have so many herbivora that there was considerable doubt about the Greenies' ability to survive in such a predator-filled environment. Nor, if they were sentient, *should* they be placed in a situation where they'd have to fight for survival.

Her preliminary reports caused Psychology is set up a few more experiments, in each of which various herbivores were turned loose on the Greenies. Most disdained the little plants, but the few that showed any interest in eating them had merely to catch them. The Greenies, it was concluded, may have been masters at evasive maneuvering, but they lacked any form of offensive or defensive weaponry that would be effective against anything larger than their normal prey.

When the first phase of her job had been completed, Ulice sent in her recommendations: *If* the Greenies were an intelligent species, they must perforce be evacuated; and if they were evacuated, an artificial planetoid simulating their own world must be provided. It would take approximately one million men, working around-the-clock shifts, about five months to evacuate all the Greenies. They could be transported, again in shifts, on a minimum of two thousand cargo ships, and preferably three thousand. The operation could not be done any faster, her report continued, because in addition to 45 billion Greenies, the Oligarchy would also have to move the entire rodent population of Bareimus III, and a goodly number of its insects as well.

She was not surprised when the recommendations were not acted upon.

The Oligarchy assured her that were the Greenies truly sentient, they would spare no expense in relocating the race and all that it needed to survive; but in light of the phenomenal expenditure in money and manpower required, they simply couldn't authorize any action until they knew, beyond any shadow of a doubt, that the Greenies were indeed an intelligent race.

She requested a firm opinion from Psychology, and got only a muddled "Maybe." The general attitude was that the Greenies probably were possessed of some form of intelligence, but they were so different, so completely alien in outlook, that no objective answer could be made until more conclusive tests could be devised . . . .

The Military politely but regretfully informed her that while they would indeed like to lend a hand, and doubtless had the capacity to do the job with fewer men and in less time than she had estimated, their budget was stretched to the limit already, and they were barely able to carry out their mundane day-to-day chores. Of course, they added, if she could wrest an executive order out of the Oligarchy, together with an ample appropriation, they'd be delighted to pitch in and help. . . .

The Treasury coldly informed her that they had more than the requisite funds, and of course they would spend any amount to protect any race that fell under the sanctions of Oligarchic Law. Was that the case with the Greenies? No? Well, that made things a little more difficult; but all she had to do was get Psychology to proclaim officially that the Greenies were an intelligent race, and then the money would flow like water. . . .

The Bureau of Education and Welfare didn't know what *it* could do to help, but should anyone find a way of communicating with the Greenies, they'd be happy to do whatever they could. And in the meantime, could she possibly spring loose some of Botany's and Psychology's findings so that the Greenies could be incorporated into some of the textbooks and tapes. . . .

Only the media came to her aid. They took up the Greenies' case with a single-minded vengeance. Within weeks every planet had its "Save the Greenies" committees, and three campuses actually erupted in violence over the Oligarchy's refusal to commit itself.

As for the alien races, they had their own problems, and weren't about to stick their necks out fighting for the right to life of a plant species which might or might not be sentient. Besides, they were as far removed from the intellectual state, if any, of the Greenies as Man was. . . .

So the problem remained in her department, on her desk. She was tempted at times to declare that Greenies were non-sentient and wash her hands of the whole affair, except that, like everyone else, she had a sneaking suspicion that they were indeed capable of thought. After all, who could know what kind of thoughts occupied the mind of a plant?

There was no doubt that sooner or later Psychology and Botany between them would determine the Greenies' status. However, *later* wouldn't do the Greenies any good. Given the amount of time it would take to get the wheels of evacuation and planet-building going, plus a safety factor in case Bareimus went nova a little sooner than expected, she figured that she had, at most, three months in which to break through the mile upon mile of red tape and get the project off the ground.

Psychology was doing its best, to be sure, but in this case its best just wasn't good enough. Aware of the time factor, they had leaped ahead to trying to force the Greenies to show a capacity for creative thought. They supplied them with all the requisite tools and apparatus for creating artificial light, and then cut off their sunlight. Fully one-third of the Greenie colony died before they called a halt to the experiment. They cut the Greenies' food rations by eighty percent and tried to get them to breed their remaining rodents and insects rather than eat them on contact. A quarter of the remaining Greenies died of starvation before that experiment was called off. They injected DNA molecules from similar plants into a number of Greenies; those that didn't die immediately showed absolutely no change whatever. They kept the Greenies under constant surveillance in an attempt to discover how they communicated, and were unable to determine their method. They introduced an especially poisonous species of vegetarian wasp from Balok VII, hoping to force the Greenies into displaying some defense mechanism other than flight, and destroyed five hundred more Greenies before the wasps were removed. They tried everything their combined minds could think of with no visible effect, and yet were unable to state conclusively that the Greenies didn't think, or even that they simply didn't think along those particular lines.

Then, two months prior to Ulice's deadline, Psychology made its first real breakthrough. Experimenting with ultrasonic vibrations, they discovered that the sounds had a soothing effect on the Greenies. A number of buttons and levers were set up, and the Greenies immediately figured out how to manipulate them to produce more ultrasonic waves.

141

Then different frequencies were added, and within a matter of three days the Greenies were creating melodies of greater and greater complexity. They were beyond the range of human hearing, to be sure, but oscilloscopic instruments were able to detect every note, every variation, every subtle nuance of the orchestrations.

Anxious to either begin the evacuation or abandon it, Ulice started pressing her demands for a decision as to the Greenies' intellectual capacity. It seemed obvious to her that any being capable of producing such intricate symphonic arrangements must be sentient, but Psychology still wasn't willing to commit itself. After all, they pointed out, numerous birds on Earth and myriads of other planets also created lovely melodies without anyone's claiming that this particular art was a manifestation of intelligence. Admittedly, no birds—and probably no Men, either—had yet come up with any music as complex as that produced by the Greenies, but that didn't necessarily prove . . .

On her own initiative, Ulice hired a number of musicians to transpose the oscilloscopic readings of the Greenies' symphonies into a score that could be played to an audience of humans. More money went to hire an orchestra, and, after a week of rehearsals, the premier performance of the Greenies' Symphony No. 6, the most sophisticated of their creations, was given to an audience consisting entirely of psychologists and musicians. The symphony was unlike anything ever heard before; fully half the audience walked out before the evening was completed, while most of those who remained gave the orchestra—and, by implication, the composers—a standing ovation.

When questioned, opinions were split right down the middle. Rostikol, perhaps the greatest conductor ever seen on Deluros VIII, claimed that it was a work of absolute genius; to his mind there was no doubt that the Greenies were intelligent, quite probably more intelligent than Man. Malor, the uncrowned king of the serious composers, found it interesting but incomprehensible. And Kirkelund, foremost of the critics from the alien culture of Canphor VII, found it a hideous cacophony of sound indicating nothing more than random selection of discordant and atonal thematic material, hardly the type of music on which to base a case for intelligence.

The seven members of the Oligarchy, as well as the Military, were completely noncommittal, awaiting a decision from Psychology. Psychology was leaning toward a statement declaring the Greenies to be a sentient race, but still wasn't ready to make it without further data.

Ulice decided that she couldn't wait any longer, and two days later the Department of Alien Affairs publicly proclaimed that the Greenies were intelligent and every effort would now be made to evacuate them from Bareimus III prior to its sun going nova. She had her executive assistants make out the proper requisition forms and sent them to the various branches of the Oligarchy from which she required assistance.

The first to reply was Treasury. It had placed the money in escrow, but was not prepared to relinquish it on the say so of a woman who possessed virtually no experience or expertise in the field of alien psychology. Next to report was the Military. They were still more than willing to help, but their hands were tied until the Oligarchic Council gave them its written approval. Psychology responded with a scream of rage. What right did Ulice Ston think she had to preempt *their* function? The Greenies would officially become an intelligent race if and when *they* said so, and not until then. And the Council simply threw up its collective hands in dismay and turned its attention to other business.

The question was still unresolved when Bareimus went nova two years later, becoming the brightest star in the local heavens for almost a month.

The Greenie colony on the Science planetoid continued to thrive and turn out more complex and masterful symphonic works. Psychology still refused to make a judgment concerning their intellectual capacity. The Education Department decided not to incorporate the Greenies into their textbooks until a decision was reached, if indeed it ever was. That portion of the Military concerned with the evacuation of planets turned its attention to more pressing problems. And Ulice Ston resigned as the head of the Department of Alien Affairs, married a man who had never set foot on any world or planetoid within the Deluros system, and had eight children in the next eleven years.

12: The Media

    ... With more than one million worlds under Oligarchic control, it was inevitable that the news media should take on new power and authority. For the most part this power was used to educate and inform the public, but there were occasional abuses, such as the notorious affair in the Aldebaran system, where the duly-elected Coordinator, Gile Cobart (5406–5469 G.E.), was denied all access to ...

        —Man: Twelve Millennia of Achievement

    ... It was Jorg Bomin (5389–5466 G.E.) who realized to the fullest the power of the media, and proved that, even among such a race as Man, the pen was mightier than the sword. Later discredited by his own race, and even by his own financial empire, the fact remains that it was Bomin who stood alone against the tyrannical regime of ...

        —Origin and History of the Sentient Races, Vol. 8

Cobart had launched another attack, to nobody's great surprise. It was his fifth in four weeks.

It wasn't a military attack, for Gile Cobart wasn't at war with any external force. As the duly elected Coordinator of the Aldebaran system, his borders were secured by the greater presence of the Oligarchy. But within the system itself, he reigned supreme.

Or, rather, he tried to.

His problem, like that of all political leaders, was the media. His approach to his problem, which made up in forcefulness what it lacked in originality, was to strike out against his critics, castigating them whenever possible and trying to rally public opinion to his side. And in the Aldebaran system, unlike most other worlds where trusts and monopolies were outlawed, he had only one enemy: ASOC, the Aldebaran System of Communications. ASOC controlled, in whole or in part, every newstape, every video and radio channel, and every one of the old-style newspapers.

And ASOC didn't like Cobart any better than he liked it.

There had never been much love between the two. During the past election, ASOC had thrown up its hands in dismay at the slate of candidates offered, refused to endorse any of them for Coordinator, and sat on the sidelines as the people elected Cobart with a mere twenty-nine percent of the vote. But while he may have had minimal support, once in office he began gathering a maximum of power about him.

He was forced to hold, tacitly at least, to the laws of the Oligarchy. But the laws were vaguely worded in many instances, and any man hungry for power could find ample ways to get around them. Such a man was Gile Cobart.

First came a systematic centralization of government. Aldebaran VII was made the capital world of the system, and the seventeen other planets became mere economic satellites. The plights of the native aliens on Aldebaran II, IV, V, and XIII were shunted aside, though given ample lip service. Soon the petty accouterments of dictatorship—brilliantly uniformed bodyguards, refusal to speak to the press, denial of voting rights to previously enfranchised portions of the population, trials of political enemies—began to take shape and form.

Only ASOC stood against him, and he felt it his duty—and his pleasure—to publicly attack ASOC at every opportunity.

ASOC and its chairman, Jorg Bomin, viewed neither the attacks nor the attacker with equanimity. The corporation was the biggest in the system, and its assets were almost as great as the planetary assets of Aldebaran VII. If Cobart had been looking for an opponent worthy of his time and efforts, he couldn't have picked a better one.

Every day Bomin's stations, tapes, and papers would attack Cobart and his policies. Every afternoon one of Cobart's spokesmen would respond with varying degrees of hostility. The battle between the non-free press and the non-free government was reaching a fever pitch when Bomin called his board of directors into session.

He didn't make a very heroic picture, standing there before them. In an age where Man's average height was well over six feet, he barely reached five; in a society where a man's economic and social standing could usually be determined by the fashion of his clothes, he dressed more plainly than the most common of menials; in a profession where style was at least as important as substance, he was bald and underweight and spoke with a slight lisp. In fact, the only thing he had to recommend him was that he always delivered the goods.

He'd been delivering the goods for ASOC for quite some time now. Beginning as a lower-level executive, he had swiftly climbed to the top of the corporate ladder, stomping on as few sets of fingers as possible in the process. Once in full control, he had properly ascertained that tape and periodical distribution held the key to all nonvideo media, and had built up a system-wide distribution empire that rivaled ASOC's control of the airwaves. Never once did he allow ASOC to branch out into any non-media-related investments; excess capital, and there was a lot of it, was funneled back into existing corporate enterprises; more newspapers, more newstapes, more video stations, more distributional outlets. ASOC and Bomin were totally self-sufficient entities, continually feed on themselves, always growing but always controlled.

"Gentlemen," he said, after taking a sip of water, "I won't mince words. The Coordinator has requested a private meeting with me tomorrow evening. There can be precious little doubt as to the subject matter of this interview. He will almost certainly threaten to nationalize ASOC. I will just as certainly refuse to yield to any threats he may make. Are there any questions?"

He waited an appropriate length of time, and, when he had determined that no one had anything to say, he continued:

"I will assume that your silence can be taken to imply full support of my position. I had hoped for, and would have accepted, nothing less. However, you must realize that I cannot simply reject his demand and walk out. To do so would be totally ineffective, and would hardly be likely to improve our position. After all, he must know that my reaction will be negative just as surely as you knew it. Therefore, I feel that we can expect something in the nature of a threat to our continued existence. After all, if he can't own ASOC himself, his next step will doubtless be to destroy it."

"There's no legal way he can do it," said one of the board members.

"There was no legal way he could both try and sentence Pollart last week, but I notice that he seems to have accomplished it," replied Bomin mildly.

"We can go to the Oligarchy," said another.

"Indeed we can," said Bomin. "However, if he denies his threat, how are we to prove otherwise? I have discarded the possibility of surreptitiously trying to record our conversation. I'm sure he has quite enough safeguards to prevent it. Are there any other suggestions?" He looked around the room. "No? Then since no one has anything further to suggest insofar as a defense or counterattack is concerned, I would like to know if the board will support whatever I find I must do or say during the meeting."

The various board members studied him intently. The old bird had something up his sleeve, that was for sure; and it was just as sure that he had no intention of telling them what it was. He had allowed them to offer what few ideas they may have had, shot them down, and now presented them with their only alternative: to trust him blindly and implicitly. They knew Cobart and they knew Bomin. It was a pretty easy choice: They gave Bomin a free hand to do as he wished.

Which surprised him no more than did Cobart's latest attack on ASOC. His first act was to instruct his staff that no advance mention was to be made in the media of his meeting, nor was there to be any coverage of the meeting itself. Out of respect for the office of the Coordinator, though not the current officeholder, he showered and shaved before leaving.

He was ushered into Cobart's office by a circuitous route. Then the door was closed behind him and he was alone in the huge, ornate room with the Coordinator.

"I'll get right to the point," said Cobart by way of greeting. "I want you and ASOC to get off my back."

147

"Easily done," said Bomin with a smile. "Return the power you've illegally usurped from the people of the Aldebaran system."

"That's just the kind of inflammatory remark I'm objecting to. If you know what's good for you, you'll stop taking pot-shots at my Administration."

"And that's just the kind of heavy-handed threat *I* object to, Mr. Cobart," said Bomin. "Surely you didn't invite me here just to make it."

"I didn't invite you at all," said Cobart. "I commanded your presence."

"And I, having weighed the pros and cons, decided of my own free will to accept your invitation."

"Bomin, I've had enough of your rabble-rousing. Some of the statements you've made through ASOC amount to nothing less than treason."

"Certainly not treason to the Oligarchy," said Bomin mildly. "Or are you implying I've committed treason against the people of the Aldebaran system? Because if you are, then you have only to prefer charges formally and—"

"What would you say," interrupted Cobart, "if I told you that it is within my constitutional power to nationalize ASOC?"

"First, that it is definitely not within your real or implied powers," said Bomin, "and second, that your desire to do so anyway hardly comes as a surprise to me."

"I've only to say the word and ASOC will become an official government agency," continued Cobart. "Oh, the courts will probably knock it down, and if they don't, the Oligarchy will. But knocking it down will take time—possibly a year, possibly more. By then the people would have heard both sides of the case, and most of your bright young men would have found nice secure jobs in other fields. Think about it, Bomin."

"Oh, I assure you I *have* thought about it. Subtlety is not one of your more noteworthy qualities, Mr. Coordinator. We at ASOC foresaw this move long ago."

"I don't doubt that you did," said Cobart. "Have you come up with any alternative solution which I would consider satisfactory?"

"It's entirely possible that we have," said Bomin. "You claim that we present your case unfairly, correct?" Cobart nodded. "What would be your response if, in exchange for your written promise never to raise the issue of nationalization of ASOC again, I promised you—also in writing, to be sure—that ASOC will give you equal time to present your side of the story? In other words, we will guarantee you one minute of air time for every minute we criticize you, one inch of newspaper column space for every anti-Cobart inch we run."

Cobart rejected the offer, as Bomin had known he would do. Then came the clincher.

"What if I further promised that for the three years prior to the next election, no section of the media owned by ASOC or any of its affiliates will criticize you or your Administration, either directly or by implication?"

Cobart stared at him. "You mean it?"

"I was never more sincere in my life," said Bomin. "I'll further add that should ASOC's end of the agreement be broken at any time prior to the next election, we will offer no resistance to nationalization."

"Put it in writing," said Cobart.

"Most assuredly," said Bomin, producing a number of documents from a small titanium-alloy briefcase. "As you can see," he said, spreading them out on a table before Cobart, "I brought with me a document for every agreement we might possibly reach. Naturally, I didn't expect you to accept halfway measures, but I was prepared just in case you were feeling philanthropic. Ah, here it is." He pulled one of the papers out, signed it, and then signed a copy. "If you'll just put your signature and the seal of your office on these, our business will be concluded."

"You gave in awfully easily," said Cobart, staring at the documents. "I never expected Jorg Bomin to surrender without a fight."

"The end result was inevitable," said Bomin. "With or without an agreement, ASOC wouldn't be able to get after you in a few days' time. At least this way I can see to it that you don't manage *all* the news."

Cobart looked at the document again. "Add a clause about keeping this a secret until either party breaks it, and I'll sign it."

"Are you planning on breaking it, Mr. Coordinator?" asked Bomin mildly.

"No," said Cobart. "But the day *you* do, I'm going to crucify you with this damned paper."

"And in the meantime," said Bomin, "you'd just as soon the people didn't know that we had agreed not to tell them

149

the truth about you. However, I have no objection to inserting a paragraph addressed to that point." He scribbled it in, initialed it on both the original and the copy, and handed them over to Cobart, who read them, signed them, and placed the official seal of his office upon them.

"I'd better not read about this, or hear about it, or see it, tomorrow morning," snapped Cobart, returning the copy to Bomin.

"Oh, you have my assurance that you won't," said Bomin, and left.

The next morning Bomin called another meeting of his board of directors, and brought in the heads of the various news media as well. As soon as all were assembled, he read them the agreement he and Cobart had signed.

"You've ruined us!" cried one of the directors.

"What the hell got into you?" demanded another.

"Quite the contrary, gentlemen," said Bomin gently. "Last night, when he affixed his signature to this agreement, Gile Cobart signed his political obituary, although neither he nor you have figured that out yet."

"You wouldn't want to explain yourself, would you?" asked his newstape head.

"Indeed I would," said Bomin. "That's the reason I've called this meeting. Now, to understand what has happened and what will happen, you must understand the agreement in its totality, both what it says and what it does not say. For example, we have agreed to give Cobart equal time or equal space in the media; in other words, every time we blast him, he gets a chance to hit back. We have further agreed never to blast him."

"Isn't that contradictory?" asked the newstape head.

"I hardly think so," said Bomin. "ASOC will never again attack Cobart or his Administration, nor will Cobart ever be able to demand time or space to defend himself."

"If that means we're going to spout the government line," said the head of the video division, "I'm tendering my resignation here and now."

"You feel I've sold ASOC out?" asked Bomin.

"I do."

"If that's what you think," said Bomin coldly, "then you're not bright enough to run your department and your resignation is accepted forthwith. Now, to continue: We will never again attack Cobart. Nor will we ever again praise him. In brief, from this moment forward, no section of ASOC will ever again mention his name. Whether his Administration rises in triumph or falls in ignominy, from this day until the next election, all news concerning Cobart will be noted, filed, and forgotten. I realize this will present some problems, such as the new farm bill passed for Aldebaran IX. However, the bill can and will be reported; credit for it will be omitted. No air time or tape time or newsprint will be given to Cobart or his government for any reason whatsoever. Is that understood?"

"He'll scream bloody murder," said the head of the video division."

"Young man," said Bomin gently, "you have already been dismissed from all duties. However, I'll assume that someone else in the room may be considering that very question, and will address myself to it. Cobart cannot possibly do us any harm by objecting to our policy. For one thing, he cannot reach the people except by personal appearance, and to reach enough of them that way would preclude his being able to function as Coordinator. He cannot show them the agreement for three reasons: first, because he has given his word, in writing, not to; second, because we won't give him access to any segment of the media; and third, because he doesn't dare let the people know the gist of our agreement. And if you want a fourth reason, we're on sound legal ground. Nothing in the agreement prevents us from this course of action, and as we are a nongovernmental monopoly, the government cannot legally object to our editorial discretion.

"I would personally suspect that Cobart will try to get news from neighboring systems piped in, but no matter where the news originates, even if it comes directly from the Council chambers on Deluros VIII, it must reach the people through our affiliated media. And this we will firmly refuse to allow. Are there any questions? No? Then the meeting is concluded. My office will issue a set of precise directives to be channeled throughout the organization by the end of the day. As for you," he added, pointing to the video head, "clear out of your office within a week, and pick up a year's severance pay." He said it so mildly that anyone who didn't know him would have sworn he was joking; but Jorg Bomin never joked about ASOC.

Within three days the Cobart Administration began to sense what was happening to it. Cobart himself decided to challenge ASOC by requesting an hour of video time for a speech of vital importance to the system. His request was neither accepted nor refused, but merely ignored. All reporters from all media were shortly withdrawn from their duties at his mansion, and the weekly news summary was edited to exclude any mention of Cobart.

For seventy-eight days Cobart fought futilely against the media boycott. Then, in desperation, he set up a governmental department to publish its own newstapes and newspapers. ASOC countered through its distributional channels. They couldn't legally forbid their outlets to handle the Administration tapes and paper; but they pointed out that their ships, which delivered literally thousands of other tapes and papers each day, were in a sad state of repair, and it was possible that some deliveries might be late. . . .

The retailers balanced the profits from selling two government publications against the loss of every other publication they handled, and reached the only financially sane decision. Cobart was denied outlets for his tapes and papers.

The Administration's next step was, through private channels, to take out advertisements in the media proclaiming support of the government. ASOC neither accepted nor refused the ads, but simply returned the payments with no explanation.

A minor attack was launched on Aldebaran X, ASOC's headquarters. ASOC appealed to the Oligarchy for assistance without ever naming the enemy, and Cobart withdrew his forces before the Navy arrived on the scene.

Finally Cobart tried to nationalize ASOC. Bomin immediately went to the Oligarchic Council, showed them the agreement, argued his case passionately and forcefully, and got the Council to rule that Cobart's action was illegal.

Soon numerous polls began appearing in the media, polls expressing voter choices for the next election. They were widely publicized, with one exception: Cobart was not listed as a candidate for reelection, and his name, where written in, invalidated the sample ballot.

Within a year the Administration was reeling; within two it was crumbling; and by election day it was totally dead. Cobart did indeed run for reelection, but even though his name appeared at the top of the ballot, as befitted the incumbent, he drew only four percent of the vote. His party, which had previously exercised a hairbreadth control of the system's legislature, retained less than a fifth of its seats. Only the briefest mention of Gile Cobart could be found in the history books, and he died a defeated, broken, and forgotten man at the age of sixty-three.

Of course the next Coordinator, who until three years before had been the head of ASOC's video division, signed no agreements, mended the system's political fences with the Oligarchy, had Jorg Bomin assassinated within three months, nationalized the media, and went on to enjoy a reign undreamed of by Gile Cobart even during the halcyon days of his Administration.

13: *The Artists*

. . . In a way, the artists can be considered the revolutionaries of the middle Oligarchic period. Literature had just begun to reflect the fact that Man was dominant in the galaxy, and the classics of the previous few centuries had shown him overcoming, in various ways, the many threats posed to his primacy. Now it was the artists who began to buck the government line by finding beauty in alien forms and outrage in alien living conditions, and by showing tolerance of alien ways. They were, in a very real sense, the conscience of Man—and a very lonely conscience at that, distrusted by their own kind and frequently ignored or misunderstood by the very beings they wished to aid.

Certainly the foremost writer of the period was Fillard Niis (5427–5510 G.E.), whose immortal cry of outraged conscience, *The Steel Boot,* sold more than six billion copies and was undoubtedly the most widely read book in human history up to that time . . .

—*Man: Twelve Millennia of Achievement*

. . . Of Niis himself, very little is known other than the fact that he was considered to be the greatest author of his time, both in that peculiarly human literary form known as fiction and in the more traditional fields of documentary writing and philosophical essay. Even today, copies of *The Steel Boot* still exist. What little we know of Niis and of the book's origins are contained in the transcript of a video interview made in 5502 G.E., some three decades after the book's first publication....

—*Origin and History of the Sentient Races,* Vol. 8

THORRIN: Good evening, ladies and gentlemen, and welcome to another edition of "Retrospect." I am your host, Lornath H. Thorrin, and my guest this week is Fillard Niis, the author who achieved literary immortality during his own lifetime with the publication of *The Steel Boot.* Mr. Niis, for those of you who have been living in some other universe for the past three decades, is the author of nine best-selling novels plus literally hundreds of essays. He ran for the legislature on Earth in 5466, was elected by a narrow margin, and then resigned after claiming that wide-scale corruption made it impossible for him to function efficiently in that capacity. He then moved to the Deluros system, where in 5472 he wrote a book that dwarfed all his other achievements: *The Steel Boot.* It sold more than a billion copies during its first four years of existence, and is fast approaching the six-billion mark, making it the best-selling book in the history of the galaxy. Looking back, what do you suppose accounted for the book's initial success?

NIIS: To be honest, Lornath, I wasn't exactly an unknown writer at the time, and as I recall the book was given a pretty large publicity budget, which certainly didn't hurt matters any. However, I think the prime reason was that the book touched the conscience of the human race, a conscience that had been dormant for too long a time. For the past few centuries Man had been concerned only with clawing his way to the top of the galactic heap, to assert his dominance over the other intelligent races. When *The Steel Boot* was published, it was time to look around and examine the carnage we'd left in our wake.

THORRIN: As everyone knows, the book concerns the despicable treatment that the various alien races suffered at our hands during our periods of galactic expansion. But not many people know exactly what it was that triggered the writing of the book. Would you care to tell us?

NIIS: Certainly. I had just put the finishing touches on *A Handful of Dust*—which, incidentally, was the last novel I ever wrote—and felt the need to get away from Deluros, to totally free my mind from my work. I decided to take a vacation to Pollux IV, which was being heralded as one of the better new resort colonies. Once there, I checked in at the fanciest hotel I could find and spent the next few days just soaking up sunlight and alcohol. One night, after I had been there a week or so, I decided to take a walk around the city. I was never much for conducted tours, so I just set off on my own. I never had much sense of direction, and I was soon totally lost. I wandered into the alien quarter of the city, and suddenly, within sight of the towering peak of my hotel, I found myself surrounded by almost unimaginable squalor and poverty. The living conditions were absolutely shocking. There were corpses littering the street, and garbage was piled up in front of all the dwellings. The water was so foul I could smell it from two hundred meters away. To my untrained eye, I felt that many of the Polluxans were in dire need of medical attention.

When I finally got back to the hotel I found our ambassador-in-residence and complained to her of the outrageous conditions I had seen. In fact, I literally begged her to send a medical team to the alien quarter; after all, the Polluxans were oxygen-breathing humanoids, and I felt that even nonspecialized human medics might be able to alleviate their suffering to some degree. The ambassador replied that the Polluxans were happy the way they were and that it wasn't our business to interfere with them. Her comments were that the Polluxans couldn't ingest pure water, but instead required the numerous minerals that were found in the foul-smelling stuff that came from their lakes. She also stated that, far from neglecting their dead, they were simply unemotional and irreligious, and that the bodies would be carted off and incinerated by the next morning. And she also opined that, since the alien quarter was centuries old, they obviously felt no inclination to repair it or institute a program of sanitation and hygiene—and since Man was a virtual newcomer to the planet, we had no right to impose our values on the native inhabitants.

Her answers made a great deal of sense, but I decided to look into the problem a little further anyway. I discovered that she was correct about the corpses, but that everything else was either a deliberate lie or a gross misinterpretation of the situation. For example, the Polluxans do indeed require certain minerals that are not to be found in pure H_2O—but the water they were drinking contained not only the requisite minerals but massive amounts of industrial waste, enough to increase their death rate by three hundred percent. As for their sanitary conditions, they had been placed in what amounted to a reservation, and were not allowed to leave it, even to dump their waste and garbage on an empty plain beyond the city. The only time it got removed was when the stench became so great that it reached the resort area and annoyed the guests. It was then that *The Steel Boot* began to take shape in my mind.

I spent the next year touring a number of planets we had recently assimilated into the Oligarchy, and found conditions deplorable on a great majority of them. Frequently we didn't even know we had harmed the aliens in any way, but that didn't alter the facts. We used populated alien worlds to dump deadly radioactive wastes, to test new weapons of war, to experiment with various ecological systems and mutations. We even had some sentient chlorine and methane breathers in our multi-environmental zoos. Everywhere I looked, Man had ground the dignity and self-respect of intelligent alien races into the dirt. Usually there was no malice intended, but occasionally such actions were a result of a carefully thought-out and programmed policy. For example, during the years 5300 through 5500 we signed 10,478 treaties with alien races. Do you know how many we broke?

THORRIN: No.

NIIS: All but sixty!

THORRIN: As the author of the best-selling book of

157

all time, what effect did the success of the book have on you personally?

NIIS: First of all, it made me and the next few generations of my family incredibly wealthy. And, to be honest, I'd have to say that it's secured a place in literary history for me. But it also had some deleterious effects as well. For one thing, no book, no matter how potent or timely, sells as well as *The Steel Boot* without an intense publicity campaign. Spending promotional money was just a small part of the procedure. For almost three years after its publication I was forced by contract to tour the worlds of the Oligarchy, making personal appearances, being interviewed on video shows, pushing both the book and the ideas behind the book to as many people as I could reach. It was financially successful, but physically and artistically debilitating. I wanted to get back to work, to keep hammering at my theme, but I simply couldn't find the time.

THORRIN: But wasn't there a rash of similar books published shortly after the success of *The Steel Boot* became manifest?

NIIS: There were, but they never had much effect, and in fact they were so one-sided and passionate in their approach that they almost turned the whole subject of mistreatment of aliens into the private property of an elite cult. Perhaps I'm being less than generous, but I honestly feel that these books and authors lessened the potency of the arguments and the poignancy of the aliens' plight.

THORRIN: In other words, none of them could push a noun up against a verb as beautifully or as effectively as you could. And, lacking your literary skill, they failed where you succeeded. We won't be letting any secrets out of the bag by noting that no other book on the subject sold more than nine million copies.

NIIS: Still, it wasn't from a lack of sincerity. You might view it as a legal case: even the most sincere barrister will hurt his client's cause if he argues with insufficient skill. Nonetheless, they reached a number of readers that probably hadn't seen or bought *The Steel*

Boot, so I've no objections to their jumping on the band-wagon, as it were.

THORRIN: Now, in retrospect, have you noticed any change in our policy toward the other races since the publication of your book?

NIIS: Not a hell of a lot, to be blunt about it.

THORRIN: Why do you suppose that is?

NIIS: I don't know. Maybe the wrong people read my book. When we began to realize just how well it was selling, I really had hopes. I was naturally pleased from a professional point of view, but I had also entertained the thought that perhaps I had struck a responsive chord among the readership, had confronted them with the truth of our treatment of nonhuman beings and elicited from them the desire to make some amends. As it turned out, that wasn't the case.

THORRIN: But what about those billions of readers? Are you saying that you don't feel the book had any effect on them at all?

NIIS: For all practical purposes, that is precisely what I am saying. I think the huge majority of them read the book, felt a very justifiable racial guilt, and having thus undergone a painless mini-catharsis, ambled off to bed and forgot the whole thing.

THORRIN: Obviously this feeling is nothing new. What was your reaction when you first decided that the book, though admittedly a best-seller, was not the dawn of a new era of racial harmony?

NIIS: There was no single day that I looked around me and said: Hey, what's the matter with everybody? The Oligarchy didn't act, but hell, since when do govern-ments act because of books? I founded a group to aid the aliens, and I know that literally hundreds of similar groups were initiated during the first rush of *The Steel Boot*'s popularity. Some of them raised quite a lot of money, and began work on some pretty comprehensive plans. The depressing thing was that seven years later, my own group was the only one still in existence, and our income, which was derived solely from contributions, had dropped from forty million credits the first year to a mere sixty thousand credits the seventh. It was as if everybody had donated just enough time or money to clear his conscience and pay his dues, so to speak, and then, having done so, immediately forgot about the problem. The pity of it is that the problem is still with us, and it's not getting any better.

THORRIN: What of the aliens themselves? I hate to sound melodramatic, but are there any insurrections or revolutions being plotted these days?

NIIS: Against the Oligarchy? You must be kidding! How do you fight an attitude that spans a million worlds, or a Navy that could demolish half the galaxy in two years' time? How do you fight an economic system that, through no fault or desire of your own, is all that stands between you and even greater squalor than already exists?

THORRIN: Then what's to become of them?

NIIS: I don't know. I hope this creeping paternalism will begin creeping back the way it came, though I doubt that it will. In the meantime, they'll simply have to put up with things as they are, and as they threaten to become.

THORRIN: I'm sorry, but I just can't imagine their not getting up on their haunches one of these days and screaming "Death to the tyrants!" or some such thing. Didn't *they* read your book too?

NIIS: Some of them did. Most couldn't understand it.

THORRIN: Surely your publisher could have translated it—

NIIS: I didn't say they couldn't read it; I said they couldn't understand it. You have to remember: They're aliens, with all that the word implies. Their hopes, dreams, goals, life-styles, their very thought processes are *alien* to our understanding. I had hoped my book would make this clear: that in some cases we had gone out of our way to subjugate them, but in most instances they thought and reacted on such different levels that there was never any conflict. We just moved in, did as we wanted, and they simply permitted—or, as was more often the case, ignored—us.

THORRIN: It must be very frustrating to be the messiah of a people who want no salvation.

NIIS: I've never set myself up as a messiah. As for the alien races' wanting salvation, some of them—such as the Canphorites—very actively desire it; and who is to say that the others don't? *The Steel Boot* was about Man's inhumanity to his fellow beings, not their reaction to it. In other words, I'm saying that we can be moral or immoral without reference to an alien's acceptance or rejection of his condition, merely because of our actions themselves.

THORRIN: And yet, despite the book's fabulous success, your pleas have been rejected by one side and ignored by the other.

NIIS: True. My only hope, the only hope Men have ever had, from the first cavemen who couldn't handle fire to the last author who can't mobilize moral outrage, is for the next generation. Maybe the great awakening will come tomorrow.

THORRIN: I'm sure we'd all like to think so.

NIIS: So would I. But . . .

THORRIN: Yes?

NIIS: I won't say that tomorrow never comes, but I suspect that it's going to arrive too late to do anyone much good.

14: The Biochemists

... Sometime around 5600 G.E. the life sciences, and especially biochemistry, seem to have taken a wrong turning, this in spite of the fabulous Project that had captured the imagination of men for centuries. Gains were made in numerous related fields, but ...

—*Man: Twelve Millennia of Achievement*

... It was in the field of biochemistry and its sister sciences that Man came close to achieving a masterwork, and sharing his results with the other races of the galaxy. Millennia-old problems in the artificial production of cellular life were solved with sober single-mindedness, and parthenogenesis allowed literally billions of females of all species to have the offspring that a cruel Nature forbade them to bear. Indeed, if Man was an inspiration anywhere during the years of the Oligarchy, it was in the biochemical sciences ....

—*Origin and History of the Sentient Races,* Vol. 8

It sure didn't look like a superman.

"Failure Number 1,098," said Rojers, turning away from the incubator with a grunt of disgust.

"Shall we destroy it, sir?" asked one of the lab assistants.

"Might as well," said Rojers. "A maximum intelligence capacity of a ten-year-old, and a body that'll never get out of a wheelchair. Yes, give it six cc's of the lethal solution, injected directly into the heart . . . wherever *that* may be."

Rojers walked desolately out of the incubation room, down the long, well-lit corridor, past his own office, and stopped before Herban's door. He looked briefly at the "Chief of Biochemistry" sign painted on the door in neat gold lettering, grunted again, and walked in. Herban, a small man with medium brown skin, short black hair—what there was left of it—and deep furrows on his forehead, was waiting for him, his feet up on his desk, his hands behind his head.

"Well?" said Herban.

"Can't you tell by looking at me?" asked Rojers wryly.

"So you go back to the drawing board," said Herban. "It's not the end of the universe."

"It's damned near the end of mine," replied Rojers disgustedly. "Today marks my tenth anniversary here, you know." Herban nodded. "That means I've averaged 109.8 failures for each and every damned year!"

"Feeling sorry for yourself?" chuckled Herban.

"I don't see anything particularly funny about it!" snapped Rojers.

"No, I don't suppose you would. Yet."

"What do you mean, yet?" said Rojers. "I've had it. I'm through. Consider my notice given."

"Given, but not accepted," said Herban. "Sit down and have a cigar."

"Don't you understand?" said Rojers irritably. "I'm quitting."

"Then consider the cigar a going-away present," said Herban. "Actually, I'm surprised it took you this long. The first time I decided to quit, I'd done only about three hundred experiments. It's all a matter of self-confidence, I suppose. I knew how good I was, and I figured if I couldn't pull the trick off in three hundred tries, I'd never manage it. It took another thirty years to realize that I'd had three hundred successes. You, if my mathematics don't betray me, have had just two shy of eleven hundred successes, give or take a few.

Your jaw's hanging open, boy. Why not fill it with a cigar and we'll have a little talk."

Rojers sat down heavily, staring at his mentor. Without thinking, he bit off the tip of his cigar and lit it up.

"Ah, but I do like a good smoke," said Herban, taking a deep puff and uttering a sigh that was as close to ecstasy as he ever got. "I do indeed. You destroyed the body, I presume?"

Rojers nodded.

Herban shrugged. "Just as well, I suppose. No sense letting it grow up or we'd all be out of work around here."

"I don't understand," said Rojers slowly. "I mean, the thing was a freak, just like all the rest. Minimal intelligence, low reaction to stimuli, legs quite stunted. What exactly are you trying to tell me?"

"The truth. With a capital *T*, not the small t they use around here. It took me more than half a lifetime to stumble upon it, probably because it's so bloody simple. And, of course, all of my predecessors figured it out as well, and kept their mouths shut for the same reason I do. But you're the brightest lad around here, even though you're only in your thirties, and since I plan on retiring in the next few years and blowing my pension on fat cigars and fatter women, it seems only logical that you'll be taking my place—if you decide to withdraw your resignation, that is. Which is why we're having this little talk. No reason to let you stumble around in the dark for years the way I did."

"I assume," said Rojers coldly, "that there is some part of the Project that I fail to understand."

"*Some part!*" Herban laughed. "Why, boy, you don't understand the whole damned thing! Now, don't give me a sour expression like that. You're in good company. Nobody else in the galaxy does either, except me. And even though I'm a goddamn genius, I took almost thirty years to figure it out myself. I often marvel that it didn't dawn on me after the third or fourth experiment." He took a deep drag on his cigar, opened his mouth slightly, and allowed the smoke to trickle out at its own speed. "But hell, I was young and idealistic and all that sort of nonsense. I suppose I couldn't be blamed for believing in the Project any more than you can."

"Are you trying to tell me that the Project is a fraud?" demanded Rojers, a sense of moral outrage beginning to creep across his mind.

"Well, yes and no," said Herban. "Yes and no."

164

"Just what is that supposed to mean?"

"Exactly what I said," said Herban. "Let's see if we can't get you to use a little of that brain of yours. After all, if you're going to become the next Chief Biochemist of the Oligarchy and points north, nobody should have to spoon-feed conclusions to you. Tell me what *you* think the Project is all about."

"Every schoolboy knows what it's all about," said Rojers irritably. "What I'm trying to figure out is what you're driving at."

"Bear with me for a little while." The older man grinned, relighting the cigar. "And tell me about the Project."

"I feel like an idiot," said Rojers. "Okay. The Project is attempting to hasten the course of evolution by artificially developing *Homo superior*."

"A fair enough description. And, in that, the Project is absolutely legitimate. Well, 'legitimate' is a misleading word; let me say, rather, that in that respect the Project is sincere. Its motives are of the purest nature, and its virtue—if not its efficacy—is beyond question."

"Then I still don't understand what you mean."

"Well, let's begin at the beginning, shall we, boy?" said Herban. "Do you know when the Project began?"

"Not exactly. About four hundred years ago," said Rojers.

"Try four *thousand*." Herban grinned. "You'll be much closer to the truth. It began, secretly to be sure, in the waning days of the Republic. Originally, only four men worked on it, and the number always remained under a dozen until about four centuries ago—388 years, to be exact—when the Oligarchy decided to make it public because of political expediency."

"Four thousand?" mused Rojers. "But why was it kept secret?"

"For reasons of utmost necessity," said Herban. "You see, originally the idea was to create a true race of *Homo superior*, a race that would supersede Man. Well, not really supersede him, since no one was all that anxious to bring about our own extinction; but to, shall we say, represent Man among the myriad worlds, to take and conquer huge new domains for us, and then to move on while we took over the fruits of their labor. Nifty idea, that. They must have dreamed of making a race of men with the intellect of a Robelian, the physique of a Torqual, the ESPer abilities of a Domarian, and, with all that, total loyalty to humanity." He shrugged. "Well, the science was young then, so I suppose they can be excused for their dreams. And the need for secrecy was twofold: to avoid alarming good old *Homo sap*, and to avoid giving advance warning to the various other races that we were planning to spring our little surprise on. And it stood to reason, naturally, that with limited funds and a miniscule number of trained biochemists, they made so little progress for thirty-six hundred years as to make no difference at all.

"Then came the Setts. Everybody knows about them now, but originally it was all hush-hush. After all, they were the first race ever to defeat us in anything resembling a major battle. It happened something like five centuries ago, and, since it occurred so far out on the Rim, the Oligarchy managed to cover it up for more than a century without much difficulty. Then the news finally got back to Deluros VIII, Sirius V, and some of the other major worlds, and all hell broke loose. The people demanded that the Oligarchy do something. For a decade or so the whole damned government racked its collective brain to come up with an answer before they were overthrown, and then some pigeonholer remembered the Project. Overnight, we were given a staff of two hundred men, which gradually increased to three thousand, and our budget was absolutely astronomical. The science of biochemistry learned more in the next ten years than it had in the past seventy centuries, and the Oligarchy had sold the public on a pipedream: we were going to create a race of supermen that would blast the Setts to kingdom come. Worked out beautifully all the way around. Of course, we found out a little while later that the Setts were terribly vulnerable to measles, and they surrendered without any trouble once we sprayed their home world with about a million tons of the virus. But the people had bought the dream of a super race, and the government found it politically expedient to keep up work on the Project."

"Is that what you meant when you implied it was all a fraud?" asked Rogers hotly. "That the Oligarchy really doesn't want to come up with *Homo superior?*"

"Not at all," said Herban. "They probably *don't* want any supermen knocking about—and, if they thought about it, neither would the populace at large. But no one has tried to hinder us in any way. If God Himself popped out of one of our incubators, there's no way anyone could make us put Him back. Nor," he added with a chuckle, "could they make

166

Him go back if He decided He didn't want to. But that's not the case. God isn't about to crop up around here. At least not as a direct result of our experiments."

"You keep saying that," said Rojers, feeling more lost than ever. "Why?"

"It should be obvious," said Herban. He pressed a series of buttons on his desk computer, waited for a moment, then glanced at the readout. "As of this minute, we have made 1,-036,753 experiments involving human genes. We have tried to force evolutionary patterns on DNA molecules, we have tried to create out-and-out mutations, we have bombarded genes and chromosomes with preset patterns and at random. We have tried well over three thousand approaches, and hundreds of thousands of variations on these approaches. In the process, we've done a hell of a lot for the science of parthenogenesis, but we haven't come up with our supermen yet. Did it ever occur to you to ask why?"

"No more than once an hour or so."

"Well, the problem is too simple for a bright young feller like yourself to solve. Now, if you asked some savage descendant of one of the Delphini II colonists, he'd probably tell you right away."

"Since I don't know any aborigines on a first-name basis," said Rojers, "I'll have to put the question to you. With no comparison intended."

"No offense taken." Herban smiled. "The solution to the problem is simply one of definition, which is doubtless caused by our somewhat more sophisticated background."

"I don't follow you, sir," said Rojers.

"Let's put it this way. Our idea of a racial superman would differ considerably from an aborigine's, wouldn't it? I mean, his ideal would be a man who could kill a large herbivore with his bare hands, survive under extremes of temperature, have the sexual potency to father a whole world, and so forth. Agreed?"

"I suppose so."

"Our idea, however, reflects the needs we seem to feel. What qualities, in your opinion, might a superman reasonably be expected to possess?"

"First of all, an intellectual capacity far beyond our own. And," Rojers went on, scratching his head thoughtfully, "a number of ESP qualities: telepathy, telekinesis, and the like. And, as his brain power increased, his physical performance

167

would diminish proportionately, since he'd have less need of his body. But hell, that's basic. We all know that."

"Not quite all of us," said Herban with a small smile. "Our aborigine would disagree . . . always assuming he had the intellect to follow your argument. Otherwise, he'd probably interrupt you in midsentence and throw you into a handy cooking pot. And the really interesting part of it is that for all his lack of intelligence and sophistication, he'd be right and you'd be wrong."

"You don't sound like you're kidding," said Rojers dubiously, "and yet it has to be a joke."

"Oh, it's a joke, all right," said Herban. "But it's on us. You see, Man has evolved mentally as far as he's ever going to. From a standpoint of intellect, *Homo sapiens* and *Homo superior* are one and the same. I'll qualify that in a moment, but it's essentially correct as it stands."

Rojers was staring in disbelief, making no move to interrupt with a protest, so Herban took another long puff on his cigar and continued. "What, my bright young man, is the most basic cause of natural evolution?"

"Environmental need," said Rogers mechanically.

"Correct. Which is the precise reason why we're not about to create a mental superman. Man has never used much more than thirty percent of his potential intellect; as long as the remaining seventy percent is there, waiting to be tapped, there is absolutely no cause for any evolutionary process which would increase our basic intelligence. Ditto for telepathy. Man originally had no need for it, because he had the power of speech. Then, as he became separated from his companions by distances too great for speech to carry, he made use of radio waves, video, radar, sonar, and a dozen other media for carrying his words and images. Why, then, is there any need for telepathy? There isn't.

"Telekinesis? Ridiculous. We have machines that can literally destroy stars, that can move planets out of their orbits. What possible need can we have for the development of telekinesis?

"Take every single trait of our hypothetical superman, and you'll find that there is absolutely no environmetal need for it. Now, as I said before, I'll qualify the statement to this extent: Telepathy and even mild telekinesis can be induced under laboratory conditions, at least on occasion. But to do so we must so totally change the gene pattern and environment of the fetus and child that it is literally cut off from the world: no sensual receptors of any kind. In such cases, the brain will usually come out totally dulled or quite mad. On occasion, the insane brain will draw on some of its reserve potential and develop telepathic traits, but of course the mind is so irrational that any meaningful contact with it or training of it is quite impossible.

"On the other hand, it's not at all difficult to develop our aborigine's superman, because we *can* control the physical environment and tamper with the DNA molecules. We turn them out every day in the incubators. We can create hairy supermen, giant supermen, three-eyed supermen, aquatic supermen, and if we worked on it, I've no doubt that we could even create methane-breathing supermen. In fact, we can create damned near every type of superman except supremely intelligent ones."

"Then it's a dead end?" asked Rojers.

"Not at all. You're forgetting our untapped seventy percent. Even before space travel in the ancient past, there were numerous documented laboratory experiments dealing with telepathy, prescience, and many other ESPer abilities and talents. Every human body undoubtedly has the potential to perform just about every feat we ask of our hypothetical and unattainable superman, but we've no way to tap that potential. It's the same problem: You, if the need arose, would have the potential to send out a telepathic cry for help, and possibly even teleport yourself out of danger. However, you'll never do it if you can scream and run, or press an alarm button and hop into a spaceship. And even if no means of aid were available to you, you simply have a storehouse of special effects; what you lack—what we all lack—is any rational means of getting the key into the storehouse door. Poor *Homo superior!*"

"Then why the facade of trying to develop supermen?" asked Rojers.

"To hide our greater purpose, of course," said Herban.

"Our greater purpose?" repeated Rojers. "You make it sound positively sinister."

"It all depends on your point of view," said Herban. "*I* think of it as extremely beneficial. But come along, and you can make up your own mind."

With that, the little man put out his cigar, swung his feet off his desk, arose, and gestured Rojers to follow him out the door. They proceeded farther down the corridor to a horizontally moving elevator, and took it about halfway around the massive biochemical and genetics complex. From there they transferred to a vertical elevator and plunged down at a rapid speed.

Rojers had no idea how fast they were going, but estimated that they were at least seven hundred feet below ground level before the elevator showed any sign of slowing up. At least, he decided, whatever was going on here wasn't too well hidden. But then, he continued, why should it be? After all, the Oligarchy was paying for it, and the politics of the Project demanded that everything be aboveboard and open. In fact, the Project had been created and maintained solely because of the demands of the populace.

The doors opened, and Herban led Rojers past two security checks, and into still another horizontally moving enclosure. There were three more changes of direction, all accompanied by increasingly rigid security inspections, until at last they arrived before a massive lead portal, which slowly slid back before them when Herban inserted his identification card into a small, practically invisible wall slot.

"This is it," grunted the Chief of Biochemistry as he walked through the doorway.

Rojers looked around and was unimpressed. It didn't seem all that different from the portion of the complex he was familiar with: corridors going every which way, numerous doors with signs indicating the departments and subdepartments contained within, and what seemed to be a fair-sized auditorium at the far end of the largest corridor. An occasional technician in a lab smock walked out of one door into another, and once Rojers thought he saw a woman scurrying down a corridor in a lead body suit. By and large, however, there didn't seem to be any of the frantic hustle and bustle and frenzied activity that marked the huge incubator room and its surroundings.

Still, there were a couple of oddities. Like the girl in the lead suit, and the fact that two of the doors he passed as he followed Herban seemed to be made of lead, while the others covered a whole range of plastics.

They came to a corridor marked MAXIMUM SECURITY and turned down it. Herban nodded to a couple of technicians who were speaking in low tones outside one of the doors, then stopped at a large, unmarked panel. Another insertion of his identification card was followed by another sliding of the barrier, and the two men walked into what gave every indication of being an extremely sophisticated laboratory, though it

170

was filled with equipment that was, for the most part, totally unfamiliar to Rojers. There were far fewer pieces of apparatus for working on genetic structures, but considerably more devices which seemed, on the surface at least, to bear some resemblance to encephalographic and cardiographic machines. Unlike the sterile laboratory atmosphere Rojers had become used to working in during the greater portion of his adult life, this place seemed built for comfort as much as efficiency. All around him were padded chairs, ashtrays (though that could simply be an offshoot of Herban's assumption that everyone—but *everyone*—should smoke cigars), food-dispensing machines, books and tapes of popular fiction, and the facilities for bathing the room in music, light images, or both.

"Have you any idea where you are?" asked Herban pleasantly, seating himself by an ashtray.

"No," said Rojers. "Though I must admit I've often thought your bedroom would bear a resemblance to this place."

Herban chuckled and lit up another cigar. "Afraid not. My bedroom is usually filled to the brim with the fattest, nakedest women money can buy. No, boy, you're in one of our basic testing rooms."

"Who do you test here," asked Rojers, "and for what?"

"We test people," said Herban. "And we test them to see if they're your hypothetical supermen."

"Now I'm thoroughly confused," said Rojers. "I thought you said we couldn't create supermen, and you sounded damned convincing. Are you telling me now that you were lying?"

"Not at all."

"Then how do these so-called supermen come to be? What lab produces them?"

"No lab does. When I said Man will not evolve into a mental superman, I wasn't lying to you. I did not, however, say that a mental superman cannot exist."

"I feel as if I were back in school," said Rojers in exasperation. "Every time I think I know what you're talking about, you stick another stone wall in front of me."

"Well, I'll admit you've had to discard a lot of wrong assumptions," said Herban, "but everything I've told you today is both true and noncontradictory. For example, I said that we cannot evolve into mental supermen. That's true. Now

171

I'm telling you that there are indeed mental supermen, and that we work with them down here. That's also true."

"If we didn't create them, how did they get here?" persisted Rojers.

"Pretty much the same way you and I got here: natural selection, natural conception, and very likely natural childbirth as well." Rojers just stared at him. "You see," continued Herban, "these supermen aren't mutations—or at least, not in the sense that *you've* been working on mutations. I'll make it simple for you. Possibly a million human mutations are conceived every day. Probably half of them are reabsorbed within hours. Of the others, most are such minor mutations as to go virtually unnoticed: a child born with a yellow spot in a head of otherwise red hair, or maybe with a weird-looking birthmark. Some get minor attention, like a baby with six fingers, or with a thin layer of flesh over its anal outlet, or with the potential for only twenty-six teeth at adulthood. Usually they're so minor we don't even notice them. And, to be sure, very few mutations breed on. We still have the appendix, we still have tonsils, we still have hair on our bodies. Despite the fact that there have been some families where no mother has nursed her baby in eighty or ninety generations, the female children still develop breasts, sometimes rather large and lovely ones. No, as I said, mutations rarely breed on, and no mutation has yet produced a superman with any more mental capacity than you or I possess.

"However," he said, stabbing the air with his cigar, "no mutation is *needed* to produce a mental superman. As I mentioned upstairs, all that's required is for a man or a woman to use one hundred percent—or even fifty percent—of the potential he or she is born with."

"And you've found such people and test them down here?" asked Rojers.

"We've been finding such people for four millennia or more," said Herban. "And yes, we test them here."

"And what talents have you found?"

"Oh, a little bit of everything. Except for prescience. Usually the hunchers, as we call them, can sense impending events, but never the details. Most often it's simply a feeling of almost unbearable expectation, and rarely does it apply or relate to anyone but themselves. But we've gotten telepaths who can send, receive, or both. We've gotten levitators. We've found teleporters, though there have been only three of them, and two of the three had to be threatened irrevers-

172

ibly with death before they could find the wherewithal to teleport themselves. We've found far more people who are adepts
in telekinesis. And, of course, we've gotten some intelligences
that have gone right off the scale, brainpower so high that
we've still no real way of measuring it."

"Fantastic!" said Rojers. "And wonderful!"

"Fantastic, at any rate," said Herban dryly. "Still, most of
them go home intact."

"What do you mean, go home intact?" demanded Rojers.

"Just what I said. Why do you think we're doing all this
testing?"

"I assume for the same reasons we've been trying to force
evolution in the incubator rooms: to create a superman."

"But *these* supermen have already been created," pointed
out Herban.

"Then I would imagine you'd want to train them to use
their talents to the best of their abilities, for the good of the
Oligarchy."

"What an absolutely childish answer!" Herban laughed. "If
enough of them used their abilities to their maximum potential, the Oligarchy—and Man—would be finished within fifty
years or so. No, my idealistic boy, we definitely do *not* help
them become supermen and then turn them loose on society."

"You mean you *kill* them all?" demanded Rojers.

"Don't look so damned horrified," said Herban. "Let's not
forget that you have killed just about every single life you've
created."

"But those were just babies," protested Rojers. "And more
than half of them were still in the fetal state."

"It comes to the same thing," said Herban. "However, if
it'll put your mind at ease, we don't bring them down here
for the express purpose of killing them. We have a galaxy-
wide structure set up to spot every human with what you
might call a wild talent. And considering how many billions
of humans there are, we don't miss very many. Anyway, once
they're found—and adolescence is usually the earliest that
such traits can be determined by outside observers—they're
either brought here or to one of seven similar labs scattered
throughout the galaxy.

"Once here, they're tested thoroughly. Before we're done,
we know the absolute limits of their abilities; quite often, we
find talents even they didn't know they possessed. We also
run a comprehensive analysis of their genetic structure, DNA
code, sperm, ovum, everything that could possibly influence

their offspring, though I must admit we've found nothing unusual as yet. That done, we are free to reach one of three decisions. If there is any chance that the talent will breed on—and since we can't determine it genetically, we simply assume it is possible if anyone in the past five generations has displayed any odd talent—they are sterilized. Without their knowing it, of course. And if it seems pretty certain that the talent will not breed on, we'll usually let them return to society, especially if it isn't too spectacular a talent, such as mild telepathy. If it's something really interesting, something that might lead people to demand that we find a way to unleash it, such as levitation, we usually ship the subject off to a frontier world."

"That's two decisions," said Rojers. "You mentioned three."

"The third should be obvious."

"Death?"

"Quickly and painlessly, if the talent warrants it," said Herban. "And, in answer to your next question, it warrants it if it can ever, in any way, prove inimical to Man. For example, if a man's intelligence is so great that no device in our technologically oriented culture can measure it, he's too dangerous to live. Admittedly, that intelligence could conceivably make meaningful communicative contact with some of the races we just can't seem to get through to, or possibly cure every disease known to us . . . but it could also mount a navy and a political following that would overthrow the existing order of things. And it's not just intelligence. A man who possesses the power of telekinesis to the ultimate degree can manipulate elements within the core of a star and cause it to go nova. This could be a boon if we get into another war with the Setts; but what if he decides that the government of his own system is totally corrupt? And the same goes for other talents. A legitimate case of prescience—and we haven't come across one yet—would destroy the economic structure of any world that deals heavily in financial speculation. Teleportation? More than half our economy is bound up in interplanetary and interstellar transportation. The ability to master involuntary hypnosis? It would lead to absolute control of a system, possibly of the entire galaxy.

"No, boy, these talents can't be allowed to survive. We don't destroy every highly intelligent man, or every man capable of telekinesis, or every telepath. Only those that can be considered a clear danger. And notice that I didn't say a clear and present danger; clear and future dangers are no damned better. And if we can discover the outer limits of a dangerous man's abilities before he does, it's a lot harder for him to erect defenses, mental or otherwise, against us."

"About how many people do you destroy?" asked Rojers.

"We bring in about a million a year to each lab center," said Herban. "There are far more, but most of them are eliminated from further consideration at lower levels. We just get the stinkers. Of that million, we'll return about eight hundred thousand intact, and another hundred and eighty thousand sterilized. As for the other twenty thousand . . . well, we potentially save the galaxy a million times every half century or so."

"Save it from what?" said Rojers disgustedly.

"We don't save it *from* anything," said Herban very slowly, very seriously. "We save it *for* something: for Man. Don't look so morally outraged, boy. I know you're thinking about all the poor innocent supermen who have gone to their deaths down here, all those fine talents who could have made Paradise happen right here and now, and maybe they could have. But I think of three hundred billion Men who aren't about to give up their birthright to anyone, including their progeny."

"And what about the incubators?" demanded Rojers. "What about all those tiny lives that we create and snuff out every day?"

"They serve their purpose," answered Herban. "And their purpose is only partially to train you fellers and further develop the subscience of parthenogenesis."

"Oh?" Rojers was still suspicious.

"Absolutely. The talents we deal with down here are very rare sports, even those that might possibly reproduce their traits. But if you ever find a genetic method of unlocking that seventy percent, the human race will happily advance as a whole. It's just that no member of it is going to let his neighbor move up ahead of him."

"But we haven't found a way to do that in four thousand years!"

"And you may not for another four thousand," agreed Herban. "But it's worth trying. And, in the meantime, Man isn't doing all that badly with his cunning, his sticks, and his stones, is he?" He arose abruptly. "I'll leave you here to think about what I've said; I'll be back in a few hours."

Herban stopped at the doorway and turned to Rojers. "You now have the power to expose a secret that's been kept

175

for quite a few centuries. So consider all aspects of it very carefully." He left, and the panel slid shut behind him.

Rojers sat and thought. He considered the revelations of the day logically, philosophically, practically, idealistically, morally, pragmatically. Having done so, he frowned and thought some more.

When Herban returned for him, he rose silently and followed the Chief of Biochemistry back up to his own level. As they were approaching the incubator room, a brash young man representing the newstapes of a distant system walked up and asked for an interview.

"I'm a little busy now," said Herban, "but I'm sure Dr. Rojers would be happy to spend a little time talking to you."

Rojers nodded his acquiescence.

"Fine," said the reporter. "Can you fill me in on the whole operation right from the start?"

"Certainly," said Rojers quietly, walking toward the incubators. "Although there's really not much to tell. The Project was set up nearly four hundred years ago to develop a race of supermen, mental giants who could take some high ground that's beyond our reach just now. We haven't come up with our ideal yet, but we're still working on it, to be sure. In fact, you can tell your readers that we may be on the verge of a major breakthrough. I wouldn't be at all surprised if we synthesized a telepathic allele on a human chromosome by the end of this century . . ."

Herban remained where he was until they were out of earshot. Then, with a sigh, he lighted a cigar and returned to his subsurface office. There was a lot of work yet to do before he could go home for the night to his fat naked women.

176

15: *The Warlords*

. . . Thus, as the Oligarchy paused to consolidate, scores of warlords sprang up on the outskirts of the empire. All but one were either ignored or summarily dealt with. . . .

—*Man: Twelve Millennia of Achievement*

. . . About Grath (?—5912 G.E.) himself, very little is known, except that, though woefully under-manned and outnumbered, he stood up to the imperialistic empire of his race and came within a hairbreadth of triumph. He was unquestionably possessed of the most brilliant military mind of the Oligarchic era—and perhaps of *any* era—and most of Grath's historic battles are standard textbook reading to this very day. . . .

—*Origin and History of the Sentient Races*, Vol. 8

By all rights, it should have been as close to utopia as made no difference. The Oligarchy had divided, conquered, and consolidated, and for the first time in his galactic existence Man had run out of enemies.

Alien enemies, that is.

But two million worlds constituted a lot of territory to belong to one political entity, and so Man fell to fighting against himself once again. Literally hundreds of warlords began springing up around the periphery of the empire; most were beaten down almost immediately, but a handful—such as Grath—began piling up a number of minor triumphs.

He stood now, hands on hips, looking up at the heavens from the surface of an uncharted world half a galaxy away from Deluros VIII. The lights of the stars ran together, becoming a vast white blur that seemed to stretch outward to infinity. But that was a visual illusion, nothing more. Grath knew exactly where Deluros was, knew every possible means of approach, knew the long and bloody path he must hew to be able to stand thus on any world from which Deluros was distinguishable from the massive white curtain that he planned someday to rule. First there would be Altair, then the Spica mining worlds to keep up his flow of supplies. These conquests would be followed up by a quick feint toward Earth. The birthplace of the race served no useful military purpose, but it was cherished with an almost religious intensity by the hundreds of billions who had deserted it for more promising worlds. The Navy would respond to his move, and then his main forces would wipe out Sirius V in half a day's time. Next it would be on to Binder, Canphor, Lodin, and finally Deluros itself. Caliban alone would be left unscathed, for Caliban alone was too valuable to destroy.

It would be accomplished neither quickly nor easily. Deluros was not at the geographic center of the galaxy, but it was the very epicenter of the Oligarchy. No approach could be made without passing at least a quarter of a million worlds of the empire, each under the protection of the Oligarchy's vast naval fleet. And, too, there were the other warlords, who in the beginning would probably cause him even more trouble than the Navy. Once, years ago, he had arranged a meeting between them in the hope of presenting a united military front to the Oligarchy, but nothing had come of it. Their vision was too small, too short-sighted. They merely wanted a piece of the action; he wanted it all.

He had started out with nothing but forty-three followers and one ship. Two years of piracy had increased his personal navy to seventeen ships and more than six thousand men. Piracy was lucrative, and he could easily have continued such an existence indefinitely, but his dreams were grander than the accumulation of mere wealth; and to his gnawing hunger for power he added a shrewd military mind and a forcefulness of character that commanded instant, unquestioning obedience.

It was after his first successful clash with the Navy that he began to think in terms of conquest rather than mere looting. True, the odds had all favored his side, but that was inconsequential; it was the first time the Navy had lost even a minor skirmish in more than three centuries, and it shattered the myth of invincibility that had grown up about the forces of the Oligarchy.

He next staked out a small area well out on the galactic Rim. Its boundaries encompassed 376 stars which included some 550 planets, about 35 of them inhabited. He allowed himself half a year to become the total master of the area, and beat his self-imposed deadline with more than a month to spare.

From there his empire expanded, always on the Rim, always far from the supply bases of the Oligarchic Navy. He avoided any confrontation with the Navy for almost five years, moving slowly, carefully, securing each new addition before moving out once again. Other would-be warlords learned from his successes, and soon they, too, were staking out territorial claims. Some of them, giddy with power, moved too soon against the Navy and were demolished; others tried to pry loose some of Grath's possessions, with a similar lack of success. Grath always executed the leaders; those underlings who were willing to join him were assimilated into his ranks, and those with exceptional abilities were given better treatment than they had known under their former commanders.

At last it was economics that forced him to move against the Oligarchy. He had almost five million men to feed, and was acutely aware of the increased rate of defections among those soldiers stationed on the habitable planets in his domain. The Rim had been all but taken, and no single system, or group of systems, could stand up to his military might. There had been one surrender after another, and his men had grown bored with these bloodless victories. He felt they needed to have a purpose once again, and the only goal remaining that could fire their imaginations and appeal to their lust was the Oligarchy itself.

He took his eyes from the stars and turned back to his associates, who were awaiting his orders.

"Gentlemen," he said, "the first blow must be a telling one. To attack a poorly manned outpost or a small convoy of Navy ships would offer no test to our strength, and would probably not even cause a ripple of concern on Deluros."

"And what's wrong with having Deluros slumber on while we go for its throat?" asked one of his subcommanders.

"Because, ironic as it seems," said Grath, "a slumbering Deluros is impregnable. The only way we can get within striking distance is to lure the Navy out from the core of the galaxy. If they fear us, if they mobilize the bulk of their forces, then we've got a chance. The trick is never to let them know our true size and strength, to make them nervous enough to seek us out but not smart enough to realize that we've got almost half a million ships."

He paused, looking slowly about the table. "In order to accomplish this, we shall make a massive strike upon Altair VII."

"You certainly don't believe in easy objectives, do you?" said an aide.

"There are a million easy objectives in this galaxy," replied Grath, "and not one of them—or all of them put together, for that matter—would do us the slightest bit of good. The Oligarchy controls almost two million worlds; they control five-sixths of the galaxy's economy; and they have a Navy of more than fifty million warships with an average crew of two hundred men per ship, not to mention billions of other soldiers and mercenaries on those planets that are under martial control. To make any kind of dent in the Oligarchy at all, we've got to hit something big, something vital. Do you think they really give a damn about what we do here on the Rim? We're so far away from the core of things that we don't even count as a minor irritant yet. We've wasted enough time seeking after loot; if we're ever to achieve empire, we're going to have to get on with it. Time is probably our greatest enemy. It's a big galaxy, big enough to take even our fastest ship more than a year to cross it unopposed. To cross it when we're outnumbered by more than a hundred to one, when we have precious little ability or opportunity to replace ships or men . . . that, gentlemen, is the situation. We're going to have to do in a handful of years what is rightfully a task for generations. And we shall begin," he concluded, "with Altair VII."

Altair VII was the political and economic center of an area almost 725 light-years across. It was the farthest from Deluros VIII of all the major Oligarchic worlds, and hence was the coordinating ruling body of tens of thousands of frontier worlds reaching out to the Rim. As such, it was considered to be of vital importance in the Oligarchy's scheme of things, and merited a fleet of almost 35,000 Navy ships for its protection (and its occasional forays against an insubordinate frontier worlds).

Altair VII held very little strategic value to any military force other than the Oligarchy itself. It was too far from the galactic core to make a useful base of operations, and it required three farming worlds to supply it with its needs. Its sole value lay in its complex and highly efficient bureaucracy. Almost six billion humans, practically all of them employed by the government in one form or another, worked in the huge, endless, glass-enclosed buildings, living out their lives amid file cabinets, desk computers, and fear of demotion or termination.

And yet power lay here too, the power to move unruly worlds into line, to expand Man's domination to a planet here or a system there; and, unstated but never forgotten, there was the greatest power of all—that of the Oligarchy.

The battle of the Altair system was brief, as space battles went in those days. Grath had made his plans well, feeding the coordinates of the star, its capital planet, and every ship of his own armada into scores of computers. Distances were established, times computed, the minute curvature of space accounted for, and eventually flight plans were programmed into every vessel. They did not all take off at once, nor at the same speed, nor even in the same direction. But each was programmed to reach the Altair system within seconds of all the others.

To the naked eye, the arrival of Grath's fleet would have seemed like magic; in one instant the system was empty, in the next it was alive with almost half a million ships braking to sublight speeds. But the technology of spacial conflict had long since ceased to rely on the naked eye, and the Oligarchy's Navy was not totally unprepared.

A number of Grath's ships overshot the Altair system by light-years; some plunged into the sun; and a few crashed into the largest of the system's sixteen planets. But the bulk of the fleet arrived when and where they were supposed to, and after a brief flurry which saw relatively heavy casualties on

181

both sides, the battle settled down—as such battles usually do—to a series of manipulations, englobements, three-dimensional phalanxes, and all the complex military formations that the most sophisticated computers and minds in the galaxy could conceive.

It took almost three weeks, weeks of long and intricate maneuverings broken by short, unbelievably violent clashes. At the end of it, Altair VII, and indeed the entire Altair system, was Grath's.

It had cost him twenty-one days and 46,000 ships.

He spent the next few months regrouping his forces, reestablishing what meager supply lines he had created, and waiting for a reaction from the Oligarchy. There was none.

"Our next target," he announced one evening, "is Valleux II. It's a mining world specializing in platinum, and it's about a hundred light-years closer to the core than Altair. Also, I've decided to give up our Rim bases for good."

"But why?" asked an aide. "We're almost impregnable here."

"Precisely," said Grath. "It's possible they felt we had some grievance against Altair, but once we hit Valleux they'll know we mean business. Now, if I were commanding the Navy, my first thought would be to contain my enemy until I knew the size and strength of his forces and could mobilize against him; and the most obvious place to contain him would be on the farthest reaches of the Rim, where he feels least vulnerable. Also, if I knew his base, I could decimate him every time he returned from a strike. No, gentlemen, from this day forth, until we land on Deluros VIII itself, our only base will be our armada. And now," he concluded, "I think it's about time to check with the computers and coordinate our attack on Valleux."

The Navy forces protecting Valleux II were considerably smaller than those that had been in the Altair system, and the battle, though furious on both sides, didn't last as long.

Counting the regrouping interim, Valleux II cost Grath 126 days and 12,450 ships.

In rapid order his forces took Ballion X, Hesperite III, and Quantos IX. They cost him 152 days and 16,050 ships.

He made one last major strike, overrunning the entire Belore system, at the expense of 93 days and 22,430 ships.

And still there was no response from the Oligarchy.

"And yet, why should there be?" he mused, half to himself, at a conference aboard his flagship. "What were their losses?

Absolutely minimal, compared to what they possess. Even with Altair and Belore in our pocket, I'll bet we're still so unimportant that no one's even bothered to tell the seven Oligarchs about us yet. They galaxy's so damned big and we're so damned little . . ."

He looked up.

"Gentlemen, none of us is getting any younger. We've proved ourselves in battle, and I now propose that we go after a target so important that they'll have to react to it: the Spica mining worlds."

His subordinates were unhappy, as he knew they would be. Altair and Belore were one thing, but Spica . . . it was protected by a fleet as large as their own, and was so deep into the Oligarchic empire that there could be no clear, easy line of retreat in any direction. On the other hand, Spica VI was a ship-building world, and to continue the war (which, each acknowledged grimly, had not yet even been noticed, let alone joined, by the opposing side) they needed ships above all else.

The Battle of Spica was the bloodiest ever fought in space, before or since. At long and weary last, Grath emerged with what the history books termed a victory.

He knew better. It had cost him 495 days, and 360,450 ships.

And it cost him more than that. He spent almost four years waiting while the huge plants on Spica VI rebuilt his fleet. In the meantime he returned to piracy, though his loot now consisted of weaponry and ships rather than credits and gemstones. His hair was streaked with gray now, the firm lines of his face more deeply emblazoned. Once again he held a conference of the various warlords, and once again found unity and the dream of Empire beyond them.

His original master plan had called for a feint toward Earth while the main body of his forces attacked Sirius, but there was no need to feint. Earth was unguarded, sleeping sublimely as the business of the race to which it had given birth went on unbothered half a galaxy away. It was a totally bloodless coup, but it cost him 200 more days . . . 150 to change the feint into a conquest, and 50 to reunite his armada for the attack on Sirius.

And finally it happened. Sirius was too vital to the Oligarchy, too close to the heart of things, to be lost. As the maneuvering and battling reached their sixth indecisive week, his scout ships reported that Oligarchic reinforcements were on the way, to the tune of at least three million vessels. Withdrawing as quickly as he could, he returned to the Spica system, a quarter of a million ships weaker than when he had left it.

For three more years he darted in and out of the main body of the Oligarchy, picking off a Navy fleet here, destroying a world there, replenishing his arms and his men.

The Oligarchy, cold, aloof, uncaring, merely tolerated him.

He waged some battles that would live long in the annals of warfare. Outnumbered by more than eight to one, he fought the Navy to a standoff in the Delphini system; with one flank demolished and another crippled, he led his forces to safety from an abortive raid on Balok XIV; and always, when the odds were equal, or nearly so, he emerged the unquestioned victor. When outworlders spoke of the Warlord, it meant Grath and no one else; and yet the Oligarchy paid him scant attention, and his deeds were considered so trivial in the scheme of things that they went unreported in the Deluros media.

"Gentlemen," he announced one night when his subordinates were gathered in his quarters, "behind me is a Tri-D chart of the galaxy. This"—and he pointed to a tiny spot on the Rim—"is where we began. And this"—he pointed to another—"is where we are now. What can be gleaned from that?"

There was a momentary silence. Then a voice spoke out: "Well, we've come almost half of the way."

"Wrong!" snapped Grath. "We've done nothing. Nothing! What do we actually possess? A handful of worlds, no more than eight thousand of them, in a direct line of our military conquest. We have no spheres of influence, no buffer zones, no economic power. If you stood in the complex at Caliban and eliminated every system we own from the map, it could take years before anyone noticed the difference.

"This is no way to destroy the Oligarchy. Sure, we've cost them almost three million ships, but they've probably replaced them tenfold by now. We've been going about it all wrong. It can't be done in a military campaign. No one man, no one group of men, can hope to conquer, step by step, what it's taken Man six millennia to assimilate. No wonder the Oligarchy doesn't bother with us; they expect us to die of old age long before we can pose a real threat to their security."

"Then what do you propose?"

184

"I suggest that we make a swift, sudden, all-or-nothing strike at the very heart of the Oligarchy—at Deluros. If we control Deluros, we control the Oligarchic empire. If not, then we're just a bunch of pirates, a little stronger and more successful than the others, but pirates nonetheless."

"That's a pretty tall order," offered an aide.

"What would you have us do? Hit Sirius again? If they protected it once they'll do so again, and they'll protect every planet, habitable or otherwise, between Sirius and Deluros. That will mean about one hundred and fifty thousand pitched battles before we get within striking distance."

"There *is* an alternative," said another aide.

"What?" asked Grath.

"Create our own empire, beginning on the Rim and assimilating as many worlds as we can, while always spreading toward the outskirts of the Oligarchy. In time, we'd be able to challenge them on far more even footing."

"No," said Grath adamantly. "First of all, we're soldiers, not administrators. Any empire we tried to build and nurture would crumble before it had fairly begun, whereas Deluros is already capable of administering an existing empire. We won't destroy the billions of tentacles that reach out from Deluros to the rest of the Oligarchy; we'll simply take control of them—which is far easier than creating those tentacles on a world of our own choosing. And second, I'm not so sure that future generations would hunger for the Oligarchy as we do. They haven't fought as we have for what we possess, and there's a strong possibility that they'd become complacent. I seek after empire; my sons may seek only comfort. Finally, we don't have a stable society here. We have a military unit, a living, breathing entity that can remain cohesive only as long as it is given military goals. No, gentlemen, our target is Deluros."

He, perhaps more than any other, knew the problems involved, the microscopic chance of victory. For almost a decade the Spica factories turned out ships and arms, while he kept his men busy with minor skirmishes and conquests. When at last he felt he was ready he organized his armada, some six million ships strong, and began his drive for Deluros. His hair was now white and his once-erect posture was a little stooped, but the brilliant mind and magnetic personality that had conceived and structured this final thrust were unimpaired. Such inviting targets as Binder and the Canphor Twins were bypassed as his fleet plunged straight toward the empire's jugular. No move was made against him as he passed Rigel and Emra and Terrazane and Zeta Cancri. It was almost as if the Oligarchy was watching, bemused, to see just how close this upstart really dared to come.

They passed a million stars, five million, twenty million, and the light from the galactic core became more brilliant. And then, suddenly, came the Navy. Millions upon millions of ships descended upon him, so many that they blotted out the stars. They came from his sides, from above and below, they rushed forward to greet him with a barrage of firepower so great that half his armada was demolished in the first minutes of battle.

Calmly, coolly, he began issuing orders. A feint here, a quick engagement there, a minor sacrifice here, a major bloodbath over there. And always, when he moved, it was toward Deluros.

Within a day his fleet had dwindled down to half a million; by the end of a week, there were less than sixty thousand . . . and still he drove toward Deluros. Eight days into the battle the computers could find no alternative to complete surrender, and so he directed his remaining handful of ships himself. At last, brilliant as his resistance had been, he was surrounded and englobed. His eyes darted to the viewscreen, trying to pick out the huge, shining star that was Deluros, but it was still too far away, totally lost amid the light of a million of its neighbors.

He stared dully at the screen. It was just too big, too much for one man to take, to even dream of taking. The only word that occurred to him was *presumptuous*.

"And to think," he mused wistfully, just before the firepower of the Navy tore his ship apart, "that Alexander wept because there was nothing left to conquer. . . ."

16: The Conspirators

... It was Admiral Ramos Broder (5966–6063 G.E.) who not only brought some measure of stability to the military after the fearful events of 5993, but also managed to ferret out Wain Connough, the prime mover in the death of the Oligarchic Era ...

—*Man: Twelve Millennia of Achievement*

... It is this author's opinion that neither Connough and Boron were so black, nor Broder so white, as history paints them. For while it is true that Connough was executed for treason within a month after the fall of the Oligarchy and Broder's conduct during that period and for the next seventy years was exemplary, it seems unlikely that the entire situation could have arisen without the mysterious death of Broder's superior, Admiral Esten Klare (5903–5993 G.E.).

Be that as it may, it can safely be said that no other body of similar power ever fell as swiftly as the Oligarchy ...

—*Origin and History of the Sentient Races*, Vol. 8

"Blame it on Grath," said Broder, looking at a small, illuminated, three-dimensional map of the galaxy.

"He's been dead for more than eighty years," replied Quince. "I don't really see what he has to do with it."

"He was the first," said Broder. "He showed them how far one man could come. It was only a matter of time before the other warlords would figure out just how much farther they could get if they banded together."

"But even Grath never managed to win them over to his side," protested Quince. "He tried right up until his final push toward Deluros."

"First they had to see that it could be done," said Broder. "They had to know that an outlaw force, properly marshaled, could attack the Navy and get away with it. Also, Grath didn't need them."

"In the end he did."

"They wouldn't have done him any good," said Broder. "There couldn't have been a hundred million men in the employ of all the warlords in Grath's heyday. Now things are different. They number between four and five billion. Look at the map." The two men turned their eyes to the illuminated spiral. "They've made huge inroads, absolutely huge. And since they haven't got anyone with Grath's talents, they're content to pick the Oligarchy to shreds, bit by bit, along the outskirts of the frontiers."

"Then why worry?" asked Quince. "It'll be eons before they turn their eyes toward Deluros."

"I doubt it."

"Why?" asked Quince.

"Two reasons," said Broder. "First, sooner or later they've got to realize what Grath knew all along: that the quickest way to conquer the Oligarchy is to conquer Deluros. And second, that the only other way to conquer the Oligarchy is to pick it to pieces, which means they'll be thirty generations removed from the warlords who finally land here."

"Then you expect a strike on Deluros?"

Broder shrugged. "If it was me, yes, I'd buck the odds and attack. With them, who knows? Hell, they probably spend more time fighting among themselves than against the Navy. Still, they'll be coming one of these days."

The conversation ambled on a little longer, and then Broder returned to his office. As second in command of the Navy's defense forces at Deluros, it was his job to keep troops and fleet in a state of preparedness . . . and wait.

188

It had been a long wait. Grath had made it to within almost two hundred light-years before the Navy lowered the boom, and no warlord had had the temerity to come that close again. Sooner or later they'd try again, get a couple of light-years closer, and be repelled or destroyed again. And he, Admiral Ramos Broder, honor graduate from the Deluros Military Academy, author of two highly praised volumes on the tactics of space war, former ambassador to Canphor VI, would grow old and die, awaiting the opportunity to prove his mettle in battle.

On course, he thought with a tight grin, there was job security aplenty. But one of the problems with job security was that the men ahead of you also had it, and you weren't likely to advance until they died or retired. That was all right for men like Quince, but not for him: He wanted a position commensurate with his abilities, and he wouldn't be getting one unless and until those abilities were tested. At which time, he concluded, half the people above him would have been killed and he'd advance anyway.

Neither the thoughts nor the frustrations were new to him. Far from it. He'd lived with them for years now, though the passage of time hadn't exactly mellowed him.

Which was why he had agreed to see the man who was being ushered into his office.

"Connough?" he asked, extending his hand.

The man nodded. He was very tall, quite rangy, with large blue eyes that darted back and forth across the office, taking in windows, intercoms, and all the paraphernalia of bureaucracy.

Broder turned to his aide. "No calls, no visitors, no communication of any sort, and no monitoring. Understood?"

The aide acknowledged the orders and left the office.

"I realize that you've taken a great personal risk in coming here," said Broder. "May I assure you that no record of this meeting will be kept, and that should your presence become known, I will authorize safe passage for you to whatever destination you desire."

Connough grunted, still looking around.

"You are free to examine the room," offered Broder.

Connough took one last look, then shook his head. "That won't be necessary."

"Fine," said Broder. "Now let's get down to business. First of all, just how did you manage to get here without credentials?"

189

"I have credentials," said Connough, flashing them.

"I expressed myself poorly," said Broder. "I realize, of course, that you would have the necessary identification to reach my office. What I'm curious about is how you ever got out to the Rim and back without being detained at one end or the other."

"I have my ways," said Connough.

"Not good enough," said Broder. "If I am even to consider entering this enterprise I must have straight answers. Otherwise you're just wasting my time and yours."

"It's a big galaxy, Admiral, and it's impossible to guard every spaceway. My organization has numerous small trading ships, and it was a simple matter to forge credentials to the effect that I owned and operated one, and that I had trading rights to several of the frontier worlds. Belasko knew I was coming, and I had no problem getting through his military cordon around the Belthar system."

"Belasko!" said Broder. "You met him in person?"

Connough nodded.

"Can you prove that to me?"

Connough withdrew a small plastic card. "You'll find Belasko's thumbprint on this. Run it through your computer and check it out."

Broder did so, and a few minutes later the computer reported that the thumbprint did indeed belong to Belasko, the kingpin of the loosely knit confederation of warlords.

"How did Belasko react to your proposition?"

"Pretty much as I anticipated," said Connough. "In exchange for Sirius V, Lodin XI, and their spheres of economic and military influence, he'll do what we ask."

"And what, precisely, is that?"

"That he make a feint at the Binder system when instructed, and that he publicly acknowledge his loyalty to Deluros in exchange for total amnesty."

"In that order, I hope." Broder grinned.

"This is deadly serious business, Admiral," said Connough. "I fail to see any humor in the situation."

"No, I don't suppose you would," said Broder. "All right, on to the next point. How many men are in your organization?"

"That, I am afraid, is privileged information until such time as you commit yourself," said Connough.

"Fair enough. Answer this much: Do you have at least twenty thousand men on Deluros VIII?"

"No."

"I thought not," said Broder. "Ten thousand?"

"I'm not here to play guessing games, Admiral," said Connough. "Let's just say that we have more than enough."

"I very much doubt it, though I'll let it pass for the moment," said Broder.

"You haven't asked the question that must be the most important to you," remarked Connough.

"Oh?" said Broder. "And what is that?"

"Why, of all people on Deluros VIII, we contacted you."

"The thought did cross my mind," said Broder. "However, it wasn't all that difficult to deduce. To begin with, nothing in my writings or speeches could have given you any indication whatsoever that I might be sympathetic to your cause, or that I wouldn't have you put to death for treason. And with an enterprise of this nature, you sure as hell didn't draw my name out of a hat. So it wasn't too difficult to figure out that what you wanted wasn't necessarily me, but the man holding my job. I just happened to be here; depending on the timing, you could have used my predecessor or my successor just as easily.

"The only question remaining was: Why *my* job? After all, I'm only second in command to Admiral Klare. But Klare's brother-in-law is on the Oligarchic Council, which means he's probably too loyal to chance even sounding him out. It also means, or so I surmise, that Klare will probably be murdered at the earliest opportunity, placing me—temporarily, at least—in charge of the system's defense fleet.

"Now, why should it be essential to your plans to have me in that position? The only answer I can come up with is that at the proper moment I will be expected to misdirect it. Most likely," he added, looking sharply at Connough, "when Belasko feints toward Binder. Correct?"

Connough nodded.

"Let me continue, then," said Broder. "Since Belasko has neither the strength nor the inclination to fight the main body of our forces, the only reason you want the fleet kept busy is so that they won't be tempted to interfere with whatever it is you're planning to do on Deluros VIII, and will return to a *fait accompli*. And, with less than twenty thousand men—and probably only a quarter of that total—I imagine you'll try to kill the seven Oligarchs."

"Not quite, Admiral," said Connough. "Only six of them."

191

"Who gets to live?" asked Broder.

"It doesn't make much difference. But if we kill all seven, everything will be up for grabs. Whereas . . ."

"Whereas if you leave one alive, you'll have succeeded in turning the galactic Oligarchy into a monarchy in one swift stroke. Under those circumstances, I'm sure none of them will turn you down. Especially," he added, grinning again, "with a swift and certain death as the only alternative."

"That is correct," said Connough.

"Not necessarily," said Broder. "The whole thing hinges upon whether or not you can really deliver six swift and certain deaths to the best-protected men in the galaxy. What makes you think it can be done?"

"We have men highly placed in each of the Oligarchic staffs. It won't be too difficult."

"I doubt it. They have one hell of a lot of bodyguards highly placed on each staff as well. Furthermore, the matter of timing becomes a vital factor; all six must be killed before any of the others becomes aware of the situation and strengthens his security. How do you plan to circumvent that little problem?"

For almost an hour Connough spelled out every detail of the planned assassinations. Broder listened intently, occasionally asking a question, less frequently offering an opinion. At the end of that time Connough leaned back in his chair. "Well?" he asked.

"Personally, I think the odds are somewhere in the neighborhood of a thousand to one against you," said Broder. "First of all, you've no idea how the remaining Oligarch will react to it. Even if he liked the idea of playing Emperor, he'd probably have you executed before you caused him any embarrassment. And, of course, if he was truly outraged at your actions, he'd have you executed for that.

"Second, with the Oligarchy in a state of momentary chaos and the chain of command in doubt, Belasko might very well carve out a huge chunk of our territory. Or he might expose the whole thing and be swept to power on a tide of public sentiment.

"Third, I very much doubt that you'll be able to kill more than one Oligarch before the sky falls on your whole organization. I figure that with exceptionally good luck, you'll kill two of them. Certainly no more than that.

"Fourth, your scheme depends, to a considerable degree, on my complicity. As yet, I see no reason why I should come over to your side, and I see numerous reasons why I shouldn't."

"I cannot answer your first three objections, Admiral," said Connough. "But as for your last one, I will give you my pledge—in writing, on voicetape, or in any other form you desire—that upon the successful completion of this affair, you will be made commander in chief of the entire armed forces of the Oligarchy. Or of the Monarchy, as the case may be."

"That's very impressive," said Broder. "It would be even more impressive if I knew you would be in power, or even alive, at such time as I wished to assume command."

"Well, we can't very well get whichever member of the council we decide to spare to make that promise," said Connough. "We are talking, Admiral, about overthrowing the most powerful single political and military establishment ever to exist. It is only natural that uncertainties as to its accomplishment and aftermath should exist."

"What's to stop the media and the public from assuming that the surviving Oligarch engineered the whole thing himself?" asked Broder, changing the subject.

"An attempt will be made on his life as well, and doubtless he will sustain serious but nonfatal wounds. The would-be assassins will not live to tell what they know. Blame for the incident will be laid on a certain radical fringe group which, though innocent, will be only too happy to take credit for it."

"How soon are you ready to move?"

"Within the next thirty days," said Connough. "This means that Admiral Klare must be assassinated almost immediately."

"It's a harebrained scheme," said Broder. "What makes you think I won't turn you in the moment you've left my office? After all, this conversation hasn't been monitored or recorded. I could deny any complicity whatsoever and become a hero overnight."

"Indeed you could," agreed Connough. "However, that is a risk I must take."

"You're a cool customer, I'll grant you that," said Broder. "When must you have my decision?"

"By this evening. You needn't contact me again. If you decide to join us, find some way to have Admiral Klare admit a man named Deros Boron to his office tomorrow afternoon. Everything else will be taken care of, and you will receive further instructions at the proper time. If Boron cannot gain admittance to Klare's office, you will have rejected my proposal."

"Is there any way I can get in touch with you?" asked Broder.

"None," said Connough, rising and leaving the room.

Broder sat and stared at the wall. It was a crazy proposition, a million-to-one shot. It probably wouldn't get off the ground at all. The odds were even that Klare would come out unscathed. The odds were astronomical that the Oligarchy would survive. And the odds extended almost to infinity that even if Klare and six of the Oligarchs were successfully gotten out of the way, the seventh Oligarch wouldn't see eye to eye with the men who had so swiftly turned him into the most powerful sentient entity in history. And, he grimaced, the odds of *his* surviving were considerably longer than the odds on any of the intended victims.

So much for the negative side . . . but was there even a hint of a positive argument? There was. It was preceded by half a hundred ifs, but it ended with him in total charge of the entire military complex of the Oligarchy.

Unlikely? Hell, yes. Improbable? Certainly.

But not impossible.

The likelihood was that the Oligarchy would survive intact, and if it did, there was the certainty that he would remain second in command of the Deluros VIII defense fleet. The less likely outcome—by far—was that the Oligarchy would crumble, and that he would ascend to a position that, under existent conditions, was completely out of his reach.

He pondered every aspect of the situation and realized that logic had taken him as far as it could. Now instinct, intuition, experience, everything that made him Man rather than machine, took over.

He pressed the intercom button on his desk.

"Admiral Klare? This is Broder. There's a fellow named Boron who's got some pretty interesting information about Belasko. Could you possibly see him tomorrow afternoon?"

Seventh Millennium: MONARCHY

17: The Rulers

... Vestolian I (6284–6348 G.E.) was one of the less ambitious rulers during the early period of the Commonwealth. Quiet and introspective, his reign took on the characteristics of his personality. Upon assuming the Directorship he immediately issued a number of proclamations which, depending on one's interpretation, might have strengthened his office immeasurably or weakened it fatally. Unfortunately, we will never know the effects these proclamations might have had, for in 6321, the second year of his reign...

—*Man: Twelve Millennia of Achievement*

195

. . . Though the seventh millennium of the Galactic Era was called the Commonwealth, it is now more properly known to historians as the Monarchy. The words differ considerably; the facts do not.

One of the most enlightened and foresightful of the early monarchs was Vestolian I, who ruled from 6319 to 6348. It was he who tried to return some portion of the power his immediate ancestors had usurped from the people with his dramatic proclamations of 6320. Two advisers, Zenorra and Oberlieu, are generally credited with reawakening within him the lust for absolute authority and the subsequent repeal of . . .

—*Origin and History of the Sentient Races*, Vol. 8

A monarchy can be far and away the most efficient form of government. It can also be the most inept. In both cases, the determining factor is the monarch. An intelligent, selfless, and decisive monarch can take swift and sure actions without spending days—or years—working his way through miles of red tape or compromising with multitudes of legislative factions. A well-meaning but unenlightened monarch must rely on his advisers, each of whom has a certain amount of self-interest at stake. And a stupid, petty, self-serving monarch has more capacity for mischief, misrule, and out-and-out evil than the holder of any other office.

During the early centuries of the Monarchy, the race of Man had known all three types of monarchs, and several others of intermediate shadings. The Monarchy was officially established in 5994 (Galactic Era); by 6013, there had been seven assassinations and/or insurrections, and it wasn't until the reign of Torlon II, beginning in 6067, that any true line of succession was established. Torlon II gave stability to a crumbling galactic economy, solidified and reasserted Man's hold on his possessions, dubbed Man's empire the Commonwealth, and gave himself the title of Director. He also outlived his two sons and four daughters, and was succeeded in 6126 by his grandson, Torlon III, whose major contribution to the Monarchy was the Floating Kingdom, a huge planetoid which had originally been one of the remnants of Deluros VI, but which he sealed with a dome and equipped with the motive power to navigate throughout the Commonwealth. The

Floating Kingdom became the home of all future Directors, though most of the bureaucratic business was still carried on on Deluros VIII—and, in point of fact, the Floating Kingdom rarely left the immediate vicinity of the Deluros system except on official visits of state.

Torlon III proved sterile, and his niece, Valla I, became the first Directrix in 6148. She was followed by eight more Directors and another Directrix before Vestolian ascended to the Directorship in 6319. A small, studious man, soft-spoken and uncomfortable in public, he reached his position of power only after two older brothers had died in the same tragic life-support-system malfunction that claimed the life of his mother, Biora I. Unprepared both by temperament and training to direct the affairs of the race, he was nonetheless a man of goodwill who resolved to master the intricacies of his office and preside over the Commonwealth to the best of his not inconsiderable abilities.

He had been Director for exactly five days when he found himself embroiled in a war against three star systems he had never even heard of.

"All right," he said, when he had finally managed to assemble the bulk of his mother's advisers before him. "As most of you probably know, I was awakened in the middle of the night and informed that the Commonwealth is at war. Admittedly it's not much of a war, since there are a lot of us and not very many of them, but it's a war nonetheless. Now, would somebody here like to tell me just what is going on? I didn't authorize any war, and I've hardly been in office long enough to offend anyone. Who are the Argaves, anyway, and what is the reason for their actions?"

Oberlieu, the Prefect of Alien Affairs, stepped forward. "If I may, Director?" Vestolian nodded, and he cleared his throat. "Director, the Argaves are a humanoid race, at least as high on the evolutionary scale as Man. At present they control three systems, and their own birthplace is thought to be on Darion V."

"What seems to be their problem?" asked Vestolian.

"They were incorporated into the Commonwealth almost two centuries ago," said Oberlieu. "It was soon decided that they were not contributing their fair tax load to Deluros, and your great-great-uncle, Jordin II, imposed a heavy tariff on all agricultural products exported from their systems." He paused, seeming ill at ease.

"And?"

"It appears," said Oberlieu slowly, "that the Argaves have been petitioning for an audience with various Directors for the past sixty years to get the tariff repealed. They claim that their economy has been in a state of continuous depression since its instigation, since all the Argave worlds are basically agrarian."

"I assume no audience was ever granted," remarked Vestolian.

"That is correct," said Oberlieu.

"Continue," said Vestolian.

"It appears that they have been threatening to revolt for the past few years unless the tariff was repealed. They have now done so."

"Why was the tariff not repealed, nor at least reconsidered?" asked the Director.

"Only a Director can repeal a law that he himself has passed," answered Oberlieu.

"Why was the Argaves' grievance never brought before a Director?" asked Vestolian.

"According to my records, it was," said Oberlieu. "Jordin II and Wilor I both refused to meet with the Argaves."

"They've both been dead for more than half a century!" snapped Vestolian. "Are you trying to tell me that no Director has been aware of this situation for the past fifty years, despite the open threat of war?"

"Yes, Director," said Oberlieu. "I think that is precisely what I am trying to tell you."

"I consider this to be nothing less than gross and criminal negligence," said Vestolian. "We shall immediately eliminate the tariff and do everything within our power to set the Argaves' economy back on its feet. We must also set up channels of authority to make sure that no such situation can ever arise again."

"I'm afraid that's out of the question, Director," said Zenorra, his Chief of Protocol.

"Explain yourself," said Vestolian.

"I'd prefer to do so in private, Director," said Zenorra.

"I haven't been Director long enough to have any secrets," said Vestolian. "I see no reason for a private discussion."

Zenorra shrugged. "If you insist."

"I do."

"To begin with, Director," said Zenorra, "you can call yourself any damned thing you please: Director, Protector, First Citizen, or anything else. What you are is an absolute emperor. Now, this can be very beneficial, but it is also a two-edged sword.

"For example, there are some twenty or so advisers gathered in this room with you. We are, in all immodesty, experts in our various fields. Between us, we know everything there is to know about presiding over an empire the size and complexity of the Commonwealth. Nonetheless, even if all of us were in complete agreement on a certain course of action, you could overrule us and make it stick. You are the most powerful human being, in fact the most powerful sentient being of any race, who ever lived, and you'll remain so until you are succeeded by the next Director."

"I don't see what you're getting at," said Vestolian.

"I'm coming to that. As I was saying, you are the most politically powerful being in the galaxy. Now, the first—and perhaps the only—purpose of power is to perpetuate itself. Study your history and you'll find that no leader during the Oligarchy, Democracy, or Republic, or even when the race was still Earthbound, ever willingly relinquished any portion of the power he had accumulated. Political power is not unlike water: It ebbs and flows along the path of least resistance. Under normal circumstances this path leads to one man, the man at the top; but if he makes a conscious effort to reverse the process, even with something so trivial as a tariff applied only to one race of beings fifty thousand light-years distant, he has put a small hole in the dike, so to speak, and begun the reversal of the power flow.

"I realize that it's tremendously inefficient for you to be forced to make such minor decisions, and certainly each of us has the right to speak in your name. But if it's done too frequently, then our underlings will soon be speaking in your name as well, and before long you'll have literally billions of Men giving edicts in the name of the Director."

"You'll forgive me if I ask a number of questions," said Vestolian, looking unconvinced.

"Certainly," said Zenorra.

"First of all, if I am the only man in the Commonwealth with the authority to make a decision, what the hell do I have almost two million planetary governors for? Why are we employing thirty billion bureaucrats on Deluros VIII and the Deluros VI planetoids if they can't even pick their noses without my permission? Half our Navy is so far from the Floating Kingdom that they can't be contacted in less than a month; if they can't use their own initiative, just what in blazes are they doing out there?"

"May I answer the first part of that, Director?" asked Oberlieu. Vestolian nodded. "Insofar as governorships and alien affairs are concerned, each governor had autonomy in the internal affairs of his planet, as long as he remains within the broad guidelines issued from Deluros. It is when interplanetary problems arise that the governor's hands are tied, though of course he is free to make recommendations, and indeed it is expected of him."

"As for the Deluros bureaucracy," said Zenorra, "they do indeed make decisions every day. But these are relatively minor decisions, decisions that are confined to their particular field or fields of expertise. The Navy is of course empowered to defend itself, and to interject itself as a peace-keeper in interplanetary strife among Commonwealth planets, but it may not initiate any offensive action except on your direct orders."

"I repeat," said Vestolian, "that this is the most inefficient system conceivable. We have two million governors, and more than a quarter of a million admirals, to say nothing of generals of planetary forces. I would die of old age before I could pronounce each of their names once, let alone give orders to all of them. How has the Commonwealth managed to function all these centuries?"

"You seem to be laboring under the false impression that there is no chain of command," said Zenorra. "In point of fact, you need issue only one brief military order to one admiral in command of a certain sector of the galaxy, and the order will be channeled down to the man who can perform the job."

"What's to prevent the admiral in charge from issuing such an order on his own?" asked the Director.

"Security," said Oberlieu.

"I'm afraid I don't understand you," said Vestolian.

"This isn't the Oligarchy or the Democracy," said Oberlieu. "The change may seem slight, but it is not. You see, in all previous governmental structures, the possibility of advancement was unlimited. Every man, from the lowliest laborer to the most brilliant demagogue, could conceivably rise to the top of the heap through his own efforts and initiative. That is no longer so. You are the absolute ruler, and even if all your most trusted aides were to conspire to take your life, none of us would succeed to the Directorship until every last member of your family, which is spread across half a galaxy and under phenomenally heavy guard, was also eliminated. Thus, to one extent or another, every member of the Commonwealth is subject to your whim, and, to be blunt, the potential for advancement or reward does not quite equal the potential for demotion or punishment. The bottom of the heap is a huge and infinite abyss; the top has room for only one man, and the job is not only taken but also spoken for for the next hundred generations. Does this make the situation somewhat clearer, Director?"

"Quite clear," said Vestolian dryly. "You're telling me that no one in the Commonwealth has the guts to change the way he combs his hair without first clearing it with me."

"You insist on trying to simplify the situation," said Zenorra, "and it's far from simple. For example, to examine the other side of the coin, you have the capacity to reward a member of the Commonwealth to a far greater degree than was ever previously possible. You can take a congenital idiot and elevate him to the head of any military force or scientific department, give him a planet of his own to rule, or do just about any other thing you please."

"But along with your ability to reward or to punish," interjected Oberlieu, "is your capacity to ignore. In fact, it's more than a capacity; it's a built-in shortcoming to the system. You received your power due to an accident of birth. You were born into the right family at what turned out to be the right time, and nothing short of the termination of your life, or a galaxy-wide revolution, can abrogate your position. You are the only man in the Commonwealth who is not ultimately responsible to either a higher authority or a planetary electorate. Hence, unlike all your billions of underlings, no decision you make can cause a change in your status, even if it were to plunge us into a real war, rather than this piddling little disturbance with the Argaves. Therefore, is it any wonder that the buck is now being passed upward at a higher rate than ever before?"

"And," put in Zenorra, "with a galaxy to rule, it is only natural that, even with a different political setup, you wouldn't have the time to attend to a tenth of the problems that can be decided only by a Director. As things stand now . . ." His voice trailed off.

"Correct me if I'm wrong," said Vestolian, "but as nearly as I understand it, it is you and the other members of my advisory staff who decide which problems have priority and which are to be ignored."

"To an extent," agreed Zenorra. "Though, of course, you are free to act—or, rather, to not act—on any problem that eventually reaches your desk. Similarly, you can issue directives on those problems that have not yet been placed before you."

"That, essentially, is the system as it now stands?" said Vestolian.

His advisers nodded.

"Then we're going to make some changes around here," he said, staring defiantly at them. He was not by nature a man of action, this Director, nor had he even yet begun to realize the scope of his power; but he had gleaned enough to know that his word was absolute law, and that something had to be done to disseminate that law more rapidly and more equitably. He terminated the meeting after once again issuing orders concerning the Argave situation and returned to his quarters to think the situation out.

He set up a meeting with Zenorra and Oberlieu three days later. In the interim, he received news of a skirmish in the Belthar region which had been ordered by his mother two decades earlier but which had only now been acted upon; of an entire alien population being destroyed when its sun went nova because the governor had been hesitant about ordering an evacuation without written approval from the Director; of some three hundred planetary heads of state who were mortally offended by his inability to meet privately with each of them during the week after his mother's death; and of a mysterious race of gaseous entities living in the Greater Magellanic Clouds that had not been contacted, befriended, studied, and/or exploited because no one knew the Director's views on the matter.

"Gentlemen," said Vestolian when his two highest aides had arrived, "I must admit that I've been sorely tempted to abdicate. The only reason I've decided against so doing is that I'm very fond of my daughter, and can think of no crueler legacy to leave her than the Directorship as it now stands. Therefore, I have prepared a list of directives—directives, mind you, not suggestions—that I would like implemented as quickly as possible. I must, at the risk of being redundant, stress the urgency of these directives; if each and every one of them is not in effect within thirty days, you will both be discharged from your positions. Is that quite clear?"

"Perfectly," said Zenorra, looking disturbed. Oberlieu merely nodded and frowned.

"To begin with, planetary governors will have autonomy to deal with all disturbances not just on their planets but within their star systems."

"What if there are three governors within a system, and they don't see eye to eye?" asked Zenorra.

"Don't interrupt until I'm finished," said Vestolian. "There will be an overseer, to be given any title you deem fitting and proper, for every ten systems; he will have autonomy to settle any dispute brought to him by the governors. Every ten overseers will also be responsible to one man, who will be in charge of a hundred star systems, and will also be empowered to act on his own initiative. This ratio and chain of command will continue right up to Oberlieu's office.

"The Navy will be authorized to take any action it considers necessary, including offensive action, the only stipulation being that it be officially approved within thirty days or be terminated by that time. Set up a chain of command, of from four to seven men, leading up to me, for approval of military action, and see to it that I'm not bothered with any action that could be considered a skirmish rather than a war."

"Director, I *must* interrupt at this point," said Zenorra.

"For what reason?" demanded Vestolian.

"To point out that you must qualify your statement. What may wipe out the entire populace of a planet may seem like the ultimate war to them, and may simultaneously appear to be a mere policing action to you."

"An excellent point," said Vestolian. "You, Zenorra, will have fifteen different definitions of war and skirmish drawn up and submitted to me tomorrow morning; I will choose the ones we shall use.

"To continue: All scientific departments will report only major breakthroughs to me. To encourage such breakthroughs, they will be given whatever money is required, within reason, by the Budget, Finance, and Treasury departments. Should there be disagreements concerning the amount of appropriations to be allotted, a three-man board of arbitrators, consisting of one economist, one scientist, and Oberlieu, will reach a decision. The decision cannot be appealed to me without just cause, and only Oberlieu will be able to determine whether the cause is just.

"Next, I want a chain of command set up among our ambassadorial corps. We shall issue a set of broad directives, and every ambassador, as long as he acts within those directives, will be free to use his judgment and act accordingly."

"You're making it almost impossible for all but a handful of men to see you," said Oberlieu.

"Correct. I suspect that handful will keep me busy enough." He paused and stared at his two advisers. "Gentlemen, I have neither the time, nor the training, nor the inclination to preside over the run-of-the-mill day-to-day business of the Floating Kingdom. I shall certainly not interject myself into the even more mundane daily affairs of the galaxy at large. My final directive is this: If any problem reaches proportions of great enough import to receive my personal attention, and if it is determined that said problem arose due to an absence of initiative, or the inability to make a decision, on the part of a bureaucrat of the Commonwealth, that bureaucrat will be summarily executed. Given the current state of affairs, I would prefer incorrect actions to inaction."

"Is that all, Director?" asked Zenorra.

"For the moment. When we see how these orders work, we'll be better able to further modify the present system. I'm surprised," he added, "that some such system hasn't been proposed by any of my predecessors."

"It has been," said Oberlieu.

"By each and every one of them," said Zenorra.

Vestolian glared coldly at them for a moment and then dismissed them.

It would take time, he knew, for the orders to reach all concerned parties. He estimated two years, but admitted that it might well be a decade before the Commonwealth showed any noticeable change. Once it happened, though, he might even enjoy being Director.

As it turned out, he was wrong on both counts: It didn't take ten years, and he very definitely didn't enjoy it.

Item: The insectoid population of Procyon II, suffering from the pangs of overpopulation, had found some pretext to go to war with the humanoids of Procyon III. The governors, unable to reach an agreement, had put the issue before the overseer, but before he could decide the merits of the case, the Navy had stepped into the picture, breaking up the war by bombarding Procyon II with deadly radiation. Not only were some ninety percent of the insectoids destroyed, but antihuman pogroms broke out spontaneously on seven of the other nine insectoid worlds in the Commonwealth. When Vestolian looked into the matter, he found that the governors had pursued his chain of command, and that the Navy had very definitely avoided any charge of inaction.

Item: The Department of Microbiology had requested an appropriation of seventeen billion credits; the Department of the Budget had agreed to four billion. The Arbitration Board had settled on a figure of six billion, and the entire Microbiology Department went on strike pending a meeting with the Director. Since they produced most of the vaccines used by humans on alien planets, a strike was intolerable, so Vestolian was forced to hear their arguments. He upped the appropriation to nine billion, and since there was no higher authority to appeal to, the microbiologists willingly went back to work. In the meantime, three expeditionary forces on the frontier worlds died for lack of vaccine.

Item: The ambassador to Alioth XIV, a world not yet incorporated into the Commonwealth, had succeeded so well in imparting his notions of a utopian democracy into the minds of the populace at large that a bloody civil war was instigated, resulting in more than 29 million deaths before the totalitarian leadership beat and starved the opposition forces into submission. When brought before an enraged Vestolian, the ambassador protested that he was merely using his initiative as directed. Why had the problem not been reported in its earlier, solvable stages? Because the Director had made it clear that he wanted to be consulted only when all other courses of action had failed—and by that time it was, regrettably, too late.

Item: A loosely knit union of two hundred worlds threatened to secede from the Commonwealth, claiming that the Director had made himself virtually inaccessible to them. When it was pointed out that all two hundred planets were economically sound and militarily strong and that the Director was preoccupied with smoothing over the problem spots of the Commonwealth, and that, further, no previous Director had ever seen delegations from any of the planets in question, the response was that at least none of the Director's predecessors had made it a matter of policy not to see them. It was all a matter of semantics and viewpoints, but Vestolian had to waste three days with ambassadors from the two hundred worlds rather than commit his military forces to the only viable alternative.

Item: Those problems that reached his desk were rarely

complex situations requiring executive decisions that only Vestolian could make. More often, they were diplomatic and bureaucratic misunderstandings that had been blown up all out of proportion.

Item: The serious problems, the ones Vestolian should have been dealing with, were being acted on—and frequently created—at far lower levels, and were usually buried somewhere along the complex chain of command, ready to rise flaming to the surface generations hence.

Once again he called Zenorra and Oberlieu into his presence.

"Good God," he muttered, more to himself than to them. "It's even worse than before!" He looked up at Zenorra. "I issued good, intelligent, proper orders, orders specifically designed to avoid bureaucratic turmoil and stagnancy, orders that should have freed me for more important matters than the stuff I'm dealing with every day. What went wrong?"

Zenorra shrugged. "What's wrong has nothing to do with you or your intentions, Director," he said. "What's wrong is the nature of Man and of his empire. Have you noticed that, paradoxical as it seems, when Man and his possessions are at their smallest and weakest, his government is usually a democracy, giving the people the broadest and most vocal representation. As Man and his empire grow larger and more powerful, quicker and more forceful decisions are required, and the government grows progressively less representative, from republic to oligarchy. And now, with an empire that literally encompasses the entire galaxy, the crying need is for one ultimate authority. There are too many diverse races and diverse interests for any form of fair representation; all that is left is the iron rule of one man. Call it what you will, but the proper word is 'monarchy.' Admittedly, you can handle only the tiniest percentage of the decisions personally, but in this case the appearance must be of a single leader whose rule is not subject to question or debate, whose power is absolute. I'll tell you something else, Director: When you repeal your orders, as you surely will, the problems will not abate one whit. Our means of governing will remain inefficient, literally thousands of worlds with legitimate problems and grievances will be ignored or mishandled, and problems sown decades and centuries ago will continue to crop up to embarrass us.

"On the other hand, abdication of any of your powers will ultimately result in anarchy. Inefficient as our system is, it is still more effective than any other means of governing an empire this size. We've simply come too far to go back. Any form of election would take half a century, and the power void created by fifty years without an ultimate authority would be intolerable. The worlds of the Commonwealth are too economically and culturally interdependent upon each other ever to go back to isolationism. Even the alien races have been bound to us militarily and economically. No, the only alternative to this is a galaxy-wide state of anarchy, and I do not consider that to be an acceptable one."

"Nor do I," said Vestolian with a sigh. "I suppose, though, that every Director has to find it out for himself."

Zenorra nodded sadly.

"Cancel all previous directives," said Vestolian presently. "We'll simply have to make do with things as they are, and drink an occasional bittersweet toast to things as they could never have been."

And the Director of the Commonwealth, wishing that he were anyone else in the universe, ate a solitary dinner and retired early.

That evening an emigration proclamation issued sixty-three years earlier by his grandfather was finally put into effect on a world that had not yet been incorporated into most maps of the Commonwealth. He was awakened in the middle of the night to be informed that he was at war again.

18: The Symbiotics

> ... It was inevitable that Man should ultimately
> turn his eyes toward other galaxies. The problems
> confronting him as he attempted to reach outward
> beyond his immediate stellar group dwarfed in both
> magnitude and difficulty every other challenge he had
> ever faced. Indeed, the mere act of survival on a trip
> of more than a million light-years to the nearest
> neighboring galaxy required the most innovative
> approach. . . .

> —*Man: Twelve Millennia of
> Achievement*

> (No mention of the symbiotics can be found in
> *Origin and History of the Sentient Races*.)

Things had been going pretty well for Man. He owned,
and ran, about as much of the galaxy as he was ever going
to. There were still some worlds and a few entire systems that
he had not assimilated, but only because he had thoroughly
examined them and found them wanting. There were still a
handful of races that existed outside the Commonwealth's
enormous economic web, but only because they had so little
of value to offer that Man hadn't gotten around to them yet.

And so, seeking new challenges, Man turned his vision outward. The notion had existed for centuries, perhaps for millennia, and had finally been put into words by the current Director of the Floating Kingdom: Man's destiny had only begun in this galaxy. It would come to fruition with nothing less than the entire universe.

There was a lot of patriotic and philosophic gobbledegook, but the gist of it was quite simple: Man, for all practical purposes, now ruled the galaxy as completely as the galaxy could be ruled. The next step was the exploration and ultimate annexation of the Andromeda galaxy.

The most immediate and serious problem was the unbelievably vast distance which, for the first time in Man's history, would not be measured in inches or feet or miles or parsecs, but in hundreds of thousands of light-years.

The initial plans called for a miles-long spaceship, populated with ten or twelve couples to begin with, and able to hold not only them but five generations of their progeny. The cost was prohibitive, but what the Director wanted the Director usually got, regardless of cost.

Then, a few years into the project, an obscure scientist on one of the domed Capellan colonies came up with another breakthrough in spaceflight, or rather, with the first truly major improvement in almost seven thousand years. It was nothing more than a complex formula for a Reduced Tachyon Drive (which, paradoxically, produced far greater speed than the standard model), but it seemed to check out and was submitted to those in charge of the project. They tested it, discovered to their surprise that it worked as well in fact as in principle, and incorporated it into their plans.

Now the trip would be made not in generations, but in years: eleven of them, to be exact. A three-year survey of the new galaxy would follow, and the crew would be home to report their findings a quarter century after they left.

Then the plan had to be modified once again. There would be no crew, and possibly no flight at all. The requisite engines were so huge, so unstable, so incapable of working at anything other than achieving an undreamed-of speed, that excess weight simply could not be accommodated. Man found himself back at the dawn of the Space Age in that respect: He had the firepower to reach Andromeda in years rather than eons, but the firepower couldn't accommodate an extra ton beyond its own weight.

Science grappled with the problem, and there was no doubt that it would eventually be solved. But the Director had no interest in eventualities; his idea of a fitting footnote in the history books would be the attainment of an Andromeda colony within his lifetime.

Which was where Bartol came in. A lot of people wondered what a biologist was doing on the Andromeda Project, but the fact of the matter was that, for all practical purposes, he *was* the Project. Miniaturization of controls and compression of air and foodstuffs had gone about as far as they could go, and they still took up a hundredfold more room than was available. Even a Deepsleep chamber took too much room and power, and while the supplies required for a "frozen" pilot were greatly diminished, they were still too much for the ships to hold.

Then one of the bright boys in the lab suggested that the Project look into utilization of the Hunks, and since Bartol was the leading Hunk authority around, he was commandeered and put to work forthwith.

Nobody, not even Bartol, knew exactly what made the Hunks tick. They were as weirdly constituted a race of beings as had ever been discovered, and Psychology had taken more than four centuries to finally declare that they were sentient. The average Hunk looked like a large, green, slimy amoeba. It possessed no sensory organs that had yet been detected, though it was obviously able to sense the presence of others. It moved by the most awkward and inefficient crawling mechanism yet devised by Nature, and seemed to have no discernible top or bottom.

But it did possess one thing that made it invaluable: a body chemistry that inhaled a carbon dioxide compound, exhaled an oxygen-nitrogen compound, ingested the constituents of human waste, and excreted the constituents of human nourishment.

In brief, it could be hooked up to a human pilot in a totally symbiotic relationship. Obviously neither life form would exhale or excrete quite as much as it inhaled or ingested, but the difference was slight enough so that the ship could carry the extra amounts that were necessary. It was the only possible means of salvaging the Andromeda Project in the forseeable future, and both the Floating Kingdom and the Project scientists were quick to embrace it.

The pilots were another matter altogether.

Softly and infrequently at first, then ever more vocally and incessantly, they objected to the symbiotic relationship.

They object, said Psychology, to the concept of living off

another's creature's leavings, of eating its excrement and breathing what it exhales.

"Then condition them," said Bartol.

So Psychology took the potential pilots away for a month, and when they came back they had no objections whatsoever to the less tasteful physical aspects of symbiosis.

And they still didn't like it.

They now object, said Psychology, to the fact that their health and well-being depends on the health and well-being of a totally alien being. They don't want to die simply because a Hunk gets sick.

"Then teach them Hunk physiology and medicine," said Bartol.

So Biology took the pilots off for a crash course in Hunk physiology, and made sure they knew even more about keeping Hunks healthy than about themselves.

And they still hated it.

Bartol finally called Jesser, the pilot most likely to make the first voyage, into his office and offered to discuss the problem with him.

Jesser entered the room, a chip on his shoulder and a baleful glare on his face.

"I understand we still have a problem of sorts," said Bartol, offering the pilot a drink, which Jesser refused.

"None that can't be solved by getting rid of the Hunks," said Jesser.

"I'm afraid that's totally out of the question," said Bartol. "There is simply no practical way of making an intergalactic voyage without them. Besides, the Hunks aren't making any trouble for the Project; it's you and the other pilots."

"Then get yourself some new pilots," said Jesser. "Because I'm not tying into any Hunk, not for twenty-five years, not for twenty-five minutes."

"So I've been told," said Bartol. "I don't suppose you'd like to explain your reasons to me. I know that you feel no physical revulsion to a life-giving symbiotic relationship, and I know you are every bit as capable of keeping a Hunk partner alive as I am. So what seems to be the problem?"

"I'm just not going to do it," said Jesser, softly but firmly. "Go ahead and fire me if you want. I can get work elsewhere."

"If you were the only pilot with this attitude, I'd fire you in two seconds," said Bartol. "But you're not, so I'm going to get to the bottom of this. What is your objection to having a

Hunk keep you alive long enough to be the first sentient being to visit another galaxy?"

"You don't count very well, do you?" said Jesser.

"Now what the hell is that supposed to mean?" said Bartol as Jesser turned and left the room.

He consulted Psychology again, and shortly thereafter the answer came back to him.

The pilots had no objection to letting the Hunks keep them alive. They had no objection to the threat of death facing them should a Hunk sicken or die.

But they objected like all hell to the thought of a Hunk being in the first ship to reach Andromeda.

"But that's crazy!" exclaimed Bartol.

"Maybe so," said Lavers of Psychology. "But that's the problem in a nutshell. This is going to be Man's finest hour, his greatest achievement, and they are totally unwilling to let any other race share in it."

"It's the stupidest thing I've ever heard of," said Bartol. "We can't get there without the Hunks."

"You know it, and I know it, and *they* know it. Their answer is that we should wait until we have the technology to do it on our own, as Man has always done things."

"So condition it out of them."

"No chance," said Lavers.

"What are you talking about?" demanded Bartol. "You got them conditioned to accept a symbiotic hookup, which is much more repugnant."

"It's *physically* more repugnant," said Lavers. "And we've reached the point where we can condition people to withstand just about any physical hardship. And I won't deny that it's probably mentally more repugnant, at least to most of us, and we can overcome that too. But when you talk about the current problem, you're asking me to change everything that makes Man Man, and I don't think I can do it. Oh, I can put them into the deepest hypnotic sleep you ever saw, and drill it into them a million times an hour that Hunks are necessary cogs in the operation, and not only don't want credit for the mission but won't even understand that a mission is taking place. And the conditioning will hold up for a while—a year, or two years, or ten years—but sooner or later they're going to break through it. It's easier to condition a man to eat and breathe when the alternative is starving and suffocating than to share a triumph with another race when the alternative is to not share that triumph."

"Rubbish!" said Bartol. "Just condition them and get them halfway there, and I guarantee they're not going to pull the plug once they break through it."

"Well, you're the man in charge of this part of the project," said Lavers with a sigh, "so I'll do what you tell me to do. But I'll make you a little side bet."

"Oh?"

"I'll bet you five hundred credits that the ship doesn't make it there and back."

"I confidently expect to be dead and buried long before that eventuality," said Bartol. "Twenty-five years is a long time."

"It won't take twenty-five years," said Lavers.

"You're on," said Bartol. "You know, I think you're as odd as Jesser is."

"Perhaps," said Lavers.

So the pilots were conditioned again, and within a year the *Andromeda I* had left the orbit in which it had been constructed and was hurtling through the intergalactic void at an unimaginable speed.

Jesser had indeed been chosen to pilot the mission, and when he was two years out from port with no untoward incidents, four more Andromeda ships were launched, each responsible for charting a different section of the neighboring galaxy.

Bartol spent most of the next year in the Project Control Building, checking the daily readouts of the five Hunks, while Lavers did the same for the pilots. The ships were exactly on course and on schedule, the inhabitants were in perfect physical health, and the Director finally made news of the Andromeda Project available to the media.

The people ate it up. Once again a new sense of purpose, of competition, was stirred within them. Andromeda, most of them agreed, would do for starters, just as Sirius had done some millennia back. But Andromeda was just one galaxy, and not such a big and impressive one at that. There were more than fifty galaxies just in our local group, and then . . .

"And then I noticed this fluctuation," said one of the minor functionaries on the Andromeda staff.

Lavers looked at the readout and shook his head.

"Not good," he said. "Not good at all."

"What seems to be the problem?" said Bartol, who had wandered over.

"Encephalogram," said Lavers.

"On who?"

"Jesser."

"What does it mean?" asked Bartol.

"Perhaps nothing," said Lavers. "But if you'll recall a wager we made some years back, I think if I were you I'd get my money ready."

"Based on one slight deviation from the norm?" said Bartol.

"When you're hooked into an alien being three hundred thousand light-years from the nearest star, there is no such thing as a *slight* deviation," said Lavers.

The deviation remained so long that it finally became accepted as a standard reading—until the other pilots began showing the same deviation, all between two and three years into their flight.

"But it isn't the same at all," said Lavers grimly. "It's smaller, slighter. Jesser's has changed so minutely over the past couple of years that it's hardly seemed like a change at all, until you compare it to the other four."

Bartol merely grunted, and expressed confidence in the basic self-preservational instinct of the five pilots.

And then one day Jesser's encephalic reading went right off the scale and came back to his original norm, all in the space of four hours.

"That's it," said Lavers. "He's broken through. In a couple of years the others will do it too."

"So he's broken through," said Bartol. "It changes nothing. He'll evaluate the situation, realize that turning back without being able to slingshot around a star or a black hole will take more fuel than he's got, and he'll keep going. After all, he's a Man, and Men preserve themselves."

"Men do a lot of things," said Lavers quietly.

And, 350,000 light-years away, Jesser took one last baleful look at his companion and slowly unhooked his breathing apparatus.

19: The Philosophers

   . . . It was with the establishment of the University at Aristotle that the Commonwealth began churning out a steady stream of brilliant philosophers as regularly as clockwork. In fact, in retrospect we can say with some assurance that it was during the middle of the Seventh Galactic Millennium, and more specifically 6400–6700 G.E., that philosophy graduated from the vague realm of an art and joined the sciences. Some of the more brilliant treatises are still on file, both on the various Deluros VI planetoids and also at the huge library on Deluros VIII. . . .

          —*Man: Twelve Millennia of Achievement*

   . . . The subject of philosophy seems to have taken a very unphilosophical, and eventually fatal, turning somewhere around 6500 G.E. The dividing line can be drawn with the career of Belore Theriole (6488–6602 G.E.), unquestionably the last of the great human philosophers. . . .

          —*Origin and History of the Sentient Races*, Vol. 9

"Brilliant!" said Hillyar. "Absolutely brilliant!"

He put the thick sheaf of papers down on the large table, leaned back, and gave the impression of a man trying very hard to strut without moving his legs.

"I told you it was," said Brannot. "I'd like to see us offer him a spot on the faculty right now, before some other school grabs him."

The other two members of the examining board nodded in agreement.

"Before I make it official," said Brannot, "I'd like it on the record that we're all in accord."

"Absolutely," said Hillyar. The others echoed him.

"Good. Then it's settled," said Brannot. He turned to the small figure seated silently in a corner of the room. "Professor Theriole, while the affairs of our university can hardly be of more than passing interest to you, we would nonetheless be honored if a person of your stature would add her name to our recommendation."

Belore Theriole looked up, brushing a wisp of graying hair from her forehead. "With no offense intended, I believe I am not inclined to do so."

"Have we done something to offend you?" asked Brannot with a note of worry in his voice.

"No," said Belore thoughtfully, "I don't think I would go so far as to say that you have offended me."

"Then could it be that you don't agree with our assessment of the thesis?" persisted Brannot.

"Oh, I'm sure that the student in question and the thesis in question are equally brilliant," said Belore.

"I detect a note of distaste there," said Brannot. "Could I prevail upon you to clarify your statement?"

"If you insist, Professor Brannot," said Belore with a sigh.

"Insist is too strong a word," said Brannot. "Let us say that I earnestly request it. After all, when a philosopher of your stature does our humble university the singular honor of sitting in on our examination board, it behooves us to learn everything we can about ourselves and our school from the viewpoint of such a distinguished outsider."

"It's too bad I gave up blushing when I was still a young girl," said Belore wryly, "or you would quite turn my head, Professor." There was a general chuckling among the learned men, and Belore continued:

"When I was asked to come here, I was only too happy to

216

accept your invitation. After all, the planet Aristotle is a pretty fascinating concept, and I had never been here before.

"And I must say that, physically, Aristotle has even surpassed my expectations. I suppose the thought of a university world, a planet the size of old Earth being turned into a garden of *academiae*, has to be seen to be appreciated. Your libraries alone would be the envy of any system in the galaxy, and the architects of your buildings have undoubtedly secured themselves that special corner of heaven reserved for artistic geniuses. Furthermore, from what I've been told of your entrance requirements, there isn't a dullard on the whole planet, if you exclude such so-called dignitaries as myself. Aristotle draws only the cream of the Commonwealth's young intellectuals, and it obviously treats them as befits their potential.

"So much for the physical aspects. As for the curricula, certainly there is no more thorough or varied course of studies available anywhere. The students, or at least those few I've spoken with, seem relatively well-balanced and incredibly quick-witted. The faculty, it goes without saying, is the finest that could be assembled.

"Having said this much, I will now go one step further. I cannot, of course, speak for other fields of study, but in my own specialty, philosophy, I think you unquestionably have the most able minds the race of Man has yet been able to produce."

"Then you approve of what we're doing here?" said Brannot smugly.

"On the contrary," said Belore with a smile. "I find it stifling and irrelevant."

"What!" The four men were on their feet at once, more in surprise than outrage.

"I have never seen such potential for good so flagrantly wasted," said Belore. "It seems almost inconceivable that a race of sentient beings capable of creating such a world as Aristotle could so blatantly misuse and misdirect it."

"Professor Theriole," said Brannot, struggling to regain his composure, "would you care to explain yourself?"

"I'll try," said Belore, "though I doubt that it will do much good. If you were to agree with me, then this situation would never have arisen in the first place."

"Why not try us and see?" suggested Hillyar.

"I intend to," said Belore. "Let me begin by asking a couple of questions, if I may."

"Proceed," said Brannot haughtily.

"Professor Brannot, what is the position of the Philosophy Department on the works of St. Thomas Aquinas?"

"A brilliant primitive philosopher," said Brannot. "Unmatched in his day, but definitely discredited."

"Discredited?" said Belore. "You mean his religious views and arguments?"

"Yes."

"Including the First Cause argument?"

"Certainly. It can be disproved with the set of all negative integers, the set of all proper fractions, the—"

"I quite agree," interrupted Belore. "What of Plato?"

"We study him, of course. As Man's first great philosopher—"

"He wasn't the first, but let it pass," said Belore quietly.

"Anyway, we do study him. But again, the man has been disproved, in practice as well as in theory, many times over. Why, the Bonite colony of a couple of centuries ago was set up according to his *Republic*, and lasted only a handful of years."

"Too many philosopher-kings and not enough streetcleaners, as I recall it," said Belore. "How about the works of Braxtok of Canphor VII?"

"He wasn't even a Man!" said Brannot.

"Does that make his view of the universe any less valid?" asked Belore.

"Not at all," said Hillyar hastily. "And, in fact, we do have a number of courses in alien philosophies."

"Oh?" asked Belore. "How many?"

"I haven't got the figures before me," said Hillyar, "but there are quite a few."

"I had the figures before me a few hours ago," said Belore. "I found seventeen. Seventeen out of more than six hundred."

"I don't know what you're driving at," said Brannot.

"Simply this," said Belore. "I've been going over the various doctoral theses that have been presented to this board, and I find them very disquieting."

"I thought you said you found the students to be singularly brilliant," said Hillyar.

"I do," said Belore. "The same cannot be said for their theses."

"I found them exceptionally well-reasoned," said Brannot.

"So did I," agreed Belore. "Those I bothered to read."

"Then I fail to see your objection."

"I thought you might," said Belore. "I looked at some fifteen doctoral dissertations. Seven of them concerned the ethics of our conduct toward alien races. Three more examined Man's relationship to his technology. The other five dealt, to some degree, with justifying some of the political, military, and economic excesses of the Monarchy."

"You mean the Commonwealth," said Hillyar gently.

"I know what I mean," said Belore. "And, similarly, I know what I don't like about those papers. Gentlemen, whether purposely or not, the subject of philosophy seems in grave danger of being turned into a branch of the political sciences."

"Nonsense," scoffed Brannot. "How can an intellectual of your stature draw such a conclusion based on a handful of treatises?"

"If this particular handful differs appreciably in content from last year's, or the year before that, I'll change my opinion," said Belore. "But I suspect that it doesn't. And that is what disturbs me. That, and your attitudes.

"For instance, I mentioned Aquinas, and you spouted off a mathematical rebuttal to an esoteric theory beside which the whole of mathematics dwindles into insignificance. *Is* there a relationship between cause and effect in the universe? If so, *is* there a first and original cause of all Creation? Don't bother me with negative integers, or some astronomical theory of contracting and expanding universes. I want to know: Is there or is there not some intellect or life force which, purposefully or otherwise, set the entire process in motion? Aquinas proposed this argument, rightly or wrongly, from a combination of intellect, faith, and empiricism, and you answer it with mathematics and astronomy. I say to you that your answers don't amount to a hill of beans.

"Plato proposed a utopian republic, with its own set of idealized ethical imperatives. And because one small group of disillusioned radicals failed to put it into practice, you consider Plato to be archaic and discredited. Rather I should say that a philosophy department that negates the works of Plato because of what happened to the Bonite colony has discredited itself without doing the last bit of damage to Plato.

"As for Braxtok, he—or, rather, it—came up with perhaps the most complex ethical argument ever devised for the assumption of divinity. Admittedly it wasn't a divinity that would appeal to any Man, but that hardly makes the argument any the less valid.

"What I'm getting at is this: It seems to me that philosophy has forgotten not only its roots but also its purpose. No one is asking questions about the nature of Man, or his place in the universe, or the existence or need for a deity. Just because Descartes concluded that no one could doubt his own existence doesn't make it true—or false, for that matter. Why is no one asking these vital questions, examining these vital arguments, any longer?

"Gentlemen, you are not turning out philosophers. Far from it. What you are doing is creating the most brilliant crop of pragmatists in our history. But pragmatism is not the only branch of philosophy, and political and social doctrines are not the only—or even the legitimate—purposes of philosophy.

"Your young men and women—and you yourselves—want to know how something works, or why it works, or if it works, or what the effect of its working will be. All other considerations—such as is it right or wrong, good or evil, consistent or inconsistent with the nature of Man—are either ignored or restructured to fit into the basic pragmatic concept under consideration.

"And that, gentlemen, is why I will not add my name or influence to your petition to get one more nonphilosopher added to this staff of nonphilosophers. I weep for the Critique of Pure Reason in this day of Pure Practicality."

"My dear Professor Theriole," said Brannot, "do you really feel that we on the staff, or our students for that matter, have no understanding of what you would doubtless term the pure philosophers? Perhaps my knowledge of them is not as great as yours, but I am not totally unversed in these aspects of philosophy. But the difference between understanding them and appreciating them, in a positive manner, is considerable, and it is here that you part company not only with us, but with the bulk of our students. After all, we don't hold a gun to their heads and tell them that their doctoral theses must have some applicability to the real world."

"One would never know it to read them," said Belore dryly.

"Professor," continued Brannot, "we stand at a crossroads in the field of philosophy. We can continue to rehash the old unanswered and unanswerable questions, and philosophy will then remain what it has always been: a parlor game of mental gymnastics, played by ivory-tower intellectuals. Or, on the other hand, we can try to apply both old and new philosophical concepts to our daily lives and make them work for us."

"I was laboring under the obviously erroneous impression

220

that we've already put philosophical concepts to work for us in the past," said Belore. "The Ten Commandments come to mind, but I'll wager that there must have been one or two others during the past ten thousand years."

"I grant you that," said Brannot, "but it only supports my argument: that philosophy can and should deal with reality. Take, for example, Bishop Berkeley's proof of God, which is the one human argument for deity not as yet disproven. I ask you, not as one professor to another, but as one human being to another: Who really gives a damn if there is some mystical Unseen Observer or not? Or take the hallowed Descartes, who thought and therefore was. I have no doubts as to my own existence: I've got ulcers, aches, pains, and worries to prove to my satisfaction that I'm here. But Descartes carried it one step further, inferring the existence of the entire universe from the singular fact that *he* existed. More power to him. But I can infer the existence of a large block of granite sitting in front of this building from my own existence, or I can not infer it; and in either case, it has no effect whatsoever on the truth of the inference.

"On the other hand," he continued, "if I were to say, 'I hunger, therefore I am,' it would have a little more relevance, because my next step would be how to assuage my various hungers, and this would lead me not only into practical proposals but ethical considerations as well. What I am trying to say, Professor, is that philosophy must *do* something. It can't just lie there as a logical toy for academic dilettantes."

"Needless to say, I disagree," said Belore. "What you are describing is simply not philosophy. Practical politicians determine our public ethics and behavior whether we like it or not, and half a hundred sciences tend to our hungers and comforts. Philosophy, true philosophy, is concerned with the soul, and I use the word in a nonreligious sense. Or, if you prefer a more palatable definition, it is concerned with that section of the mind—and notice that I didn't say the human mind—that is not the concern of the psychiatrist or biologist. Its purpose is to give an overview of the Universe and of Life and of Being, all spelled with capital letters. Its purpose is no more to answer questions than to ask them, no more to solve problems than to give new insights into them. I repeat: Pragmatism is a philosophy, but it is not the only philosophy, nor even among the most important."

"Then why do the vast majority of our philosophers seem to disagree with you?" asked Hillyar.

"Because they've been conditioned by men like you," said Belore bluntly. "Besides, this isn't a field like politics, where the majority rules. The fact that most of them agree with you means nothing except that more of them are wrong than might reasonably be expected to be wrong under other circumstances."

"I perceive," said Brannot, "that neither of us is about to convince the other of the correctness of our viewpoint."

"I suppose not, more's the pity," said Belore. "Gentlemen, I think we might as well cut this short before tempers begin rising. You may send more dissertations to me, and I shall comment on the correctness of the arguments, since I have said I would do so. However, I think we would all be happier if I had nothing further to do with them, or with you."

And with that she arose and walked from the building, alternately feeling younger and older than her years.

"Well!" said Hillyar after a few minutes' silence. "What do you make of that?"

"She was a brilliant woman in her day," said Brannot slowly. "It's rather disconcerting to see her so out of touch with reality. Philosophy would forever be an art rather than a science if she had her way."

"What gall!" said Hillyar. "As if we had no knowledge at all of Plato and Kant and Aquinas. What does she want us to do—insist that every doctoral candidate spend half a lifetime contemplating the lint in his navel?"

"Let's not be too harsh in our judgment of her," said Brannot loftily. "Remember—that frail, wrinkled shell of a body once housed a truly superb mind."

And with that, he picked up the next thesis, which presented some telling arguments justifying the economic subjugation of the natives of Broward III, and was soon lost in rapturous fascination at the intricate chain of reasoning put forth.

20: The Architects

... Unquestionably the greatest of the Commonwealth's architects was Ebar Mallow (6700–6755 G.E.), who for reasons unknown seems to have vanished from the ranks of the profession after the completion of the unfortunate Bureau of Alien Affairs project. Nonetheless, that single edifice assures him a place in the vanguard of the history of human architecture ....

> —*Man: Twelve Millennia of Achievement*

... The ill-conceived Bureau still stands today, and is in many respects quite the most remarkable building ever erected by any race. Much of the credit for its design, if not its ultimate fate, must go to Ebar Mallow, perhaps the most brilliant architect to come on the scene since the creation of Caliban. Even now, the Bureau still functions as it was designed to do; the pity of it, of course, is that ...

> —*Origin and History of the Sentient Races*, Vol. 9

"What the hell is *that*?" asked Mallow, gesturing toward the huge structure that was being moved into his office.

"That, my bookish friend, is a chair," said Verlor, walking into the office as the workmen left.

"A chair for *what*?" demanded Mallow, trying to picture the type of creature that could fit comfortably into the thing and failing dismally.

"The ambassador from Castor V," said Verlor.

"I didn't even know Castor had any intelligent life," said Mallow.

"According to our psychologists, they crossed over from nonthinking beast to thinking beast about three thousand years ago. According to the Castorites, they've been an intelligent species for longer than Man has been around."

"Surely he's not coming here to debate the issue," said Mallow disgustedly. "I'll be happy to grant his species intelligence since the Big Bang if it'll make him happy. Especially if he can fill that chair."

"He's got other reasons for seeing you," said Verlor. "As I understand it, he wants to talk about the Bureau."

"Not a chance!" snapped Mallow. "I spent seven years getting those plans approved by the Floating Kingdom, and I'm not about to make any last-minute changes because of some elephantine bigwig from Castor!"

"Calm down," said Verlor. "We don't even know what he wants."

"It doesn't matter," said Mallow. "No changes!"

"Look," said Verlor. "We've all got orders. Yours are to design and build the Bureau. Mine are to see that our guest is treated with every courtesy. This is no small-time bureaucrat; he's the Castorian ambassador to the Commonwealth."

"You mean Castor's not even a member of the Commonwealth?" said Mallow.

"Its status is up in the air at the moment. They've been asked—politely—to join. If they decide not to . . ."

"They'll be asked *un*politely," concluded Mallow.

"In all likelihood," agreed Verlor. "At any rate, any unpleasantness with the ambassador is to be initiated by the Floating Kingdom, not by you. Understood?"

"Understood," said Mallow distastefully. "When do we expect this visitor of yours?"

"If I may be so bold as to intrude upon your discussion," said the cold, noncommital tones of a T-pack, "I am quite ready to proceed with our meeting."

The two men turned to the doorway, and saw a huge, thick-limbed being standing there, its blunt, broad head covered by a combination plastic mask and T-pack, its heavily armored skin exposed to the air. It had the three-legged, tripodal structure and stance common to most of the denizens of high-gravity worlds. Affixed to the mask were small medallions that obviously represented medals and official status.

"How long have you been standing there?" demanded Mallow.

"My name is Krotar," said the Castorian, ignoring the question. "May we proceed?"

"I'll leave you two gentlemen for a few minutes," said Verlor. "Buzz me if you need anything."

"I object to being termed a gentleman," said Krotar, "but since the T-pack may be translating Terran inaccurately or too literally, I shall offer no formal complaint."

Mallow shot Verlor a who-the-hell-does-he-think-he-is look, then turned back to Krotar.

"Well, Mr. Krotar," he said, "just what can I do for you?"

"You may begin by referring to me as Ambassador Krotar," said the Castorian.

"Whatever you wish, Ambassador," said Mallow, wondering what the *less* diplomatic Castorians must be like.

"And," said Krotar, nodding an acknowledgment, "you can show me the plans for the Bureau of Alien Affairs."

"Is there some particular reason why you're interested in them?" asked Mallow as he darkened the room and threw the Tri-D mockup of the Bureau's exterior into the area separating him from Krotar.

"I would not ask without a reason," said Krotar. "You will explain the plans."

"As you wish." Mallow shrugged and began to recite the stock speech he had given perhaps a thousand times during the past two years. "The new Bureau of Alien Affairs, to be erected on Deluros IV, will be rectangular at the base, and will remain that way although tapering by almost fifty percent by the time it reaches its peak, which will be almost two kilometers above the ground. At its base the Bureau will be four kilometers long and three kilometers wide. The outer facade, as you can see, will contain various bits of art from almost all of the known cultures of the galaxy."

"Including Castor?" asked Krotar.

"If Castor is adopted into the Commonwealth, I have no doubt that its art will be incorporated into the facade," said

Mallow, devoutly hoping that the Floating Kingdom would require a better display of manners before welcoming it into the fold.

He flicked a number of switches on his desk, and the Tri-D picture changed, now showing a miniaturized cross-section of the huge lobby of the building.

"Now, although the Bureau will be multi-environmental, the lobby through which all entities will enter and exit will not be so treated. The atmosphere on Deluros IV is almost nonexistent, and the gravity is about half that of Deluros VIII. It would be an easy matter to supply it with an atmosphere and artificial gravity more to Man's liking," he said, getting in the dig, "but there will be no favoritism in the Bureau.

"Throughout the lobby will be numerous signs and recording stands, in all the known languages of the galaxy, directing the various member races to the proper areas. There will be literally hundreds of moving courseways crisscrossing and encircling the lobby, each of them ending at a designated elevator. The elevators are designed to hold a minimum of ten members of any race at a time, and in the case of some of the smaller races, they will accommodate almost one hundred of them.

"The elevators will respond to each race's own language, or to a T-pack using Terran or any of the five recognized forms of Galactic. Once an elevator is told that no more entities will be entering, it will hermetically seal its doors, and within a matter of thirty to sixty seconds the atmosphere of the entities' home world will be established and its gravity put into effect. Unless otherwise directed, the elevator will proceed to the floor or sector reserved for use by that species. Incidentally, most of the elevators can move horizontally as well as vertically, since very few species will need an entire floor of their own.

"Each elevator, as well as each office, will be supplied with an ample number of protective suits designed to fit that elevator's—or office's—race, plus atmospheric helmets and facemasks."

He flicked two more switches, and the view of the elevator's interior was replaced with a cross-section of one of the upper levels of the building.

"Now here we have a typical floor plan—the 288th, as I recall. Each section is more than ample to hold up to three hundred members of a race, although it can easily be compartmentalized by so programming one of the desk computers. As you will notice, there is an impenetrable barrier about midway up the south hallway; this separates the environments between races sharing the floor. The only way for a being to cross from one section to the other is by means of the horizontal elevator. I should also point out that the elevators will move to their destinations immediately, but will not open until their atmosphere has been drained and until each passenger is wearing a protective suit. To borrow an old military term, it might be construed as a fail-safe system.

"Each office can be placed in immediate communication with any other office. All interoffice communications will be translated instantaneously en route unless caller or receiver designates otherwise.

"Every race will have its own cafeteria and sleeping quarters, as well as libraries and, where possible, commercial video transmissions from its home planet. And, of course, each race will be provided with recreational and medical facilities."

"Will there be a security force?" asked Krotar.

"Absolutely," said Mallow.

"What will be its composition?"

"Men," said Mallow.

"I see," said Krotar. "Why, if I may ask, is the Bureau of Alien Affairs to be erected on Deluros IV, when Deluros VIII or the Floating Kingdom would seem to be the more logical place to build it, if the race of Man is truly interested in convincing the other races of the galaxy of its goodwill?"

"I'm not a politician, Ambassador Krotar," said Mallow. "I'm just an architect. I was told to erect it on Deluros IV, and that's where it will go. If I might offer an unofficial opinion, I would estimate that the cost of placing the Bureau on Deluros VIII, which has a far greater gravity, would be so high as to make such a move impossible."

"Are you trying to tell me that a race that could build the Floating Kingdom and the Deluros VI planetoids, and can keep a standing army and navy numbering in the tens of billions, could not find the economic and architectural means to erect a single dwelling for nonhuman races on Deluros VIII?"

"I'm not trying to tell you a damned thing, Ambassador!" said Mallow in exasperation. "If you want to create a scene, why not hunt up Verlor? He's in charge of racial incidents. I just design buildings."

Krotar stood up, towering over both Mallow and the Tri-D image of the 288th floor. For just an instant Mallow feared for his safety, but the Castorian merely stared at him. If there was any expression of rage or indignation on his face, Mallow couldn't detect it.

"I think," said Krotar, and his tones came out infuriatingly flat and unemotional through the T-pack, "that you need not bother adding any Castorian artwork to your Bureau."

"I hadn't really planned to," said Mallow. "Now suppose you tell me just what you came here for."

"That is my business," said the Castorian. "Yours, as you pointed out, is erecting buildings."

After he had left, Verlor came back in.

"Well?" he asked.

"Well what?" asked Mallow.

"What did he want?"

"I haven't the foggiest notion," said Mallow. "He came in, acted uppity as all getout, looked at the plans for the Bureau, found out that the security police will be Men, and told me that he didn't want any part of it."

"I thought so," said Verlor. "He's the ninth one to back out—and he wasn't even in."

"I don't understand," said Mallow.

"Neither do I," said Verlor. "But, for whatever reason, there seems to be some movement afoot among the aliens. It's not open rebellion or anything like that. It's more that they've decided to make some trivial gesture of independence, and they've hit upon the Bureau."

"That sounds awfully farfetched."

"Maybe," said Verlor. "And yet, not one of them has given a decent reason. The Canphorites backed out because they wanted four entire floors, and we only offered them one and part of a second. The Lemm objected to having to import members of their own race to prepare their food. The Emrans didn't want the Bureau to be anywhere near the Deluros system. And so on."

"Why didn't you tell me before?" asked Mallow.

"Because the Director has ordered us to go ahead with the construction of the Bureau as scheduled."

"Well," said Mallow disgustedly, "I suppose I can always reconvert the Canphorites' floor to some other environment, and—"

"No," said Verlor. "It's to be built as approved. If certain

228

races don't occupy it willingly, well, we have certain pressures that can be applied."

"You sure you don't want me to turn a couple of floors into a hospital?" said Mallow sardonically.

"Don't joke," said Verlor. "You may have to."

"Is there anything we can do to make the Bureau more attractive to them?" asked Mallow. "It sure doesn't sound as if it's the Bureau itself they object to, but I'd hate to see it go to waste."

"It won't be wasted," said Verlor. "Don't forget: With no atmosphere on Deluros IV, the damned thing could stand for ten million years and look as new as the day it was built. Which, among other reasons, is why we picked an airless world. They never thought of that at Caliban, and the Cartography complex is under continual repair and renovation. That won't happen with the Bureau."

"No," said Mallow grimly. "It'll just be built and forgotten. What the hell is the matter with these creatures, anyway? Don't they know that this is going to be the greatest single architectural feat since Caliban? Maybe even greater, since Caliban never was multi-environmental."

"The problem," said Verlor, "is that you're viewing it as an architect, and they're viewing it as political and racial entities. You know, the Commonwealth has gotten so huge that it's getting damned near impossible to administer it efficiently, and so the aliens are feeling their oats, pushing until they find a weak spot. They know how much publicity the Bureau has gotten in the media, and how much fighting we had to do to push through the appropriation. What better way to embarrass us than to refuse to take part in it?"

Verlor's words proved uncomfortably prophetic. In the next few days thirty more races decided not to avail themselves of the Bureau's facilities, and within a year each and every nonhuman race in the Commonwealth had found some pretext or another for withdrawing its support.

Mallow had given too much of himself to the Bureau to surrender without a battle. He journeyed out to Lodin XI and was granted an audience with the native leaders.

"I am not unaware of the reasons for your action," he began. "I'm no politician, so I can't say whether you are fully justified in your goals or not. What I am is an architect, and what I have to offer you is a building unlike any ever before created or even conceived.

"You say you wish to live in harmony and equality with

229

Man," he continued, "and I will take you at your word. Well, this building, this entire concept, will allow you to do just that. And you—and all the other races, including Man—will be doing so in a public fishbowl. We will all function in harmony because we will have to do so; the only alternative will be to admit before the eyes of the galaxy that it cannot be done. Perhaps it can't, but we will never have a greater opportunity to try than now, with this building."

The Lodinites listened politely, and just as politely declined his offer.

Next on his list were the Canphor Twins.

"If nothing else," he pleaded, "don't use this noble project as a symbol of your spite for the race of Man. If you must be political, so be it. Don't pay your taxes, don't accept a human governor, don't allow the Commonwealth to keep military bases on your moons. But allow this Bureau to come to pass. It is the last best hope for the races of the galaxy."

The Canphorites jeered him out of the room.

By the time he reached the insectoid world of Procyon II, he had decided upon different tactics.

"Your life has undoubtedly been bitter," he told them. "I am just as disgusted and outraged at what our Navy did to you during the reign of Vestolian as you are. But you can't just withdraw from the marketplace of ideas and culture. Come to the Bureau. Prove that you're better than we are! You'll be given every opportunity to do so. Every facility will be open to you, every comfort will be provided. If you want to plot the downfall of the Commonwealth, what better place could there possibly be to do so than the Bureau, where you'll be in instant contact with other races who feel equally wronged?"

The Procyons, being insectoids, could not understand why the Bureau had been created in the first place. They bore Man no malice; indeed, they had replaced their decimated population in a handful of years. They simply could not relate to the problem. Why travel to the Bureau to eat and breathe? They could do that right here.

His next stop was Domar, but he didn't even get a chance to get out of his ship. The Domarians, one of the few ESPer races in the galaxy, knew everything he was prepared to say, and weren't buying any. After all, what need had a race of telepaths for close physical contact with other races?

At Terrazane he felt he had the means with which to finally strike a responsive chord.

"The people of Terrazane," he said, "are known throughout the galaxy for the magnificent edifices they construct in their cities. You, of all races, must understand that a project such as the Bureau has been designed to be used. To let it stand, an unused, sterile monument to futility, would border on the criminal. Surely the Terrazanes will not boycott the Bureau."

But he was wrong again, for the Terrazanes' racial art was nonfunctional. Huge, minutely embellished edifices covered the planet, but for no purpose other than the appreciation of the populace at large.

On Aldebaran XIII the reaction of the natives against what they felt to be a structure built by Man to assuage his conscience was so violent that he needed an armed guard to escort him back to his ship.

On Gamma Leporis IV, he met with a race of aquatic beings that had never been exploited by Man, had never been at war with Man, and had no reason whatsoever to feel inimical to Man. Garbed in a protective undersea suit, he used a modified T-pack to address their delegation.

"I am at a loss to understand why you have withdrawn your support from the Bureau," he told them. "We have always had an amicable relationship between our races, and since so very few races are aquatic, the potential to learn about the thousands of other sentient species is severely limited even for those of you who have journeyed to other worlds. But here at the Bureau, your opportunities to increase both your knowledge and your alliances would be virtually limitless. Ample living space would be provided you, and all of your needs—medical, social, religious, even sexual—would be provided for. Surely you, who have the most to gain from the Bureau and the least reason to embarrass my race, will reconsider your position."

They agreed with everything he said. The Bureau would make the task of contacting other races infinitely easier, and certainly they had nothing against Man, who had freed them, ages ago, from the tyrannical yoke of the Lemm. But, on the other hand, those few other races they had been in contact with felt that a gesture must be made against Man's iron-fisted control of the galaxy, and while they personally had only the highest regard for Man, they would not go against the will of the majority, especially in a situation such as this, where they were physiologically prohibited from gaining a full appreciation of the problem. They intended no offense, but under the circumstances . . .

And so it went, on world after world, with race after race. By the time he visited the twentieth alien planet, he found out that he was far from the only emissary of the Commonwealth trying to persuade the aliens to reconsider their stand. He struck paydirt on the twenty-seventh planet, Balok VII, only to have his work undone when the Commonwealth began putting economic sanctions on all alien worlds that had not yet come back into the fold. The Balokites, who had been all set to rejoin the Bureau, dug in their heels and again withdrew their support. The Setts actually went to war with the Navy, and held their own for almost a month before they were totally exterminated.

As failure after failure greeted Man's efforts, work nonetheless proceeded on the Bureau. Foundations were laid, walls and facades erected, environmental systems laid in, communication and translation systems set up, food synthesis laboratories installed, medical centers created, decorations and furniture imported.

Within a decade the Bureau was complete, a huge, proud, unbelievably complex monolith of a building, towering many thousands of feet above the rocky surface of Deluros IV, visible for miles in every direction, all of its internal systems functioning smoothly, its exterior a paean to the art of a thousand sentient races.

Thus it stood. And thus, Mallow knew, it would stand for all eternity, an empty, unused monument both to Man's brilliance and his shortcomings, an edifice so mature and far-sighted in its conception and execution that neither Man nor his neighbors in the galaxy would ever be ready for it.

The night it was completed Mallow got rip-roaring drunk and stayed that way for a week. When he finally sobered up he resigned his position, left the Deluros system, set up shop some forty thousand light-years away, and made a fortune designing inexpensive but highly efficient group housing for the colonists of Delta Scuti II.

21: The Collectors

... With the Commonwealth entering a period of severe unrest, it was primarily the duty of the planetary governors to hold their native populations in check.

They were a remarkable lot, these governors, charged with the responsibility of speaking for the Commonwealth on their respective worlds. One of the greatest of them was Selimund (6888–6970 G.E.), who, in addition to his political abilities, founded the Museum of Antique Weaponry on Deluros VIII. ...

—*Man: Twelve Millennia of Achievement*

(No mention can be found of either Selimund, his fabled collection, or collectors and collections in general in *Origin and History of the Sentient Races*.)

Being a governor had its advantages, reflected Selimund, even when one was sitting on a powder keg like Mirzam X. For one thing, damned near all the alien worlds were powder kegs these days, and since Mirzam X was a little bigger than most, the job held a little more prestige than most. For another, the natives despised humanity so devoutly and so openly that he perforce had very little contact with them.

And, too, there was his collection.

Man had always had the urge to collect things, to surround himself with ordered series of possessions. Possibly it was an intellectualization of the primordial territorial instinct, possibly not. Selimund himself called it the "pack-rat urge," although no member of that long-extinct species had ever carried the fetish quite so far as Man had done. There was something in his nature that reveled not only in pride of ownership, but in the painstaking formulation of lists of objects to be procured, lists of objects already procured, and numerical, alphabetical, or other orderly arrangement of both possessions and lists. It wasn't exactly avarice, for most collectors spent enormous amounts of time and capital on the accumulation of objects—or, more often, sets and series of objects—that most other people considered either trivial or worthless.

Collecting, over the eons, had become highly specialized, just as had all other forms of endeavor. There was once an era when it was possible for a man to know, in his own lifetime, the sum total of all scientific knowledge. By the time the race had left its birthplace and begun to permeate the galaxy, no man could even know his own highly specialized field with any degree of completeness, and the concept of the true Renaissance Man was lost forever. So, too, did collections become more and more specialized. It was still possible to collect the entire works of a single author or painter, or representative stamps from every period of a planet's history—but to try to collect *all* the literary works of a single genre, or *all* the stamps from a certain point of galactic history, was an out-and-out impossibility.

Undaunted, Man continued to yield happily to the joy of ownership, the striving toward completion of some fancy or other which had pricked his imagination or awakened his greed. From stamps and currency to masterpieces of art to any other objects, no matter how unlikely or intrinsically worthless, Man collected.

And very few men collected with the skill, passion, or success of the current governor of Mirzam X. Selimund, whose closest association with military life was the armed guard around his executive mansion, had for reasons probably not even known to himself decided early in life that there was nothing quite so fascinating as the study—and, hence, the collecting—of alien firearms. The production and possession of all such weapons had been strictly prohibited since the inception of the Commonwealth, but that merely made their acquisition all the more challenging.

He had begun with handguns from the Canphor Twins and Lodin XI from the Democracy, and had gradually increased his possessions, moving both forward and backward from that historical point in time. He was acknowledged to be the greatest living authority on the weaponry of the late Democratic period, and more than once he had been called in to determine the authenticity of a piece from that era. His collection was on permanent display back on Deluros VIII, and had been willed to the Commonwealth upon his death. Its value had been placed at some 22 million credits, but, like all collectors, the evaluation of his collection was dealt with in terms of emotion rather than currency, for no piece would ever be offered for sale.

Some pieces, however, might well be offered in trade, and it was for this purpose that he had cleared his desk early this afternoon, and was awaiting the arrival of Baros Durmin, a dealer in antique weaponry who had supposedly come upon an unbelievably valuable cache of ancient firearms. Durmin was finding it harder to replenish his stock, and so he had proposed a trade rather than an out-and-out cash transaction. Selimund didn't know exactly what Durmin had to offer, but the man usually delivered high-quality items, and so the governor was willing at least to take a look at his wares.

Durmin, a huge man with hamlike hands and a deep, booming voice, was ushered into Selimund's office, followed by two assistants who carried in a large, ornate container the size of a trunk.

"Hello, Baros," said Selimund. "Now, what's this fantastic find you've been raving about?"

"You won't believe it until you see it, Governor," said Durmin. "Okay, boys, open it up."

The two men unlocked the container and opened it. Selimund looked in, trying not to appear too anxious, and Durmin withdrew a small object wrapped in Toranian spider-silk. He removed the covering without a word and handed it over to Selimund, who began examining it gingerly.

"A laser pistol," he murmured, holding it up to the light. "Early Democracy . . . no, make that late Republic. Handcrafted. Good for about four minutes without repowering. Trigger device fits a near-human hand, probably a little

235

smaller. Emra IV, I'd say, or possibly Lemm." He paused, lost in thought. "No, it couldn't be Lemm. They never developed laser weapons. Probably Emran. Well-built. Looks almost new." He looked up at Durmin. "What else have you got?"

Durmin handed him another weapon.

"Lovely!" exclaimed Selimund. "Absolutely gorgeous!" He handled it as if it were made of the finest crystal, apt to shatter at any instant. "An explosive-projectile hand pistol! I've only got one in my whole collection. They went out of fashion early in the Democracy. Never understood why. It was a deadly little weapon. Where did you get all this stuff, Baros?"

"Sorry." Durmin grinned. "Professional secret."

Selimund nodded. He hadn't really expected an answer to the question.

He spent the next few hours going over the remaining seventeen weapons, studying each, appraising their craftsmanship and market value in his mind. The condition of the pieces was beautiful, as if they had just been turned out of a factory that morning. Moving parts were well oiled, metal parts glistened, stocks and handles were smooth as glass. All had been used by the Emrans, or a race very similar to them, for all were made for the same type of hand: three or four fingers, with a short thumb, somewhat smaller than a human hand.

"What are you asking for the lot?" asked Selimund at last.

"Well, Governor, if I were to name a price, it would be in the neighborhood of half a million credits," said Durmin. "However, as I said, I'm not putting these up for cash sale. They're for trade only. I might consider the atom cannon from Doradus IV that you have on display at Deluros, plus two early Republic hand weapons from Torqual and Procyon III."

"Not the cannon," said Selimund emphatically. "You'd have to offer twice as many weapons for that."

"That could be arranged," said Durmin. "This isn't the sum total of the cache."

"Why not bring the rest tomorrow morning, and we'll talk business," suggested Selimund.

"Fair enough," said Durmin. "I've got fourteen more pieces."

"Then I think we'll be able to do some dealing," said Selimund. "If you like, you can leave these weapons overnight. I'll have them placed under heavy guard and will personally guarantee their safety."

236

Durmin seemed to be debating the matter for a moment, then agreed and left with his assistants.

Selimund had a late dinner, then tried to relax with a newstape. It didn't work. His thoughts kept going back to the weapons sitting in his office, and finally he yielded to the urge to examine them again. He dismissed the guard, closed the door behind them, and carefully laid the firearms on his massive desk.

He decided that three of the pieces were definitely Emran, probably as many as seven of them. The others had belonged to similar species, but he was at a loss as to why all the weapons had been unearthed in a single spot. Well, finding them was Durmin's business; his was acquiring them.

And acquire them he would. Durmin's estimate had been somewhat low; he mentally priced the lot at three-quarters of a million credits, and tomorrow's addition would up the value to almost twice that.

He sat back and gazed lovingly at the weapons, imagining how they would look on display at his museum back on De-luros VIII. What a find! He hadn't honestly expected to accumulate this many early Democracy and late Republic hand weapons during the remainder of his life. As for the cannon, he could always replace it, and besides, he'd never cared for it that much. Hand weapons were his specialty, and this was like a magical windfall from some benevolent deity.

Carefully, lovingly, he picked up another of the old-style explosive-projectile pistols and examined it again. The balance was exquisite, and the restoration job Durmin had done was unbelievable. There was absolutely no sign of wear, of corrosion in any of the moving parts.

He began disassembling it, marveling at the workmanship that had gone into it. This was no showpiece, this weapon; it had been made for one purpose and one purpose only—to destroy; and it was as neat a little engine of destruction as had ever been built.

He noticed that he had gotten some fingerprints on the pistol while examining it, and he opened one of his desk drawers, withdrawing a soft cloth with which to clean it.

It was as he was cleaning the barrel prior to reassembling it that he saw the powder.

Something was wrong. The weapon was thousands of years old, and had been cleaned at least once in the past few weeks. There shouldn't be any trace whatsoever of gunpowder.

He laid the pistol down gently and stared at it. He knew enough about the restoration of ancient weaponry to be sure that the powder wasn't a residue from the cleaning or restorative process. No, while there wasn't enough to smell or taste, there was no doubt in his mind that it was gunpowder.

But why? The pistol wasn't used in target ranges; one explosive bullet from its barrel would take out the side of a building the size of a governor's mansion.

He signaled for the guards, and asked them to find out if there had been any armed rebellions since the Setts went to war with the Commonwealth over the ill-conceived Bureau of Alien Affairs project. The answer came back in a matter of minutes: There had been sporadic disturbances on the Canphor Twins and perhaps a dozen other worlds, but all had been put down almost instantly.

He spent the next two hours tracing Durmin's movements during the past year. Durmin was a well-traveled man, but at no time had he set foot on any of the worlds that had had disturbances.

And *that* meant that there was more to this than met the eye. Much more.

For one thing, it meant that there was more alien trouble brewing. For another, it meant that whoever Durmin had gotten the weapons from was pretty well supplied with firepower, or they'd never have let so many pieces go, no matter what price Durmin was willing to pay. And *that* implied that, far from being weaponless, the aliens had some seven millennia of firearms to draw upon, and that most if not all of them were in working order.

Which led to other thoughts. Such as: Why did Durmin want the Doradusian cannon? It wasn't worth anywhere near as much as the hand weapons—at least, not to a collector. But to a gunrunner whose clientele needed some really heavy firepower, it was probably worth hundreds of pistols. And the two pistols that Durmin wanted in addition to the cannon? His commission for effecting the trade. Not a bad commission, either, decided Selimund; they were worth about 35,000 credits for the pair.

One by one Selimund began disassembling the other weapons. He couldn't tell about the laser pistols, but seven of the eleven explosive pistols showed traces of recent use. Probably these were rejects, he decided, weapons that were too inefficient to be used by the rebels.

But rejects or not, they were beautiful, masterpieces of the

238

ancient weaponers' art. What a display they'd make at the museum! Except for the Republic laser pistol; that one would stay in his office, hermetically sealed in a transparent showcase. Possibly he'd add a little bronze plaque at its base, describing its use and manufacture.

He shook his head vigorously. That was enough pipedreaming. The first order of business was to find out where these rebel forces were, what their strength was, and when they planned to mobilize. This would then be reported to the Floating Kingdom, and if all went well, it would be good for a handsome raise in salary.

The problem was that he didn't need any more money. What he needed was things to spend it on. Things like weapons from the Republic and Democracy. . . .

He reassembled all the weapons, called the guards, and went to bed, a troubled man. He woke up feeling no better.

He skipped breakfast and went back to his office and looked at the weapons again, touching each one lovingly, regretfully. They were so damned beautiful!

He had already considered arresting Durmin on the spot and confiscating the weapons as evidence. But they'd have to be turned over to the court, and that would be the last he'd ever see of them. He had even toyed with assassinating the dealer and his aides, but decided against it on strictly practical grounds.

No, he'd have to follow the thing through. Collection or no collection, his first loyalty lay with the Commonwealth.

Not that the Commonwealth would really need his help or his loyalty. After all, what could one planet—even a well-armed one—do against the combined might of almost two million worlds? It wouldn't amount to much more than a policing action. Of course, the cannon could do an enormous amount of damage, but that could be taken care of by the simple expedient of destroying the trigger mechanism before turning it over to Durmin. In all likelihood any race that had been able to recondition the firearms before him would be able to repair the cannon, but there was always the chance that such an intricate mechanism was beyond their abilities. At least, he liked to think so.

Furthermore, the galaxy was in a state of flux. Rebellions were cropping up with greater frequency, and surely Durmin's contacts weren't the only aliens who had been surreptitiously stockpiling weapons over the centuries against the day that they would finally dig in their heels and strike back at the oppression of the Commonwealth. Blowing the whistle on this operation wouldn't solve anything; in all probability, it wouldn't even delay the uprisings on any of the other worlds.

There were a thousand races that sooner or later would take up arms against Man—but there was only one collection, and probably only this one opportunity to add such precious treasures to it. Besides, in these days of instant interstellar communication, there wasn't a ghost of a chance that the aliens would still have their arsenal around by the time the Navy got there. Turning Durmin in would just be a gesture in futility, an act of misplaced nobility.

He picked up the explosive pistol again, caressed it lovingly, cradled it in his hands. He was still holding it when Durmin returned with another container.

"Here are the rest of them," he said, carefully unloading the items on Selimund's desk.

Selimund looked them over one by one. Suddenly he froze.

"Is that what I think it is?" he asked softly.

"I thought you'd like it, Governor," said Durmin, smiling.

"A pistol from Twenty-seventh Century Earth," whispered Selimund. He reached out a trembling hand and touched it gingerly, reverently. "I've seen a couple of drawings, but . . ."

"It's a beauty, isn't it?" said Durmin.

Selimund nodded.

"I know your specialty is alien weapons," Durmin continued, "but when something like this comes along . . . well, it's the prize of the whole lot. That's why I've got to ask for the cannon."

Selimund looked long and hard at him, then found his gaze drawn back to the pistol.

"It's a deal," he said.

A moment later he was working meticulously over the newest treasure in his collection, polishing and shining it, completely oblivious to a galaxy that had once again found it expedient to stockpile weapons.

22: The Rebels

. . . As the millennium drew to an uneasy close, Man was girding for the greatest challenge yet to his primacy in the galaxy; and, strangely enough, this challenge came not just from the alien races, but also from a number of misdirected Men as well.

Among the first of the turncoats was Loran Baird, a former naval officer, who for reasons known only to himself . . .

—*Man: Twelve Millennia of Achievement*

. . . It was the alliance between two visionary beings, Brastillios of Canphor VII (6977–7202 G.E.) and Loran Baird of Aldebaran X (6955–7020 G.E.), that led to the first step in the downfall not just of the Monarchy, but of the whole of Man's tyrannical hold over the races of the galaxy. Members of warring races, they nonetheless managed to form a bond of mutual trust and friendship which resulted in . . .

—*Origin and History of the Sentient Races*, Vol. 9

Everything was going to hell.

Castor V hadn't joined the Commonwealth, and neither had some fifty other planets that had seemed to be teetering on the brink. Not only that, but some of the frontier worlds, feeling their oats, had actually tried to throw the Commonwealth out. It hadn't worked, of course, but each act of rebellion got a little farther than the previous one before it was surpressed.

Then came the real shocker. Spica VI, that huge and hallowed ship-building world, populated only by the race of Man, declared independence from the Commonwealth. The Floating Kingdom, its back to the wall, responded in the only way open to it—with might and more might. The Spicans fought to the last man, and when the brief but bloody war was over, almost two million men lay dead on the surface of the planet, a once-industrialized surface that was now and forever covered with rubble and debris.

"The problem," said Baird, "is that no one is taking the trouble to organize these damned uprisings, to coordinate them for maximum efficiency."

His companion looked across the table at him.

"How do you expect any coordination?" he asked at last. "You've got a thousand alien races, plus a goodly number of Men, who have nothing in common except their enmity toward the Floating Kingdom and Deluros. They've never worked together, never trusted one another, never before fought against a common enemy. Why should they start now? Or, to put it another way, you're a Man. What Canphorite or Lodinite or Emran in its right mind would trust you?"

"I see your point, Jannis," said Baird, "and yet in the end they're going to have to trust me, just as I'm going to have to trust them."

"Ah, but are you?" Jannis smiled.

"If I have to, I will," said Baird grimly. "That's why I've contacted you. You're a merchant on Canphor VII. You deal with the damned creatures. Can you set up a meeting between me and one of their underground leaders?"

"I figured as much," said Jannis. "Why Canphor? Why not some race that doesn't have a five-thousand-year history of insurrection, some race that won't be predisposed to murder you the instant you walk into the room?"

"Because the Canphor Twins are the leaders of the nonhuman races, and if we're ever going to overthrow this tyranny we're going to need their help."

"You keep talking about some mysterious 'we,'" remarked Jannis. "Just who do you represent?"

Baird's eyes narrowed. "That information is for the Canphorites," he said at last.

"I take it that I have been scrutinized and found wanting," said Jannis dryly.

"The less you know, the less trouble you'll be in if the roof comes tumbling down," said Baird. He slipped a large roll of currency across the table. "Will you do it?"

Jannis looked at the roll, then nodded. "I imagine it will have to be on one of the outworlds. They won't come to any planet of your choosing, and you certainly won't go to the Canphor system."

"The hell I won't," said Baird. "I want them to know we mean business."

"How about Canphor III, then?" said Jannis. "That way it won't seem like a total capitulation."

"No," said Baird firmly. "One of the Twins, VI or VII, I don't care which."

Jannis shrugged. "It's your funeral."

But that, decided Baird after his companion had left, was where Jannis was wrong. It was the Commonwealth's funeral. Not today, not next year, perhaps not even in a century, but it would be the start.

Jannis contacted him a few days later. The Canphorites had, to his amazement, agreed to the meeting. The two Men would go to Canphor VI, where Jannis would escort Baird to a certain building and then leave him. No arrangements had been made for Baird's departure, which Jannis found distinctly ominous, but Baird readily consented to the conditions.

Baird had never been to either of the Canphor Twins, and as Jannis's ship landed at a Canphor VI spaceport, he was amazed by the lack of structures to be seen. He had thought, considering the Canphorites' long and variegated history, that both populated planets would be teeming with life and activity.

"Don't be misled," said Jannis when Baird questioned him on this point. "Most of Canphor VI is underground. I guess they got understandably tired of rebuilding their cities after we kept razing them to the ground. Pretty much the same situation exists on Canphor VII. In fact, over the past few hundred years, property values have skyrocketed in direct relation to depth. Only the most impoverished portion of the populace lives on the surface, which actually serves a double purpose."

"And what is that?" asked Baird.

"It keeps the Commonwealth happy and ignorant. Happy, because the portion of the planet they have access to is so tranquil and obviously unequipped for violence; and ignorant, because if nothing else the surface is totally unrepresentative of the planet." He opened the hatch of the ship and stepped down. A windowless vehicle was awaiting them. "It works by remote control," Jannis informed Baird. "The reason for it is so that nobody will be able to see in. Less chance of an incident this way."

"How do you survive in your business?" asked Baird.

"I assume you mean physically and not financially." Jannis smiled. "I never leave the surface, and I work out of our embassy."

They entered the vehicle, which immediately raced off across the red, barren landscape. After a few minutes it began descending at a 45-degree angle, and when it leveled out again Baird estimated that he was at least four miles beneath the surface. There followed a number of sharp turns, so many that he concluded it was being done to confuse him in case he had been trying to remember the way back, which indeed was the case. At last it stopped and the doors opened automatically, to reveal the interior of a large building of totally inhuman design.

"I'm not supposed to get out with you," said Jannis. "I suppose I'll be kept here until you've finished with them, or vice versa."

Baird nodded and stepped out. No Canphorites were around, so he walked to the only door he could find, opened it, and stepped through. He heard the door close behind him, and found himself in a small, darkened room. Standing a short distance away was a Canphorite. The being was typical of its race, all of which looked alike to Baird: tall, incredibly slender, with a large, bulbous head, small dark eyes, and a round, protruding mouth. It was humanoid in type, but very definitely inhuman.

"You are Baird," it said, the tones coming out dull and unaccented through a T-pack.

"Yes," said Baird. "And you?"

"I am Brastillios."

"I am pleased to meet you," said Baird.

"Are you indeed?" said Brastillios.

244

Baird nodded. "Where are the others?"

"What others?"

"I was under the impression that I was to meet the leaders of your underground," said Baird.

"I am empowered to speak on their behalf," said the Canphorite.

"All right," Baird said, making the best of the situation. "Let's get down to business."

"And just what *is* the business at hand?" asked Brastillios.

"I think you know, or you wouldn't be here," said Baird. "However, if you want me to spell it out for you, I will. My business is the overthrow of the Commonwealth."

"And why should a Man wish to overthrow another Man when there are still so many non-Men in the galaxy, non-Men that your race delights in slaughtering?"

"What my government does and what my race approves of are not necessarily the same thing," said Baird.

"I wonder," said Brastillios. "Certainly you seem to have many of the trappings of your government. You cannot speak my language nor I yours, but it is I who have the T-pack."

"I was told to bring nothing with me," said Baird.

"Nothing," agreed Brastillios, "except the desire to meet a Canphorite. And now that you have, do you even know whether I am native to Canphor VI or Canphor VII?"

"What difference does it make?" said Baird. "There are only two sides involved here. Canphor VI and VII are on the same side, so why should I prefer one to the other?"

"A noble sentiment, and an adroit evasion," said Brastillios. "I am native to Canphor VII, and I agree that it makes no difference. There is Man, and there is everything else."

"Correction," said Baird. "There are some Men, and there is everything else."

"You have not yet answered my original question," said the Canphorite. "Why should you wish to help us?"

"Because a large body of Men finds the Commonwealth as intolerable as you do. Our economy is unstable, our culture is stagnating, our ambition has been misdirected and stifled."

"Tell me about your ambition," said Brastillios. "Men have always hungered for distant worlds. Why should I believe that you do not hunger for mine?"

"Men have better goals to strive for than the subjugation of other races," said Baird.

"It is unusual, is it not," said the Canphorite, "that in all of

245

Man's history he has not yet set his sights on some of those better goals?"

"I'm not here to apologize for the rest," said Baird. "My concern is the future. You want to overthrow the Floating Kingdom. So do I. You can't do it alone. Neither can I. But together, we just might cause a few ripples."

"And after these ripples have caused a wave that washes the Commonwealth away, what are your intentions then?" asked Brastillios.

"I might well ask you the same question," said Baird. "If the Commonwealth crumbles, Man will be virtually powerless in a galaxy where he is vastly outnumbered by a populace that probably will have a few scores to settle with him."

"The concept of punishment is alien to most races' way of thinking. I think Man has very little to fear from us once the Commonwealth is destroyed," lied Brastillios.

"Similarly, I can assure you that the Men I represent are not the type to turn on their allies," lied Baird.

"Who *will* they turn on?" asked the Canphorite. "Man always turns on someone."

"Governing the race of Man will be time-consuming enough," said Baird. "We've already got a pretty big chunk of the galaxy. We don't need any more."

"And who will rule this philanthropic new order? You?"

"The thought has crossed my mind."

"It is an unrealistic thought," said Brastillios. "We can strike a painful blow to the Commonwealth, but it will nonetheless outlive both you and myself by centuries, probably millennia."

"Then there's no time to waste," said Baird. "Shall we lay our cards on the table?"

"Even in translation I do not understand this idiomatic expression."

"It means that our meeting has reached that point where we must be frank and open with each other," said Baird. "And since you still seem somewhat dubious, I'll begin. Through various contacts I have in the Navy, I can present our side with a force of approximately twelve million men, about two million ships, and a considerable arsenal. No single unit will amount to more than five percent of the whole. They are scattered around the galaxy, but this may prove to be an advantage, as they will thus prevent the Commonwealth from massing its forces. Now, how many planets do you control or can you influence?"

"I find it interesting that you speak in terms of numbers of beings, while I am expected to reply in terms of planets," said Brastillios.

"I am speaking in both cases in terms of strategic units," Baird pointed out. "I fully realize, as you must, that neither my humans nor your allied races can militarily overthrow the Commonwealth as things stand now. But a well-orchestrated series of attacks and rebellions may give other Men and aliens the idea that it can be done."

"Why would other Men come over to your side?" asked Brastillios. "Why would they not defend their primacy to the death?"

"Men side with winners," said Baird. "And they wouldn't view it as surrendering their primacy, but as overthrowing an unpopular government. So I repeat: How many worlds can you influence?"

"Perhaps three thousand, perhaps more," said Brastillios.

"There can be no terms such as 'perhaps' involved," said Baird. "We've got to coordinate this entire operation down to the last detail. Each rebellion, both in the Navy and among the nonhuman worlds, must appear spontaneous, and they all must be strategically mapped to cause the most difficulty and confusion to the Navy. Nor must they all be military actions; we don't want the first ten planets that rebel to be blown to kingdom come—it would discourage the rest of them. Now, what kind of weaponry do you have at your disposal?"

The Canphorite listed the contents of his arsenal and made some educated guesses at what the other alien worlds possessed. Baird was surprised to find them so well armed, but said nothing. After all, it just made his job that much easier.

"Your history books will not speak too highly of what you have done today," remarked Brastillios, when the broad lines of the strategy had been agreed upon.

"If we win, I'll be the author of those books," said Baird. "And if we lose, someone else will overthrow the Commonwealth sometime in the future, in which case I'll be considered a visionary born before his time. If we take a smashing defeat, what will the books say about you?"

"They have been written for millennia," said Brastillios. "We have only been awaiting the proper time to publish them."

For just a fleeting instant Baird thought he might have bitten off more than he could chew. Then he shrugged. The aliens wouldn't cause any problem. They'd be in the vanguard of the fighting for the next few centuries, and if they still were feeling their oats after the remnants of the Commonwealth had decimated their ranks . . . well, Man was not totally without experience in dealing with alien races.

Brastillios stared hard at the Man. He, too, had his doubts about this alliance. Men, after all, were Men. Then he, too, shrugged. This temporary partnership was a necessary evil, no more, no less. Sooner or later there would be a redress of power in the galaxy, and if some Men wished to bring it about sooner while helping to destroy others of their race, why should he object to it?

They made arrangements for a series of future meetings at which every minute detail would be hashed out. Then, for the first time in galactic history, Man and alien shook hands in mutual friendship and brotherhood.

Both of them had their fingers crossed.

Seventeenth Millennium:
ANARCHY

23: The Archaeologists

> . . . Thus, as Man's empire dwindled, no central
> governmental body was formed among the other
> races, and a galaxy-wide state of anarchy came into
> being. . . .
>
> It was during the Seventeenth Millennium (G.E.)
> that the race of Man, no longer possessed of its
> once-mighty military and economic power, turned
> toward more peaceful pursuits. There was a general
> reawakening of interest in the species' racial roots,
> and Earth and the early colonies were at last thor-
> oughly explored and examined by scores of archae-
> ologists. One of the most successful of these was
> Breece, a female from Belthar III, whose published
> works are still read today. . . .
>
> —*Origin and History of the Sen-
> tient Races,* Vol. 9

Breece stood on Earth and wondered where the tens and
hundreds of centuries had gone.

Earth was not deserted—exactly; and the race of Man was
not on the verge of extinction—exactly. But oh, she reflected,
how the mighty have fallen! So high had Man ascended that
it had taken him many long millennia to lose every last ves-

tige of his primacy, his power, his property. In fact, some tiny portions of the latter still remained: the Deluros system, a series of ghost worlds, all shining and efficient and unused; Sirius V, whose frontiers had retrogressed until it now housed only one vast city; Caliban, a still-living, still-functioning anachronism, a mechanism that would wait for all eternity to report the movements of a Navy that had been dead and forgotten for centuries; the Floating Kingdom, its imperial palaces converted into factories, its motive power no longer operational, doomed to float aimlessly from system to system until some star finally reached out and dragged it to its bosom; the Capellan and Denebian colonies; some four thousand scattered worlds; and ancient old Earth itself.

Over the ages, after the fall of the Commonwealth—or the Monarchy, as it had come to be known—race after race began reasserting itself, taking back some or all of what Man had appropriated. Many of them didn't really care about Man or what he had done to or for them, but there were those—the Canphorites, the Lodinites, the Emrans, and a hundred others—who cared passionately enough to make up for the lethargy of the other races. Bit by bit, with the patience of Job and the skill of Grath, they had begun pushing Man back, forcing him into planetary alcoves, denying him access to a world here, a system there, nationalizing a factory on this world, destroying a laboratory or college on that world.

Man fought back, as Man would always fight back. At first his losses were minimal, but he had reached his peak, had held the galaxy in the palm of his hand, and there was no place to go but down. He did it much the same way he had gone up: scrapping, fighting, bluffing, lying, with just enough isolated instances of nobility and of barbarism to make the galaxy wonder if he was either a god or perhaps some killer straight out of hell, rather than just another sentient race.

And indeed, reflected Breece, Man wasn't just another species to be recorded and forgotten in the history books. He was something special, something very different. No other race was capable of such generosity, such idealism, such achievement; and, too, no other race could produce such examples of pettiness, bestiality, dishonor, and dishonesty Whatever else could be said for Man, he was unique—which, when all was said and done, was why she stood on Man's mother world, cold and rain-soaked, searching for whatever it was that had given shape to this strange, intelligent ape, that had made him better than the galaxy's best, poorer than its worst, had made him reach out to the stars and scream his defiance in the face of Destiny.

She stood in the twilight, staring out across what had once, eons ago, been the Serengeti Plains. This now-barren piece of land, stretching from the still-picturesque Ngorongoro Crater to the dry bed of Lake Victoria, had seen almost all the history of Man while he was still Earthbound. Here he had been born, had first invented the wheel and the bludgeon, had first discovered fire. Here he had pitted himself in naked battle with the legendary black-maned lion, and had sold his fellow Man into bondage. The First and Fourth World Wars had extended far enough south and east to turn the Serengeti into a temporary battlefield. It was here, six hundred years before the beginning of the Galactic Era, that Man had exterminated the last of his competing land-dwelling species, and it was here, a century later, that the initial research was done on the Tachyon Drive.

And now the Serengeti stood lonely and deserted again, knee-high in jungle grasses, bordered by wait-a-bit thorn trees, hiding a million years of human debris and artifacts beneath its soil.

It seemed a good place to search for answers.

With a sigh, Breece turned and walked back to her dome. Tomorrow, if the rain let up, she'd begin digging, marking, cataloguing. And maybe, just maybe . . .

She jumped as she heard the cracking of some twigs behind her.

"Who's there?" she demanded.

"I saw your camp and took the liberty of coming over," said the cold, clear tones of a modified Terran T-pack.

"Who are you?" she asked, peering into the gathering darkness.

"I am Milnor, of the moon Kormonos, system of Atria, race of Rinn," said the voice.

She peered again, and finally could make out the Rinn's figure. It was vaguely humanoid in shape, a bit squatter and more muscular than a Man, with a greenish tint to the skin. There was considerable hair on the body, which was unclothed but for a pouch suspended from one shoulder. The Rinn spoke into a T-pack, which was strapped around a protuberance which appeared to be a chin, but wore no face mask or helmet, and seemed quite at home breathing Earth's air.

251

"I am Breece, race of Man," she said. "What are you doing here?"

"I am an archaeologist," said Milnor. "I have spent the past seventeen years on Earth, digging through ruins, rummaging through still-standing buildings, even interviewing those Men who still cling to this world. I have been in the Serengeti for almost two months. One of my robots informed me of another camp. I came to ascertain your motives for being here."

"I have as much right here as you do," said Breece. "Perhaps more."

"I do not deny this," said Milnor. "I only wish it known that I am totally nonpolitical, and am interested only in my work. If my presence here will offend you, I can easily move my base of operations elsewhere until such time as you leave."

"That won't be necessary," said Breece, feeling a sudden rush of guilt. "I'm noncombative. In fact, it appears we are members of the same profession."

"I had hoped as much," said the Rinn. "Still, with no intention of offending you, I felt it best to make sure, though certainly no one but another archaeologist would have any reason for being here."

"Oh, I don't know," said Breece. "It seems like a lovely place to live."

"I would think, based on my knowledge of Man and supported by my findings on Earth, that you would crave the community of your fellow beings."

"Most Men would," agreed Breece.

"But not yourself?"

"No. I'm different."

The Rinn's mouth curved in its equivalent of a smile, then straightened suddenly. "If you crave solitude . . ."

"Your presence doesn't upset me, if that's what you're driving at," said Breece. "In fact, I think I'd find exchanging ideas with an archaeologist of a different race most stimulating."

"Excellent," said Milnor with another smile. "Would it offend you if I were to consume some food first? My metabolism is such that I must feed at least five or six times a day."

"I wonder that you have time for your work," said Breece.

"I never sleep," said the Rinn. "May I summon one of my robots?"

"Of course," said Breece, and a moment later a robot, almost indistinguishable from the Rinn, approached with a small container.

"It is only vegetation," said Milnor. "However, if the sight of my eating it will affect you adversely, I can withdraw."

"It's not necessary," said Breece. As Milnor devoured a number of plants and grasses, Breece's eyes examined the robot. "That's a fabulous machine," she said at last. "It's amazing how much progress has been made in the science of robotics."

"Indeed," agreed Milnor. "And yet, it was a science devised by Man. Why is it that your race made only minimal use of it?"

"We preferred to do things ourselves," said Breece.

"True." Milnor nodded. "Man never gave quarter, but he never asked for it either. A fascinating race."

"What was it that led you to devote so much time to the study of my race?" asked Breece.

"So many of the sentient species are so busy blindly making war against Man that I felt that somebody ought to try to understand you."

"I thank you for the sentiment," said Breece. "And what have you learned about us that has increased your understanding?"

"That is a very difficult question," said Milnor.

"Oh? Why?"

"Because the more I discover about your race, the less I am able to comprehend it."

"Welcome to the club," said Breece with a bitter laugh.

"Perhaps you can enlighten me on some points," said Milnor eagerly—or at least he looked eager. The words coming through the T-pack were totally devoid of emotion.

"I'll try," said Breece, "but please don't be too disappointed if I'm just as puzzled as you are."

"Well, for example," said Milnor—and now they were not Man and non-Man, but merely two professionals discussing their field of expertise—"very few races of the galaxy have believed in religions, though many accept the philosophical notion of deity. Yet Man had not just one religion, but literally hundreds of them. Many of them issued very reasonable ethical codes and directives, from which most civil law on Earth, and ultimately the Commonwealth, was derived. Also, all the great religious figures, from Jesus and Buddha almost to the end of human history, have preached a doctrine of love and tranquillity."

253

"You forget Moses, who figuratively took the sword of God in his hand to slay the Egyptians."

"But even Moses did not allow his people to fight," said Milnor, "and it was Moses who gave his nation the Ten Commandments. Now, my question is this: given such ethical codes and moral leaders, and threatening what seemed to most Men to be the very real alternative of hellfire and eternal damnation, it would seem to me that Man would have evolved socially and morally into the most peaceful and ethical of species. And yet this obviously is not the case, despite rare examples to the contrary. Can you possibly explain this to me from a Man's viewpoint?"

"Not as an archaeologist, I can't," said Breece. "But perhaps archaeology is the wrong science to apply to that question."

"Which science would suit it better?" asked the Rinn.

"Anthropology, perhaps. Or psychology. Or possibly even philosophy. At any rate, I think the answer lies in more than one place. First of all, Man was a carnivore. He still is, though he calls himself an omnivore. The conditions of ancient Earth were such that Man either had to evolve certain seemingly physically impossible abilities, such as geometrically multiplying his strength and speed, or he could develop into an intelligent being. No evolution occurs without prior environmental need, and in this case the need was for a physical equalizer, some method by which Man could kill the animals he had to kill in order to survive. This led to the creation of weapons. Some people, in fact most people, would say that all human history follows from that."

"But this is not necessarily so," said Milnor. "Man is not the only intelligent carnivore in the galaxy."

"True," said Breece. "As I said, that's only part of the answer, only one influence upon the race."

"And what of religion, of the noble philosophic systems Man devised?" asked the Rinn.

"Religion was an emotional crutch, and an emotional weapon as well. It was a crutch in that it offered a catch-all explanation for the inexplicible, and a weapon in that far-sighted men such as Moses were able to invoke the authority of God Himself to gain acceptance of their ethical systems."

"This I realize," said Milnor. "But where did it break down?"

"That's hard to say. But every time Man achieved something new, such as air travel, the birds and clouds were no longer things of wonder to us and another page of the Bible became just so much pretty poetry. As for the ethical systems, I can't really give you an answer. Possibly when Man moved out into the galaxy he felt he was greater than God, and hence under no ethical imperative to obey his Earthbound and Earthmade laws."

"But Man ignored these two laws during most of his existence on Earth," Milnor pointed out.

"I know," said Breece. "Maybe the laws were made for perfect things, and Man is not perfect. If I knew the answers, I wouldn't be here."

"I understand," said Milnor. "If you could tell me what period you are most interested in, perhaps I could be of some assistance in directing you to the most likely places to begin your digging."

"That's very generous of you, Milnor," said Breece, "but the truth of the matter is that I simply don't know where to begin. My race is dying, falling back on every front, losing everything it once held dear. I want to know why. I want to know what made us do it all in the first place, why we succeeded, why we failed. If you can point to a spot anywhere in the galaxy and say, 'Dig there and you'll discover what it is that makes Man Man,' I'll be forever in your debt. But I don't think you can do that, can you?"

"Alas, I cannot," said Milnor.

"Then I suppose I'll just have to proceed in my own haphazard way." She turned her head into the mild breeze, breathed in the cold, clean air. "This very spot we're standing on might have been the Garden of Eden. I wonder if we'll ever know why Man wanted to leave it. He didn't slink out of Paradise, you know; he walked out proud and erect. Isn't that curious?"

"You are not like most Men I have met," said Milnor after a thoughtful pause.

"There's a little of me in all Men, and a little of them in me," said Breece. "I want to know. Isn't that the very trait that started Man on the path that led him to where he is now?"

"Was it truly the urge to know?" asked the Rinn. "Or was it the drive to possess?"

"I don't know," said Breece with a shrug. "And yet, with all my race has done that I feel ashamed of, I can still feel pride at their accomplishments. From the Pioneers to the Olympians to the Warlords, they bucked the odds. Maybe they

255

went places they had no business going, maybe they stepped on some toes—and far worse—but they won, and in a perverse way I'm proud to be one of them. Is that sinful, I wonder?"

"I cannot offer an answer," said Milnor. "But let me in turn ask you one final question, and then I shall leave you to the sleep you must need by now. Granting all that you have said is true to one degree or another, why is it that you are spending your life studying a species that we both admit is in its twilight? What will an understanding of Man's virtues and flaws and foibles benefit you?"

"You mean me personally?"

The Rinn nodded.

"I'm not sure," said Breece. "If I am to be totally honest about it, I could very well be doing this because I'm resentful."

"Resentful?" asked Milnor. "Of what?"

"Of all the Men who lived during the zenith of our race. There was a time when we owned it all, and we let it slip away. Or, rather, *they* let it slip away. Maybe I'm bitter about their losing my birthright."

"Truly?" asked Milnor.

"Perhaps," said Breece. "Or perhaps it's the feeling I get when I look out across the Serengeti, and see it as primitive Man must have seen it eons ago. But with one difference: his future, as a race, lay before him; mine lies behind me. I think it's very sad that nothing will ever grow here again except grass: no animals, no birds, and no Men."

"To use an expression of your species, you weep for the passing of your race," said the Rinn. "Is that not correct?"

"No," said Breece. "First I want to know how and why it happened, what made it inevitable. Then I'll decide whether or not to shed a few tears. And now, if you'll excuse me, Milnor, I must get some sleep."

"I understand," said the Rinn. "However, if it will not offend you, I should like to present you with a gift."

"A gift?"

"Yes," said Milnor. "It is a human artifact." Suddenly her face radiated interest. "I think," continued the Rinn, "that if you study it until you know it in its entirety, a number of your questions may be answered."

"I very much doubt that any one artifact can do that," said Breece.

"This one can," said Milnor. He removed his shoulder

256

pouch, stuck a stubby hand into it, searched around for a moment, and withdrew the artifact, which he rubbed carefully with a soft cloth and then handed to her.

It was a mirror.

24: The Priests

> . . . About the middle of the Seventeenth Galactic Millennium, as the race of Man was in danger and disarray everywhere, there was a rebirth of interest in religion, though this incarnation had none of the trappings of Man's ancient, Earthbound religions. It was simple, straightforward, possessed of very few dogmas, and was in truth far more of an ethical doctrine than a religion in the established sense of the word.
>
> One of the unsolved mysteries about Man is why, at a time when the comfort of religion should have been so avidly sought after, it should have flourished for so short a time and gained so few advocates. . . .
>
> —*Origin and History of The Sentient Races*, Vol. 9

It was a dirty little village, surrounded by scores of other dirty little villages, all of them standing out like leprous sores on the surface of Raxar II. Crumbling stone structures surrounded what had once been a city square, and in the middle of the square was a dust-covered fountain which had not operated in decades.

Mihal scurried along, looking neither right nor left, trying not to think of all the filth he would later have to remove from his robes. He carried a number of books in his left hand; in his right hand was a finely embroidered white handkerchief with which he was constantly mopping the sweat off his face. He longed for a cigar or a pipe, anything to keep his mind off the oppressive heat, but tobacco had been increasingly hard to come by in recent years, and since its cost had risen correspondingly with its scarcity, he had broken himself of the habit, though not the desire for it.

A little girl peeked at him from behind a decrepit building, and he smiled at her.

"Can you tell me where I can find Rodat?" he asked.

She wiped a runny nose with an unwashed forearm, then pointed to a nearby structure. Just before she ducked out of sight, he thanked her and approached the building. He looked for a door on which to knock, but could find none and, with a shrug, he walked inside.

"Hello?" he said. "Is anybody home?"

"In here," came a hoarse voice. He followed it and soon found himself in a small room. A number of insects were flying in and out through the holes where windows had once existed, and the heat grew even more unbearable, if possible. Sprawled on the floor atop an exceptionally grimy blanket was an old, emaciated, bearded man, whose age Mihal estimated at eighty or thereabouts.

"I am Per Mihal," said Mihal, trying to avert his eyes from the man's naked body.

"A new one, eh?" said the man. "What happened to Per Lomil?"

"He was transferred to Spica II," said Mihal, mentally adding: Lucky devil!

"And Per Degos?"

"Dead," said Mihal. "You are Rodat?"

The man nodded, and was suddenly wracked by a coughing seizure.

"This is my first day on Raxar II," said Mihal when the man sank weakly back on the blanket, "but I'll be here for quite some time. I was told that . . ." He paused, searching for a delicate way to phrase it.

"That I was dying?" asked Rodat. "Well, they told you rightly, priest. What can I do for you?"

"For *me*?" said Mihal in astonishment. "I am here to ease

259

your suffering, to bring you peace and solace in your . . . ah
. . . last hours."

"I'm good for three or four more days yet, priest," said
Rodat. "Don't go rushing me off before I'm good and ready
to go."

"That's quite all right," said Mihal, seating himself on the
floor beside the old man. "I'll stay right here with you to the
end."

"Going to give me a real good send-off, eh?"

"View it as helping you prepare to be taken to the bosom
of your Maker," said Mihal.

"Let Him wait until I'm good and ready," said Rodat. "I'm
in no hurry."

"I don't mean to be presumptuous," said Mihal, "but I
can't help thinking your attitude is all wrong. This is God
you're talking about, not some landlord to be put off with a
sneer. This is the Creator of all things, who is preparing to
take you into His kingdom."

The old man stared at him for moment, then turned and
spat on the rotting floor. "Priest," he said at last, "you've got
a lot to learn. I believe in the same God you do, and I believe in Him more devoutly than you do."

"Then ask his forgiveness, and surely it will be given," said
Mihal, wondering what kind of madman he was ministering
to.

"Ask His forgiveness?" said Rodat. "For what?"

"For Man's transgressions against God's law," said Mihal.

"Do you believe all that, or are you just spewing it out by
rote?" asked the old man.

"I beg your pardon!" said Mihal.

"Don't," said Rodat. "If I can get along without begging
God's pardon, you certainly don't have to apologize to me.
Maybe you ought to just leave me and peddle your religion
elsewhere."

"I'm not in the peddling business," said Mihal hotly.
"Whether or not you believe in the religion has absolutely no
bearing on the truth of it. If all the Men who ever lived did
not believe in God, would that make His existence any less
real?"

"Don't confuse God with religion, priest," said the old
man. "God has always been around. It's religion that comes
and goes with the seasons."

Mihal leaned over and wiped some sweat from the old

260

man's brow. "You're burning up with fever," he said. "Is there anything I can do to make you more comfortable?"

"Shutting your mouth would be a pretty good start," said Rodat.

"What have you got against me?" asked Mihal. "All I want to do is help you."

"You can help me by leaving me alone. I'll give you plenty of warning so you can be in for the kill."

The old man closed his eyes and lay motionless for a number of minutes, and Mihal opened one of his books and began reading aloud. It was a prayer of penitence.

"I hope you're doing that for your own benefit," said Rodat, reopening his eyes. "I don't mind being kept awake, but I'll be damned if I'll let you beg God to pardon me."

"You *may* be damned if I don't," said Mihal. "Please allow me to aid you in the only way I know. Your soul may not matter to you, but it's vitally important to me."

"Why?" rasped the old man. "Yours couldn't matter less to me."

"Because I entered the priesthood to serve people," said Mihal. "That is my only goal in life, and my greatest pleasure."

"Then I feel even sorrier for you than you do for me." He closed his eyes again, and soon his breathing, although weak, became regular.

Per Mihal sighed. It seemed so futile, sitting here with a man who wanted nothing that he had to offer, and yet that made the offering no less important. He wondered, as he sat and stared at the dying man, why religion was having such difficulty in reestablishing itself after a six-millennium hiatus. Originally it had died off because it tended to pile dogma atop dogma, pyramiding them up to the sky. Then, as Man learned to live in the air and beneath the sea, as he controlled first his environment and then his destiny, more and more of the dogmas fell by the wayside. The basic laws of religion began eroding, and when Man finally reached the stars and performed acts that religion had reserved only for God, it spelled the temporary end of religion. But religion was more than just a series of dogmas and rituals; it was a means to comfort the oppressed with the promise of a day of judgment when all wrongs would be righted and all losers made over into winners. Man didn't need that comfort when he ruled the galaxy, but now he was a loser once again.

But this time, reflected Mihal, Man didn't grab for the bait as readily. He was willing to worship God, but on his own terms, not God's. Mihal had seen many things in his brief life: poverty, lust, greed, pride, fury, resignation, nobility. The one thing he *hadn't* seen, outside the cloistered walls where he took his training, was a single Man who felt any need or desire to ask God to forgive the race for what it had done. Love, devotion, and worship were all parts of Man's spiritual makeup; apology, it seemed, was not.

And yet, did that make him any the less worthy of salvation? After all, Man was what he was, an animal that would always remain true to his nature. And since God had provided him with that nature, surely there must be a purpose to it. And what God created and gave purpose to, God must love. Mihal disdained ivory towers, but he was an idealist nonetheless, and his job was to bring comfort to God's downtrodden children. If they didn't particularly want that comfort, that just made his job all the more challenging.

He became aware of a sound behind him, and turned to see a girl of sixteen or seventeen standing in the doorway, a woven basket in her hands.

"Is he dead yet?" she asked.

"My God, what a callous question!" said Mihal.

"A practical one. I've brought food for him. There's no sense leaving it here if he's dead. There's barely enough to go around as is."

"I see," said Mihal, wondering whether an apology was called for and deciding against it. "He's just sleeping."

She placed the basket by the old man's side. "My name is Pilar," she said. "He's my uncle."

"I'm Per Mihal," said Mihal, extending his hand.

"Oh. The new priest?"

He nodded.

"Have you been here long?"

"I arrived this morning," he said. "I have spent most of the day wondering how you can put up with these living conditions."

"Nobody told us we had a choice," replied Pilar.

"As long as Rodat seems to be sleeping comfortably, would you care to go for a brief walk?" asked Mihal. "I haven't seen much of the village."

"All right," she agreed. "Though there's not much to see."

They stepped outside, and Mihal felt the huge sun beating down on him again. He was amazed by the poverty surrounding him. Even for a ghetto it was bad. He wondered what some alien race, finding traces of Man here in the far future, would make of it. Would there be any sign that this hapless creature had once ruled the galaxy? He doubted it.

"How long will you be with us, Per Mihal?" asked Pilar as they wove their way in and out of the dilapidated buildings.

"Until I'm reassigned," he said. "Which means anywhere from a week to a lifetime."

"Well, you won't be hurting for business," she said.

"I wish that weren't so."

"Oh?"

"I suppose priests are like doctors," he said. "Nothing would make us happier than a lack of patients."

"Not very likely in this day and age. Our empire is gone, our primacy is just a distant memory, we're hunted like animals on some worlds and shoved into ghettos on others. As long as things don't get any better, you can keep your shingle up."

"We don't feed on misery," said Mihal gently. "We fight it."

"You'd look pretty silly fighting empty air, wouldn't you?" Pilar laughed. "You'd be like a navy without an opponent. It's people like us that keep people like you in business."

"Believe me, Pilar," he said, "nothing could make me happier than seeing an end to all poverty and misery."

"And what would you do with all that spare time?"

"I would spend all my waking hours praising God for His benevolence," said Mihal devoutly.

"Really? And do you spend all your present waking hours condemning Him for forsaking us?"

"Of course not!" said Mihal. "I ask Him to forgive us for the sins we have committed during our long and bloody history, and for which we are now suffering."

"Oh," said Pilar.

"Do you feel that this is incorrect?"

"I'm not a priest, and I don't know very much about religion," said Pilar, "but if it was me, I'd ask Him to keep His hands off and let us climb back to the top of the heap if we can."

"I find it very disquieting to see so many people who possess this sort of attitude," said Mihal. "After all, if you can acknowledge God's existence, then surely . . ."

"Oh, I believe in God, all right," said Pilar. "I just believe in Man more."

"Isn't that a little inconsistent?" asked Mihal gently.

"Look around you, Per Mihal," said Pilár, gesturing toward the dust-covered streets and crumbling buildings. "This is God's handiwork. Then look at Deluros, or Caliban, or Earth. Man built them."

"Man built them," agreed Mihal, "but only by the grace of God. Only God can create a world."

"True," said Pilar, "but only Man can put it to use. I view it as a kind of partnership. God provides, and we dispose. Only God hasn't been providing very well these days."

"Then we must ask His forgiveness for whatever we've done to offend Him."

"I respect God too much to lie to Him, and I'd be lying if I said I was sorry for anything Man has done. Religion is supposed to be a spiritual crutch, Per Mihal. If it forces us to lie and grovel, it's not acting as a crutch—it's amputating our legs in order to attain God's sympathy. What kind of deity could be fooled like that?"

"Nobody wants you to lie, Pilar," said Mihal. "What religion tries to do is give you an awareness of your relationship to God. Once you understand that relationship, asking forgiveness won't be a lie."

"Don't you feel a certain measure of pride in what we've done?" asked Pilar. "Man, in his time, has walked on a million alien worlds and bent Nature to his will. He gave shape and scope and meaning to the galaxy. Why should I be ashamed of that?"

"Look where it got us," said Mihal.

"Next time we'll do it better."

Mihal shrugged. "I think we'd better be getting back. We've been gone almost forty minutes."

They returned to Rodat's side and took turns watching him throughout the remainder of the day. As night fell his breathing became more uneven, and his left arm started twitching spasmodically. Finally he opened his eyes.

"Still here, priest?"

"I'm not about to leave you," said Mihal solemnly.

The old man muttered something unintelligible. Its tone was not complimentary. Suddenly his body stiffened, as if riddled with intense pain.

Mihal reached out and held his hand. "Have courage," he said softly, as Rodat began to relax.

"I wish you the same," said the old man. "And strength."

"Me? Why?"

"Because, priest, you're going to need it."

He sat in silence for a few minutes. Then he started reading from his prayer book again. Rodat told him to keep quiet and stared boldly out at the darkness, eyes unblinking, jaw set, ready to meet his Maker on his own terms.

Mihal closed the book and sighed. He suddenly had a terrible apprehension that he was going to spend the rest of his life being tolerated.

"I think you're right, old man," he said at last.

"Eh?"

"It's going to be a long tour of duty."

25: The Pacifists

(No mention of the Pacifists can be found in *Origin and History of the Sentient Races*.)

The huge room was filling up. Here was a Canphorite, tall, slender, dignified; there sat an Emran, muscles bulging, shifting uncomfortably; walking through the doorway were ambassadors from Lodin XI, Castor V, and Procyon III, looking as unalike as any three sentient beings could look.

And standing in the midst of the gaudily dressed beings who had come from all points of the galactic compass were two Men.

"Looks like a pretty good turnout," said Lipas, the smaller of the two.

"It's even better than I had hoped for," said Thome. "We just may come out of this in good shape."

A Teroni, its face obscured by the chlorine gas inside its helmet, approached them.

"Where is your delegation?" it asked.

"They'll be here, never fear," said Thome in Galactic-O.

"They had better be," said the Teroni, walking away to where a number of other chlorine-breathers were gathered.

"I wonder what *is* keeping them," said Lipas softly. "We're not going to be able to stall much longer."

266

"They're only about half an hour late," said Thome confidently. "And besides, a third of the aliens aren't here yet either."

"But *they* aren't vital to the meeting," said Lipas. "*We* are."

That was indeed the crux of it. It was Man who was the focal point of the meeting; any other race or even any group of races was merely window dressing.

Man had fallen upon hard times in the past century, hard even compared to those that existed at the beginning of the millennium. From four thousand worlds he was now reduced to less than five hundred. His military might, which during the heyday of the Oligarchy and early Monarchy could not even be computed, was now a matter of record: 53,305 battleships, a standing army of less than a billion, and some seventeen billion hand weapons. These were still formidable figures, but precious few of the races assembled in this room had any reason to be envious of them; most possessed far more firepower, and incomparably better communication systems.

Man's economy had suffered even more than his military power. Of his 489 worlds, some 368 were in the throes of a severe depression, while most of the others were fighting a losing battle against runaway inflation. The Deluros VI planetoids, with no finances available to maintain them, had finally been cannibalized and sold to alien scientific establishments.

On every front, Man's star was fast approaching its nadir. Isolated antihuman pogroms had turned into widescale wars of extermination, economic sanctions had turned into galaxy-wide boycotts, and treaties were signed and broken by alien races with the regularity that had once characterized the race of Man.

Man responded with bluff, guile, and pressure in proportions that he thought would do the most good; but the aliens had possessed a master teacher for millennia, and had learned their lessons well.

So Man resorted to force. Half his meager Navy was lost in one brief battle around Praesepe VI. The entire planet of Aristotle was blown up. The worlds of the Spica system were taken, one by one, in less than a week. Torn and reeling, bloody but unbowed, Man fought on.

Or rather, most Men did. But there were a few, such as Thome, who could see no sense in absorbing defeat after defeat, humiliation after humiliation. He did not preach surrender, for no Man—including himself—ever surrendered. But he spoke in favor of reaching a political accommodation with the other races of the galaxy, and soon had so many followers that he was encouraged to form a political party. It ran candidates for offices on Sirius V, Delta Scuti II, and Earth . . . and lost every election. After an appropriate interval his followers ran again, and lost again.

Determined to prove to Mankind that pacifism was a viable alternative to a bitter series of wars that could end only in the extermination of the race, he went over the heads of his constituency and approached the aliens directly.

If he could arrange a conference between all the races of the galaxy, Man included, would they be willing to participate?

The aliens were in the driver's seat, and they knew it. Only if certain conditions were met, they answered, would they consent to such a meeting.

The conditions?

All delegates would speak with T-packs. Not modified Terran T-packs, but Galactic ones.

Thome agreed.

The meeting would be held on Doradus IV, symbolic of the first worldwide population that Man had wiped out through sheer carelessness, rather than malice.

Thome agreed.

The delegation of Men must be empowered to speak for the entire race. They'd had enough experience in signing agreements with one representative of the race and then having other Men deny that anyone had spoken for their specific interest groups.

Thome agreed.

The race of Man must totally disarm prior to the meeting.

Thome explained, time and again, that he did not have the influence or the power to make his race lay down its arms. That, after all, was one of the hoped-for goals of the meeting. However, he would guarantee that no Man attending the conference would bear arms.

After considerable procrastination, the aliens agreed.

There were, including Man, 13,042 intelligent races in the galaxy. Some of these, such as the insectoids of Procyon II, who had no interest in the affairs of other races, or the ichthyoids of Gamma Leporis IV, who bore Man no ill will, were not invited to the conference. But of the 11,039 races invited to send delegations, 9,844 had responded favorably.

268

Even such far-flung and exotic beings as the Vasorites, who spent their entire lives following their small red sun over the horizon on incredibly long, untiring legs, agreed to attend.

In fact, Thome had more trouble getting Man to agree to the meeting than any of the aliens. After all, Men were the reason for the meeting. They would be expected to disarm, to make territorial concessions, to pay economic tributes, and they weren't happy about it. Thome kept hitting away at the only alternative—racial death—and at long last the leaders of the loosely knit Interstellar Union of Man, a conservative government that ruled more by consent than any effective manifestation of real political power, agreed.

There had been a lot of stipulations. The aliens must be informed that Man's presence should not be construed as any form of weakness or surrender, but merely a willingness to discuss the situation across a conference table instead of a battlefield. The aliens must realize that paltry as Man's armaments were, the race was in no way willing to leave itself totally defenseless. The aliens must understand that the use of a Galactic T-pack was only a temporary affectation, not a permanent reversal of the long-standing human policy. The aliens must understand this, the aliens must do that, the aliens must yield on such-and-such a point . . .

Thome smoothed over as many points of disagreement as he could, then returned to the aliens with those demands which were not negotiable. The aliens gave in on a number of points, and he finally persuaded Man to yield on the remainder.

It had taken almost three years to set up the conference, years during which Man had lost seven more worlds, years during which Thome despaired almost daily of bringing the project to fruition, but at last the appointed moment had arrived. He looked around him, smiling at the humanoid delegation from Emra, nodding to a passing Torqual, bowing low to a crystalline being from far Atria.

"It's going to work!" he whispered excitedly to his companion. "I can feel it in my bones. Look at them, Lipas. They're not out for blood. They want an end to the killing as much as we do."

Lipas surveyed the room. "It's possible," he admitted. "I shook hands with one of those Leptimus V creatures, and it didn't even flinch. A couple of years ago it would have raced off to its equivalent of a bathroom to wash away the taint of a Man's touch."

A three-legged Pnathian lumbered over to Thome, an unbelievably complex T-pack arrangement attached to its helmet.

"I have been here for almost half a day," it said. "When will the conference begin?"

"There are almost eighty races that have not yet arrived," said Thome. "Once all are in attendance we shall proceed with our business, Ambassador."

"And *your* delegation?" asked the Pnathian. "Is it here yet?"

"No," said Thome. "It is one of the delegations we are waiting for."

The Pnathian stared at him for a moment, then walked off to join one of the Lodinites.

In another two hours all but fourteen races had arrived, and Lerollion of Canphor VII, the leader of the Canphor Twins, approached Thome.

"Where is your delegation?" he said, and even the T-pack seemed to resonate with anger.

"They'll be here," said Thome. "They are coming from almost half a galaxy away. I don't think being a few hours late constitutes a breach of trust."

"Nonetheless, we cannot delay the conference any longer," said Lerollion. "Have you any reason why we should not begin without your delegation?"

"Absolutely," said Thome. "My delegation is the whole reason we're meeting here today."

"Just the same," said Lerollion, "it is time to begin."

The Canphorite walked to the rostrum and, turning on the amplifier, requested the delegations to take their seats.

"Delegates," he said, "I, Lerollion of Canphor VII, now declare this conference to be in order. The clerk will read the roll."

The clerk, a squat little being from Robel, began calling out the names of the worlds, from hot, dusty Aldebaran II to Zeta Piscium IX. Only six delegations were absent.

"I had written an introductory speech," said Lerollion, "a speech of friendship and conciliation. With no offense to these assembled delegates, the speech was not written on your behalf, for you are all my friends, as well you know. It was written for one particular race of beings"—here he paused long enough to cast a hostile look at Thome—"a race from which I perhaps expected too much.

"And yet," he continued, "if I am to be disappointed, the

fault is undoubtedly my own, for nothing in that race's history has given me any indication that it would either seek, recognize, or appreciate the words I had prepared. It is a race of barbarians, a race that is being given one last chance to join our peaceful community of worlds. I do not know why, under the circumstances, this race was not the first delegation to arrive. I do not know why it has not arrived yet. But I do know what the inevitable result will be should this race offend us this one last time." He paused. "I see that Thome of the race of Man is requesting the floor. It is given."

The Canphorite sat down, and Thome walked up to the amplifier.

"I am aware that the regrets and impatience Lerollion has expressed echo the sentiments of many of you," he said. "This is understandable, and perfectly justified. The race of Man has indeed brought most of its current sorrows upon itself by its actions over several millennia of galactic rule and misrule. But it is for precisely that reason that this conference has been arranged. We come to you with new insights, new humility, new——"

"But you don't come to us at all," said an Emran.

"Where is your delegation?" demanded a Domarian.

"They *will* be here, I assure you," said Thome. "Characterize our flaws and faults in any way you wish, but grant us a certain degree of intelligence and self-preservation. My delegation will be here because there is no viable alternative."

"In that you are correct," said a Castorian. "There is no viable alternative."

"Then let us proceed in a spirit of brotherhood," said Thome. "I wish only to assure you of our sincerity. I now return the floor to Lerollion of Canphor VII."

He walked back to the empty area reserved for his delegation, and seated himself next to Lipas

"Any word from them yet?" he asked nervously.

Lipas shook his head.

"Well, damn it, they'd better get here soon!" snapped Thome.

"Did it ever occur to you that Lerollion might be right—that they're not going to show up?"

"They've got to," said Thome firmly. "If they don't make an appearance, it's the end of everything."

One after another, the alien delegations took the floor. Some of the speeches were conciliatory, some were noncommittal, some were overtly hostile. For hours they droned on, as Thome waited for his delegation.

Darkness fell, and Lerollion rose to speak once again.

"Several of the assembled races must indulge in a recess for purposes of sleep and nourishment," he said. "However, if Thome of the race of Man will still offer his assurance that his delegation is expected to arrive, I am prepared to wait for them."

"I don't know what has delayed them," said Thome, "but I know they will come."

"I understand that the psychology of your race is such that their appearance here will be extremely painful and humiliating to them, which is why I offer to wait," said Lerollion. "However, if they are not here by sunrise tomorrow, I have orders to return to my home world, regardless of whether or not the conference continues."

With that, he recessed the meeting and took his seat.

As night fell, Thome dozed sporadically. From time to time he awoke with a start, expecting to see his delegation entering the huge hall, but except for Lipas, Lerollion, and ten or twelve other beings, it was empty.

At daybreak Lerollion left, and most of the other alien delegations walked out with him. A handful remained until midday, and the ambassador from Quantos IX stayed until twilight.

Then Thome found himself alone with Lipas.

"Come along," said the smaller man gently.

Thome shook his head vigorously.

"But it's obvious that they're not going to come," said Lipas.

"Go ahead if you want," said Thome. "I'll wait here by myself. Somebody should be here to greet them."

Lipas looked at his friend, then sighed and walked out of the hall.

"They'll come," said Thome softly, staring at the door through which no one would ever enter again. "They *must* come."

He leaned back in his chair and waited.

26: The Destroyers

    . . . It was not without sincere regret and a deep
sense of guilt that a war of extermination was waged
against the remnants of Man's once-proud race. But
in view of his capacity for violence and carnage,
which continued unabated despite his fall from galactic primacy, no other alternative seemed feasible.
For of all the thousands of sentient races, only a
handful had descended from carnivora, and of these
only Man remained true to his heritage. . . .

          —*Origin and History of the Sen-
tient Races*, Vol. 9

On a nameless world far out on the Rim of the galaxy,
Man made his last stand.

Or, to be more precise, one man and three women. There
had been more when they had reached this world, hundreds
more, but now all except these four lay dead near the entrance to the cave.

The cave was about two hundred feet deep, with an opening so narrow that the man had momentarily gotten stuck
trying to follow the women into it. It was very cold and dark,
and filled with a fine powdery dust that made breathing a

painful chore. But it was defensible, at least until their supply of food and water ran out, and that made the dust very easy to put up with, considering the alternative.

The cave was situated high on the side of a jagged mountain, accessible to the four humans only by extremely precarious handholds and footholds, and totally inaccessible to the Kragan squadron that was besieging them, huddled together for warmth and comfort at the mountain's base.

The Kragans, a large, chubby, hairless species of intelligent marsupial, weren't by nature a hostile race. But like almost all intelligent races, they liked to side with the winners, and Man hadn't been a winner for centuries. One by one he had lost his bases on the periphery of his empire, and in the last eighty years the core of his power: Caliban, Earth, Deluros VIII, the Floating Kingdom, all had been toppled. None had given up without a fight, but all were lost nonetheless: dead, desolate memories of a strength and a glory that had blossomed, flowered, and withered in the seasons of Time.

And slowly, over the years, Man had become the hunted rather than the hunter. It was not to his liking. The galaxy showed Man no more mercy than he had shown it, and entire worlds were exterminated. Then came the search-and-annihilate missions. Sixteen humans had erected a small done on Vega IX, which had never been able to support life or atmosphere; a proton bomb wiped them out. Two thousand human refugees found shelter on the surface of a long-dead star in the Betelgeuse region; they were destroyed within hours of being discovered.

Man fought back, of course; Man always fought back. But with no central governing body, no military leadership, no coherent organization, even Man found the odds too high. There were 13,042 sentient races or mutations in the galaxy; no more than a dozen disavowed Man's extinction, and not one would do battle on his side.

"Still, we didn't do too badly," said the man, looking out across the rocky mountainside. "All things considered, we made them pay for every goddamned inch they took."

"And they'll pay dearly for the last inch too," said the first of the women, looking thoughtfully down on the device that they had painstakingly carried to the cave and lovingly reassembled in almost total darkness the previous night.

"Don't be too quick to give up yet," said the man. "We're all that's left. After us, there is nothing more."

274

"So says the father of a new race," said the second woman sarcastically.

"Let's just worry about keeping the old race alive a little longer," said the man. He gazed down on the Kragans. "Hell, they look so fat and gentle."

"Maybe we can reason with them," suggested the third woman without much enthusiasm.

"You mean tell them we're sorry and that we can't be blamed for what our ancestors did?" asked the first woman.

"Hell!" snapped the man. "We're not sorry, and we're proud of what's gone before us! I just wish we could have lived during the Republic, back when we were just flexing our muscles for the first time."

"I prefer the Monarchy," said the second woman. "You heard those Kragans threatening us in Galactic, didn't you? In *Galactic*! There was a time when the only language they'd have known was Terran. A Kragan who spoke to a Man in any other tongue would have been killed. And the slower the better," she added with a glint of fire in her eyes.

"This is ridiculous," said the third woman. "We live *now*, and if we want to keep living, we've got to do something about it pretty damned quick."

"What would you suggest?" asked the man. "You want to shoot it out with two hundred Kragans? Or trigger *that* damned thing"—he gestured to the device—"and blow the whole goddamned planet to hell?"

"It's better than letting them take us without a fight," said the first woman.

"Five years ago it would have been," said the man. "Even three months ago, before they got that colony in the Delphini System. But now we're the last. If we die, Man is through. He's over. Forever. We've got a responsibility."

"To whom?" asked the second woman. "We're the only four people we owe anything to. Nobody else counts. And I say that we fight."

"You're not talking about fighting," said the man. "When you fight, somebody wins."

"So you just want to sit here and wait until we starve to death, is that it?" said the second woman.

"No, of course not," said the man. "All I'm saying is that whatever else happens, we have to stay alive." He paced the cave restlessly, then walked to the tiny entrance. "Look, there's nothing on this world we can use, that anyone can use. Maybe I can persuade them to leave us here, to post a guard ship to make sure we'll never go back into space."

"If the positions were reversed, could a Kragan convince you of it?" asked the first woman.

"Could anyone?" echoed the third woman.

"No," admitted the man. "But . . ."

"But what?"

"But I'm a Man," he said. "They're Kragans."

"That's the whole problem," said the first woman.

"What's the Kragan truce sign?" asked the man.

"You mean it!" said the first woman incredulously. "You're really going to go down and talk to them!"

"Hope your Galactic's fluent," said the second woman contemptuously. "Yes, sir. Hope it's real good. Maybe if you bow and scrape enough they won't know what you are. They might think they've stumbled onto a whole new species."

The man spat on the floor, carefully maneuvered his body through the opening, and began the slow descent. His foot kicked a loose rock that tumbled down the mountainside, and he immediately stood up in full view of the Kragans, waving his arms wildly.

"Don't fire!" he yelled. "I'm coming down to talk. I have no weapons."

To his mild surprise, he was allowed to complete his journey unmolested, and within two hours his feet rested on solid ground.

"Who is your leader?" he asked of the assembled Kragans.

"I," said one of those nearest to him.

"I have come to talk," said the man, trying to keep from breaking into Terran.

"Why?" asked the Kragan.

"To ask for mercy."

"Is that all?" said the Kragan. Had its face been at all manipulable, it would have looked suspicious.

"Not quite," said the man. "You know that we also have the power to destroy this planet and everything on it."

"We know that."

"I'll make you a deal," said the man. "If you'll let us remain here, alive and unharmed, I'll allow you and your forces to leave. We have no desire to die, nor to kill anyone else."

"You have no desire to kill anyone," said the Kragan emotionlessly, "and yet you came down here to threaten us with

276

complete and total destruction. Is it any wonder that we cannot allow you to survive?"

"But we are the last!" said the man. "When you have killed us, the race of Man will have ceased to exist."

"Yes," said the Kragan. It did not sound regretful.

"It was Man that gave form and structure to the galaxy. We've played too important a role in the scheme of history to die as a race. Surely you must be able to see some value in keeping a remnant of us alive."

"As you kept remnants of other races alive?" asked the Kragan. "How many species has Man exterminated in his brief lifetime? How many worlds has he ground to dust and ash?"

"But damm it, *I* didn't do those things!" cried the man in exasperation.

"Left to live, you would," said the Kragan. "You already contemplate doing so with this very planet."

"Give me an alternative," pleaded the man. "Any alternative."

"The alternative," said the Kragan patiently, "is *not* to destroy the planet."

"Then let us live in peace!"

"You are a Man," said the Kragan. "For you to live in peace is a contradiction in terms."

"Keep us imprisoned on this planet, then," said the man. "Destroy our ship and patrol the skies so that we can never leave again."

"Your ship is already destroyed," said the Kragan. "And you will never leave again. Have you anything further to say?"

The man looked up at the stars for the last time, sighed, and shook his head. "No," he said.

"Then return to your companions," said the Kragan. "We will not honor any further truces."

The man trudged slowly up the mountain.

"Well?" asked the second woman.

"We're no worse off than before," said the man.

"That's not saying a hell of a lot," said the second woman. "I assume we're also not any better off?"

"No." He looked around the cave. "How long is the food good for?"

"Two days if we eat hearty," said the third woman. "Maybe a week if we scrimp."

"Why scrimp?" said the second woman. "If we're going to die, let's at least do so with full stomachs."

"Right," said the first woman. "Death by slow starvation isn't one of the nicer ways to go."

"There is no nice way," said the man. "If only those damned Kragans would listen to reason!"

"But they won't," said the third woman.

"Damn it!" said the man. "We've meant too much to the galaxy just to die like this! They could save us. Keep this place a planetary prison or zoo or whatever they wanted to do with us, and just let us live. It can't end like this! We've gone too far, done too much, to die in this forgotten little hellhole with nobody around to notice. Damm it all—we're *Men!*"

"Bravo!" said the second woman, clapping her hands sarcastically. "What a pity those words can't be engraved on the wall of the cave."

"You may be content to sit here and wait for death," said the man, "but if we can't live, then I think we should at least die with some kind of gesture, something they may remember us for."

"We could all kneel down in front of the Kragans and pray while their firing squad mowed us down," said the second woman with a laugh.

"Or write your touching little speech up and put it in a bottle in the hope that someone will find it someday," added the third woman.

"Stop your snickering!" snapped the man. "If we're going to die, at least we ought to go about it right."

"And what is the right way for a race to die?" said the second woman.

"Not by sitting around moaning and cackling, that's for sure!" said the man. "Don't you want somebody to know we've been here, that this is where Man met his end?"

"Who do you propose to tell?" asked the second woman.

"I don't know," said the man. "Somebody." He looked around the cave and his eyes fell on the device. "Everybody." He walked over and knelt down next to it. "At least they'll know we didn't go out like lambs to the slaughter, that we fought to the very end to preserve all that was Man."

He reached out and pressed the button.

It was glorious.

EPILOGUE:
587th Millennium

Eons passed, and Man—or something very like him—
slithered out of the slime, sprouted limbs, developed thumbs.
He stood erect, saw the stars for the first time, and knew
that they must someday be his. . . .

MIKE RESNICK was born in Chicago in 1942, attended the University of Chicago (where, in the process of researching his first adventure novel, he earned three letters on the fencing team and was nationally ranked for a brief period), and married his wife, Carol, in 1961. They have one daughter, Laura.

From the time he was 22, Mike has made his living as a professional writer. He and Carol have also been very active at science fiction conventions, where Mike is a frequent speaker and Carol's stunning costumes have swept numerous awards at masquerade competitions.

Mike and Carol were among the leading breeders and exhibitors of show collies during the 1970s, a hobby which led them to move to Cincinnati and purchase a boarding and grooming kennel.

Mike has received several awards for his short stories and an award for a nonfiction book for teenagers. His first love, though, remains science fiction, and his excellent science fiction novel, THE SOUL EATER, is also available in a Signet edition.